Somehow his

Dylan willed himself to stop, but hadn't the power to obey his own edict. When his arms encircled her, she looked up at him.

What did she think of him? Did he dare to think she might have wanted his embrace? He cared not, he told himself, but in fact he did. He hoped she was as caught in the moment as he, as ensnared by the moonlight, the circumstances, the scent of jasmine and gunpowder.

He bent toward her, knowing that he should pull away and run, but unable to do so. In the distance, guns flashed, cannons thundered, but he continued on until his lips were pressed gently against hers. When he finally forced himself to draw away, he expected her to slap him, to demand that he leave the inn at once and never return. He expected many things, but he never expected what she did.

Dear Reader,

Welcome to another great month of the best in historical romance. This February brings us four great titles sure to add spice to your Valentine's Day!

First, don't miss *Defy the Eagle,* the long-awaited reissue of Lynn Bartlett's enthralling saga of epic passion and ancient rebellion. Caddaric, a son of Britain, and Jilana, a daughter of Rome—lovers by destiny, enemies by birth.

For those of you who enjoyed Deborah Simmons's *Silent Heart,* her new release, *The Squire's Daughter,* is sure to please. Marquis Justin St. John is cursed by a tragic past, but when he marries Clare Cummings in a marriage of convenience, his new wife begins to unravel not only his heart, but an old mystery, as well.

If you've got a penchant for the exotic, have we got a book for you! Set in the Mediterranean during the medieval era, Claire Delacroix's *Honeyed Lies* weaves the tale of Rebecca, a young widow who accidentally finds a mysterious book everyone seems to want— including the honorable and handsome Jacob.

And last but not least, in *Dylan's Honor* by Kristie Knight, patriot Honor Richmond is determined to unmask the Tory spy operating out of her tavern— but Dylan Alden's smoldering passion keeps her guessing if he is friend or foe.

We hope you enjoy all our February titles. Next month, keep an eye out for our 1994 March Madness promotion, featuring four exciting new books by up-and-coming first-time authors.

Sincerely,

Tracy Farrell
Senior Editor

DYLAN'S HONOR
KRISTIE KNIGHT

Harlequin Books

TORONTO • NEW YORK • LONDON
AMSTERDAM • PARIS • SYDNEY • HAMBURG
STOCKHOLM • ATHENS • TOKYO • MILAN
MADRID • WARSAW • BUDAPEST • AUCKLAND

ISBN 0-373-28810-7

DYLAN'S HONOR

Printed in U.S.A.

Books by Kristie Knight

Harlequin Historicals

KRISTIE KNIGHT

is a native of South Carolina. She believes that laughter makes the world go round. Though she resolved long ago never to take herself too seriously, the one exception to that philosophy is her writing—which she takes very seriously. Kristie, a former secretary and office manager, now makes her home in Decatur, Georgia, with her husband, Bob.

DYLAN'S HONOR

is dedicated to all my friends at
Southeastern Writers Association, Inc.,
who make my summers so special.
The creative energy generated during
our workshop week at St. Simons Island,
Georgia, is too valuable to measure, but the love,
support, and friendship they offer so selflessly is a
treasure. To these people, I wish great success,
however they choose to define it.

In addition to the people who attend this
workshop, there is a small group within SWA I
wish to acknowledge: The Southeastern Orphans.
These wonderful, loving people mean a great
deal to me.

Special thanks must go to Patricia Laye,
Peggy Mitchell, Danielle Iserman,
Sandra Chastain, Marion Collins,
Emily Sue Harvey, Amy Munnell, Harry Rubin,
Leroy Spruill, Becky Weyrich, and
Dorothy Worth, my board of directors, whose
sound advice, support, and sense of humor have
lighted my path for many years.

Chapter One

Charleston, 1780

The times were exciting . . . dangerous and exhilarating. The war for independence had been going on for four years now, and Honor Richmond felt that the most critical battles were yet to be fought. Honor wanted more than anything to help the Patriot cause, so she listened to everything that was said and absorbed it. She might hear something that would prove to be vital later.

The young woman eagerly scanned the faces of the men seated near the fireplace. She placed fresh tankards of ale in front of each of them, hoping to hear something of value in their conversation. Some of the men were angry, some serious and some, like Honor, were hopeful. For months, she'd listened to the patrons of her father's inn as they asserted the value of their service to either the Loyalists or the Patriots. At times, she heard something worth remembering; more often than not, the stories passed around were simply boastful tales.

Honor, now twenty-two, had been serving many of these men since she was ten years old. Her father had put her to work at a young age because he couldn't afford to hire a serving girl. Honor didn't mind an honest day's work, but there were times when she would have liked to play with her friends instead of working so hard. The White Point Inn and Tavern was a busy place in these unsettled days.

Honor smiled at the strange man who had entered the tavern and was making no move to seat himself. She strode toward him. He removed his hat, revealing a shock of sandy brown hair caught in a tie at the nape of his neck, but his eyes were what drew her attention. Blue. As blue as the sky over Charleston Harbor in midsummer. Almost as dark as the cornflowers that grew wild outside the back door of the tavern and along the roads in warm weather.

"Welcome to the White Point Inn and Tavern, sir," she said, smiling up at him. "Are you interested in a room for the night or food and drink?"

He looked down at her and studied her for a moment. "Good evening, miss. How is the food?"

"Best food and lodgings in all of Charleston," she replied with pride. Honor and her father, Henry Richmond, ran the best tavern in town. "I can give you my personal guarantee on that, sir."

"Then I'll be delighted to sample your fare. There's precious little palatable food to be found in these troubled days."

"Follow me." Honor led him back toward the fireplace, to the only vacant table. She saw, as she turned around, that he favored his left leg, but tried to pretend she hadn't noticed. "If you'll give me your cloak, I'll be happy to hang it up for you."

"You're very kind."

"I recommend the fish stew," Honor said, taking his cloak. "We've the best-stocked larder in town and we buy our fish fresh."

"Then that's what I'll have. And a tankard of ale." He sat down in the chair that allowed him a full view of all the other patrons of the tavern, as well as the door. Stretching his left leg out before him, he reached down and rubbed the knee gently. "Injury from the siege of Savannah."

"Many have been less fortunate," Honor replied, carefully avoiding looking down. She hung his cloak in the back of the tavern and then went to dish up his meal. The spicy aroma of the fish stew, ladled in healthy portions over rice, made her recall that she'd been working for eight hours without stopping to eat and that she was starving.

Placing the bowl on her tray, along with the ale, she wondered about the stranger. There were plenty of them in Charleston. Since the war had started, the port city had been a hotbed of activity, drawing strangers from everywhere. This man seemed different. His alert eyes constantly searched the room, as if he were looking for someone. She instinctively felt

...at little happened without his knowing about it. She liked ...at in a man. She smiled as she hefted the tray.

When she reached his table, he grinned up at her. "I'm ...ylan Alden. Pleased to meet you."

"Honor Richmond," she answered, placing the stew and ...e in front of him. He sounded very English. A quiver of ...ution touched her spine. Was there something of value she ...uld learn from him? "Nice to meet you, too. Are you stay-...g long or just passing through?"

His eyes narrowed almost imperceptibly, but Honor no-...ced. For some reason he didn't seem to want to answer her.

"What?" he asked, as if buying time to decide how to re-...ly. His gaze met hers, lingering for moments too long.

"Are you planning to stay or are you just passing through ...harleston?" she repeated, finally averting her eyes from his ...aptive gaze.

Honor knew she was probably reading more into his hes-...ance than she should. He might just be shy or wary of ...rangers asking questions. Who wasn't these days?

"Oh, yes. I'm staying." Dylan breathed in deeply. The stew ...nelled great. Mingled with the spicy aroma was the faint ...agrance of flowers. "Came here to settle after I was able to ...alk again. They say my leg will never be the same. I can't ...em to get rid of the stiffness."

He gazed at her. Her ebony hair was pulled back from her ...ce in a braided chignon of some sort, darkly framing her ...elicate features and warm brown eyes. Her wide mouth, ...arted slightly, was sensuous, kissable. Realizing that she was ...atching him as closely as he was studying her, he cleared his ...roat and grinned again. "I hope this is as delicious as it ...nells."

"Oh, yes. I have to admit it would be better with a little ...ore salt, but you know how precious salt is these days. Al-...ost im-impossible to get," she stammered quickly, feeling ...e color spring to her cheeks. "I'll get you some bread."

Honor fled into the changing room. This man was danger-...us, she concluded. She should simply stay away from him. ...e was handsome, certainly—more handsome than any man ...e could remember coming to the tavern, but in a different ...ay. Before, she'd always managed to keep herself at arm's ...ngth from the tavern patrons, but she felt instinctively that ...ith Dylan Alden it would be difficult.

"What are you daydreaming about, Daughter?" Henry Richmond asked, heaving a heavy stack of wood into the bin.

"Me? Nothing. I was just—just trying to decide whether to stop now and eat or wait awhile." Honor cut several thick slices from a fresh loaf of bread. "I'll be right back."

She sped through the doorway of the changing room back to the public area. She didn't want her father to question her further. Honor threaded her way among the tables and placed the platter of bread on the newcomer's table. "Just holler if you need anything, Mr. Alden."

Spotting several empty tankards, she hurried forward and picked them up. Though many of their patrons drank a lot, causing her to have to work harder, she was glad. Men who consumed large quantities of ale often had loose tongues. She brought back fresh drinks, placing them on the table without comment.

Honor finally ladled some stew into a bowl for herself and her father. "Della," she called to the cook, who was placing fresh bread in a warmer by the fireplace. "What happened to Papa?"

"Faith and begorra, he's gone again."

Knowing that her father would return at his own leisure, Honor poured his stew back into the kettle and settled down to eat her own supper. As she leaned back in the chair, fatigue spread quickly through her muscles. In addition to the excitement of the times, the war brought in many customers, and she had to work harder and for even longer hours. Never one to let opportunity pass by, her father had expanded the hours in the common room and had crammed extra beds into some of the sleeping rooms upstairs.

Honor didn't complain. She concentrated on the excitement, instead. Of course, women couldn't fight in the war; nevertheless, she had vowed to make a difference and she would—if she could only convince someone to give her a chance.

"Has Mama been fed?" Honor stopped eating and waited for Della's answer.

The stout woman nodded and scowled. "Not that she eats enough to feed the leprechauns. No wonder that woman's so sick."

Honor took another mouthful of her stew. She hadn't been up to see her mother since before breakfast. Ruth Richmond had been ill for a long time. Honor couldn't remember when her mother had been well enough to participate in the running of the inn, much less in simple, everyday pleasures.

Many times Honor would visit her mother and the frail woman wouldn't speak at all. Those days were even more disturbing than when her mother ranted and raved about every subject under the sun. Honor was thankful that Della had assumed much of the burden of Ruth Richmond's care.

The Irishwoman had been with the Richmond family for years. In many ways, she was more a mother to Honor than Ruth Richmond ever had been. Honor took her bowl and placed it in a bucket filled with soapy water. Impulsively, she hugged Della and received a groan and a scowl for her efforts. Knowing the matron as she did, Honor laughed and scooted away before the grumbling could start.

The patrons in the common room wouldn't remain silent for long, so she returned to her job as quickly as possible. As she had expected, every tankard was empty or nearly so. Wearing her most cheerful smile, she went from table to table replacing the empties with full ones. This war was certainly good for business.

Jeffrey Sheridan arrived shortly before midnight and sat alone at a table. She brought him a bowl of stew and some ale, knowing he'd be hungry as usual. Soon men began leaving the tavern, some struggling to stand. The stranger, Dylan Alden, dropped a handful of coins on the table, smiled to her and touched his forehead in salutation as he threaded his way among the revelers and left. Once again, she tried to pretend she didn't notice his limp, but she could see in his expression that the leg still pained him.

She watched until he was gone. Though he had exchanged several words with other men in the tavern, he'd mostly kept to himself all evening, just taking in the atmosphere. He was an enigma, and she'd probably be wise to stay away from him. Drawing her attention back to the task at hand, she cleared away the dishes and wiped down the tables, until she glanced around and noticed she was alone with Jeffrey.

"Busy night, Honor," he commented as she neared his table.

"They're all busy these days, Jeffrey," she answered, sitting down with him. "If this keeps up, we're going to have to find more help. Della has her hands full in the kitchen and I can hardly keep up out here. With all the extra beds upstairs, I spend nearly the whole morning there."

Jeffrey looked at her and smiled. She knew that he wanted to marry her, but she could never do so. They'd been friends for too long to ruin a nice friendship with wedding vows. She patted his hand. "Let me get you another ale."

Without waiting for his answer, she went to the bar and filled the tankard. When she returned, she was conscious of his gaze following the sway of her hips as she walked. She said nothing.

"Thank you, Honor." Jeffrey sipped the ale for a moment and then stared into its amber depths. "I fear things are getting worse."

Honor slid into a chair beside him and stared. "How? What's happened, Jeffrey?"

"A short time ago we heard from our sources that many British ships were nearing Charleston. Today, they landed on John's Island. We're digging a canal from the Ashley to the Cooper for protection. We're pretty vulnerable from there if we don't get the hornworks finished in time."

Unable to speak for a moment, Honor simply stared at Jeffrey. Her thoughts skimmed from one subject to another, each a different aspect of what his implication could mean to her, to the White Point Inn, to the people of Charleston. When she could finally speak, she whispered, "How many? What are they here for?"

Jeffrey shrugged. "I know little about this. I fear we'll find out soon enough, though."

Honor stared at the fire for a few moments, her thoughts whirling with excitement. Then she looked at Jeffrey. "Now is the time, Jeffrey. You can use my help."

Once again, Jeffrey gazed at her with new wonder. "What are you talking about, Honor?"

"Don't you see? It's perfect, Jeffrey." Honor could hardly contain her glee. "You need me. I can listen to the men who come in here, pass on information to you."

Jeffrey shook his head. "Honor, I've told you a hundred times. It's too dangerous."

"What's so dangerous about it? These men know me. They come in here day after day, bragging about all they're doing for the war effort." Honor clasped his hands in hers. "I can do this, Jeffrey, if you'll give me a chance."

He looked at her as if he were looking at a petulant child. 'No, Honor. It's far too dangerous. Women just aren't equipped for war.''

Honor jerked back her hands and crossed her arms. "Why are you being so pigheaded? You know I can be as tough as you.''

Jeffrey smiled and patted her shoulder consolingly. 'Honor, I know you want to help, and you are, you truly are. Just being here when I come in is help enough. I imagine many men feel that way. To come in and see your pretty face is enough to make us realize what we're fighting for.''

How could she make him understand? Honor knew that she was worth more than simply looking pretty for the men who were taking all the risks. She wasn't stupid; she understood the dangers. But she also knew that if the war effort were to succeed, everyone would have to become involved in some way.

"You're very kind and gracious with your compliments, Jeffrey, but that isn't enough for me." She stared at him with determination. This time, she simply must find a way to convince him of her value to the Patriots. "If you don't find something for me to do, then I'll find something myself. I don't have to depend on you or anyone else. I'll not sit home and embroider while the world battles around me.''

Jeffrey's features grew hard, and he sighed with exasperation. "For God's sake, Honor, you can't— Don't you understand? You're a woman. Women don't charge off to war with bayonet fixed and musket loaded. Women are too soft, too gentle. The realities of war would damage your soul irreparably. I cannot let you do this.''

"I swear this to you, Jeffrey," she said, beginning to understand what she was up against in her quest. "Either you give me a job to do, or I'll find one. The decision is yours to make. Either I fight this war under your direction, or I fight it on my own terms. I *will* serve the Patriots in our struggle for freedom. With you or without you.''

"Honor, do you know what they do to spies? That's what you'd be, you know." Jeffrey knew he was going to have to make his case strong enough to convince her of why he was reluctant to accept her help. "First they interrogate you, an extremely painful process. Then they try you, without really allowing any defense. Then they either shoot you or hang you as a traitor. This isn't mere gossip you'd be spreading.''

The realization of her determination finally dawned on him. Deep wrinkles furrowed his high brow as he stared at her, first in disbelief and then with grudging admiration. Finally, when he could meet her level stare no longer, Jeffrey bowed his head. ''All right, Honor. It will be as you demand, though I am completely against this. I shall find something for you. Give me a few days.''

''One week, Jeffrey,'' she said, fighting to control her exultation. ''I'll give you one week before I make my own choices.''

Honor could hardly sleep that night, so thrilled with anticipation was she. What would Jeffrey find for her to do? Though he'd often denied the possibility, she knew that women could do many things to help during a war; women had been doing so for centuries. There were camp followers who cooked and washed and nursed. That role didn't really appeal to her, but if he told her that she must take on those tasks, she would without complaint. She had heard stories of women who actually fought, but she didn't think she was ready for that unless she had no choice. Given a little more time, she would take up the musket alongside the Patriots and do her duty as she saw it.

Jeffrey Sheridan was a resourceful man. Faced with her unrelenting demands, he'd give her a job to do. He'd never been able to refuse her anything she truly wanted.

She decided it was too bad she wasn't in love with Jeffrey. He'd make a nice, pliable husband, just the sort she needed— if she needed a husband at all.

Her thoughts turned then to the stranger, Dylan Alden. She said the name several times, letting it curl sweetly around her tongue as her eyes closed and his image filled her mind's eye. Now there was an interesting man. She suddenly sat up and stared into the darkness. Why? What made him interesting above others?

She lay back onto her warm feather pillow and mattress, closed her eyes and imagined him as she'd first seen him. Everything about him seemed normal—his nose, his high cheekbones, his lips, his blue eyes. His face was comprised of all the usual components, but the combination took on a nearly devastating appeal that was lacking in others. Dylan Alden. Dylan Alden. Beware...

Dylan Alden's night had hardly begun when he'd met her. The lass was a beauty, no doubt about it. There were dozens of tavern wenches like her, ample bosom, shapely hips, hair the color of obsidian by firelight, eyes almost as dark. Why had he remained there, fascinated by the trill of her laugh, the shimmer of her hair, the exciting twinkle in her eye, the spirit of her presence, which seemed to dominate the common room of the tavern?

Dylan cursed himself for a fool and, ignoring the pain in his leg, strode toward his lodgings. The evening had been useless to him. Not only had he failed to obtain the information he sought, he'd been smitten like a schoolboy with his first infatuation.

It wouldn't happen again. He simply wouldn't allow himself to be distracted from his purpose. His job in this war was far too important for a mere flirtation to obscure his purpose.

British ships had reached John's Island; the time for Dylan to act had arrived. For the past month, since he'd arrived from Savannah, he'd done nothing other than acquaint himself with the city of Charleston and her citizens. He'd become friendly with many of the townspeople and with some of the soldiers. He liked the people here, which made his task all the more difficult.

His duty was, however, for the best. He must continue to believe that, never doubting his purpose. With luck, and a generous portion of his skill in aid of the best army and navy in the world, the war would end soon. Once again, the British Empire would reign supreme, undivided and unchallenged.

When he'd first come to Charleston, he'd been surprised at the division of loyalties, with half the population on each side of the dispute. Nobody trusted anyone else—well, hardly anyone.

For the first time in Dylan's life, he had a true goal, a meaning beyond his simple day-to-day existence. The sovereignty of Britain's rule was being challenged. Dylan also saw his chance to rise above his father's low opinion of him. He would fight with everything he had to assure that Britain's forces would not fail in their quest to uphold the empire.

He didn't question the colonies' right to disagree with their king; in fact, he was adamant that the lines of communication remain strong. But this insurrection was nothing less than treason, and no matter how much he loved the land and its people, he could never condone treason.

After the war was won, he intended to settle here. Land was inexpensive and fertile. The people were open-minded and intelligent. The women... Again his thoughts returned to Honor Richmond. She was beautiful, her eyes filled with alert understanding. But she was a serving girl, nothing more to him. He must keep reminding himself of that. He would continue to see her, because she could help ease his way into the small groups of men that gathered in her father's tavern. That was all. Nothing more.

He rubbed his knee gingerly. The injury had been indeed inflicted during his escape from Savannah, but it wasn't as bad as he pretended. His limp made people trust him more quickly. It helped to explain why he wasn't fighting for either side. He unwound the tight bandages and flexed his knee. Keeping it bound so tightly might cause a permanent stiffness, and he didn't want that. But for now, he had little choice. He couldn't go out without the bindings.

He hobbled about, stretching and exercising his leg. The girl in the tavern, Honor Richmond, had noticed his injury. Everyone did. As he'd planned, even after his leg healed, he would have to continue his ruse. People would begin to talk about him. Unless he could find something useful to do as a civilian, he'd have to continue to limp, maybe even pretend his leg was worse. *Damn, but he hated the deceit he was forced to practice.* He hated lying and he hated liars.

As he removed the rest of his clothing and slid into his cold bed, his thoughts were on the serving girl. He'd simply have to avoid the White Point Inn and Tavern. There was no other answer. He couldn't risk everything for dalliance with a wench. Dylan was made of stronger stuff. He took his duty too seriously.

As his eyes began to close, he saw her again. Honor Richmond's image was emblazoned on his eyelids, tormenting him with her beauty. Scowling, he opened his eyes and thrust bac' the quilts. Cold air surged around his nakedness, and he cursed his weakness, his inability to banish the vision of her face from his thoughts. Bare feet touched the floor, and his toes curled in protest.

"Damnably foolish," he murmured, and strode to the window to peer out into the darkness.

He'd get little sleep this night. Too much had happened. Dylan felt that he was on the crest of a wave, speeding ever forward.

He'd always been a careful man, a man in control of his life. He'd emerged from his father's rule and sworn he would thereafter be master of his own fate. His attraction to Honor was dangerous. Dylan swore to simply avoid her. There were other women whose charms he'd sampled—though not of late—and he could do so again.

Returning to his bed, he lowered himself onto the straw mattress and groaned. He needed better lodgings. He'd never before been forced to sleep on a ticking filled with straw. Down was more to his liking. He recalled the White Point Inn and Honor's boast that it provided the best lodgings in town.

He was tempted to move there, but she'd cause him nothing but trouble. A man in his position needed to slip in and out of places unnoticed. Honor saw everything, he felt sure. Groaning, he pounded a lumpy place on the mattress and tried unsuccessfully to fall asleep.

Opening his eyes once again, he stared into the darkness. Honor might be of real help to him, in fact. If he was correct and she did notice everything, as he suspected, he might be able to glean information from her without her ever knowing what he was about. The idea appealed to him. With that thought in his mind, he finally drifted into a fitful sleep.

Honor sidled among the men seated comfortably around the tables. Many had been sitting there all evening and were becoming more and more boisterous with each refilling of their tankards. She'd long since cleared away the supper dishes. The blowing rain outside kept her customers from their favorite pastime these days: standing at White Point and staring across the harbor to watch for Clinton's approach.

John's Island, located just beyond James Island, was too close for the city's citizens to feel invulnerable, as they perhaps had a few scant days ago. Clinton's navy represented a real threat.

The debate about the significance of Clinton and his ships continued relentlessly. Tonight, as usual, the Patriots seated near the fireplace were fervent in their discussion of this latest turn of events in the ongoing war. Men of Charleston were rightly concerned that Clinton meant to lay siege to the city. Women were terrified.

Without seeming to be eavesdropping, Honor hovered around the tables, listening to everything being said. Excitement sizzled in the air, almost a physical presence that commanded her attention. Other women might be afraid, but not Honor. *Well,* she admitted to herself, *perhaps a bit.*

As she served more rum to the table nearest the fire, she heard someone mention the name Clinton. " . . . not sitting around waiting this time," the voice went on.

Honor caught her breath. What did the man mean? Suddenly, he stared straight at her. For a few seconds she was unable to move, then she smiled sweetly and hurried on her way, mentally cursing herself for being so obvious. From now on she'd have to be make doubly sure to appear to be paying no attention to the conversations.

The door swung open, and Dylan Alden entered the tavern with a gust of wind and rain. He smiled to her in greeting and closed the door behind him.

Honor hurried over to conduct him to a table. "Welcome again to the White Point Inn, Mr. Alden."

"Thank you." Dylan gazed down into depthless, brandy-colored eyes that glistened in the firelight. "I couldn't pass by the warmth of your hospitality and hearth on this wickedly cold night."

"I'm glad you didn't." Honor surveyed the room and spied an empty table near the fireplace. "Come. We'll make you happy you stopped in."

She led him to the table and asked, "Will you be supping with us again or will you have a mug of hot buttered rum?"

Dylan smiled. Her face was lovely, with a strength he found appealing. *This woman wouldn't back away from adversity,* he decided. *She would attack it head-on.* "Thank you for your kindness. I'll have both."

"We've a fine oyster soup this cold night. It's the best in all of Charleston." Honor waited while he looked at her. Was he trying to make a decision about his supper or was he day-dreaming?

"Again, you've caught my fancy. I'll have the soup. Have you any biscuits?" Dylan almost hated for her to leave, but she nodded and sped away to the kitchen. When she returned, she placed a steaming bowl of soup in front of him. He inhaled deeply and smiled. "Smells wonderful."

"It is." Honor smiled back with obvious pride.

Dylan laughed. "Are you as positive about everything as you are about the fare at this inn?"

"No. But I know what it takes to please a weary traveler—a warm supper and a clean bed." Honor stood beside the table, hands on her hips, and grinned. "Since I work here and upstairs, I assure you that we have both and that both are the best."

Dylan stopped with his spoon halfway to his mouth. "Are your mattresses by chance of feather?"

"That they are." She shook her head. "From your question, I presume that you are unhappy with your present lodgings?"

"If that, Miss Richmond, is your presumption, then you are correct. I'd give nearly anything I own for a featherbed this night."

"You can be assured it won't cost that much." Honor tried to remember that he was a patron of her father's inn, but her eyes kept meeting his, drawn there despite her will. "We've a vacant room that has but one small bed. The room is small, too. It costs a bit more, since you'd be having the room to yourself."

With a smile that he couldn't hide, Dylan said, "I'll take it. I've had my fill of sleeping on a mattress stuffed with straw." He sipped his soup thoughtfully as she went about her business.

When she returned to check on him, he smiled warmly. "Excellent stew." He looked at her for a few seconds and wrinkled his brow thoughtfully. "I say, miss, I'll bet you hear lots of interesting war tales here."

"A few," she answered, wondering why he'd ask a thing like that. She remembered Jeffrey's warnings about saying nothing to anyone about what she heard. "Nothing reliable. You know how drunks are. And whatever I hear passes over me as quickly as the March winds."

Dylan was surprised to hear that and wondered if she was telling the truth, though he had no real reason to believe she was lying. "Is that right? I've noticed quite a few officers have stopped by."

She was wary of anyone asking questions of her. "Now, who would think of discussing the war with a serving girl? Not much reason for that, is there?"

Dylan eyed her speculatively. "I think you underestimate yourself."

Honor hurried into the back room, where Della was bringing in another kettle of soup. "That's going quickly, Della. I hope we have plenty."

"I'll be swearin' I shucked enough oysters today to fill up the Cooper River." Della hung the kettle beside the small hearth. "I know how the men like my soup."

"Everybody likes your soup," Honor corrected, and left to refill the tankards of ale and mugs of buttered rum. Somehow, her spirits seemed higher since Dylan had come in for supper, but his questions still puzzled her. Maybe he was just making conversation.

She hummed a jaunty tune to herself as she threaded her way among the tables and chairs, stopping here and there to replace an empty mug or tankard.

When she next found herself at Dylan's table, she hesitated a moment. "How long will you be staying with us, Mr. Alden?"

He grinned and winked at her. "As long as the beds are soft and the food is this good."

"Ah, then you'll be here for an extended visit." Honor returned his smile. "I'm glad."

"I think I am as well." Dylan rose and dropped a few coins onto the table. "I must go and retrieve my belongings. So eager am I for the comfort of your beds, I'll tarry no longer than I must."

"We'll be awaiting your return. Goodbye." Honor stacked the plate and bowl and turned the mug onto its side. She brushed away the crumbs, preparing the table for other guests who might arrive.

Then she continued her rounds among the tables, tending to her customers as she usually did. Jeffrey came in, once again near midnight. This evening, nobody seemed to want to go home. The tavern was still packed with people discussing the ramifications of Clinton's move. She shook her head. *Talk. That's all they do. Why isn't someone actually doing something?*

As the patrons finally began to leave in twos and threes, she had more time to spend with Jeffrey. "What have you heard this evening, Jeffrey?"

"Not much, Honor," he admitted, scanning the room slowly. "Clinton seems to be content just sitting out there. I understand his ships are damaged and his troops are weary from their long trip."

"Where did they come from?" she asked, sitting down. She and Jeffrey were alone now in the tavern. "Why did they stop here?"

"They sailed from New York." He shrugged. "Who can know why they're here, except for Clinton himself?"

She studied her friend for a few moments, watching him eat his soup. "Have you decided what I can do to help, Jeffrey?"

He wiped his mouth and stared at her. Inhaling deeply, he closed his eyes briefly and then said, "As much as I hate to, I do have something for you to do."

She edged forward on her chair. "What, Jeffrey, what? I'll do anything to help."

"Honor, this isn't a child's game. This is serious, deadly." He hesitated for a moment and then continued, "I want...we need for you to listen to the conversations here as you suggested. Men speak freely around you. Try to remember everything. Write it down if you must...just a word or two, so you won't forget anything. I realize this isn't as exciting as you might wish, but let's start with something manageable and we'll see what happens."

"I already have information. A man was here earlier and said something about Clinton not sitting around and waiting this time."

Jeffrey's eyes opened wider. "Honor, please be careful. I appreciate the information and I'll pass it on, but I warn you to take care."

"I will, Jeffrey." She reached over and hugged him impulsively. As she did, the door swung open, and Dylan stepped inside the tavern.

Honor sprang to her feet and swung around to face him. "Mr. Alden, I—I didn't expect you back so soon."

Dylan removed his cloak and shook the rain off it. "Well, the thought of your featherbeds hurried my footsteps."

"My, but you're favoring your leg even more. Does the weather affect it?"

How alert she was to have noticed. Dylan realized he'd have to be very careful around her. "Yes, I'm afraid it does."

She took his cloak and quickly introduced him to Jeffrey. While the two men talked, she waited patiently. With a smile for Jeffrey and then for Dylan, she said, "Well, Mr. Alden, let me show you to your room."

She took a candle and strode to the staircase that led off the back of the common room. "When you're ready, Sir."

Dylan nodded to Jeffrey and followed Honor up the narrow stairs. He tried to avoid looking at her figure as she climbed ahead of him, but he couldn't avert his eyes. The graceful swing of her hips was entrancing, almost magnetic. When they reached the top of the stairs, she hurried to the end of the hallway. "Here we are."

She opened the door and hung Dylan's cloak on the hook provided. For a moment she gazed up at him, intensely aware of his vitality, his presence—and the close confines of the small room. "If there isn't anything else . . ." she murmured, hoping that he would stop staring at her as if she were a tasty bit of cake.

"What?" he asked, jolted from his reverie. Dylan glanced about and nodded his approval of the room. He shouldn't be here. He'd known all along that he should forgo comfort and stay at his previous lodgings. Something about her reached down inside him and touched a chord that hadn't been struck in too many years. He leaned upon the bedpost, as if his leg pained him too much to stand erect.

Honor gazed tentatively at him, trying to understand his sudden loss of composure. "Is there something else you need? An extra quilt is in the drawer there. Can I bring you a poultice or something?"

He tried to smile, as if to say that he was tired and would like nothing more than to go to bed. "Nothing. No. Nothing at all. You're too kind. I appreciate everything you've done."

"Fine. I'll have Ezra bring up some water." She smiled tentatively. "Meals are included in the price of the room, Mr. Alden. You can pay by the day or week."

"Call me Dylan," he requested, feeling himself founder in the depths of her eyes.

Her smile was captivating. Dylan fought the urge to reach out and caress her cheek, trace the fine-boned jaw to her sensuous lips. "Call me Dylan," he repeated, as if the sound of his words could steel him against the effect she seemed to have.

"Oh, I couldn't. My mother... my father would beat me if I did something so ill-bred." Honor shook her head. She could imagine what her parents would say if she called a gentleman as fine as Mr. Alden by his first name. She'd been brought up to respect her elders and her betters. Though she truthfully considered nobody any better than the next man— or woman—she still understood the system that made Dylan Alden different from her. "I couldn't. I simply couldn't."

"Nonsense. I insist." Dylan's gaze never left her face. Her mouth opened slightly, as if to protest again, and he could see her tongue moisten her bottom lip. Without stopping to think what he was doing, he placed his index finger across her mouth. "Shh! I insist."

"Dylan," she whispered, the word a caress that replaced the warmth of his fingertip upon her lips. "Dylan."

Chapter Two

As the sun started to rise, Honor was standing at her window high above the city. Staring out across the harbor, she watched the sky change from black to a delicate blue-gray, followed by a luminescent pink and lavender. Mist rose like dancers clad in diaphanous gauze, whirling gently across a silver stage.

She loved Charleston in the morning. No place on earth could be more beautiful, she thought, hugging herself against the chill that stole through cracks in the window frame. There was much to do today, but Honor couldn't tear herself away from the scene just yet.

Somewhere on an island about thirty miles from where she stood, Clinton and more than eight thousand men were preparing to move steadily toward Charleston. Despite her excitement, Honor acknowledged that Clinton's inevitable siege of Charleston might succeed. The leader had been rebuffed before, but his army was stronger this time.

She considered his chances realistically. Should he win, what would happen to her? Last night Jeffrey had finally accepted her offer to help. What could she really do? He'd asked her to listen to any conversations that might have an impact on the Patriots' cause. She'd already been doing that for some time. Most frequently, the men she served were merely boasting—or so she thought. Now, every conversation would have to be weighed carefully before being discarded as bragging.

Honor couldn't complain. She'd asked to help. Jeffrey thought that the patrons of the White Point Inn trusted her enough to speak freely. *More likely they ignored me rather han trust me,* she thought wryly. As far as those men were oncerned, she was harmless.

I'll show them. She smiled then as the sun broke vibrantly bove the sea. Turning away slowly, she decided that the best ay to prove the men wrong was to do the very thing they hought she couldn't do. Honor had the advantage: she alone new what she was capable of.

As she dressed for the day's work, her thoughts turned to)ylan Alden. Knowing that he was no more than a flight of tairs beneath her somehow sent little chills racing down her pine. He was far too handsome, far too secretive for her. At ge twenty-two, she knew enough to avoid that kind of man, nd she planned to avoid Dylan whenever she could.

She pulled on her cotton chemise, caught the back tail of it, rew it between her legs and tucked it into a tape she tied round her waist. After donning her best pleated petticoat, he slipped into her blue bodice and apron. Honor studied erself in the wavery mirror as she crossed her kerchief over er breasts and tied it at her waist in back. "Well, that's all ou can do," she told herself finally.

Plain cotton stockings kept her legs warm, and she was hankful for them. Her black slippers were cold as she slid her eet into them, and the leather was hard and cracked from ough use. Maybe one day soon she could buy another pair. 'Clothing costs too much these days," she said aloud, reeating her father's often spoken words. She touched her ingertip to a flagon of floral-scented cologne and then to her eck. The fragrance made her feel feminine, and she enjoyed hat feeling. She considered it her one weakness. She loved retty scents.

"Good morning," Dylan Alden called as he stepped from is room on the second floor and spied her heading downtairs.

"Good morning to you! How is your leg this morning?"

"Better. I guess the damp weather really affects it." Dylan
nhaled deeply and caught the scent of flowers. The soft fra-
rance seemed to surround her. Dylan smiled as he followed
er down the stairs. If this young woman only knew how
nany matrons had thrust their daughters his way, she would
augh. With the sweet fragrance of her cologne and the gen-
e sway of her hips clad in simple homespun, she'd garnered
nore of his attention than the daughters of dukes and earls.

"We're having ham and hominy grits for breakfast." Honor sniffed the air as they reached the common room. "Isn't that the loveliest smell ever?"

Nodding in agreement, Dylan couldn't help wondering if she knew how her sweet smell completely occluded the odors associated with breakfast. "I'm sure," he said, taking a seat at the same table as the night before.

Watching Honor go about her chores, he decided he was saddened by her choice of wearing a cap. The white cap was pretty enough, but he longed to see the rich, satiny shimmer of black hair he knew it hid. When she placed a plate of food before him, he just smiled.

The food, as always, was exceptional. The hominy grits were generously laden with butter, and the slice of ham nearly covered the plate. He took tea with his meal, but noticed that several men, undoubtedly Whigs, were drinking coffee. The choice amused him.

Liberty tea, they called it. The colonists had been heavy consumers of tea until the tea tax was levied, followed by the outbreak of war. Now, many of them drank coffee in protest. Dylan stared at his mug. If he intended to blend in with the Patriotic crowd here, he should be drinking coffee, too. The idea repulsed him. It was somehow uncivil.

Honor smiled as she passed near his table, and he called out to her, "Miss Richmond!"

A startled look crossed her face as she approached his table. "Is something wrong? If there is, I'll be happy to—"

"No, nothing's wrong." Dylan wondered how he could explain that he preferred coffee to tea, and decided that he should simply say that he'd reverted to old habits when he'd placed his order. "I hope this doesn't inconvenience you, but I'd rather have coffee. I must say that old habits are hard to break, especially when you give them little thought."

Honor smiled broadly. These days, coffee drinkers were usually ardent Patriots. She liked knowing that she and Dylan were on the same side. "Liberty tea?" she asked with a hopeful smile.

Dylan felt a little uncomfortable with her question, but smiled broadly in return. "That's what they call it."

When Honor entered the changing room, her father was standing there glaring at her. "I heard that, Daughter."

"Heard what?" she asked, wondering what she'd done now to invoke his anger.

"I heard you call the coffee 'liberty tea.'" Henry Richmond put down the iron kettle of hominy he had brought in from the kitchen and hung it near the fireplace. "If I've told you one time, I must have told you a thousand—we can't take sides. That's why we serve tea *and* coffee."

Honor grimaced. He always raised such a ruckus over little things. "I didn't mean anything by it, Pa."

"It don't make no difference what you meant. Everybody knows the rebels call it 'liberty tea.' Anybody with a brain bigger than a pea knows that." Henry placed his hands on his hips and glared at her. "I won't have it said that the White Point is taking sides. Why, half our patrons would quit us."

"Yes, Pa," Honor said meekly, knowing that he was probably right. So far, they'd kept all their former customers, and even gained some, because they were strictly neutral. These days, that was difficult to do. "I'll try to do better."

"If anybody should be of a mind to ask which side you favor, just tell them the truth." Henry wiped his brow with the back of his hand and peered through the door to the common room.

"What's that, Pa?" she asked, though she had heard this very same speech so many times she could mouth the words right along with him.

"Just tell them you're a woman and don't have sense enough to have an opinion." Henry glared at her for a few seconds. "And that's the truth. Women's brains was made for tending babies and pleasing their husbands. Politics is too logical for them."

Honor turned around and ladled herself a bowl of hominy. Trembling with anger, she tried to hide her feelings from her father, but it wasn't easy. He often spoke his mind without regard for her sensitivity. Honor wasn't like other women. Even her best friend, Miriam, was more inclined to patter about babies and dresses than politics.

As she sat at the table, Honor's shoulders sagged. Why was she different? Why couldn't she be like other women, content with their station in life? In that moment, she felt so very alone.

She toyed with her breakfast for a few moments, then abandoned the effort. Her father sat there, wolfing down his food as if nothing had passed between them except pleasant conversation.

Thank goodness he'd given up trying to find her a husband. She imagined he still thought that she'd eventually marry Jeffrey. At times, she thought that Jeffrey felt the same way. *Well, let them think it if they will. I've told them both often enough that it's out of the question.*

She pushed back from the table and looked down at her father, trying to quell her anger with little success. "I'm off to the market, Pa."

He glowered at her. "Just be back quickly, Daughter. I'll not be paying you for dawdling down at the fortifications."

Honor stared at him. What could he possibly mean? First of all, he never paid her anything at all, but that wasn't the comment that intrigued her. "What do you mean 'dawdling at the fortifications?' "

"I heard about how all the women from town's been down there to see if they can see Clinton." He stared at her, as if he realized he'd made a mistake in giving her the information. "I won't have a daughter of mine hanging about like common trash down there. You understand me?"

"Yes, Pa," Honor lied, crossing her fingers behind her back. "I understand."

She pulled on her woolen cloak and headed out the door. "Well, I do understand. I wasn't lying," she consoled herself as she reached the street.

"Lying about what?" came a deep, masculine voice from behind her.

"Oh," she gasped and whirled around to see who had heard her. "Mr. Alden!"

"Dylan," he reminded her as he strode to her side. "I believe I heard you correctly, didn't I?"

What could she tell him but the truth? "Yes, you heard me correctly."

"Ah, I thought so. And what brought on that angry retort to the wind?" he asked, drawing his cloak more closely about his shoulders.

Honor smiled. He had a way of making her feel more cheerful. "Well, Mr. Alden—Dylan—the wind and I were discussing a statement I made to my father moments ago."

"Aha!" He exclaimed, playfully shaking his index finger at her. "Lying to your father, eh? Not a good sign, my dear."

My dear. The two words rang musically in her ears. She liked Dylan Alden. He seemed to have a sense of humor about life that was refreshing in this time of war. "Not exactly," she explained. "I didn't actually lie to him."

"Continue. Remember, the severity of your punishment will be commensurate with the offense, so state your case well." Dylan linked his arm with hers.

He stopped suddenly and gazed down at her. What was he doing? Had he taken leave of his senses? His cheeks warmed, and he realized that for the first time in his life—well, in many years—he might be blushing. Dylan Alden blushing?

Preposterous.

Honor looked up at him. Why had he stopped so suddenly? Could it be his leg? "Is something wrong?" She tried not to think about his arm linked with her own, but she couldn't avoid it.

"Wrong?" Dylan felt foolish. "Nothing's wrong. You were saying about your non-lie?"

"Non-lie? I like that. Well, my father mentioned something about the women of Charleston going down to the fortifications to see if they could spot Clinton." Honor went on to explain what he'd said. "So, I just said I understood. I didn't say I wouldn't do it myself. He thought I meant that I'd go straight to the wharf."

"I see. The plot becomes clear." Dylan laughed. He'd seen the women of the city staring out over the harbor, too. He thought it a dangerous occupation, but none of them seemed frightened in the least.

"Well, when word of Clinton's arrival reached Charleston, I think everybody went through a period of fear, but we're confident that our troops can..." Her voice faded into the moaning of the wind. "What I mean to say is that the, well, the Patriots aren't afraid of Clinton, and the Loyalists will welcome him."

Neutrality. The White Point Inn and Tavern was strictly neutral in this war, or so Henry Richmond had explained. Dylan knew it wasn't so, had known it for some time, but he had to admit that they succeeded in being as courteous to the Loyalists as to the Patriots. Whatever the political leanings of the management, they never let it show. "Sort of something

for everyone," he murmured, agreeing with her about th
Charleston people's sentiments.

"I suppose." Honor realized that both of them had bee
walking toward the fortifications without ever having dis
cussed the direction of their stroll. She knew that her fathe
would have fits if she were gone too long. "Maybe we'd bet
ter hurry. My father is expecting me back shortly. Will i
bother you if we walk faster?"

"No, I'll be fine." Dylan smiled at her. She was a thought
ful woman, he was discovering. "I have longer legs, remem
ber?"

They walked faster and quickly reached the fortifications
From there, Honor could see little. The American fleet, a
contingent of seven ships, was supposed to be at anchor in th
harbor, though she couldn't see them. Several small ships ha
been sunk out at the entrance to the Cooper River, to preven
the British ships from stopping supplies coming into the port
On the left, Fort Moultrie, along with the treacherous sand
bar, guarded the entrance to the harbor.

"Commodore Whipple and the cannon of Fort Moultri
won't let the British ships get past," she murmured, hardl
realizing she spoke aloud. She glanced around the harbor. Th
American ships still weren't to be seen. They must have gon
out to meet the British fleet, she decided hopefully.

Dylan shook his head. "You wouldn't expect so, but I thin
the townspeople should be doing more to prepare." H
glanced around at the gathering crowd. "These women an
children should be sent out of town, for I suspect that whe
the battle begins, not even the gates of hell could contain th
British this time."

Honor looked up at him. Deep down inside, she had to ac
knowledge that he might be right, but the Patriot in her re
fused to believe him. "We...I mean, the Patriots defeate
Clinton here before."

"Honor, Clinton's naval support couldn't get into the ha
bor at the time because of the unfavorable winds and th
cannon fire from Fort Moultrie. We can't count on that thi
time." Dylan wanted her to be aware of the danger. In fac
he realized she should probably leave town until the threa
passed. Once Clinton had defeated the Patriots, Charlesto
would be a much better place to live. Order would be n

tored, and people could go about their business without fear
f reprisals.

Honor could say nothing. He was right. When Clinton had
ried once before to defeat the city of Charleston, he'd failed,
ut a big part of that failure had been due to the weather. She
fted her chin. She had confidence in the Patriot forces.
Commodore Whipple would prevent the British from enter-
ig the harbor. Anyone could see that a ship coming from the
Atlantic Ocean couldn't get past the sandbar with the wrecked
hips *and* past Fort Moultrie. Even if they did, the American
leet would be firing at them from the harbor. Impossible.
Defeat was unthinkable.

"Not so long ago, when I was a little girl, cattle used to
raze there on the *faussebrai*. Pa says the man who built it
omplained and complained about the cows, but nothing was
lone for a long time." Honor shook her head sadly. "How
imes change."

"That they do." Dylan looked at the fortifications, or
aussebrai, as she'd called it. "Hard to imagine cattle there."

"Children, too. They had a hard time keeping boys from
Jlaying there. They liked to slide down the steep bank. And
tow we're depending on that high grassy bank as a part of our
lefense." Nothing much seemed to be happening—at least,
tothing they could see. Honor glanced up at Dylan. "I sup-
Jose I'd better go. My father will already be angry. I've been
one too long."

Dylan looked along East Battery Street at the throng of
Jeople. Among the merchants, ordinary citizens and soldiers
vere groups of seedier-looking men. He smiled at Honor. "I'll
valk you to the wharf."

"That won't be necessary." Honor hoped he'd come any-
vay, but she didn't want him to think he had to feel respon-
ible for her. She'd been going to the markets and wharves for
ears to order the foodstuffs for the tavern. She certainly
ould handle herself against the riffraff that always seemed to
e around.

Dylan realized she was an independent sort of woman, so
e tried to soften the impact of his pronouncement. "I just
teant that I'd like to walk along. I need employment. Maybe
ne of the warehouses could use my help. Even though I can't
ght, I can serve in other ways."

Honor nodded. She agreed wholeheartedly with that sentiment. There were many people—her father, for instance—who felt it was important to concentrate on keeping the city operational for the citizens. Without the taverners and merchants, people would starve. There were others of like mind who served in other capacities. Now even Honor was working for the Patriot effort.

As they walked along, her eyes were drawn to the steeple of St. Michael's. Once a proud monument, gleaming in the sun, it was now a blackened monolith.

Near the wharf, they ran into Jeffrey Sheridan, who was walking with a small boy. "Hello, Jeffrey. You remember Mr. Alden?"

Jeffrey glanced at her and then at Dylan. "Of course. How are you this morning, Mr. Alden?"

"Call me Dylan. I'm fine." Dylan noticed the looks that Jeffrey kept giving Honor.

He's in love with her. Dylan knew that he was right in his assessment. Jeffrey was in love with Honor, but Dylan suspected that the young woman didn't share that feeling. He also sensed that Jeffrey knew as well.

Jeffrey placed his hand on the small boy's shoulder. "This is Paddy, a young friend of mine."

Honor smiled at the boy. She'd seen the street urchin many times. He seemed an industrious sort, always running errands or helping someone. "Nice to meet you, Paddy."

"Oh, I seen you about, miss." Paddy grinned. One of his teeth was missing, but it didn't deter him. "And you, too, sir."

"I believe I've noticed you as well," Dylan replied. The boy was observant. Dylan had seen him all over town and suspected that he didn't have much of a home if he had one at all. He felt sorry for the lad. "I—I'm staying over at the White Point Inn. Stop by now and then. I might have an errand for you to run occasionally."

Paddy grinned again. "That's my job. Running errands."

Dylan ruffled the boy's hair. "I thought it might be."

"Well, we won't keep you." Jeffrey gazed at Honor.

"I should hurry," Honor said, remembering her father's instructions. "I hope to see you again soon, Paddy."

Honor and Dylan hurried on their way. As they walked along the wharfs on the Cooper River, she noticed several ships anchored there. "The American fleet. They're anchored here."

"What?" Dylan asked, following her gaze.

"I wonder why? Oh, well, I suppose it doesn't matter. They're here. That's what counts."

Dylan nodded.

They reached the fish market and she selected several fish, a bushel of oysters and some shrimp. From there she went to the vegetable market. With the war going on, food was becoming more and more scarce, but she bought what she could. She took a small portion of the order, things Della needed right away, wrapped in brown paper. "Deliver the rest today, please," she called as they were leaving.

Dylan walked almost all the way back to the inn with her, but stopped at Tradd Street. "I've some errands of my own to run, so I'll see you later. Perhaps at supper."

Honor agreed and went on her way. She knew that by now her father would be furious, but there was little she could do about it. When she went through the gate into the back yard, he was digging furrows for a vegetable garden.

"Well, it's about time you came home!" he shouted, leaning on his hoe.

"I ran into Jeffrey Sheridan near the fish market." She held up the parcel to show that she'd gone where he'd sent her. "I need to take these to Della."

She left her father grumbling about the unreliability of women. "Della, here are the onions and radishes you wanted."

Henry Richmond walked into the kitchen and smiled at Della a moment before he turned to his daughter. "Have you nothing else to do?"

Without waiting for her father to get angry with her, Honor hurried out of the kitchen. Della called after her, "Send one of those lazy girls down here."

"All right," Honor yelled back as she continued into the house. She had beds to make, her mother to check on and the tavern to set up for dinner. As she was making beds, she remembered that Dylan had mentioned that he'd see her at supper. She supposed that meant he wouldn't be home for dinner.

She found one of the servant girls gathering dirty linens to be washed. "Della needs you for a while."

"Yes, miss," the girl answered, hurrying down the stairs.

Suddenly, Honor stopped. Why had her father, who'd seemed so grumpy when she returned from the store, changed so radically when he'd entered the kitchen? Trying to remember the way her father treated Della, Honor sank into a chair. The thought was staggering. Her mother had been frail and ill for so long, might her father have taken comfort elsewhere? In Della's bed?

Could that be why the Irishwoman didn't seem interested in other men? Honor suddenly felt ill. How could her father . . . Her father had his faults, as did everyone, but would he stoop so low as to dally with one of his employees? If he had, how did Della feel about it?

Honor began to see the truth—or what she thought was the truth. Henry Richmond and Della must have loved each other for many years.

She could never hate Della. The older woman had been more of a mother to Honor than Ruth Richmond could ever be. When Honor had been hurt as a child, it was Della she ran to for comfort. When Honor was happy about something, she'd gone first to Della. When her mother became ill, Della had assumed the extra duty of caring for her. The cook worked tirelessly to encourage Honor's mother to eat, to sit up awhile each day, to take an interest in life, though most of her ministrations were met with a blank stare.

Should she ask Della or her father about their relationship? Honor knew she couldn't do that. She was certain, however, that she'd just discovered a secret that must remain a secret.

Dylan slipped away from town, carefully picking his way along a path that paralleled the Ashley River. He'd spent too much time with Honor, but he couldn't regret it. She was a cheerful girl, and much more intelligent than most women he knew.

He peered across the fortifications, knowing that he still had a good distance to walk. Dylan hoped that his route hadn't been noted by anyone who might be in a position to understand why he was going this way.

When he was more than a mile away from the fortifications, he slowed his pace. His leg was troubling him more than he wanted to acknowledge. The tight bandages caused pain in his lower leg, but he didn't have time to stop and loosen them. He was already too close to the appointed time to dawdle.

Dylan soon reached a path that led through a copse of palmettos down toward the Ashley River. He stopped, bent over and rubbed his leg while he peered behind to make sure he wasn't being followed. After a moment, he straightened and quickly took off down the path. He didn't want to appear on the bank of the river, so he waited among the rushes and palms for Cedric Hillard, his contact from Clinton's camp, sitting on a fallen tree in the meantime. He wasn't really in a hurry to see the man as he didn't particularly like him; he had to admit, however, that Cedric Hillard was good at his task.

After a few moments, he heard the sounds of someone coming through the rushes. Dylan pulled out his pistol and remained very still. From his position, he could see almost everything in the direction of the river and also back toward town.

Then he spotted Cedric's head bobbing up and down. Dylan waited until the man was closer and then called quietly, "Cedric!"

Cedric's head turned quickly and he moved toward Dylan's hidden position. "'Ello, Dylan, old friend—er, London, I mean. Got to remember to call you that! Good to see you again."

Dylan ignored the greeting and asked, "What of preparations to attack?"

"To the point, eh?" Cedric chuckled and looked down at Dylan. "Still angry with me about the leg? I 'ad to do it, you know. Would 'ave give you away as a Tory if'n I hadn't."

"I think, Cedric, you could have done less damage." Dylan grimaced as he remembered fleeing with a small band of Patriots and being shot by one of his own men. He understood the reasoning, or thought he did, but he knew that Cedric was a much better marksman. Still, they had to work together. Dylan refused to allow his personal feelings to interfere with the job he had to do.

Cedric shrugged. "Here's the news. We've taken John's Island without resistance. Nobody much there, anyway. Now we're on James Island. Clinton's men are fording Wappoo Creek. Soon they'll be in place to cross the Ashley River and attack from the west. The fleet is in place outside the Charleston bar, waiting for an opportunity to cross.''

Dylan listened carefully. The plan was sound. With the British ships preventing further help from the American navy, Clinton's plan should succeed. Dylan related the details of what he had seen that morning, and the two men parted with a promise to meet again in two days.

Leaving Cedric behind, Dylan returned to Charleston. Tired though he was, he went about town to see what information he could glean. By the end of the day, he was hungry and worn out. He wanted nothing more than a good meal, a soft bed...and maybe a little conversation with Honor Richmond.

Chapter Three

Honor hurried among the tables, laughing and talking with the patrons who had become friends. Dylan walked in. She smiled at him and raised her hand in greeting.

He looked worn and haggard, as if he'd been working hard all day, she thought. "Good evening, Miss Richmond," he said as he took his usual seat.

"Gracious, Mr. Alden, but you look as if you'd fought Clinton...or Francis Marion all by yourself today." Honor added Marion's name in order to comply with her father's edict about not taking sides. She placed a mug of ale on the table before him, leaned down and whispered, "That was for another man, but you look as if you need it more."

"Thank you, Honor," he murmured in reply, before taking a swig of the cold ale. He ordered his supper and waited for her to bring it to him. Over the past few days, he'd come to enjoy these evenings spent watching her work. As she bustled about, she was as graceful as the tall palmetto palms that danced in the breeze blowing off the Atlantic.

He noticed that several men reached out to pat her on the fanny, but she seemed to know which men to avoid and always slipped past just out of their grasp. Dylan frowned. He thought the men's behavior was in extremely bad taste and wondered why Henry Richmond didn't do something about it.

Honor skirted around another table and came to a stop beside him. "Here's your supper, Dylan. Della makes the best flummery in town. Shall I save some for you?"

"I hope you will." Dylan's mouth watered at the mention of the dessert. "One of my favorites."

With a nod, Honor hurried on. The tavern was full and she could ill afford to tarry overlong with one patron, even if he did happen to be the most intriguing man in the crowded common room.

The evening passed quickly. She was more tired than she could ever remember being in her life. Della and one of the girls had cooked and cleaned dishes until they were exhausted, too. The three women sat around the kitchen and ate their supper well after midnight.

"I can't recollect when I seen as hungry a bunch of men in my life. I'm thinking I never set down for one minute since dinner." Della sipped from her glass of buttermilk and shook her head. "Your pa's got to get us some help."

Honor was reminded of her earlier thoughts. Even though she'd complained to her father about needing more help, he always refused to listen. Maybe if Della told him, he'd change his mind. "You tell him, Della. He never seems to hear me."

"Faith and begorrah! I'll just do that." The older woman finished her buttermilk and stood. "You girls finish. I'll not be cleanin' up after you till that rooster crows ."

"I'm finished, Della," Honor said. "Here, I'll wash all our dishes. You two go on to bed."

Della ambled into the tiny room off the kitchen. She'd occupied that room ever since she'd first come to the White Point Inn and Tavern too many years ago for Honor to remember. Honor watched her go in and close the door. A peaceful feeling settled on her, a peace that came with knowledge. Della and Henry Richmond were in love.

Dylan heard footsteps on the staircase long after he'd gone to bed. He was exhausted from his day's journeys. From now on, when he was scheduled to meet Cedric, he would make sure he didn't do any extensive walking the same day, at least until his leg healed a little better.

He was sure that Honor was mounting the stairs after her long, hard day. Dylan couldn't understand how such a slight young woman could work so hard. Even though her hours were long and the work tedious, she didn't seem to object. She'd made friends with the patrons of the tavern and seemed to get along well with everyone; she could even handle the drunks. Dylan admired her more each time he saw her.

The more he thought about it, the more extraordinary she seemed. In fact, he could probably obtain a lot of valuable information from her. After all, she heard almost everything that went on. He just had to find a way to get it out of her.

He'd tried several times to get her to talk about the things the men in the tavern said, but she was remarkably close-mouthed about what she heard. Maybe she was a woman who didn't gossip at all, though he felt that was as unlikely as a snowfall in Charleston in June. If he couldn't get information from her directly, he'd just have to get her to introduce him to some of her Patriot friends.

Somehow, that thought made him feel less a man. He enjoyed being with her, and to pick her mind for information seemed to cast a shadow over their relationship. Maybe he wouldn't have to do that. There had to be other sources.

Honor bustled among the tables. She smiled at Dylan as she placed his breakfast on the table, but hadn't much time to linger. The tavern was already full of hungry people. She ladled the last of the hominy into a bowl and groaned. She'd have to go to the kitchen to see if there was any more ready.

When she stepped out the back door, she ran headlong into Paddy. "Well, hello. What are you doing here this early in the morning?"

He grinned at her and lowered his eyes briefly. Honor could almost believe the boy was flirting with her. "Well?"

"Miss Richmond, I wondered if I could do some errands for my breakfast?"

Honor's heart went out to him. The child was obviously hungry. "Sure. Wait here."

She went into the kitchen and inquired about more hominy. Della said that it would be ready in a few minutes and that she'd bring it over to the house. Honor went back outside. "Come with me, Paddy."

Leading the way, she went into the changing room and sat him down at the table. "Here. This wasn't enough for a full serving. You eat that and if you're still hungry, we'll find something else. Do you want a biscuit?"

Paddy's dark eyes widened and he licked his lips. "Yes, miss."

Honor put a biscuit on a plate along with some butter. "Here. And call me Honor."

"All right. Did you make this hominy? It's real good." Paddy ate ravenously, breaking off chunks of Della's huge biscuit, slathering them with butter and popping them into his mouth.

"No, we have a cook. Della prepares all our food." Honor placed her arm around his shoulders. "I'll tell her you like it."

"Like what?" Henry Richmond appeared in the doorway. "Who is that?" He pointed a long finger at Paddy.

"Pa, this is Paddy. He's a friend of mine." Honor silently prayed that her father wouldn't be angry with her. He didn't like beggars, even small ones. "He helped me with some packages yesterday and he's going to help me a little around here today."

"Now, Daughter, you know we ain't got no extra—"

"Aye, and that boy's hungry, Mr. Richmond. I got plenty he can do to help." Della strode into the changing room and walked right past Henry. She ladled another spoonful of hominy into the boy's bowl from the pot she carried. "Here, boy. You eat that all up. Next time, come to the kitchen. I'll take care of you."

Honor watched her father shrug and go on into the common room. She was amazed at how easily he gave up the fight. "Thank you, Della. I appreciate that."

"Me, too," Paddy said eagerly. He regarded the two women. "But I can't stay here helping all the time. I got to...I mean, I—I already told somebody I'd help him and I need to be all over town."

"Well, you come by when you're hungry. I'll make sure you get something to eat." Honor started to go into the common room, but suddenly turned around to stare at the boy. *Impossible! He can't be helping Jeffrey. He's just a child.*

Honor looked at Della. She was switching the empty kettle for the full one. Without another word, she left the changing room. "Paddy, you wait right there. I want to talk to you."

Without waiting for an answer, Honor hurried into the common room and refilled the coffee mugs and poured fresh tea for those drinking the brew. Noting that her father was deep in conversation with Jeffrey, she smiled at Dylan and went back to talk to Paddy.

She sat with him while he finished eating. "Paddy," she said finally when he appeared to be slowing down. "Tell me about this man you work for. Do I know him?"

"Sure you do, miss, I mean, Honor. He's Jeffrey." Paddy's voice was still the sweet soprano of a boy who hadn't reached puberty.

Honor swallowed hard and closed her eyes. Why would Jeffrey do such a thing? Would he let this child spy for him? This boy couldn't be older than ten or eleven years. Anger rose in her. "How old are you, Paddy?" she asked, willing her voice to remain even and low.

"I'm 'leven," he answered proudly. "But I'm little for my age."

Trying to smile cheerfully, Honor said, "I'm little for my age, too."

"How old are you?" he asked, innocently.

Taking the hem of her apron, she wiped some of the dirt from his cheeks. "I'm twenty-two."

"You're as little as me and two times as old," he said finally.

"Where do you live, Paddy?"

He frowned a little and looked down. "Around."

"What about your parents?" She couldn't bear to think that he was an orphan living on the streets.

Paddy shrugged. "Never knew my pa. Ma died of the fever 'bout two years ago."

"Where do you sleep?" Her voice was little above a whisper.

Before he could answer, Henry bellowed, "Honor! Git out here."

"Wait here," she said again, going to see what her father wanted.

The tavern was full to capacity. Her father growled something about her being a lazy daughter, but Honor didn't even stop to listen to him. She hurried around the room, taking orders, refilling cups, clearing tables while Henry stood behind the counter glaring at her.

When she finally got back to the changing room, Paddy was gone. She glanced out the back door, but didn't see him. "Cat's foot!" she exclaimed, and filled a bowl with hominy. She hadn't time to go looking for the boy now.

As she ate, she considered her earlier thought. Could Paddy be working as a Patriot spy? Despicable as it was in theory, Honor realized the brilliance of it in practice. While women were nonpersons to the bragging men around town, children were even less so. Who would notice a small boy? Who would guard his tongue for fear of the boy overhearing? Nobody. Tactical brilliance on Jeffrey's part, but dangerous for Paddy.

After the tavern had cleared out, she went searching for the boy. She stopped down at Edward's Sewing Parlor to see if her friend Miriam would like to walk down to the fortifications with her. Since the entire town seemed to gather there each day, Honor felt that it would be a good place to start her search.

"I sure would," Miriam said enthusiastically. "I've been dying to go ever since I heard about Clinton. Isn't it exciting? All this war business is sending prices too high to imagine. Why, I tried to buy a piece of lawn to make a chemise the other day and the shop owner was asking nearly three hundred dollars. It was not much more than a yard in length. What nerve."

Honor could hardly get in a word. They walked along Meeting Street until they came to the fortifications that ran from Granville Bastion at White Point to Battery Broughton farther up the Cooper River. There was already a throng of people there, so Honor and Miriam could see little. "Don't these people have anything to do?" Honor asked, craning her neck to see over the people in front of her.

"I suppose not. I'm taller than you and I can't see, either."

Honor stared at her friend in amazement. "For goodness sakes, Miriam, you're only three inches taller."

Miriam smiled wickedly and touched Honor's nose. "Poor thing. Only five feet tall. Can hardly see over the fence railings."

"Don't be silly." Honor realized that Miriam was simply poking fun at her, but she didn't like it much. "You aren't exactly as tall as a palmetto tree."

Miriam looked at her friend. "What's bothering you? You aren't usually so sensitive, even about your height."

"Why would you think something's bothering me?" Honor asked defensively.

"Because, dear friend, you're always cheerful. Today," she said suggestively, "you're positively braying at me like a donkey. So what is it?"

Honor tried once more to see and knew that there was simply no way. "Come on. I'll tell you as we walk."

They were walking up East Battery when Honor spotted Dylan. She knew that if Miriam saw him, they'd never get away. Honor tried to steer her friend in another direction, but it was too late. Dylan waved and started walking toward them.

"Who's the gentleman with the limp?" Miriam asked, turning to eye Honor suspiciously.

"Oh, he's a guest at the inn." Honor didn't want to say anything more to Miriam, who always jumped to conclusions.

"Do tell," Miriam said and smiled at Dylan as he approached.

"Honor... Miss Richmond, how nice to see you." Dylan noticed the pink tint in Honor's cheeks and felt a little like a schoolboy. Was she blushing because of him? The thought intrigued him.

Miriam turned to stare at Honor, who introduced them. Dylan acted like a perfect gentleman, but Honor could see the wheels spinning in Miriam's head.

"I don't believe I've seen you around town, Mr. Alden," Miriam said, smiling directly at him. "Have you been in Charleston long?"

Dylan studied her. There was no coquetry in her demeanor. She was as intense in her evaluation of him as Honor had been. "No, I assure you I would have remembered a lady as lovely as you."

Miriam's gaze dropped to his attire. "You have a very fine tailor, Mr. Alden. My mother and I operate a sewing parlor. If you've a need of shirts or cravats, please stop in. We're on Tradd Street."

"I will," Dylan said, suddenly conscious of his clothing. He kept his wardrobe in immaculate condition when he could. He didn't have too many clothes, but he made sure they lasted by taking care of them. "I may just do that. Thank you."

"We're the finest seamstresses in all of Charleston," Miriam added, as if he needed further convincing.

Honor suddenly remembered her pact with Miriam. Neither of them ever intended to marry. Was Miriam flirting with

Dylan? Could it be that she would change her mind and marry after all? All the plans they'd made of running their own businesses and being free to do as they chose without the encumbrance of a husband and children seemed for the first time to be in jeopardy.

"May I escort you ladies somewhere?" Dylan smiled at the two women. He looked from Honor to Miriam and couldn't help making a mental comparison. Miriam was a lovely blond-haired woman who seemed to be almost as inquisitive as Honor. She was certainly direct. It was easy to see why they'd become best friends. They both appeared eager to face the world.

"No," Honor answered as quickly as she could, but Miriam's voice chimed in nearly as fast.

"Yes, yes, Mr. Alden." Miriam nudged Honor and smiled brightly. "We'd love to have you accompany us."

"Fine. Where are you going?" Dylan asked. He didn't really have time to escort the two women on their errands, but he'd offered and now was caught very neatly in his own little trap.

"Going?" Miriam repeated, as if she suddenly realized she really had no place to go.

"Yes, Miriam." Honor glared at her friend. Honor had to return to the inn or her father would be angry because she'd been gone so long. Now it seemed that Miriam had plans for her. "Where are we going?"

Color flooded into Miriam's face, and Honor covered her mouth with her hand so that Dylan wouldn't see her smile. Miriam was forever embarrassing herself by speaking first and thinking later.

Honor tried to compose herself and then turned to Dylan. "I believe, Mr. Alden, that we were returning home. I have work to do. My father doesn't like for me to be gone for very long when we're so busy."

Miriam smiled and shrugged. "I guess she's right, Mr. Alden. I need to go back to the shop." After a few seconds, her smile brightened. "But you could accompany me and find out where it is. You said you might need some shirts."

The humor of the moment evaporated for Honor. "Well, then I must leave you. Good day, Miriam . . . Mr. Alden."

She didn't wait, but spun on her heels and hurried off toward home. Honor didn't like the feelings she was experiencing, nor did she understand them. Mr. Alden was no more than a guest at the inn. He meant nothing to her. As she walked along, she tried to analyze her emotions, but kept coming back to Dylan's captivating smile and probing blue eyes.

"It's Miriam," she said emphatically to herself as she entered the gate and crossed the yard. "It has nothing to do with him. She's going to break our pact, I know she is. It has nothing to do with Dylan," she repeated, as if confirming the truth.

Several days passed and the city of Charleston became more choked with people than ever before. Every time Honor left the inn, she was swept along with the flow of citizens heading toward the fortifications. Something was happening that she couldn't discern. Jeffrey hadn't been around for several days, so she couldn't ask him what it was.

Nobody seemed to know anything definite. Of the gossip flying about, everything seemed to be pure speculation. Frustrated, Honor continued to listen for information, hoping to hear something of value to the cause.

One evening near midnight, Jeffrey rushed in and sat at his favorite table. Honor, weary from bustling about all day, nearly fell into a chair opposite him. "What's happening, Jeffrey? Where have you been lately?"

Jeffrey closed his eyes and leaned back for a moment, as if resting from a fatiguing campaign he'd lost. When he finally looked at her again, his expression was grim. "Honor, Clinton's men have moved over the Wappoo River and have taken offensive positions across the Ashley. We're certain they're going to attack any day now."

Attack! The word screamed danger through Honor's body like a banshee. For a few seconds, she sat there staring straight ahead, seeing nothing. "When?" she asked, glancing at Jeffrey apprehensively and then at the window. "When will it happen?"

He shook his head. "How the devil should I know? We've got men trying to find out, but we don't know anything yet. They're just sitting there."

Suddenly, she gazed at him, willing him to go on, willing him to tell her something that would chase away the fear that was building inside her. Honor had always been brave, but she somehow felt that this test of Charleston's strength—of the Patriot army—would be the most significant thus far in the war. Would they be victorious?

"What can I do, Jeffrey? There must be something." She rose and began to pace near where he was sitting. "This waiting is killing me, especially now that I know that mule-headed Clinton is coming closer."

"Mule-headed Clinton?" Dylan's voice came from behind her.

Honor spun around and looked at him in astonishment. She hadn't even heard him come in. "Dylan!" she exclaimed, wondering how much he'd heard. "How long have you been here?"

He chuckled. He hadn't meant to intrude on her conversation. At first, he'd thought they were talking about private matters, but he'd heard the reference to Clinton and had begun to listen more closely. "Long enough to hear you mention Clinton. What makes you think he's mule-headed?"

Honor shrugged. She didn't feel comfortable discussing such important men with Dylan, since she hardly knew him. Even though she'd come to believe that he was a devout Patriot, she was wary of talking to him about her own part in the war. Jeffrey had warned her repeatedly against revealing anything to anyone other than himself. "He's tried to take Charleston before and failed. That's why nobody's really afraid."

"Honor," Dylan said almost in a whisper, "the past has little to do with the present. I hear Clinton has more than ten thousand men." He hesitated a moment, hating to lie about his loyalties, but knowing at the same time that he couldn't reveal the truth. "We here in Charleston have no more than six thousand or so."

Jeffrey watched the two of them carefully for a few seconds. "But six thousand rebels can beat ten thousand British soldiers anytime." He reached out and patted Honor's hand, as if to reassure her. "Don't worry, Honor."

"I won't. They've got to try to get into Charleston and we've always been well defended." She started to add something else, but a thought intruded. Honor glanced around the near-empty tavern. "We should be able to see them from upstairs. Come with me." She grabbed a candle from a table and motioned for the two men to follow.

Leading the way, she scurried up the stairs like a squirrel climbing a tree. She led them past her room and to a tiny room that faced the Ashley River. Throwing open the shutters, she fairly quivered with excitement.

Across the Ashley, on the west bank, were scores of camp fires. "Look!" she exclaimed, pointing. She sank to her knees and propped her elbows on the windowsill. Dylan and Jeffrey did the same.

Against the unfathomable darkness of midnight, only the flames were visible, but she knew that the fires must be surrounded by hundreds ... thousands of men. The three chattered excitedly about the inevitable attack. Dylan seemed a bit reticent to Honor, who took a moment to study his profile in the dim light. A shiver crept up her spine, and she glanced back at the riverbank.

Her fears were replaced by curiosity. For more than two hours, the three of them sat there and stared out the window, talking less and less as time progressed. Honor remembered her chores, but decided she could take care of them later. This was too exciting.

Finally Jeffrey drew his head inside. "I must go. Tomorrow's another busy day for me." He patted Honor's arm as if to comfort her. "Don't worry. We'll keep them out of Charleston."

"I'm not worried." Honor smiled at him, but didn't think he could see her very well. "I'll take the candle and walk you down the stairs."

"Don't bother. I can find my way." Jeffrey hugged her impulsively and rose. "See you tomorrow or the next day."

After Jeffrey was gone, Dylan and Honor sat there for nearly another hour. Even though she couldn't see much, she was unable to pull herself away. History was being made, and she was a part of it.

"Honor, I think you and your family should leave Charleston." Dylan shifted his weight to his right leg and stretched. His muscles were cramping from sitting in the same position for so long without moving, and his injury was aching.

Honor turned and stared at him. "Whatever do you mean?"

He realized that convincing her of leaving would be difficult, especially if she thought he was being condescending. "Didn't you say your mother was ill? I think when the battle begins, she will be terrified. She'll be much better off outside the city."

"We have no place to go, Dylan, even if we should want to leave." Honor glanced back to James Island, the west bank of the Ashley River. "I'm sure my father wouldn't consider leaving town right now. We're too busy."

"Business will diminish considerably when the fighting starts. People will begin leaving in droves." Dylan cast about for something he could use to convince her. "You can always go stay with relatives."

"We won't leave, Dylan. This is our home. Our only home. We have no relatives." Honor cradled her chin in her hands and returned her attention to the river. "They'll never be able to ford the river. There's too many of them. Where would they find the boats?"

From his conversation with Cedric, Dylan knew that the British soldiers were confiscating every boat or raft on John's and James islands. When they were ready to attack, they would have no problems. "I'm sure Clinton will find a way."

The next morning, Honor was up before the sun. She'd hardly slept for thinking about the British so close at hand. Even before she dressed for the day, she stood at her window and peered across the river.

Through the early morning fog, she could barely perceive the beginning activities of an awakening camp. Though her view was excellent, she was too far away to discern more than general movement. As she dressed, she wished she could see better.

To her surprise, when she reached the dining room, a young black woman was starting to set up for the day. Honor nodded. "Hello. Are you going to be working here?"

"Yes, I'm Annie." The slender woman moved from table to table, wiping each with a damp cloth.

"I'm Honor. Pleased to meet you." Honor smiled and hurried out to the changing room, where she found Della bringing in the first kettle of hominy. "Did you know that Papa hired a girl to help us?"

"Aye. I'm believin' he hired two. Got me some help in the kitchen, too. Faith and begorrah, it's about time."

"Two?" Honor was amazed at the revelation. "What happened to make him do that?"

"I told him we needed some help. This war ain't ending soon, so I reckoned how we'd have all the business we can handle and more. Wouldn't want to lose customers cause we can't feed 'em. And you know how he is about money."

Honor laughed. Della's argument was probably the only one that would have influenced Honor's father to hire additional help.

"Here, I'll take a bowl of hominy up to Mama." Honor placed the bowl and a mug of milk on a tray and went upstairs. She had little time to spend with her mother these days and enjoyed the moments when she could, taking the time to feed her mother at least one meal a day. She tapped on her mother's door. "Mama, it's me with your breakfast."

Without waiting for an answer, Honor stepped inside the cool darkness. Her mother had no candle lit. Honor placed the tray on a table and went to find one. When she returned, the dim light exposed her mother's haggard face as she lay covered to her chin with quilts. "Good morning, Mama. It's a pretty day today."

Honor knew her mother wouldn't respond unless the topic truly interested her. Ruth Richmond seldom spoke to anyone these days. Settling herself beside her mother's bed, Honor tucked a napkin beneath her mother's chin and began to feed her. "Charleston's filled with interesting people now, Mama. You should try to regain your strength and come down some evening. The tavern is always busy."

Ruth's eyes betrayed nothing of her thoughts, but she chewed her food hungrily. Her hair, once a vibrant red, was now dull and streaked with gray. Eyes, once an alert, eager brown, were now like shuttered windows, revealing nothing—not even the fragile life that resided inside the disease-riddled body.

Honor continued to chatter, knowing that her mother was listening. "I saw Miriam the other day. She said to tell you hello. We went to the fortifications to see if we could catch a glimpse of Clinton's troops."

Gasping because of the slip, Honor gazed at her mother to see if she'd understood the implication of the remark.

"Clinton?" Ruth murmured, cutting her gaze to her daughter's face.

"Nothing to worry about, Mama," Honor reassured her. So far, her mother had asked nothing of the war, not since Clinton's last attempt to take Charleston. Obviously, she felt threatened once again. "He'll never get through. Commodore Whipple and a part of the Continental navy are anchored right in the Cooper River. We have Fort Moultrie at the mouth of the harbor and fortifications all around. They're building a hornworks to the west, bordered by a canal that stretches from the Ashley to the Cooper River."

Ruth said nothing more, but opened her mouth for another bite of hominy. Honor talked about the two new employees, about how hard everyone was having to work. "We've got new people coming into town every day. Dylan said that—"

"Dylan?" Ruth repeated, her eyes narrowing as she looked at her daughter. "Who is this Dylan?"

Honor realized she'd made another mistake. Her mother had always been insistent that her daughter's conduct be proper and ladylike, even if the family was of the merchant class. "Dylan Alden, Mama. He's a boarder. A nice man who—"

"Why did you call him 'Dylan' then?" Ruth lifted a wrinkled hand from beneath the covers and pointed a too-thin finger at Honor. "Since when do you call a stranger by his given name?"

"We're friends, Mama." Honor knew that her mother would never accept so lame an excuse, but she had no other to offer.

"Friends? How can you be friends with a stranger? How long have you known this man? Who is his family? Why haven't I heard about him before?"

Honor couldn't remember when her mother had been so interested in anything and regretted that Dylan had to be the subject that ignited her concern.

"Honor, I forbid you to become friends with someone I don't know. Men are devious. He could...I'm sure you have better sense than to trust someone you don't know. How many times have I told you—"

"Are you finished eating?" Trying not to appear impatient, Honor placed the bowl back on the tray.

"Don't interrupt me." Ruth raised herself up on one elbow. "Listen well, Daughter. Don't allow this man to treat you with such familiarity. He's up to no good."

"Mama, he's not. He's just being nice." Honor didn't really try to defend Dylan. Doing so would only strengthen her mother's resolve to separate the two.

"Never has a man just been nice for the sake of being nice." Ruth collapsed against her pillow, all her strength seemingly depleted from her frail body. "Mark my words, that man is up to something no good."

Chapter Four

Honor's day passed quickly. She hardly had a chance to breathe. Her dinner was taken in bites between serving the huge crowd of men gathered to discuss Clinton's movements. Suppertime came and went nearly unnoticed, except for the gnawing hunger she felt.

Late in the evening, Dylan returned to the inn. He sat in the tavern, drinking his rum and listening to the heated conversations that had grown by that time to a roar. Every possible angle was discussed and ripped apart, new strategies developed, flaws discovered. Tempers flared.

Ale and rum contributed greatly to the lively debates. Honor had little time to listen, but she tried to hear as much as possible. The problem was that nobody really knew anything. Most of the arguments were merely conjecture.

Dylan, too, listened carefully. His job was to discover exactly how much of Clinton's plans had been leaked to the enemy. What he discovered was that those who were in a position to know anything at all weren't talking. Those closest to the center of the debates were boorish drunks who, after a few drinks, could hardly remember which side of the conflict they'd chosen to embrace.

Soon, Dylan began to concentrate on Honor. Simply watching her made him feel better. The tiresome discussions around him went on until nearly midnight, then most of the men began to leave the tavern.

Jeffrey didn't come in that night, much to Dylan's dismay and delight. Of all the people he'd met, Jeffrey probably knew the most about the fortifications, the Patriot plans, and the espionage network in the city, Dylan had decided.

In fact, the reason he'd first come to the White Point Inn and Tavern was to become better acquainted with Jeffrey Sheridan. The bonus he'd received was meeting Honor.

Dylan watched her bend across a table to wipe it off. Her neat figure attracted him, banishing all thoughts of work and Jeffrey Sheridan. On several occasions, Dylan had studied Jeffrey and Honor, hoping to discern the true nature of their relationship. They laughed easily together, talked quietly and smiled frequently.

Finding that he didn't like the thought of a romantic relationship between the two, Dylan had made his observances more focused during the past week. That Jeffrey was in love with Honor was beyond doubt, but she didn't seem to share that feeling. Dylan knew that women were seldom in love with the men they married, but grew into that emotion during the years of living together. He hoped that wasn't the case with these two. He didn't want Honor to marry Jeffrey.

"Big crowd tonight," Dylan commented as she wiped the table nearest him.

Honor stopped, turned and dropped into the next chair. "A noisy crowd. It's been like this all day. I've hardly had a chance to breathe."

Dylan shook his head. "I can't believe all these people are staying in Charleston. Why don't they leave? Some of them are bound to be injured or killed when Clinton attacks."

Honor shrugged wearily. "I don't know. I can't answer for them. Maybe they have no place to go, like us."

"Seems as if they don't believe the attack will come." Dylan tried to analyze the atmosphere in the city. In the past few days, it had grown almost festive. "They seem to feel this is a party, maybe a masquerade ball."

"I know what you mean. I've noticed that people are much more active and curious than I've ever seen them. I guess nobody believes Clinton can get past our defenses. After all, he tried once before and failed miserably." Honor toyed with her cleaning rag for a moment, thinking of all the people who flocked to the fortifications each day. The event had become a social ritual. "I hope they aren't disillusioned when the battle begins."

"I'm afraid they will be." Dylan studied Honor's face. He could see the fatigue written there. "Why don't you close up for the night?"

"I suppose we're closed, but I still have work to do." Honor looked around. "When I've wiped this last table, I have to put the chairs and benches on the tables, and then scrub beneath them. Then I'll be done."

Dylan was angry that such a lovely young woman was forced to work so hard for so little in return. He rose purposefully. "Here, I'll help you."

Honor jumped up. "Oh, no. Don't worry about it. You go on to bed."

"Nonsense. You're exhausted. The least I can do is put the chairs on the tables for you." He went from table to table doing so. "There. Now you can scrub."

He walked to the stairway and watched her. Even while doing such a menial job, she was feminine. That was the thing he found most intriguing about her. She worked as hard, maybe harder, than any woman he'd ever met, yet she was always feminine and ladylike.

Honor felt self-conscious with Dylan watching her. She'd scrubbed this floor more than a hundred times while Jeffrey stood and talked to her, but this was different. Dylan was different. He was a true gentleman, a man of wealth and fortune. A man of substance.

Honor didn't resent her position in life. In many ways, she was freer to do what she wanted than wealthy planters' daughters were. Honor could walk about the city without a chaperon or laugh and talk with the soldiers or handsome men in the town, but she paid for that privilege by being a serving wench in a tavern.

The term smarted. Even though she wasn't of the same class as the planters, she wasn't beneath them. Thinking about it, she straightened her back and stood more erect. She had her pride.

When she finished, Dylan was still there watching her. "I'm done," she announced.

"Good." He looked across the gleaming, wet floor. "You didn't miss a spot."

Honor grinned, raised one eyebrow and then winked. "Tonight, kind sir, I couldn't care less about missing a spot. I'm more tired than a dog with a host of thirsty fleas."

"Well, if you promise you don't have fleas, or that you won't give them to me if you do, I have a surprise for you." Dylan smiled back at her. When she was happy, her face lit up with a delightful joy that teased dimples into her cheeks and glorious amber twinkles in those huge dark eyes of hers.

"What?" she asked, remembering her mother's words, *He's up to no good.*

"A surprise. Come with me." Dylan turned and went up the stairs without waiting for her answer.

"Dylan, wait a minute." She blew out all the candles except for one, which she picked up. Hurrying after him, she wondered about the surprise. Nobody ever gave her anything but more work to do.

When she reached the second floor of the inn, she turned toward his room. There she met him, coming back out.

"Come with me," he said mysteriously and headed for the stairs.

Honor followed him up to the third floor, where she and her parents slept. Dylan went to the empty room she'd taken him to before, when they'd first seen the British across the river. They went inside, Honor a little hesitantly.

What's he up to? she wondered, praying that her mother wasn't right about him.

Once inside, Dylan went immediately to the window. Puzzled, Honor went with him. Then reached inside his coat and pulled out a long, narrow object. "Here, look through this."

"What is it?" she asked, trying to get a good look at the object in the darkness.

"A spyglass." Dylan showed her how to adjust the lens so that she could see better.

"Ooh, I can see the fires much better. I can even see . . ." Honor peered through the glass, trying to understand what she was seeing. "I can even see people, I think. Must be the guards."

Dylan knew he probably shouldn't have given her the spyglass, but it really couldn't hurt. People all over Charleston were peering out their windows through instruments very similar to the one he'd just given Honor. There were no secrets to be divulged by letting her watch while the troops prepared for battle, so he felt good about giving her a means of entertaining herself.

"Where did you get this?" she asked, never taking her eyes from the sight before her.

"I was in a shop this afternoon. Someone asked for one. There were several left, and I thought you might like one."

Dylan couldn't help feeling pleased with himself. It was seldom that he could make someone happy so easily. Honor deserved a little happiness. She worked too hard.

She turned slowly to face him. "You bought this for me?"

"Yes. Just today."

"I—I can't accept this, Dylan...Mr. Alden." She held the spyglass out to him. Maybe her mother had been right. Had Dylan bought this gift as a means to—to do whatever her mother thought he might?

"What do you mean? Of course you can take it." Stunned, Dylan stared down at the object. Clearly, she'd been delighted with the gift. Why was she turning it down? He placed it on the ledge between them.

"My mother told me never to take gifts from strangers." Honor repeated her mother's admonishment, though she truly felt that her parent was being foolish.

Dylan suddenly understood. A mother's way of protecting a virginal daughter. "We're not strangers, Honor. We're friends, remember?"

"We barely know each other." Honor tried to see what he was thinking, but the light was far too dim. "We just met."

"Nonsense. Time has nothing to do with friendship." Dylan recognized the hand of her parents in her actions. He knew that Honor didn't really feel that way, but convincing her that they could be friends might prove difficult. He felt the return of guilt, unable to rid himself of it even though he was doing what he considered a necessary job. "Honor, sometimes people are friends immediately after they meet. It's almost as though they've known each other a lifetime. We're like that, or close to it. Don't let your mother's prejudice ruin our relationship."

"It's not that. I mean, I know that she's just being protective, but—"

"But what? Tell me what's wrong." Dylan placed his hands on her shoulders. Sparks seemed to fly between them, as if iron had struck flint where he touched her.

"I—I don't know." Honor felt herself giving in. Things were moving too fast for her.

Dylan recognized that she was truly confused. "Look, Honor. Let's say this is mine, and I'm lending it to you indefinitely. Would that be all right?"

"Yes, I suppose it would." Honor considered his offer. "That way, it wouldn't really be a gift, would it?"

"No. Not at all." Dylan smiled at her delight when she picked up the glass and began to gaze out into the darkness again. "But I think you'd be better off looking across the river during the day. There's probably much more to see."

"You're right, of course." Honor lowered the glass. "I'm really tired. Do you want me to leave the glass here? That way, we can both use it."

"No, I'd be afraid it would get broken. Why don't you take it to your room." Dylan linked his arm through hers. "If I want to look out, I'll borrow it back from you."

Honor rose on Sunday morning before dawn. As the sun broke across the eastern horizon, she was staring through the spyglass toward the western bank of the Ashley River. When the sun began to dispel the mist, she could see more clearly. Men in red coats, tan breeches and high black boots were gathered around the fires. There were so many of them! How could the Patriots ever hope to defeat such a strong army?

Honor couldn't dwell on the hopeless feeling that all those troops gave her. She had to be positive. Somehow, some way, the Patriots would repel Clinton's advance when it came. They had to.

Today was March 12. Clinton's men had been in possession of John's Island and James Island for several days now and nothing had happened. Honor prayed that nothing would.

She could dally no longer. Her father would be on a rampage by now. He wouldn't tolerate someone who didn't do his or her job. Honor took the spyglass back to her room and then went downstairs. As she expected, Henry Richmond was already grumbling about her getting up so late.

She explained to her father that Dylan had lent her a spyglass and that she'd been watching out her window. Everyone would want to know about the British troops' movements, and now she could tell them.

The tavern was nearly empty at this hour. She began preparing for those who would inevitably stop in for breakfast. As she was working, a boom thundered forth and shook the inn. Honor felt the panic rise in her. For a few seconds, she stood there, rooted to the floor.

Then she raced up the stairs, snatched her spyglass from its hiding place and went to the window where she could see best. Puffs of smoke nearly obscured the river, but she could see British soldiers firing cannons. The rebels were returning the fire. She forced herself to calm down. Neither side seemed to be inflicting much harm on the other. In fact, most of the cannonballs were falling into the water.

Still, the threat was enough to frighten many people into the streets. Honor could hear women screaming and children crying. At last the firing seemed to slow down a little, and she relaxed. If this was all that was going to happen, she was glad. Nobody in the city would be harmed. The British cannonballs weren't getting past the earthworks at the end of Tradd Street.

Every time she got a free moment, Honor raced up the stairs and peered through the glass. There was no more firing, but everyone was eager to know what was going on. When she went back downstairs, she would tell a few of her favorite patrons what she'd seen. By midafternoon, the tavern was filled with people who wanted to know what was happening across the river.

Henry realized that here was a chance to make even more money. He began to encourage her. "The White Point Inn and Tavern will be the news center of Charleston. We'll pass the information on to our customers."

Word soon spread. By the supper hour, the common room was packed. Honor was perched at her spying post, with Paddy bringing the information downstairs to tell all the interested listeners. Henry's prediction had come true.

Dylan realized that if he didn't find a position in town that would be of vital enough importance to keep him from fighting, he might be conscripted into the Patriot force. The South Carolina Militia was a loosely organized group, but with the siege coming, the leaders would be getting desperate.

He began to look for such a post. By accident he discovered that a warehouseman was having to leave Charleston with his pregnant wife. The woman had been hysterical since the cannon firing had begun yesterday. The doctor had suggested that she might feel more secure in the country.

Dylan went to the warehouse and talked with the owner. The warehouseman was happy to offer to hire Dylan as his assistant, but Dylan insisted on buying into the venture. He felt a little guilty when he claimed to have been injured in the battle to save Savannah, but knew his job was vital to British success and lied convincingly. He realized his new partner would never have allowed anyone who wasn't a true rebel to buy into the business.

The man explained the operation to Dylan and left. From the information he'd obtained about the warehouse when he'd first heard of the man's situation, Dylan knew that many of the supplies for the Patriot force were funneled through there. His dilemma was soon solved. Even though he'd actually be giving aid to the enemy, Dylan could slow down the shipments or arrange for some of the supplies to be captured by the British.

In operating the warehouse, Dylan was in a position to learn a great deal about troop movements and supply trains. All this information would be beneficial to his side.

At the same time, he could claim to be aiding the Patriots. Though he hated using his friendship with Honor to obtain information, he was certain that she heard many things that he could pass on to Clinton's army. When the time was right, he would become so close that she would begin to pass on to him the secrets she heard. The gift of the spyglass was his first step. He was, in reality, paying for the information he obtained from her by allowing goods to be shipped to the Patriots.

When his workday was over, he hurried back to the tavern to tell her of his new job. He was certain she would be impressed.

To his surprise, the tavern was packed with people eager to hear about Clinton's army and the shelling of Charleston. Every few minutes, Paddy would come down the stairs with a full report. The child would then run through the streets, telling anyone who wanted to know, what was going on.

An efficient news network, Dylan decided, as he made his way through the throng and went upstairs. He stopped at his room long enough to wash his hands and face. After such a busy day, he felt grubby.

He knew Honor would be in the little room on the third floor. Mounting the stairs, he felt his spirits lift the closer he got to her. His reaction to her was most puzzling to him. One of these days he'd have to stop and give some serious consideration to the effect she had on him.

When he reached the small room, he found it empty. Disappointed, he started to leave, then noticed the open window. "Might as well take a look while I'm here," he said aloud.

"What?" Honor poked her head in the window. "Oh, Dylan, it's you. What did you say?"

Astonished to find Honor sitting on the roof, he rushed forward. "What are you doing out there? Don't you know it's dangerous?"

"I'm fine. The slope of the roof isn't steep here. And the British aren't firing anymore." Honor edged over slightly. "Come on out."

Dylan looked down at the roof, wondering if it would hold his weight. Taking a chance that it would, he joined her. "I suppose the view is better from here?"

"Most assuredly," she answered, handing him the glass. "Have a look for yourself."

Dylan took the spyglass and adjusted it for his right eye. He peered across the river to the encampment. The red woolen coats of the British troops were easily visible from the roof of the tavern.

"I know there's not much going on right now, but it's interesting to watch, isn't it?" Honor stared across the river. Even without the glass, she could see the soldiers, though not nearly so well. "Papa thinks this is just wonderful. We've never had so many customers." She hesitated a moment. "I must admit that I was a little afraid when the firing started, but it can't reach us here."

Dylan chuckled. His gift to her had inadvertently made her have to work harder. "Sorry. I didn't intend to add to your job. But I don't think you should sit out here during the shelling. It's much too dangerous."

"Oh, don't worry. I've been here most of the day." Honor smiled broadly. Dylan's glass had saved her from a hard day's work. "Papa thinks that giving reports about the troop movements is drawing more customers, so I've been assigned to stay here and watch them. Paddy is passing the word."

"Yes, I met him downstairs. Quite the enterprising lad, isn't he?" Dylan handed the glass back to her. Then he noticed her pink nose and cheeks. The warm sun had kissed her face with color. "You'd better be careful or you'll end up with a nasty sunburn."

"I'd thought about wearing a hat, but I haven't had a chance to go back inside to get one." Honor relaxed against the gable of the house. "I'll remember tomorrow."

Dylan looked down at her. Honor took genuine pleasure out of life, snatching bits of joy from the most uncommon places and events. He'd realized from the beginning that she was somehow different from the women he'd known in the past, but until this moment, he hadn't understood how deep that distinction went. Thinking back over his life, he decided that he'd had more fun with Honor than with anyone else. He was a long way from settling down; he might never marry. But when he did decide to take that step, he wanted it to be with a woman like her. He couldn't help the tinge of guilt that stayed with him because of the way he was using her.

Sensible, intelligent, witty, clever...these were all traits he'd connected with her during the past few days. He grinned rather foolishly as he watched her staring through the spyglass. This trip to Charleston was taking him down many paths he'd never sought to travel—and he was enjoying every step of the way.

Though days passed quickly for Dylan, the firing continued. Each day, both sides would fire their cannons and guns for about two or three hours, inflicting little damage on each other. Dylan began to wonder why they were wasting the gunpowder, but decided that they must have a strategy of their own.

His warehouse, as he now called it, was a prosperous venture. All manner of necessities were funneled through the building. The few employees were a little wary of Dylan at first, but gradually came to accept him as another Patriot who was unable to fight because of his physical limitations.

Dylan's job, his real job, was a tense, time-consuming one. Every moment of his day was devoted to listening for information, talking to people who might know something of value and passing it on to Cedric. His job had purpose. Dylan was proud to be of service to his king and country. One day soon the war would end and Dylan would find some property for himself and settle down to raise rice or indigo.

A planter. Dylan had left the antiquated class system of England to come to America. Here, even though the colony was under British rule, there was no rigid class distinction. A man was accepted for who he was, more or less. Especially here in Charleston, a second son was every bit as important as the first.

Dylan loved the beautiful, wild countryside. Much of its vast expanse was still available for settlement. Deep down, he felt that he truly belonged here. He hoped that there would be something left to own when this terrible war ended.

He worried that the war would leave a chasm between the two sides, Patriot and Tory, but could only pray that bridges would be built as quickly as possible to connect the polarized parties. At times he wondered what his part would be when that time came. Would his spying be the salt that prevented the wound from healing naturally? He hoped not.

From the window in his small office, Dylan could see the Continental navy. Henry Laurens, president of The Continental Congress, had committed a full third of the navy for Charleston's defense, and it seemed to Dylan that Commodore Whipple might possess the will and the knowledge to prevent the British navy from taking the harbor. Only time would tell.

Dylan's thoughts turned, as they inevitably did of late, to Honor. Her image was constantly in his mind, her fresh, unrestrained smile calling a grin to his own face. Though he knew he should remain at the warehouse to prepare a shipment of goods to be sent up the Cooper River, he closed his office and returned to his lodgings.

Upon entering the yard of the inn, he discovered that even more people were clamoring to get inside than before. Honor's reports attracted people from everywhere, especially those who had no access to a rooftop with a view of the Ashley River. Dylan pushed his way past the men outside and shoved his way among those fortunate enough to get a table as well as those waiting for one.

He spotted the Irishwoman, Della, and nodded. He decided to go on upstairs, rather than try to be served here in this mob scene. There'd be no information to be gotten from these men now. Perhaps later, when some of the rowdier ones had tumbled away for the evening, he'd have better luck.

When Dylan reached the third floor, he went to the little room. Honor would be perched outside on the roof, he knew. He poked his head out the window and smiled at her as she turned to look at him.

"Oh, I thought you were Paddy." She lowered the telescope and studied him for a moment. "Quite a raucous crowd in the common room this afternoon, is it not?"

"Quite." Dylan climbed through the window and settled onto the roof next to her. He accidentally brushed against her as he tried to make his wounded leg more comfortable. He gazed at her for a minute, refreshing his image of her with the true beauty of her face. Somehow, no matter how he pictured her, she was lovelier in person.

Honor smiled at him. She didn't know why he was staring at her so blatantly. The warm westerly wind ruffled her hair and she brushed it back out of her face.

She handed him the glass and he peered through it. The amount of activity had changed little. Remarkably, the people with access to spyglasses could discern very little of the soldiers' purpose as they walked about the camp. Dylan knew, however, that they were building a fortification for the coming siege.

He turned to Honor and handed back the glass. "Very interesting."

"Yes, the people of Charleston are quite interested in every move the British make." Honor turned slightly and edged toward the east end of the roof. "Come over here."

Dylan followed, a little puzzled.

"Look there." She handed him the glass and pointed in the direction of the fortifications.

Looking into the spyglass, Dylan was amazed. The throng of people gathered between Granville Bastion and Broughton's Battery had grown even larger. He lowered the glass and considered the implications. Where had all of them come from? What did they expect to see? "I don't understand what they're looking at."

Honor shrugged and shook her head. "Neither do I. The view from the fortification is not half as good as from up here. The British soldiers are too far up the Ashley."

"Honor, I really wish your family would leave town. I'm afraid that when the fighting begins, you...someone will be injured—or worse." Dylan, more than most men in Charleston, realized that the houses near White Point on the Ashley River side of town were in grave danger.

"What's going to happen, Dylan?" Honor finally asked. "I've been here for days, watching them. Most of the time they don't seem to be doing anything but sitting around."

"I suppose it seems that way." Dylan knew that the people of Charleston were speculating wildly. He also knew that the military men in town were well aware of the reason Clinton hadn't attacked. The big British ships couldn't get into the harbor, not as long as the wind blew from the west.

"Have you seen Jeffrey?"

"No, have you?" Honor had expected to see her friend sometime during the day, since he hadn't appeared the previous night. "I'm worried about him."

Dylan gazed at her, wondering once again about her relationship with Jeffrey Sheridan. "Shall I make inquiries or try to find him?"

Her face registered shock, as if his question implied some injury to her old friend or some danger. Dylan watched her as she considered how to answer his question.

Finally, she shook her head. "No. I think Jeffrey would be upset with me if I sent someone searching for him. Thank you for offering."

"What about the boy, Paddy? Have you seen him?" Dylan asked, changing the subject abruptly.

Again, Honor shook her head. "He was here earlier, but he's been gone for most of the afternoon. It's really annoying, too. He promised he'd spread the news about the soldiers, but I suppose he's lost interest."

"Oh, I wouldn't worry too much about him. He's a growing boy." Dylan pictured the lad in his mind. "I remember when I was his age. Everything was an adventure to me."

"I'm sure that's true," Honor admitted with a slight smile. "But you weren't living in a city about to become the focus of a major battle."

"I suppose you're right, but I'm sure he'll be fine. He'll reappear soon and be astonished that you were concerned for his safety."

Honor nodded, realizing that Dylan was probably right. Little boys were like that, but Paddy wasn't just another little boy. He was special. His job was dangerous, and she couldn't help being concerned for him. "Papa hired two more girls today. We can't seem to keep up with the work." She grinned sheepishly. "But he won't let me come down from here. We're the most popular tavern in all of Charleston because of the firsthand reports we give."

Honor stared out at the harbor. The British warships were out there somewhere, waiting for something. What? Once again the wind blew her hair into her eyes and she tucked it back into the bun at the nape of her neck. As she did so, her mind began to work. The wind! That was why the British ships couldn't get into the harbor.

She looked at Dylan. He knew why the ships were waiting. She expected that Jeffrey probably knew as well. Neither of them had thought to tell her. They both felt that she wouldn't understand. Well, she'd show them both what she knew and what she could do. When she got a chance.

As they sat there talking, the sun began to set. With dusk came the end of her job. She could see little except camp fires across the river at night, even with the spyglass. Honor didn't want to break the congenial atmosphere between her and Dylan, but she realized they couldn't stay on the roof much longer. "I suppose it's time to go inside."

They crawled along the roof and then back through the window. Honor took the spyglass to her room and hid it away before heading downstairs.

Dylan followed her, and when they reached the second floor, he stopped. "Will you have my supper sent up to me? I can't abide the thought of trying to dine amidst that boisterous mob in the common room."

"I'll see to it." Honor was a little disappointed. She enjoyed the friendship that had developed between Dylan and herself and had hoped he'd sit in the common room, where she could occasionally stop to chat with him.

It was just as well that he didn't come down. The room was crowded past capacity with people anxious to hear the latest news. They were looking for someone to drink with, someone to boast to and, just perhaps, someone to bolster their courage. Honor sped from table to table, having to squeeze among the men who had no chairs but were standing beside the tables to participate in the discussions.

Honor darted among them, trying desperately to remember who'd been served and who'd paid. Even though the tavern stood to make a good profit that night, she would have gladly done with about half the number of customers.

At one table she had to wait for one man to finish his lengthy explanation of sails and wind. Her senses perked up and she listened, all the while gazing around the room as if she were bored.

"Can't get in. The west wind keeps them out." He looked at the other men at the table to see if he had their attention. "Now, you see a sailor, like myself, who's familiar with the bar, might take a chance."

"Sailor like you? Hell, there ain't no sailors like you," A man smoking a cigar said, blowing smoke as he spoke. "I'd venture you couldn't sail a rowboat in Town Creek."

"Say, what do you know about me? I sailed, I did."

The other men laughed. Honor didn't know whether he knew what he was talking about or not, but his thoughts were the same as hers.

As the patrons left after midnight, Jeffrey stopped in. By this time, Dylan had come down for a glass of brandy and a cigar. The three sat at a table and talked about the people of the city and their fascination with Sir Henry Clinton and his army.

"Nobody understands why Commodore Whipple doesn't do something. He's anchored there in the Cooper River and General Lincoln can't convince him to fight," Jeffrey said, leaning back in his chair. He looked tired and worn, as if he'd been fighting a battle all his own. "What does he think Congress sent him here for?"

"I saw the ships there the other day and wondered the same thing." Honor looked to Dylan, to see if he knew anything about the problem.

Dylan privately hoped that Whipple would stay where he was. The British were already removing the water, stores, guns and cannons from the *Renown,* the *Roebuck* and the *Romulus,* so they could sail easily across the Charleston bar. The smaller ships would have no problem crossing the bar into Five Fathom Hole. "From what I can understand, Whipple has holed himself up inside the barrier he created when he sank the ships across the mouth of the Cooper River. It doesn't look like he plans to fight.''

"That's exactly what I'm talking about. He keeps telling Lincoln that the conditions right for the British ships to sail into the harbor would create too heavy a swell in Five Fathom Hole. The Americans couldn't anchor and bring their broadside guns to bear on the British fleet.''

"Why doesn't he just sail out past the bar? Can't he engage them there?'' Honor didn't understand naval tactics too well, but it seemed to her that fighting was better than waiting, especially when the stakes were so high.

Both men glanced at her and shrugged. Neither could give her an answer.

A little while later, she walked Jeffrey to the door. "Good night, Jeffrey.'' She leaned forward and whispered, "I believe Arbuthnot can't come in until the wind changes. What do you think?''

"Makes sense. Who told you that?''

"I figured it out. I was watching the ships out there, and it just came to me. Then I heard a man talking about it here tonight. He said the same thing.''

"I'll pass it on, though I'm sure that some of our men already know the reason Clinton's waiting to attack.''

A few days later, Jeffrey came bursting through the doors of the tavern and raced up the stairs to Honor's perch on the roof. "Look,'' he shouted, pointing to the bar.

Honor turned and gazed through the spyglass, only this time she didn't really need it. With her own eyes, she could see the British ships sailing past Fort Moultrie. Right into Charleston Harbor.

Chapter Five

Somewhere deep in the pit of Honor's stomach, a hard knot of fear formed. Until now, watching the British had seemed little more than a game, even after the firing had begun. In the span of one day, everything had changed. With British warships sailing unopposed into Charleston Harbor, what would happen to the city?

She spent every spare moment watching from the roof, but nothing seemed to alleviate the sense of pending doom that pervaded her every thought. Usually optimistic, Honor hated feeling that way, but she was also a realist. She offered a silent prayer for the days and weeks to come, asking for a miracle to help the city.

Foodstuffs were difficult to find and too high priced for most people to afford. Luckily, the larder at the White Point Inn was well stocked. Honor had heard that the army was taking nearly all the food that was shipped into the city. Her father kept the cellar full of all sorts of meats, molasses, rice, flour, corn meal and anything else he could find, but with having to feed so many people, his stores were being depleted faster than he could replace them.

As the prices of food went up, so did prices at the inn. Men who paid in British coin were charged less than those who paid with American paper money, which was worth less with each passing day. Honor felt a little guilty about the difference, but couldn't do anything about it.

"Paddy!" Honor exclaimed when she spotted him outside the back door.

The boy came into the changing room and sat down. He looked haggard and dirty. "Hello, Honor."

"Paddy! Where have you been?" she demanded, then was immediately sorry for her tone of voice. She stilled the shrewish quality when she spoke again, hugging him close. "I've been so worried about you."

"I've just been busy," Paddy answered, squirming in her grasp.

"Here, sit down and have something to eat." She found a bowl and ladled some hominy into it. "I want you to eat this and then come to find me."

Paddy's eyes narrowed, as if he were trying to decide what her intent might be. She realized that she sounded too possessive and that it might frighten him away. She knelt beside his chair and looked up into his eyes. "Look, Paddy, we're friends. I really was worried about you. I don't want to tell you what to do. I just want to be your friend."

"You sure that's all?" he asked after a moment.

Honor smiled and resisted the impulse to hug him again. "That's all. I promise. You can come and go as you please. No questions asked."

"All right." Paddy grinned and wolfed down his hominy. "Any milk?"

"Pour yourself some. It's there in the pitcher." Honor tried to act as if she weren't overly interested in what he was doing and went about her tasks. After a while he came looking for her.

"Honor," he said, when she'd finished with a customer. "I'm glad you want to be my friend."

They talked for a little while. Paddy told her he'd been down to the earthworks at the end of Tradd Street to watch the firing. Honor wanted to scold him for being so reckless, but thought he'd misunderstand. "I think you should be more careful. This war will get much worse."

"Aw, Honor, don't worry about me. I can take care of myself." Color flooded into his cheeks and he looked down at his feet. "Besides, I want the war to get started. I'm tired of waiting around."

"Well, my friend," she began, taking his arm and leading him up the stairs, "I think you're getting your wish. The British warships have sailed into the harbor."

"Whoopee!" he yelled, and Honor clamped her hand over his mouth.

"Shh." Honor glanced toward her mother's closed door and hoped she hadn't heard. "My mother isn't well. We don't want to disturb her."

Dylan heard a yell and went racing up the stairs. He suspected that something awful had happened. When he reached Honor's perch, he found her and Paddy taking turns with the glass. "What is it? What happened?"

Honor winked at Paddy. "Nothing. Paddy just expressed his feelings about the British warships floating in our harbor."

Dylan climbed out onto the roof to look. "Any change?"

"None. They're just sitting there." Paddy grinned. "Isn't this just fine? It's so exciting."

"I agree that it's exciting, but it's also dangerous." Dylan glanced at Honor and noticed her grimace. Apparently the two of them had discussed this prior to Dylan's arrival. "I know you're a young man of considerable wit, Paddy, but please don't become too cocky. Cannonballs are dangerous to everyone."

"The last time the British warships came into the harbor, they had to leave or be sunk." Paddy wrinkled his forehead, apparently thinking of a story someone had told him. "Some ships got caught on the bar during the battle. Two got off, but one, the *Action—*"

"*Acteon,* Paddy," Dylan corrected. He didn't know why he bothered. What did it matter that a child mispronounced the name of a ship?

"Yea, that's it. Anyway, the *Acteon* couldn't get off the bar. When the other ships sailed away, her crew set fire to her." Paddy laughed and pointed out to sea. "You should have seen it. One of our ships went out there and our men boarded her. Stole all kinds of stuff. Even fired shots at the other British ships that was retreating."

Dylan scowled at the reminder of Clinton's ignominious defeat during one of the first important battles of the war. That single defeat probably gave the rebels a taste of victory that still sustained them. It certainly had that effect on the Charlestonians. He couldn't count how many times that tale had been recounted over a tankard of rum.

"We'll run 'em off again, won't we, Dylan?" Paddy asked, much more seriously.

Noticing the tiny worry lines around the boy's eyes, Dylan smiled and ruffled the child's hair. "Maybe. You never know."

Paddy scrambled back through the window. "I'm gonna go tell what I seen."

For a few moments after Paddy left, neither Honor nor Dylan said anything. Honor decided that so much had happened during the past few days, neither of them knew where to start talking. Finally, both of them spoke at once.

"I'm sorry, you go ahead," Dylan insisted.

"I'm concerned about the boy, Dylan." Honor watched from her perch as Paddy ran out of the yard and down the street. "He's not careful enough. Something awful is going to happen to him. I can feel it."

"Don't worry, Honor. He's a smart boy." Dylan studied her and then shifted his gaze to watch Paddy disappear into the crowd. "I worry about you, too."

"Me? Why would you worry about me?" she asked, astonished that he would say such a thing.

"Well, you're a little like Paddy. Carefree and unconcerned about your own safety."

"I'm quite concerned about my safety." Honor was confused by his comparison. She always acted prudently. "Whatever are you talking about?"

"You're sitting here on this roof. Don't you think that soon the British are going to start loading the cannon with more gunpowder?" In the strong daylight, Dylan could see the lovely translucent quality of her complexion. Her eyes were dark orbs that punctuated a strong face, one that instilled trust and confidence. Dylan was suddenly glad that women weren't called upon to fight in wars. He knew beyond doubt that a great deal of strength was carefully hidden beneath Honor's tiny feminine exterior and that, given the chance, she would do a better job than most men.

"Dylan, I'm not a weakling. I can take care of myself."

"You sound just like Paddy. Listen to yourself."

Honor knew she did, but the boy was much younger, more inexperienced. But was he? He lived by his wits on the street— just how inexperienced could he be? For the moment, it didn't matter. Sitting here with Dylan was enough for her. She closed her eyes as his deep gravelly voice washed over her, touching every cell in her body with a special quiver of excitement that she knew only when he was near.

Unable to speak, she passed him the spyglass. When he took it, his hand brushed against hers, lingering momentarily before moving on. Hardly realizing what she was doing, she cupped her fingers in her other hand and stared at them. There was a slight tingling, little impulses that darted here and there beneath her skin, like lightning bugs on a warm summer night.

When she could look up at him, there was a question in her eyes. What did he do to cause her to feel this way? Why did no other man affect her as Dylan did? Where were these little tingles of excitement when Jeffrey hugged her or kissed her on the cheek?

For a few days, Honor pondered on those things, wondering if something was wrong with her, whether Dylan felt the same tingles as she. Having no answers nearly drove her mad. There was nobody she could talk to—except Miriam.

One day she walked over to Miriam's shop after the shelling stopped. There, Honor found her friend staring out the window. "Not busy?"

"Hardly. Fabric is too expensive right now. I saw some fine lawn the other day that was nearly three hundred dollars a yard."

"Well, come on. Let's go walking."

Honor and Miriam walked along the fortifications, trying to see if there was any damage. They found a little, but were more concerned with enjoying themselves. They walked all the way from Granville Bastion to Battery Broughton. From there they could see the American navy blockaded behind the ships and spikes they'd sunk at the mouth of the Cooper River.

"Seems a shame to sink all those ships, doesn't it?" Miriam asked as they strolled along.

"Sure does." This was a sore point with Honor. "I wonder why they didn't fight. I mean, we just let the British sail into the harbor unscathed."

"You know, I don't understand why more people aren't leaving Charleston. Mama said that she knew of some who were, but it seems to me that better than half the shops are still open."

"I think you're right. But who can afford anything? Papa said he saw some men's shoes that were selling for about seven hundred dollars."

Miriam gasped aloud and turned to gape at Honor. "You don't mean it?"

"How can you even question that price when you just told me about that fine lawn? Who'll be able to afford anything?" Honor realized she'd suddenly discovered one of the painful elements of war. "What'll we do, Miriam? I may never get another new dress and this one is practically hanging in tatters."

"Honor, I'll make sure you don't have to parade down Meeting Street naked." Miriam giggled behind her hand. "Although that might be an exciting thing to see."

Honor turned to stare at her friend. "You'd honestly like to see me walk down the street naked?"

"Oh, no!" The seamstress tilted her head to one side and fluttered her eyelashes coyly. "But I'd like to watch the men who were watching you walk down Meeting Street naked."

"You're a goose, Miriam Edwards." This was one of those times when Honor wished she knew some really bad words to call her friend. She'd heard plenty of them at the tavern, but she didn't know exactly what they meant. She finally settled on an epithet that was more ladylike. "Nothing but a...dirty-minded, little green goose."

Miriam laughed and linked her arm with Honor's. "Oh, Honor, that's why I love you so much. You're so serious about certain things."

"What *will* we do, Miriam?" She was serious about her question. "I mean, what if people can't pay for the food at the inn or the clothes that you make? What if we can't buy food to serve or cloth to make clothes? This is frightening. More frightening than the silly cannon fire."

"Oh, don't let's talk about such matters. Leave that to the men of Charleston." Miriam patted her hand to comfort her. "Let's talk about..." She glanced around. Something caught her eye and she smiled wickedly. "Let's talk about that fallen woman."

"Miriam!" Honor exclaimed, stopping dead and gaping at her friend. "What a thing to say! Of course we can't talk about—about one of those ... people. It isn't decent."

"They'll probably be the only ones making any money. The soldiers can pay them. Nobody else will have any money for our goods. Maybe we should join them."

Honor could only stare at Miriam. Words refused to form in her mouth. In all her life, she'd never spoken to one of those women and never talked about them. Her mother had reared her to be a lady, even if she wasn't a planter's daughter.

"Don't you think it would be fun?"

Curiosity soon made Honor turn to see the woman Miriam was talking about. She was beautiful. Several years older than them, she had a finely chiseled face surrounded by a halo of honey blond hair that looked so soft it fairly drifted with the breeze. Standing no farther then ten feet away, she turned and soon noticed the two girls gaping at her.

Honor felt the color rise in her cheeks. The woman smiled and winked. Trying to appear much more worldly than she could ever be, Honor smiled and lifted her hand in response. The woman's dress was cut far too low to be fashionable—or even decent—and exposed a voluptuous expanse of creamy white flesh for anyone to see. Cut high, the satin skirt showed trim ankles and dainty feet that were clad in fine white kid boots. As she stared, Honor decided that, in her entire life, the total cost of her clothes had been less than the value of those boots.

The woman walked toward them, and Honor fought the impulse to turn and run. "Hello, girls," she said and looked them both up and down. "I'm Echo."

Both girls muttered a response.

Echo glanced up and down the streets at the throngs of men pushing and shoving in their rush to get wherever they were going. "I think you ... young ladies shouldn't be out walking alone. Some of these gentlemen might get the wrong idea about you. Charleston isn't as safe as it once was."

"Thank you, ma'am," Honor said quickly, and started to turn away. She hesitated, then faced the prostitute again. "Miss ... Miss Echo, perhaps you should take care as well. What with the British ships in the harbor and Clinton firmly ensconced on the western bank of the Ashley River, there's no telling what will happen.''

Echo smiled. ''Thank you for caring enough to say that. Not many girls like you would have given me a moment's notice. My place is on East Bay. A large, pink house. Stop by if you ever need anything.''

As they hurried away from Echo, Honor thought that if her mother ever found out, she'd need help, all right. She'd be expelled from the tavern for associating with a fallen woman. Still, the woman was pretty, and Honor sort of liked her—as well as one could like that kind of woman.

Miriam glanced over her shoulder and chuckled. ''Maybe I should go back and offer to make her clothes. Did you notice that satin? Expensive, to say the very least. And those boots, too.''

''I saw.'' Honor gazed at Miriam for a long moment. ''Miriam, you wouldn't really make her—her dresses, would you?''

''Sure I would. Didn't we promise a long time ago to be successful? Well, with this war going on, how do you expect a dressmaker to be successful?'' Miriam stopped and crossed her arms. ''I'm not going to starve because the planters' wives and their precious daughters can't afford to buy clothes. What if she came into the tavern? Would you feed her?''

As far as Honor could recall, her father had never turned away a paying customer. She saw no reason for him to do so now. ''I guess so.''

''Of course you would. Times are hard, Honor. We have to find new ways to make money.''

A thought occurred to Honor. ''Miriam, could you really make a dress like that?''

Her friend frowned. ''Certainly I could.''

''All right, all right. I suppose I should have asked if you *would* make a dress like that, instead of if you could.''

While Miriam chatted on about dressmaking, Honor stood there for a minute, thinking about what had just transpired. For the first time in her life she'd actually conversed with a prostitute. Now she was calmly discussing the woman with Miriam. Times were hard, but they were also changing. If someone had asked her yesterday if she'd ever do such a thing, her answer would have been an emphatic no.

While they were standing there in the busy street, Honor suddenly overheard someone mention Clinton. Her ears were automatically attuned to any news about the general, so she listened. After glancing around surreptitiously, the speaker told another man that the British attack would begin soon, probably the next day.

Honor's gaze steadied on the fellow speaking. She'd seen him before—several times—in the tavern. His information always seemed to be credible. She silently prayed that he was wrong this time. Turning away so that he wouldn't catch her listening, she heard, "Everything is in place. Tomorrow is the day. Pass the word."

That cold, hard lump down deep in her belly began to grow and swell, consuming her from the inside with a fear that she fought to control. She could hardly breathe. After a while, she realized that her chest was burning as if she were in a flaming building, and she gasped for breath.

Could he be telling the truth? Did he know or was he speculating?

Either way, Honor had to get home. She needed to find Jeffrey as quickly as possible. This was something she had to pass on to him, perhaps the most important information she'd ever give him.

"Miriam," Honor said, wondering how she could leave her friend abruptly without making her suspicious. There was no simple way, she decided, nor did she have time to play games. "Miriam, I need to see someone. I'll stop by later."

Before her friend could ask questions or object, Honor rushed away. "Where are you, Jeffrey?" she murmured, wishing she knew more about his habits. "Maybe Paddy will know."

But Honor didn't know where to find him, either. She went to Jeffrey's house, but he wasn't there. From there she went to Lincoln's headquarters, but realized she couldn't just go charging in.

The only way she could think to ask for Jeffrey and not raise suspicions was for her to say her visit was personal...very personal. Working quickly, she removed the pins from her hair and shook her head, sending her ebony tresses cascading down her back in a shimmer of curls. She glanced up and down the street, then unbuttoned her bodice. The swell of her breasts was clearly visible when she marched up the steps and into the reception area.

The clerk glanced at her, shot out of his chair and then stood gawking at her like an adolescent. His mouth fell open. "'Ello, mate," she drawled, mimicking the accent of a woman she'd once heard down at the wharf. She leaned forward to give him an unobstructed view of her cleavage. "I'll be lookin' fer Mr. Jeffrey Sheridan w'at works 'ereabouts. 'Ave ye seen the bloke?"

Gulping, the young man darted a glance down the hallway. "Ahem, Miss . . . ?"

He was clearly asking her name. Honor knew better than to give her name to anyone, for fear of jeopardizing their network. "I don't b'lieve I'll be tellin' you who I am, 'less you've a mind to ask me over for . . . for tea, dearie."

The man cleared his throat. "Miss, please try to understand my position. Mr. Sheridan does occasionally come here, though I'm not sure what business it is of yours. Perhaps if you would state your purpose—"

"I'll be the judge of whose business it is. Just you take yerself off to find 'im before I forgits I'm a lady. I've 'ad run-ins with the likes of you before." Honor winked suggestively at the man. From his reaction, she felt fairly sure he'd never been close to any of the women down at the wharf who sold their bodies freely. "I'm gittin' right impatient with ye, I am. I know 'e's 'ere 'cause 'e told me so. And tell 'im to 'urry it up a bit. I ain't got all day."

The man straightened, tugged on the hem of his coat and hurried down the corridor. Within moments, he returned, scowling at her as he sat down at his desk. "Mr. Sheridan will be with you shortly. You may seat yourself—"

Honor pulled her handkerchief from her pocket, dusted off a corner of the desk and heaved herself onto it. "I'll just be sittin' 'ere with you, if your 'ighness don't mind."

"Of course," the man growled between clenched teeth.

With her back to the clerk, Honor closed her eyes briefly, willing herself to relax. What should she do when Jeffrey appeared? She hadn't much time to think. A door opened and he appeared, peering down the hall in confusion.

"Jeffy, love," she shrieked, jumping up from the desk. Honor ran down the corridor and leapt into his arms, locking her legs around his waist.

The expression on his face registered complete astonishment. For a moment he didn't even recognize her. To reassure him, she whispered his name and winked. Jeffrey firmly unwound her limbs from his body and dragged her back to the desk, where the clerk was staring in amazement. "Horace, I do not know this woman. This is obviously a ruse to discredit me. Don't ever allow her in this building again, under any circumstances."

Jeffrey then dragged her toward the door. Honor, caterwauling about the ill treatment she suffered at the hands of soldiers, screeched and squealed until they got to the porch.

Grinning wickedly, Jeffrey crossed his arms and stared. When he spoke, his words were loud enough for the clerk to hear. "Miss, I don't know who you are, but go home immediately. You are a discredit to all of Charleston. I assure you that we've never met. I frequent only respectable establishments, where I shall be with my friends this evening—not where you've likely come from. Have I any luck at all in this life, I shan't be bothered by you again."

With that, he stomped back inside and slammed the door. Honor, not to be bested by him at anything, opened the door and shouted after him. "Oh, you won't 'ave anything to do with the likes of me, eh? You'll be seein' my face every night for the rest of your life, or near to it, if I 'ave anything to do with it."

Dylan hurried to his lodgings. He wanted to be with Honor when the war started in earnest. Cedric had told him earlier today that the battle was imminent. Dylan though she might need him, whether it began today or tomorrow.

He hurried through the gate, up the back steps and into the changing room. She'd told him to use that entrance if he wanted to avoid the crowds in the common room, and at this particular moment, he did.

He found her, as he'd suspected, sitting on the roof. She wasn't peering into the glass as usual, but was simply staring out at nothing. She didn't even appear to hear him as he approached.

He stared at her for a few seconds, wondering what held her in such a deep state of thought. Finally, he called her name gently to avoid frightening her. "Honor."

"What?" She jerked around, fumbled with the spyglass, but caught it before it could tumble to the ground below. "Oh, Dylan. It's you."

For more than an hour she'd been sitting there, trying to fathom the truth about the coming attack. Jeffrey had told her, in his humorous way, that he'd be stopping by to see her. She felt that her news was urgent, too urgent to wait, but he hadn't been able to get away earlier, she was sure. She'd been thinking about her visit to his headquarters, too. Her first attempt at disguise had worked well.

The British showed no more movement today than they had for the past few days, weeks even. How could she determine whether the man she'd overheard knew what he was talking about or not? But she couldn't think about it with Dylan standing there.

He climbed out to join her. Perhaps he could help to ease the tension he discerned in her face, he decided. "What were you thinking about?"

Honor gazed at him. His blue eyes were so calm, so understanding. Could she tell him what she'd heard? Would he believe her or think her foolish? Could she trust him? For a moment, she hated herself for ever getting involved in this war, even to the small extent that she was. But she'd known the risk, and she now had to assume responsibility for her actions. She couldn't talk to Dylan about this. Jeffrey was the only person she would trust with the information.

She tried to smile, as if nothing were wrong. "Oh, I was just thinking about a conversation I had with Miriam today. You remember her, don't you? My friend who is a seamstress—Miriam Edwards."

Honor knew she was chattering to cover her uneasiness, so she simply closed her mouth. After all Jeffrey's warnings about making the enemy suspicious, she knew better.

"Oh, yes. I remember her. Pretty girl." Dylan smiled when Honor frowned. Was she a little jealous of her friend, maybe? "Not my kind of woman, though."

Now he truly had her attention. "I see. And just what type of woman is your kind, Mr. Alden?" she teased.

Dylan perceived that she was amusing herself at his expense. Well, fair was fair. He'd started it by baiting her. "Let's see. You want to know what sort of woman I like. Hmm. That's difficult to say." He eyed her critically. "Well, about your height and weight, I'd say. Maybe with hair as lovely as yours, but hanging down around her face. Brown eyes that glow with the fire of brandy in the sunlight. Do you know of such a woman?''

Now Honor blushed. He was teasing her, and she deserved it. His preference among women was none of her business, but he hadn't been unkind. He was smiling that wonderful, compelling smile of his. "Well, I do know of just such a woman. However, she has several shortcomings I think you should be wary of.''

"Truly? You know the woman of my dreams?" He edged closer eagerly. "Please, torture me no longer. Give me the name of the lass and I'll be off to rescue her from whatever tyrant or madness she needs rescuing from. Please, I implore you.''

Honor stifled a giggle and looked at him levelly. "Well, if you insist. But I warn you," she said, drawing back slightly to study his mock-serious countenance. "She may be the woman of your nightmares rather than the woman of your dreams.''

"Say it is not so, fair Honor." Dylan placed his hands over his heart. "Nothing, no matter how horrendous, could keep me from this fair maiden. I am doomed to spend my life pining after her if you don't acquaint me with her immediately.''

"Very well. I shall tell you more about this—this fair maiden." Honor smiled, but placed her hand over her mouth to hide her amusement.

"I shall be indebted to you for the remainder of my life.''

"And I, Mr. Alden, shall remember that." She took a few seconds to formulate her next words so that they would be in keeping with the tenor of their ridiculous conversation. "A true beauty, she is. That I'll grant her. A face so pure and fair as to be carved from the finest marble.''

"Yes, go on. Don't torture me like this.''

This time, Honor couldn't stifle her giggle, but regained her composure quickly. "Skin as smooth as the finest satin. But when she opens her mouth to speak, she brays like a donkey and smells worse.''

"Oh, Miss Richmond, it cannot be true." Dylan bowed his head sadly, resting his chin on his chest.

"There's more," she continued. "She bites like a donkey as well.''

Dylan could restrain his amusement no longer. His great booming laugh echoed among the houses and caught at Honor's heart. Soon, both of them had forgotten their fears and were laughing uncontrollably.

"What's so funny?"

Honor clapped her hand over her mouth and looked toward the window. Paddy's head was poking out and he wore a puzzled expression. She couldn't speak without laughing again. Soon, Paddy joined in their merriment, even though he didn't know what had set them off.

Dylan finally glanced up at the boy and tried to explain. Somehow, his words didn't come out nearly so funny this time. "Well, I suppose it isn't as funny the second time."

Paddy clambered out onto the roof, still scowling despite Dylan's explanation. "What's going on with the British?"

Honor handed him the spyglass. After a minute, he shook his head. "I don't understand. What are they doing over there? When are they going to attack? I hate this waiting."

"We all do, Paddy," Honor said, wishing she could tell him what she'd heard. Even though she knew Paddy himself was helping the Patriot cause, Jeffrey had warned her against telling anyone what she knew. She thought that a little stringent, but had agreed. Besides, she didn't want to frighten Paddy.

Dylan looked at the boy, wishing he could tell him the truth. If he could do so, and if Paddy would go, Dylan would take him out of the city, find him someplace safe to stay until all this was over. But he couldn't risk exposing himself, and he doubted whether Paddy would consider leaving Charleston. "It'll happen soon enough, Son," was all Dylan could say.

Honor wondered what sort of woman Dylan really preferred. She knew he'd been having fun with her. Her thoughts drifted to the evening they'd met. He'd never told her exactly why he had come to Charleston. She suspected that he'd had a disagreement with his family, but had no proof of that. Maybe she never would.

He was a gentleman. A man of title, most likely, or the son of a man of title. No matter what kind of woman he was looking for, if indeed he was looking, Honor wasn't even in the same class. That didn't really bother her too much, not that she would admit, anyway. She didn't intend to marry. Not ever.

* * *

Late that evening, Jeffrey dropped in. Honor stopped by his table and sat down for a moment to pass on what she'd heard. "Jeffrey, listen closely. I heard two men talking today. One of them said the British attack would come tomorrow."

"Tomorrow?" Jeffrey repeated, as if to verify that he'd heard her words correctly.

"Yes. Do you think it's true?"

Jeffrey gazed directly into her eyes. "I can't tell you, Honor. I can't say anything."

"What do you mean? I heard the information. Can't you at least deny or confirm it?" she asked incredulously.

"No. If it's true, I can't tell you. If it's false, I can't deny it. No matter what I know, I can't admit it." Jeffrey edged closer and took her hands in his. "Honor, this is all so dangerous. There are British spies everywhere. The less you know, the safer you are."

She nodded slowly. She understood what he was telling her, but it didn't make her feel any better. "I wanted to tell Paddy. He's so young and—"

"No, Honor. Tell no one. Not your father, not your mother. Nobody. Promise me."

"I promise." Honor sagged back in the chair and looked at the thinning crowd, then closed her eyes. Her whisper was barely audible. "But, Jeffrey, what if it's true?"

"If it's true, we'll deal with it." Jeffrey tried to find a way to comfort her. "Look, Honor, we've known Clinton was out there for a month. What do you think we've been doing all this time?"

She opened her eyes and looked at him. "What?"

"We've been reinforcing our defenses, importing powder, bringing in more soldiers. We're in a good position to win this battle, Honor. You have to believe that."

"That's what keeps me going, Jeffrey." She considered their position for a moment. "I just wish I could do more to help. I feel so useless."

"You aren't useless. The information you give me is vital."

She sat up straighter. "Has something I told you helped? Anything? It's the never knowing what happens with the information that drives me mad."

"Don't worry. You're helping considerably."

With that, Honor had to be satisfied. Jeffrey would say no more.

The next morning greeted Charleston with more thunderous cannon fire. Honor sat up in bed. Something was different. She sprang from the bed, removed her nightgown and pulled on her dress. Barefoot, she snatched her spyglass, hurried to her little perch and peered off into the distance.

At first, she couldn't see what was happening. Plumes of black smoke filled the air, obscuring her vision for a long period of time. As well as the ground-shaking cannon fire, there came a sound of something like muskets.

Honor edged around the roof until she faced almost due west. Squinting, she gazed into the spyglass toward the hornworks. That was where much of the smoke was coming from. After a moment she noticed the puffs of smoke appeared to be divided almost equally along two distinct lines.

Clinton had come around behind Charleston at the Neck to attack. She looked at the banks of the Ashley River and saw men still crossing far west of town. The men were British soldiers. Then she noticed some who were dressed differently. These men wore blue uniforms with tall hats. "Hessians," she whispered, wondering who else would turn against them. Combined with Clinton's men, there must be thousands of soldiers now bearing down on Charleston. Thousands of them.

Honor was happy that her mother was probably sleeping soundly through this tumult. Her thoughts returned to Clinton's first attack on Charleston. Poor Ruth Richmond had already been ill, but the sound of the firing had seemed to have a devastating effect on her. She hadn't been the same since. Now this. The doctor had prescribed laudanum on his last visit because she seemed so agitated. Honor hoped it would work.

While she was staring into the distance, Dylan came crawling toward her. "What are you looking at?"

"The British! It's begun." Her hand shaking with apprehension, she handed him the glass and pointed in the direction of the smoke. "There. Past the hornworks. You can't see much for the smoke."

Dylan had known where the first attack would come from, but he also knew that this wasn't the worst of the fighting. Both sides were merely exhibiting their strength in hopes of frightening the other. He, and probably everyone else, didn't believe it would work. The fighting would worsen as soon as the British completed digging their trenches. Soon the Royal Navy would begin its bombardment. Charleston was indeed a city under siege, a situation that would inevitably get worse within the next few days.

Chapter Six

Several days of fighting ensued. Honor, terrified at first, could scarcely tear herself away from the roof. People were leaving Charleston in droves.

Dylan came out one morning and watched the fighting for a while. "Honor, please try to convince your father to leave the city."

Honor shook her head. "He'll never do it. We have no place to go. Besides, the fighting isn't in town. We'll be all right."

"You can't believe that this is all there will be of the battle." Dylan tried desperately to think of a way to convince her that matters would deteriorate very quickly. The present shooting was simply a prelude to the true battle. "It will get much worse."

"He won't leave. Even if we had someplace to go, Mama's too sick to move around a lot." Honor smiled bravely and patted Dylan's hand, as if to assure him of their safety. "We'll be all right," she repeated. "We will. Besides, who would run the tavern if we left?"

Exasperated, Dylan nearly shouted, "Who cares about who'll run the tavern, Honor? I'm talking about your life here. You're in danger, grave danger." At her astonished expression, he softened his voice. "I'm really concerned, Honor. I—I care for you a lot and—"

Honor smiled brightly and squeezed his hand. "I care for you, too, Dylan. All the more reason for me to stay."

"No, it's not. It's all the more reason for you to go. I'll find you someplace safe." Dylan jumped to his feet and looked down at her. She simply didn't understand the danger, and there was no way he could convince her. Frustration bit at him like a nagging mosquito. Then his anger and anxiety melted away. Gazing into her eyes changed everything. Those warm brown eyes turned his anger to liquid fire that coursed through his veins. *Careful, Dylan, old boy,* he warned himself, and he tried to look stern with her. "Damn it, Honor—"

A thundering boom interrupted him and the building shook. Dylan spun around to see what had happened and took a misstep. His foot came down on the steeply sloping part of the roof and he began to slide.

"Dylan!" Honor screamed, reaching for him. In her desperate attempt to prevent him from falling, the spyglass slipped out of her hands and fell after him.

It was as if seconds turned to hours while she helplessly watched him slip over the edge of the roof and heard him crash into the live oak below. She scrambled through the window and raced down the stairs as if her own life depended upon it. When she reached the backyard, she found him lying in a crumpled heap.

"Dylan!" she shouted as she ran to him. Kneeling by his side, she reached out to touch him, to confirm that he wasn't dead. Honor didn't know what to do. She wanted to turn him over so she could see his face, but was afraid she would injure him further. "Della! Come quickly! Help!"

Della poked her head out the door and looked around. Spotting Honor kneeling on the ground, she moved toward her as fast as she could. "Lord have mercy on us. What's happened to my baby? Child, are you hurt?"

Honor didn't turn around. "I'm fine. At least, I think I am. Dylan's hurt. He fell."

"Joseph! Git your black self over to the doctor's house and bring him. Don't you be . . . Forgit it. Girl! Git to the doctor's." Della shuffled toward Honor, barking orders to a serving girl as she went. "You're a lot faster than old Joseph, I'll warrant. I'll get a cool cloth."

Honor hardly heard the commands being issued behind her. Dylan's eyes, those lovely, cornflower blue eyes, were beginning to open. For a few seconds, they crinkled at the corners as if a smile were beginning, but a groan and faint movement interrupted and the smile grew into a grimace.

"What in the—Ooh! that hurts—name of all that's holy happened?" He squinted and settled his gaze upon Honor. "Made myself look rather foolish, didn't I?"

"No, of course not. You—you just took a misstep and—"

"Made myself look foolish, as I said." Dylan finished her sentence for her. "Am I dead? Did I go to heaven? Lord knows, I see an angel."

Pain gnawed at Dylan everywhere at once, but his gaze never faltered. The angel looked like Honor, except for the spectacular halo around her head.

"Angel? No, you're not dead." Honor didn't know what to think about his words. Maybe the fall had injured his skull. "I'm Honor. Remember me?"

"No, you're an angel. Honor's just as beautiful, but she doesn't have that shiny halo." Dylan squinted and shaded his eyes with his hand. "Damn, but that hurts . . . oh, excuse me. I guess . . . You are an angel, aren't you?"

Honor laughed nervously and leaned over to keep the sun from shining so brightly in his eyes. "No. I truly am Honor. Thank you for the compliment, though. Does it hurt very badly? One of the girls has gone for the doctor."

"Don't need a—" Dylan tried to sit up, gingerly testing each muscle and bone "—doctor. Damn! What a clumsy oaf I am. Who would have thought it?"

"You're not clumsy. Just unfortunate." Honor tried to help him to his feet. He stood there, a bit unsteadily for a moment, but gradually became more sure of himself. "Don't you remember? A cannon boom occurred at about the time you were turning around. I imagine it startled you and caused you to fall. The whole house shook."

"As much as I would like to lay the blame for my fall on the cannon, I'm not sure I can honestly do so." Dylan smiled a little sheepishly. "But since you're so insistent, I'll go along, simply because a gentleman never disagrees with a lady."

Honor cocked her head to one side and looked at him pensively. "I'll remember that. I'm sure one of these days that bit of wisdom will come in as handy for me as it did for you just now."

"I may have erred in telling you such a thing." Dylan took her arm and walked back to the house with her. His body hurt all over, but he was certain there were no broken bones.

As Honor helped him up the stairs, she noticed that his limp was no worse. "I'm glad you didn't worsen the damage already done to your left knee."

Dylan shook his head slowly. "I'm glad, too. I imagine that if I'd landed on it, my knee would never have healed properly."

"How did you injure it the first time?" Honor asked, realizing that she'd known about the injury ever since they'd met, but didn't know how it had happened.

Glad that he could tell her the truth—even if it was a bit skewed—Dylan stopped on the landing. "It happened at Savannah, when the British were marching into town after the Americans surrendered. An Englishman shot me as I escaped."

"You had to flee?"

Dylan nodded and looked down at her. Even in the dimly lit stairwell, her eyes glowed with warmth. "I suppose you could put it that way. I either had to flee or be imprisoned. The fellow who shot me seemed to disagree with my decision in the matter."

"You're lucky he was a bad shot." Honor peered up into his eyes. For a long moment she said nothing. She sensed something in him, something she couldn't quite define. The same sort of feeling came over her every time he touched her. Her knees were like soft butter, and she braced herself against the wall. She shook her head in an attempt to clear her muddled thinking. "Did he...I mean, did you shoot him back? Did you kill him?"

"No...well, yes, I'm happy he wasn't a good shot, but no, I didn't shoot him. I was too busy trying to get away without being caught."

Honor helped him the rest of the way up the stairs and into his room. "I'll send the doctor up immediately when he gets here."

"There's no need for—"

"Yes, there is. Don't be silly." She wagged her finger at him as if to scold. "Now, you just lie there and rest until he arrives." She grinned and continued, "Be a good boy and do as you're told."

Dylan mumbled and sat on the edge of the bed. He realized there was no convincing her that he didn't need a doctor. However, his muscles and joints were beginning to ache and he decided that an examination might be prudent.

Honor sent Della and the doctor straight to Dylan's room. The common room was full, so she bustled about refilling mugs and ferrying food from the changing room to plates to tables. The shooting had quieted, so she had time to attend to her other duties.

When the doctor came down the stairs, she met him and offered him a mug of ale. "And how was the patient?" she asked, crossing her fingers and saying a silent prayer that Dylan was going to be all right.

"Oh, I'd wager he'll be sore for a few days, but other than that, he's going to be fine."

"What about his left leg? Did he reinjure it?"

"Don't think so. That bullet struck just above the knee, but missed the bone." The doctor lifted his tankard and drained the last of the ale. "Lucky man, he. Well, I must be going. Other patients. Some injured this morning in the shelling."

Color drained from Honor's face. "Nobody...killed?"

The doctor smiled. "Nope. Not today."

He left, and Honor had to be satisfied. She went to the changing room, ladled a bowl of soup for Dylan and cut off a thick chunk of bread. After she'd poured him a mug of ale, she arranged everything on a tray and took it to him. She hesitated at the door for a few seconds, wondering if he might be asleep. Honor tapped lightly so as not to disturb him if he was, but he called for her to come in.

"I brought you something to eat."

He sat up slowly and turned stiffly. "Thank you. I don't believe I could have walked down the stairs to eat. I'm afraid my entire body is getting stiff."

"Oh, I'm so sorry. Is there anything I can do?" Honor felt partially responsible for his condition. After all, if she hadn't been on the roof, he wouldn't have climbed out there to talk to her and to see what was going on at the fortifications. "I feel as if this is my fault."

"Nonsense. If you hadn't thought of it, I probably would have. Everyone with a view is doing the same thing." Dylan sipped the soup and then grinned at her. "Well, not everyone is falling off rooftops like me."

"Thank goodness," she said. "I'll be sure to check on you frequently in case there's anything you need. That fall must have been terribly painful."

"Not as bad as you might think." Dylan leaned forward and thought about it for a few seconds. "When I slid off the roof, I landed in the top of that big live oak. From there, I bounced down from limb to limb. Not exactly a joyful trip, you understand, but not nearly so bad as falling all the way to the ground in one go."

"I suppose not." She remembered his earlier words. "I guess you were lucky this time as well."

"Looks that way to me." He rubbed his back and sighed. "Though with the way my body aches at this moment, I might disagree."

"Tsk, tsk, tsk," she said and grinned mischievously. "I seem to recall your saying that a gentleman never disagrees with a lady."

"Then I am exposed."

"Exposed?"

"Exposed. I'm not really a gentleman."

Honor walked back toward the door and then hesitated. She turned and gazed at him. "And maybe I'm not a lady."

Before Dylan could reply, she was gone. He stared at the door for a long time, wondering what she could possibly mean. He thought he knew her well enough to know she *was* a lady, no matter what she'd implied.

He'd been tempted to forget that fact several times, today being the latest. *That* was the reason he'd fallen. It had nothing to do with the boom of the cannon. It had everything to do with looking at her and those huge brown eyes that made him forget all else. He slid the tray off the bed and onto a chair before settling back down to stare at the ceiling.

Crossing his ankles, he tucked his hands behind his head and continued to stare. What was happening to him? Was he becoming soft? His preoccupation with Honor today might have cost him a great deal of time, might have cost the British effort more than Dylan could ever know.

Lucky, she'd said. Yes, he was lucky... this time.

Several days passed and Honor settled into a routine. She spent a great deal of time on the roof, following the action out at the Neck. When the firing stopped, she scanned the west bank of the Ashley, noting how the number of troops there lessened each day.

Food shortages were getting worse in town. Honor prayed that the fighting would end soon so that nobody would starve. After she looked at the Ashley each day, she turned to the Cooper River. The river was glutted with boats heading out of Charleston. She didn't know where all the people came from. No matter how many boats left the city, its population didn't seem to lessen.

Jeffrey stopped by. He seemed so distracted, she could hardly talk to him. "What's wrong, Jeffrey?"

"Oh, nothing really. Just a little nervous. Who isn't these days?" He dropped into a chair. "So much to do." He glanced around the near empty room and whispered. "I hardly have time to stop to see my...friends," he said suggestively.

Honor understood and smiled. "Well, I'm doing the best I can to entertain everyone who comes in. I *listen* to their every wish in order to serve them better. I *see* that everything they need is at hand."

Jeffrey chuckled. "Ah, my little lynx. The Carolina beauty with the eyes of a lynx."

Blushing, Honor scowled at him. "Don't make fun of me. I'm quite serious." She proceeded to name a few men she'd been serving only that night.

Looking impressed, he leaned forward and winked. "Keep up the good work, my lynx-eyed spy. That's it—I'll call you Lynx. Your name will be know for generations to come. Lynx, the master spy."

Honor couldn't tell whether he was teasing her or not, but she liked the name. It made her feel more like a part of the network, more important. Somehow, it made her believe that everything would turn out all right.

And then came April 10.

Honor was stunned by the ferocity of the fighting. The city of Charleston was under a constant barrage of cannonballs that smashed whatever they hit into a pile of rubble. The entire Richmond household, including servants and a few guests, huddled in the cellar the first day of fighting. Ruth Richmond lay against a sack of flour, staring straight ahead. She'd been dosed well with laudanum.

Honor was concerned for Dylan. He hadn't been in his room this morning when the firing started. Nor had she seen Paddy in several days.

Occasionally, she would fly up the stairs to see if she could determine who was winning, but her flights were useless. The air was thick with smoke, black and acrid. Charleston seemed to be enveloped in a suffocating cloud that threatened never to lift.

Though she had longed for the real fighting to begin, now she regretted her wish. *Careful what you wish for, the Lord might grant it,* she reminded herself as she stared across the expanse of swirling black. She heard a whistling sound that grew louder, and she turned to see what could be causing it. A cannonball flew through the air toward her, missed the tavern and hit the corner of the smokehouse. Honor flattened herself against the floor as the ground shook and buckled as if there had been an earthquake.

Wasting no time, she scrambled to her feet and raced down the stairs, gaining the cellar more quickly than she ever thought possible.

"What was that?" came the question from everyone in unison.

"Cannonball," she replied, gasping for breath and collapsing onto a huge sack of flour. "It hit the smokehouse."

Henry leapt to his feet, peering at her in the semidarkness. "Knocked it down?"

"I don't think so." Honor tried to remember exactly what she'd seen. She'd been so frightened, she could hardly recall how it happened. "I . . . yes, I believe it hit the western corner and displaced some bricks."

Henry walked to the steps and stared upward. "Damned British bastards!"

Then, apparently recalling that several of their guests were British sympathizers, he shrugged and sat back down, cupping his chin in his hands. Honor said nothing. She wanted to remind him that he'd violated their strictly neutral policy, but decided that any Tories in the cellar were probably cursing the British as well. Nobody was safe, neither Whig nor Tory.

They spent the night in the cellar, though no one slept much. Aching and hungry, Honor prayed for the firing to cease, as it had after a few hours during the past few days. But now the fighting continued through the night. And her thoughts kept returning to Dylan and to Paddy. She was worried about both of them.

When the light of dawn filtered through the cracks in the cellar doors, Honor could stand it no longer. "I'm going to fix breakfast, war or no war."

"Praise the Lord, I'm with you." Della rose and followed Honor to the double doors. "See anything?"

Honor pushed one of the doors open slightly and peered through the crack. "Nothing. Stay here. I'll check to see if it's safe."

"Harrumph!" Della climbed the steps herself and flung the doors open. "If I'm gonna die, I'm gonna do it in the daylight with my head 'bove ground. Sure and I won't be dying like a mole."

Honor silently agreed and charged up the last few steps. Glancing around, she noted no further damage to their property. She hurried on into the house and rushed up the stairs to her perch. Guns were still crackling and cannons still booming, but she refused to huddle underground in fear any longer. She would see what was going on.

Dylan strode along, ignoring the pain streaking through his body. "Damn!" he exclaimed to no one in particular. "Shouldn't have left yesterday morning."

Expecting a shipment of goods, he'd gone to his warehouse before the barrage of fighting began. He'd waited, like almost everyone else, for the inevitable letup. He never would have predicted that the firing would continue all night.

Concern for Honor and her family hastened his footsteps. As he rounded the corner, he automatically glanced toward the Neck. Even as he watched, a cannonball sailed through the air and smashed into a home in the next block. He hated war.

Nearing the White Point Inn and Tavern, he looked up once again. None of the visible structures seemed damaged, but he couldn't see the backs of the houses or businesses. For all he knew, the edifices he was looking at were the only ones left standing.

His gaze went to the tavern as he approached. "Damn!" He cursed and began to run, his left leg protesting at the shards of pain that shot up and down the muscles. "That woman's gone mad."

Honor was crawling through the window onto her favorite spot to view the battle. Dylan wanted to cry out, to warn her to go back inside, but was afraid he'd frighten her and she'd fall. When he reached the yard, he sped across it, paused to stare at the gaping hole in the corner of the smokehouse and then ran full speed up the stairs.

Gasping for breath, he poked his head through the open window and saw her, calmly sitting there with her spyglass in hand. As much as he admired her for her fearlessness, he wanted to shake her for her recklessness. "Honor!" he called, hoping he wouldn't frighten her. Though if the firing of cannonballs didn't frighten her, nothing would. "Have you gone mad?"

"And a good morning to you, too, Dylan." She lowered the spyglass and smiled innocently. "Maybe you shouldn't come out here."

"*I* shouldn't? What about you?" Dylan wanted to drag her back through the window and take her somewhere safe, but in all of Charleston, there was no place that fit that description. "Come back in here at once before you get injured or killed."

She stared at him for a moment, wondering if he felt the same magnetism as she. Even in the midst of the thunderous cannon fire, she felt drawn to him. Without stopping to wonder why she obeyed so quickly, Honor crawled back to the window and allowed him to help her through.

Dylan pulled her into his arms and held her, closing his eyes to shut out the vivid images of blood and death that he remembered so well from other battles. He couldn't think of that now or what might have been, only that she was safe.

Honor trembled in his embrace. Her bones turned to liquid, and she leaned against him for support. What was happening to her? Why did this man affect her this way?

After a moment, she decided that she must learn to control her body when he was around. Shakily, she disengaged from his embrace and managed to walk over to a chair. She sank down into it to keep from falling. When she could speak, she looked up at him, hoping to keep her voice from quavering. "Dylan, is something wrong?"

"Wrong? You're perched out there on the roof like a crippled bird with a cat about to pounce. Don't you know how dangerous it is out there? You should be in the cellar."

Dylan wondered how to impress upon her the danger of her situation, rising from several sources. First of all, there was the cannon fire and the muskets. He certainly couldn't discount the risk of falling, not after the last few painful days. And then there were the soldiers. Not the general population of soldiers, but the stragglers, those with something other than war on their minds. If one of them spotted her out there alone, there was no telling what could happen. He didn't even want to think about it.

"Dylan, I'm a grown woman now, not a child. I can take care of myself." Honor tried to reassure him, but she wasn't positive that her efforts had any effect. "Come. Let's go down to breakfast."

Knowing he couldn't do any more, Dylan followed her down the stairs to the changing room. He realized he'd have to stay close to keep her from doing something foolish. It wouldn't matter right now if he didn't go to work. Nothing was going on at the warehouse, not with all the shelling.

She took several bowls and mugs from the cupboard and placed them on a tray. "Take these out to the big table. I'll check on breakfast."

Ignoring the cannonballs sailing over her head, she made her way to the kitchen. There she found Della stirring a huge kettle of hominy. "Is it ready?"

The woman said nothing, and Honor stared at her, puzzled at the lack of response. "Della," she called, raising her voice slightly. "Is it ready?"

Still no reply. She wondered if Della had gone deaf.

Honor walked over to where the cook was standing and touched her arm. Della jumped and spun around. When she reached up and removed the cotton that had been stuffed in her ears, Honor laughed and hugged her. "I thought you'd gone deaf or something."

"Hominy's ready." The woman took the kettle off the crane, grabbed the coffeepot and went toward the house. "You get those folks out of the cellar."

Without further discussion, Honor went to the cellar doors and called down to the people hiding there. "Come on up. Della has breakfast ready."

There were ten for breakfast. Somehow, Honor ended up sitting next to Dylan. Her mother, sagging like a limp doll, sat on her other side. Patiently, Honor fed her mother until the woman refused to eat any more.

Conversation was sparse. Everyone was too tired to make polite table talk, so they ate mostly in silence, except for the thundering and whistling and crashing of the cannonballs, which didn't let up. Some of them struck buildings nearby. Honor could tell by the way the ground shook or by the sound of the whistle. She was beginning to get used to the fearsome noise, even though she still jerked involuntarily when they hit near the inn.

Before they were finished eating, Paddy came in. His eyes were wide with excitement. "Boy, you should see the way those cannonballs eat up the ground or a building. Looks like some great monster came along and ate a big chunk right out."

Honor remembered how independent the boy was and tried not to sound like a mother hen. "Paddy, we were concerned. I wish you'd stop by more frequently."

"Aw, I thought about it, but there was so much to see. I been everywhere." He pulled a chair close to the table.

Della came into the common room and scowled at the boy. "Child, how come you haven't been here to eat? Do I have to break a hickory switch and take it to your backside?"

"No, ma'am." Paddy bowed his head.

Apparently, Della had more control over this young man than anyone else. Honor was happy that someone else cared where he'd been. "Go wash your hands," she said. "Then you can eat. Della made hominy and gravy."

Paddy raced from the room with Della following him, scolding him every step of the way. Honor laughed out loud, and soon everyone at the table was laughing, except for her mother.

Laughter. That's what's needed to keep us from quaking in our boots like children. Only the children, if Paddy is a fair example, aren't afraid. Honor watched the boy return, his face shining and his hair combed, the result, she was sure, of Della's ministrations. She made no comment, but gave Paddy a bowl of steaming hominy.

As they finished eating, people began to drift away. With the arrival of daylight, everything seemed less frightening,

Honor supposed. During the remainder of the day, patrons came into the tavern, passing along news of injuries or damage. Honor wanted to go out and see the damage for herself, but she was kept too busy waiting on tables.

Like a dark sentry, Dylan sat in the corner watching her every move. When she had a few moments to spare, she hurried up the steps and he followed her. She was beginning to feel as much a child as Paddy.

Throughout the evening, the common room was full. Men kept coming in to talk about the battle or to hear the latest news. Once again the White Point Inn was a hive of activity. It wasn't until late that night that the customers finally began to leave.

Honor was nearly exhausted. Having had no sleep the night before, she felt that she couldn't stand up another minute, but she refused to go to bed without seeing what was going on in the battle.

From her perch high above the city, she gazed through her spyglass toward the hornworks. As far as she could tell, nothing had changed. The British soldiers were still firing at the Americans and vice versa. In the indigo darkness, she couldn't ascertain how much destruction had been done to the city, but she surmised that it must be great. The many volleys that had flown into the air over Charleston must have inflicted much damage. She'd have to wait for morning to determine how much.

Though she thought she'd stolen away without being detected by Dylan, he joined her on the roof. "I thought I'd find you here," he said, and looked out at the edge of the roof.

"I couldn't go to bed without coming out here." Honor sat there, feeling the cool night air swirl around her. The moonlight was almost intoxicating, its silver glow bathing everything in a shimmering light. "You know, it's the oddest thing. I've been wondering what that peculiar smell is and now I know."

Dylan sniffed the air. "Smells like gunpowder to me. Maybe a little of something else—something sweet." The something else he smelled was the fragrance of flowers, which surrounded her like a soft cloud of invisible blossoms.

"That's it. I know exactly what you mean." Honor turned slightly and pointed to the brick wall that enclosed the backyard. "See that?"

Dylan looked at the wall, squinting as his eyes adjusted to the moonlight. "I see the wall."

"Don't you see the flowers? The jasmine?" Honor stared at the bushy vine that clung to the wall and spilled over it into the street. "Don't you smell it? There's nothing in the world that smells better than jasmine, even when it's mixed with a heavy portion of gunpowder."

Though Dylan wasn't sure he could sense the difference, he nodded. Her fragrance was enough for him. While she continued to stare at the flower, he studied her. Even in the dim light, she seemed as vibrant and fresh and exuberant as the personification of springtime. She was like a sylph, dancing on the moonbeams, daring him to catch her.

Only *she* caught *him*. Somehow his arms slid around her, seeking to capture that sweet innocence for his own. Dylan willed himself to stop, but hadn't the willpower to obey his own edict. When his arms encircled her, she looked up at him, puzzlement carving her face into somber planes and angles that softened almost immediately.

What did she think of him? Dylan didn't see fear in her eyes. Did he dare to think she might have wanted his embrace? He cared not, he told himself, but in fact he did. He hoped she was as caught in the moment as he, as ensnared by the moonlight, the circumstances, the scent of jasmine and gunpowder.

He bent toward her, knowing that he should pull away and run, but unable to do so. In the distance, guns flashed, cannons thundered, but he continued on until his lips were pressed gently against hers. When he finally forced himself to draw away, he expected her to slap him, to demand that he leave the inn at once and never return. He expected many things, but he never expected what she did.

Honor gazed up into his eyes for a long moment, with the cool air and dark smoke curling around them, holding the world at bay. And then she kissed him back. Her lips brushed his, softly, gently, a whisper of ocean breeze.

Honor Richmond had kissed him. Dylan felt as though he owned the world.

Chapter Seven

Honor didn't know what had possessed her to do such a thing last night. Kissing a man! And he a near stranger!

Ah, but what a stranger... and what a kiss.

Dylan Alden. The words rang musically in her head as she waited tables. After their kisses, she'd stammered some excuse and had rushed back through the window. She needed to think about the consequences of what she'd done.

First, she'd jokingly told him she wasn't a lady. *Well, technically that's a true statement,* she admitted grudgingly to herself. Then she let him kiss her. And, of all the forward and naughty things she could have done, she'd kissed him back. She was no better than... than a wharf woman, teasing and taunting, using her body to attract the men that passed.

What must he think of her?

Honor hadn't time to ponder that question, nor did she really want to. It was enough that she'd made herself look and feel foolish.

The thought she couldn't get out of her mind, no matter how hard she tried, was how much she'd enjoyed the kisses. As she considered that question, she decided that she must be worse than the women like Echo. Since they were paid for what they did—a job, in essence—they probably didn't like it. And her mother had always spoken of "wifely duties" as something to be endured, not enjoyed.

Honor spent the entire day in turmoil. Her mind darted from one question to another, each bringing more complications.

She hurried through her chores that night and scooted up to the roof to be alone. Honor had always been a realistic person, never taking the flights of fancy most women had too seriously. Now, she was experiencing some of those very same fantasies. She'd dreamed of his arms around her, of his lips on hers. The reality hadn't diminished that fantasy's power over her; it had, if anything, strengthened it.

How could she face him? Would he expect her to kiss him again? "Questions, questions, questions. All questions and no answers," Honor said, leaning her head back against the gable. "The world is literally being blown apart around me, and I'm pondering my own trifles. Except they aren't trifles. Oh, how foolish can one be?"

"My, but this sounds like a serious conversation." Dylan crawled out to join her. "Is this a soliloquy or may anyone participate in such lofty conjecture? And is 'one' a representative of mankind, or a particular person?"

Color crept up Honor's neck, but she raised her chin defiantly and met his gaze. She prided herself on being honest. How would that honesty serve her in this situation? "I think . . . I think you know the answer to that question. I just wish I had some answers to mine."

"Ah, just as I thought." Dylan slipped his arm around her and squeezed slightly. "Honor, don't berate yourself for something that was spontaneous . . . and wonderful."

"It's not the spontaneous and wonderful part that bothers me." Honor was glad he wasn't trying to evade the discussion completely or pretend the incident had never happened. She was also relieved that he didn't take her kiss as an automatic invitation to initiate such liberties again. Dylan seemed above that. "It's the reality of what happened. I never thought I would do such a thing."

He studied her for a few seconds. "Maybe the fact that you enjoyed it is what's bothering you."

"How would you know whether I enjoyed it or not?" she asked, watching the expression of his face soften as he prepared to answer her. "No," she said, placing her fingers over his lips. "Don't answer that. I'm not sure I want to hear what you'll say."

"Honor, the truth can't hurt you."

"No?" She smiled wryly and shook her head. "Just let word get out that I kissed you and see how much the truth can hurt."

"You don't think I would tell anyone, do you? Honor, I'm not that kind of man."

For a few seconds, she said nothing. When she looked into his eyes again, she found compassion there, or what she perceived to be compassion. "What kind of man are you, Dylan?"

"I'm a man who's found a good friend in a lovely young lady of Charleston." Dylan rested his chin on top of her head, wondering what he could say to comfort her. He knew the social implication of her actions, but he also knew enough to determine that she was motivated by emotion, not by greed or other self-serving reasons. He'd been kissed by a lot of women who had ulterior motives, seldom by one who really cared about him.

A good friend. The words echoed in Honor's mind. Was that what he wanted of her? Was that what she wanted of him? Could she ever be just a friend to Dylan Alden? Now that they'd kissed, was friendship a realistic expectation? She didn't think so. The kiss had been too exciting, too... too much of everything. Once a path had been trodden, one couldn't return and go another way.

"Honor," he whispered, as if saying her name enchanted him. "Are you angry with me?"

"Angry? Why would you think that?" Honor was truly puzzled by his question. She was many things where he was concerned, but angry wasn't one of them. She'd been realizing that her feelings went far deeper than she'd ever thought possible.

"You're just so quiet, so serious." Dylan watched the flare of the cannons firing and then listened for the boom that followed seconds later. So much had happened. So much was yet to occur. His feelings for Honor were as puzzling to him as anything he'd ever experienced, yet he couldn't step back from them, from her.

Their discussion was interrupted by a series of thundering volleys. He instinctively pulled her closer into the protective circle of his embrace and, for a few seconds, neither of them moved. Flaming orbs flew over their heads.

"Look!" Honor exclaimed, pointing to one of the fire-balls. "What is it?"

Dylan stared for a moment. He hated to see the British resort to this particular tactic, but knew that Clinton believed it would shorten the battle. "A fireball. It's called a 'carcase.' Designed to hit a structure and destroy it with fire."

"Don't they know that the whole city could burn if they do that?" Honor stared incredulously as another ball of fire sailed over her head, leaving a trail of roiling, acrid smoke behind that nearly obliterated her view of the full moon.

"Honor, this is war. I know that for weeks the people of Charleston have treated this as a social event, but it isn't. Clinton is serious." Dylan couldn't reveal too much, but he wanted to impress upon her the gravity of the situation.

"But this is inexcusable." Honor folded her arms across her chest and stuck out her chin. "Doesn't he realize that all he's doing is making matters worse? He doesn't know the will of the Charlestonians."

"He intends to break that will, Honor," Dylan explained, wondering how many others were thinking the same thing as she. "That's the nasty part, the object of war. One side breaks the will of the other."

Honor nodded, indicating that she understood his point. "But, Dylan, he doesn't know us. We'll never give in to such tactics. We're too stubborn."

Though Dylan didn't see how they could do otherwise, he said nothing more. There was nothing to be said. For a long time they sat there, and then she suddenly sat erect.

"We have to do something. What if one of those things strikes the inn and it catches fire?"

He hadn't really thought of that. "I don't know. I suppose we'll have to put the fire out."

"With what?" Honor tried to think of something that would help, but nothing came to mind immediately. Then she snapped her fingers and said, "Sand. That should work. Sand all around."

She jumped up. "Come on. We're going to fill some buckets with sand and dirt. Some with water."

They went back into the house and down the stairs. Honor led him out to the kitchen and looked around. "What do you think?"

"I think that we'll need something lightweight. Once we fill a container with sand, it should get pretty heavy. If you can't lift it, then it's no good to you." Dylan glanced around at the kitchen pots. "Maybe some of these will do." He reached for a good-sized kettle and then hesitated. "Della won't beat me if I take her pot, will she?"

"No, she won't." Della strode into the room and answered for herself. "I've seen them fireballs scooting across the sky like a hound after a fox."

"I'll go get a shovel." Honor ran from the kitchen and out to the barn. She found a couple of shovels and returned to the kitchen. "Here, Dylan. You and I can dig. Della, find us enough pots and buckets to put all around the house."

The two of them went to the far side of the yard and began to dig. Luckily, the ground was mostly sand there and easily worked. Della kept bringing containers for them and leaving with filled ones.

"You know," Honor said with a giggle, feeling a little like a lunatic as she dug beneath the full moon, "anyone watching us might think we're burying treasure out here. Silver or something like that."

Chuckling, Dylan filled one container and started on another. "Or they might think we were burying the body of someone we'd murdered."

"Either way," Honor said, "we look awfully foolish."

Tired from digging, they finished the last container and then walked slowly back to the kitchen. There they found Della sitting in the semidarkness in front of a banked fire.

"I never thought I'd see the day that people would be throwing fire at one another. It's heathen behavior." The Irish woman rocked back on the legs of the cane-bottom chair and crossed her arms. "Lord bless us and save us, what is the world coming to?"

During the next few days, the workers of the White Point Inn and Tavern distributed containers of sand throughout the house. They took empty hogsheads, filled them with water and placed them on the porches. Della found a cache of old linens and stacked them neatly by the water barrels. If the house should be struck by one of the fireballs, the linens could be dunked in water and thrown against the flames.

Della prepared meals, but with much less finesse. The firing of the cannons was too disconcerting, especially now with the threat of fire. Honor helped as much as she could, but her main job was watching for fireballs.

"I don't care if nobody don't eat, Daughter," Henry Richmond said that morning. "We're going to be prepared for the fires if they catch."

To his credit, Honor thought, *he is feeding the soldiers who stop by whether they have any money or not.*

At first, sitting on the roof had been fun. Now it was a job, a hard job. Her nose was sunburned, she ached all over from having to sit so rigidly, and she was tired. Honor couldn't remember ever being so tired that she could simply lie down on the street and fall asleep.

The shelling continued day and night, back and forth for more than forty hours. Exhaustion reigned in Charleston, not only with the soldiers but with everyone. Apparently, the soldiers on both sides became so tired the firing stopped. Honor said a silent prayer of thanks and then stumbled to bed to rest.

The days were long and hot, hotter than Honor could ever remember for April. The wind came from the south. Along with the wind came the Royal Navy, sailing right past Fort Moultrie. Even though the guns of the fort blazed, pitching cannonballs across the harbor entrance, the ships came on. One ship was hit. The resulting explosion nearly disintegrated the deck, and the fire completed the job. Another ship ran aground, and, her own crew, apparently, burned her.

Honor realized how gut wrenching that must have been for the sailors, but necessary from their point of view. As a whole, the Royal Navy sailed into the harbor relatively undamaged, their guns blasting.

Honor had a sinking sensation. As long as the ships had remained on the other side of Fort Moultrie, she'd felt that the Patriots had a chance. Now, she wasn't so sure.

Sitting on the roof became nearly impossible, but she remained as long as she could. From her vantage point, she could see some of the damage that had been inflicted by the cannonading. In this part of town, most of the homes and businesses were brick, but all of them were trimmed with wood. Black streaks of burnt wood were scattered here and there as a testament to the fireballs that blazed across the sky. The acrid smell of burning grease filled the air.

Dylan stayed at the inn as much as possible. He sat with Honor or edged further around the roof to watch for incoming fireballs.

The streets and brick sidewalks were pocked with the results of the exploding shells. Some buildings were demolished completely.

As Honor and Dylan sat there, he said, "The worst is yet to come, I fear."

"Worst? How can it get worse?" Honor couldn't imagine what would be more awful than the events of the past few days.

"The heat." Dylan looked up at the white-hot sun punctuating the dark blue dome of sky. He saw no clouds on the horizon. No chance of rain. The breeze had died to almost a whisper. "The wind is blowing from the south."

"I know." Honor wondered what he was talking about. With all the guns blasting and the cannons bombarding the city, the weather seemed irrelevant.

"As long as the wind blows from the south, we'll be engulfed in the heat." Dylan pointed to the men out at the hornworks and shook his head. "You're here where the breeze can cool you. What about them? The soldiers? Think how hot it must be down in those trenches."

Honor nodded slowly. She hadn't thought of that. She decided the heat there must be much like that in the attic, stifling and still, a palpable predator that sapped its victims' strength until a more deadly enemy could approach. "They must feel like they're being cooked alive."

The heat lingered over the next few days. Milk spoiled quickly even when kept in the cellar. Honor found that she craved water constantly.

Jeffrey came by only occasionally, but could stay no more than a few minutes. Each time, Honor forced him to eat a bite while he gave them the latest news.

When he sat down, he smiled at her. Jeffrey was genuinely happy to see her, having spent most of the past few days crawling from trench to trench, sometimes through the swamp. "Well, my little Lynx, what have you to report?"

"Just that the cannonading is ripping us apart." Honor felt a little guilty. She hadn't seen much of anything that would be of use to him and somehow felt it was her fault for not being more observant. "I promise to try harder. What's going on? I mean, what's really happening?"

"Rumors are rampant that General Lincoln is planning to surrender," he said flatly, not knowing how to cushion the blow to make it more palatable.

Honor stared blankly at him, unable to understand exactly what his revelation meant. "I—I don't . . . what will we do?"

He gazed at her for a long moment and sipped his ale. "I don't know, Honor. Why don't you leave town? Go any way you can. Head down to the wharf and take a boat, any boat, up the Cooper River."

"Jeffrey, you know we have no place to go. Even if we did, I doubt that Papa would consider abandoning our inn." Honor tried to think rationally about the ramifications of his advice. "No, he won't do it."

"Look, Honor, I know . . . I feel sure that we're going to withdraw soon. We have to." Jeffrey closed his eyes wearily and rested a moment before continuing. "We're losing men. Our supplies are getting low. Charleston is being flattened by Clinton. He promised to do that if he ever returned. He hasn't forgotten the beating he took the last time he attacked."

Honor leapt to her feet and spun around. She began to pace. A few months ago, her life had been pleasant, even though the war had been going on. Business had been good. She remembered laughing and joking about how ineffective Clinton's men were. And now he was about to march into Charleston. Worse, General Lincoln was about to withdraw, leaving the city to the British. "What will Clinton do to us? I mean, to those of us who remain?"

Jeffrey stood and shook his head. "I can't answer that, Honor."

When he was gone, she sat down at the table and stared straight ahead, seeing nothing. Her thoughts were on Clinton. What would he do? Would he round up all the citizens and slay them? Would he make servants of them? What was to become of them all?

Dylan had been gone the whole day. He'd walked throughout the city, gauging the damage in order to give his report to Cedric. "Cedric, the damage is extensive. I don't see that they can hold out much longer. Their meat is spoiling in this heat. Food is in short supply all around."

"Well, London, looks as if we're going to win this time. Wouldn't want to be a soldier in the Continental army, what with Clinton so angry 'bout his treatment before, if you know what I mean." Cedric grinned his lopsided grin and touched his cap. "See you soon, chum."

Though he hated himself for giving his report, Dylan realized that reliable information could be used by the British side to end the fighting sooner. Knowing that supplies were running out, they could increase the level of firing until the city could stand no more. Ending the battle sooner would save lives. Dylan kept telling himself that. He had to.

Honor sat with her head drooping into her hands. She couldn't remember how long she'd been sitting there at the table, the weariness stealing the last of her energy. A sharp knock sounded on the door.

Rising slowly, she walked to the door and opened it. As long as the firing continued, she had little to fear. Outside the door a small group of rebel soldiers stood looking up at her. "Yes? What may I do for you?"

"Miss, I'm Lieutenant Belton Monroe. Would you lead me to your larder, please?"

Honor stared at him for a few seconds. "My larder?"

"Yes, miss."

She glanced at the group of men, some more weary looking than she felt. "If you gentlemen will come in, our cook will be happy to prepare a meal—"

"No, miss, we're here on orders. Take us to your larder."

Dylan stepped into the common room. He understood the situation immediately, though he doubted that Honor did. "Honor," he called softly. "Do as the officer says. He is under orders and will do this with or without your consent. He's here to confiscate food for the soldiers."

Honor began to understand the soldiers' mission. "But my father is an innkeeper, Lieutenant. We must have food for our customers and lodgers. Surely the army—"

Dylan reached for her and drew her into his arms. "Honor, these men have no choice and neither have you."

She looked up into Dylan's eyes. He was trying to be gentle, but she'd gone numb when she'd realized what the soldiers wanted. "Come with me."

With Dylan to help support her, Honor led the way to the larder. There, several of the soldiers began to look at everything in the barrels, on the shelves, hanging from the ceiling. They formed a line, passing the meats out of the cellar to a wagon that had been drawn up to the cellar door.

She watched helplessly as their stock of food went from hand to hand up the stairs. All the hams, bacon, beef went first, followed by the salt. The soldiers opened the hogsheads of cheese and took them as well, until all that was left were a few barrels of rice, flour, cornmeal, sugar, molasses, coffee, tea and hominy.

After the men had gone, Honor looked at the near-empty cellar. "What will we eat?"

"Rice, I suppose." Dylan tried as best he could to comfort her. "We can live on it. Don't worry."

"With no salt?" Honor remembered the days before the war when salt had been plentiful. Imported from Bermuda, it had been inexpensive. The Carolinians used it to cure their meats. After the war began, salt became more scarce and more expensive, but it had still been available. "What does this mean, Dylan? I thought the army brought in plenty of meat when they were waiting for Clinton to strike. What happened?"

"The heat," Dylan replied, leading her out of the cellar and into the common room. "The unnatural heat wave spoiled all the meat the army brought in."

"But we have to eat, too," she protested, wondering what her father would say when he returned from wherever he'd gone.

"Honor, in times of war, the soldiers are fed first. What is left is available for the general population. Right now, there's not enough meat for the soldiers, so we do without."

"So much has already happened to us, I don't know why I'm surprised about this," she said, sinking into a chair. "What else can happen?"

Over the next few days, Honor wished she'd never uttered those words. Jeffrey stopped by with more bad news. "That bas—ah, Tarleton has closed off the Cooper River."

Honor stared at him. "Where? What do you mean?"

"A week or so ago, Tarleton's dragoons defeated the Americans at Monck's Corner, closing off all the supply routes and escape routes." Jeffrey sighed with exhaustion. "I can only stay a minute. Nobody can get out of Charleston now. But worse, nobody can get in. That means there's no fresh food coming in from the plantations. We're isolated."

"Isolated?" Honor repeated the word dumbly, as if she couldn't believe what he was telling her. She knew how much the soldiers depended on keeping the Cooper River open for supplies and as an escape route for the people of the city.

"Yes, and Clinton sent another request for surrender."

Honor's head jerked up and she stared at him for a few seconds. "We're not! Tell me we're not surrendering."

"No. General Lincoln refused." Jeffrey hesitated a little. He didn't want to tell her the rest. "Honor, he wanted to. He probably would have, except the leading citizens of Charleston refused to let him."

"Jeffrey, that's absurd. Why would he even consider it?" Honor slapped the table. "We defeated Clinton once before. We can do it again."

When Honor had the chance, she went to Dylan to tell him of the news. He nodded sadly. "I heard the same report."

"Everything seems to be collapsing around us, Dylan. What will become of us?"

Dylan didn't know the answer to her question. He wished he had food in his warehouse to give her, but he didn't. There was nothing he could do. His connections were primarily one way, though occasionally Cedric told him about something that was going to happen or had just happened. "I don't know, Honor. We'll survive . . . somehow."

"Your reassurances aren't very reassuring when fireballs are blazing through the air, apt to strike my home at any given moment." Honor didn't really mean to sound bitter, but she was tired, so tired. She'd grown accustomed to the whistling and exploding of the cannonballs, but that didn't lessen her apprehensions very much.

A few days later, more Patriot soldiers stopped by. These soldiers weren't nearly as nice as Lieutenant Monroe had been. They demanded to be taken to the food-storage rooms.

"You're too late," she told them coldly, blocking the door with her body. "Some of your men were here and took all the meat and cheese and salt we had. We've nothing left to give."

"Stand aside, miss," the soldier commanded, leveling his gaze at her. "We're here on orders and have no time to exchange pleasantries."

"I've just told you that—" Honor had no opportunity to complete her sentence. The soldier took her by the waist and drew her aside so the others could enter. "Unhand me, you devil! Whose side are you on? More likely you're with Tarleton's bunch of thieves."

Honor kicked and wriggled to get free, but her efforts were wasted. "Release me this instant!"

The soldier tightened his grip. "Sorry, miss. Orders."

He dragged her along to the back of the house and out to the kitchen, where Della was glowering at the soldiers, her eyes filled with hatred. "You let my girl go!"

"Stay out of this, old woman!"

The soldier nodded to the others and they began their search. They looked everywhere, even under the hay in the loft in the barn. "Stop it, I say!" Honor exclaimed, wishing she had something she could use to bash the soldier in the head.

Della lifted a heavy kettle and was about ready to bring it down on the soldier's head when Dylan caught her. "No, Della. You'll only go to jail." He took the pot from her hands and placed it on the table. Then he turned to Honor and the soldier holding her. "Soldier, I demand that you release Miss Richmond at once!"

"We got orders—"

"You have orders to confiscate food, not to manhandle young maidens." Dylan stepped forward threateningly.

The soldier glanced at Dylan, who was about four inches taller and much more muscular than he was. "If you'll keep this little hellion from attacking us, you can have her."

Dylan didn't meet Honor's eyes. He kept his gaze leveled on the soldier. "No bargains, Soldier. Are you afraid of a woman who's barely five feet tall and weighs no more than a hundred pounds?"

This time the soldier released Honor, who stepped away from him, balled up her fist and walloped him in the stomach. "Never, under any circumstances, are you to touch me again."

Doubled over, the soldier backed out of the kitchen, to the chuckles and ridicule of his men. "Way to go, Sergeant!"

"She's tough enough to command this unit," called one man.

Another soldier glared at the sergeant. "What about letting her take the sergeant's place? She's a better fighter."

On orders from General Lincoln's administrative staff, the soldiers took almost everything this time. They left only a barrel of rice. Honor watched the men leave with a glare in her eyes. How could they take everything? What right did they have? She glanced at Dylan, started to say something, but walked away silently. At that moment, she couldn't talk to anyone.

During the next few days, Honor learned about hunger. The rice in no way made up an adequate diet, not even with the spring vegetables that were beginning to grow in the kitchen garden. Della cooked the rice with small onions or greens, but the result was still too bland.

One day during a quiet spell and at low tide, Honor and Dylan took a basket and a shovel down to the water's edge and dug a few clams and oysters. Before they'd filled their basket, the cannonading began again and they scrambled for the safety of home.

Della fed Mrs. Richmond before the others, though she ate little. "That poor woman doesn't eat enough to stay alive. I'm worried that this war is going to kill her."

"I know what you mean. She has no interest in food." Honor watched Della fill the large bowls with rice, clams and oysters. "She has no interest in anything. The sounds of the fighting don't even bother her anymore, not like they did when Clinton attacked before."

Shaking her head, Della stopped what she was doing and looked at Honor. "Honor darlin', your ma's not long for this world. I'm afraid she's decided to die."

Tears formed in the corners of Honor's eyes, but she acknowledged that Della was right. "I've done everything. I simply don't know what else to do."

"You've done what you could. Your pa has done what he could." Della placed the bowls on a tray. "The doctor did what he could. Now, it's the Lord's turn."

Honor turned away for a moment and brushed the tears from her cheeks. "I've given her the laudanum, hoping it will protect her from the distractions. I don't even know if it's working."

Della folded her arms around Honor and held her close. "Her mind is so closed off, she doesn't even know where she is sometimes."

"I miss her," Honor whispered, feeling the tears threaten once again.

"I do, too, girl. I do, too."

Supper that night was a feast. Most of the lodgers had left for safe havens outside the city of Charleston, so Honor, Dylan, her father, Della and Jeffrey sat down to supper together. Though Henry seemed surprised that Honor invited the servants to eat with them as well, he said nothing.

Nobody said much of anything during the meal. They were so glad to have something other than rice to eat that the company didn't matter. They simply savored the flavors and textures of the succulent shellfish.

The firing came from all sides now. Admiral Arbuthnot and the ships of the Royal Navy were firing at the city of Charleston, increasing the danger to the people living near White Point. All along Bay Street and Battery Street, houses were damaged, some nearly demolished. The fireballs kept up their relentless pace, streaking across the sky with trailing orange flame and roiling black smoke.

But Clinton became even more devious. His men were firing cannonballs that split open upon impact. The shell carcasses contained rice.

Honor found one in her garden and stared at it, puzzled for a moment by the contents. Then she realized what Clinton was doing. "Damn that man! We won't give up. I would eat clover and drink water from the Ashley River before I'd surrender," she shouted. Nobody heard, but she felt better about saying the words out loud.

That evening, Jeffrey stopped by to talk to her briefly. "I just have a moment to—"

"Do you know what Clinton's doing? He's making fun of us. He's taunting us. Firing cannonballs filled with rice." Honor's face was splotched with red, indicating the depth of her anger. "We won't give up. We won't."

"Honor," Jeffrey said quietly, closing his eyes briefly as if he hated what he was going to say. "Honor, Fort Moultrie surrendered to Admiral Arbuthnot today."

"What? Why?" Honor sank into a chair. Too much was happening, too much that she'd never expected, never would have believed. Her chin rested on her hands as she thought of the last defense outside the city of Charleston falling. Somewhere across the harbor, the British were now taking over the fort the Patriots had counted on to keep Charleston free. "I didn't even know they were fighting out there."

"They weren't." Jeffrey sat down beside her and took her hands.

Dylan walked in and joined them. "Bad news, eh?"

"The worst," Jeffrey said. "About five hundred men of the Royal Navy were put ashore a few days ago. Two hundred more yesterday. With the ships in the harbor and the troops on shore closing the noose around Fort Moultrie, the soldiers in the fort had no choice."

"They gave up without fighting?" Honor was incredulous. Why, oh why, would something like that happen? "Jeffrey, are you sure?"

"Positive."

"I heard it, too, Honor." Dylan placed his hand on her shoulder and patted her gently. "I couldn't believe it, either."

Honor's chin rested on her chest. "May seventh is the worst day in this war. Nothing else can happen to top this."

Dylan sped around the craters in the brick sidewalk in his haste to reach the inn. He wanted to be there for Honor. On this of all days, she would need someone to be strong for her. He dreaded what he must do, but there was no other way.

When he reached the inn, he paused outside the gate. All around, houses were scarred with soot and burned places. Bricks everywhere had been thrown askew, making walking doubly difficult.

Charleston had once been a beautiful city, with clean, neat streets and well-kept yards. Now there were places that resembled piles of rubbish, nothing more. Gone was the grace and charm, replaced by the stench of burnt grease from the fireballs, acrid smoke from the cannon and the bitter taste of defeat.

General Lincoln had surrendered.

Chapter Eight

Honor didn't believe Dylan, even though the guns and cannons had been silent for most of the day. "No, you're wrong. You must be wrong." But the expression on his face told her otherwise. "And I thought that May seventh was bad. It was nothing in comparison to today. May twelfth has to be the low point of my life. What else can happen?"

Dylan didn't know how to answer her question. He thought, privately, that everything would soon be better, but he held his tongue. Honor was in too much pain right now.

"I'm going to do everything in my power to..." Honor didn't finish her sentence. She'd almost said that she would do everything in her power to free Charleston, but she remembered Jeffrey's warnings. Even though she thought she knew Dylan as well as she'd ever known anyone, she heeded Jeffrey's advice.

Dylan shook his head and drew her into the circle of his arms. He'd known defeat in his lifetime, plenty of it. Even though his older brother, Nathan, had hated the family estate, electing to stay in London year round, his father had refused to pass the property to Dylan. For years, Dylan had tended the land as if he would inherit it someday, and for a time, his father had even pretended that it might be so.

But, in the end, he'd refused to change his will. He simply couldn't put Dylan ahead of his older brother, no matter how sensible the idea might be. Nathan Alden hadn't set foot on Cheshire Place in more than three years when his father made his decision. Dylan, filled with despair over losing the property he loved to someone who would probably sell it, left England for good.

His personal loss, his personal defeat, made him more sensitive to Honor's feelings at the moment. "Honor, nothing bad will happen to us. You'll see. Order will be restored and our lives will return to normal. Sir Henry Clinton is an honorable man."

Honor couldn't believe such a thing. "If he's so damned—" She clapped her hands over her mouth. This was the second time she'd used that word over Sir Henry Clinton's behavior. She said a silent prayer asking for forgiveness. "If he's so honorable, why has he done such horrible things?"

"War is never simple, Honor. You must know that." Dylan really didn't know what to say now. He'd told her about the surrender, but not about the terms. If she was this upset, maybe he shouldn't continue. But he knew Honor would want to know everything. Even though she might be angry, she wasn't one to shy away from the truth. "The rebels will march out to the hornworks and lay down their weapons. Then Clinton and his men will march into Charleston. The American soldiers aren't being punished. Clinton is offering them a parole, good as long as they don't take up arms against King George again."

Honor tilted her head to one side and narrowed her eyes to a slit. "Why is he doing that?"

"As I said, he's an honorable man." Dylan recognized the signs of acceptance in her. Even though she hated the idea of surrender, she was taking all this pretty well. "Most of these men are South Carolina Militia, not the Continental army. So he's letting them go back to their homes and families. The soldiers of the Continental army will be imprisoned until they can be exchanged."

Early the next morning, Paddy came by. "Do you know what he's done, that Clinton?"

"No, Paddy, what's he done?" Honor stopped sweeping the floor and leaned on her broom.

"Everybody's got to go sign the paroles. Men, I mean. Even me."

"Gracious, I think you have that wrong. You're only eleven years old. Why would you have to sign?"

"Every man that's able, whether he fighted or not, is having to go. Even Dylan, and he's half-crippled."

Honor dropped the broom and sat down. This was something she couldn't understand at all, something totally unexpected. "Why would he do a thing like that? How do you know this?"

"There was some signs put up that said so."

"But, Paddy, surely they didn't mean—"

"There was some soldiers standing there. Red coats and shiny black boots. Said I was to report like the rest of the men."

Dylan walked in the door, his face contorted with a scowl. He glanced at Honor, then around the room. "Honor, where's Henry?"

"He's out in the barn. Why?" Honor rose slowly and walked a few steps toward Dylan. "It's true, isn't it? What Paddy says."

Inhaling deeply, Dylan nodded. "I suppose this is just so Clinton will have some idea of how many men are in town."

"Dylan!" she exclaimed, wringing her apron with her hands until it became a twisted mass. "That's not honest. You said he was an honorable man. Where is the honor in what he's demanding? Where is the honor in inflating the numbers of soldiers for the purpose of saving face?"

"Honor, I'm sure this is simply a formality." Dylan walked across the floor of the common room and stopped at the door to the changing room. "Your father will have to go, too."

Within a few minutes, Henry, Paddy and Dylan joined the group of men marching toward the hornworks. Honor watched them until they were out of sight. She wasn't satisfied with Dylan's answer about Clinton's reasons for making all men sign the paroles. There must be something else, another reason that would make more sense. She didn't know what it was now, but she'd find out. Somehow, she knew it had to do with adding to the total number of soldiers who had been fighting in Charleston.

To her surprise, many Charlestonians came out to welcome Clinton and the British soldiers. Bands played, speeches were given, guns fired in victory. Honor felt sick. The city she loved had forgiven her conqueror. People all around were joining in the celebration.

Her resolve to help free Charleston increased a hundredfold. She couldn't wait until she could talk with Jeffrey about how they could manage this, but she'd find a way somehow.

She kept thinking about all those soldiers outside of Charleston who were still fighting for the cause. There would be others here in the city who would be fighting as well, but their weapons would be completely different. Honor and Jeffrey and even little Paddy would use information, stolen knowledge passed on through the network of spies that Jeffrey had so painstakingly set up before the siege had begun.

Clinton might have won the day and would surely win others, but Charleston and the Patriots weren't through yet. The independent spirit, the rage over what had been and was being done to the people of America would rise, and the tide that it wrought would be unstoppable. Sir Henry Clinton might bask in his glory for a while yet, but his downfall loomed as surely in his future as had this bitter lesson to the people of Charleston.

Dylan was correct about Clinton, to a degree. All the men who'd fought against him were allowed to sign their paroles and return to their families. Honor found that Charleston was indeed returning to normal—if having groups of British and Tory soldiers take over your home could be called normal.

Commerce began again. Shops opened. Food was brought in. Debris was cleared from the streets. The White Point Inn and Tavern opened for business once again, though its rooms were taken by the soldiers. Honor stared at them as they came in, carrying their belongings. She could barely conceal her hatred.

"Honor, you must pretend to accept them," Jeffrey warned her late one night in the deep shadows of the barn. "You are more valuable than ever. These soldiers—all the British and Tories, in fact—must begin to trust you, or our mission will have failed."

"Jeffrey, how can you ask this of me? You're asking me to be more than civil." Honor tried to put her thoughts into words, but felt as if she had failed. "Not cordial, not pleasant, but friendly—is that what you want?"

"You've done it all along, Honor, remember?"

"Yes, but it was different then. I was friendly to the Tories that came in here before the humiliation of our defeat. Now, I'm supposed to..." Her voice trailed off into silence as she mutely accepted what she had to do. Honor had vowed to do everything within her power to restore freedom to her beloved Charleston, and here she was, balking at her first opportunity. "I'll do it."

Honor felt the first bite of the doubled-edged sword of espionage a few days later. As she was walking along, smiling and flirting with British soldiers she passed on her way to Miriam's, a thunderous explosion erupted and threw her to the ground. At first she thought that the Patriots were trying to retake the city, but the thick plume of black smoke and the flames reaching for the sky denied her wish.

Something dreadful had happened. Along with a multitude of others, Honor ran toward the scene. As she hurried toward the shaft of smoke, she began to see mangled and bloodied bodies lying all around and slowed down. What could have caused this carnage? she wondered.

Her stomach began to rumble in protest, but she swallowed back the bitter taste of gall and went on. Then she saw Miriam's mother, Ida Edwards, lying in a pool of blood on a brick staircase. "Oh, Mrs. Edwards!" Honor exclaimed, running forward as hard as she could. She knelt beside her friend's mother and took her hand. "Mrs. Edwards, it's me...Honor."

Honor couldn't tell at first whether Mrs. Edwards heard her or not, but finally the woman's fingers tightened slightly on her hand. "Honor, dear," came the ragged whisper. "Help Miriam...she'll need looking after. Tell her how much I love her."

"Of course, I will, Mrs. Edwards." Honor glanced about, spotted Paddy and waved for him. "Paddy, go quick. Find Jeffrey or Dylan." She returned her attention to Mrs. Edwards. "You can tell her yourself, Mrs. Edwards. You'll be fine. I'm sure as soon as the doctor gets here he'll—"

"No, Honor," Ida Edwards croaked, a tiny rivulet of blood trickling from her mouth down her chin. "I won't last. My time here is up."

Honor fought her tears. She knew better than to cry or get hysterical in front of an injured person. "Non-nonsense, Mrs. Edwards," she stammered. "You'll be all right. Just wait and see." She squeezed her eyes shut for a moment, willing her tears not to fall. She had to be strong for Mrs. Edwards. Now was not the time to have weeping fits.

"I was remarking to Miriam the other day how strong and fit you are. Why, you'll be up and around in no time." Honor searched her mind for something else comforting to say.

"Honor, my dearest, you're a sweet child." Ida Edwards stared up at her with soft gray eyes and tried to smile. "I've always loved you. I always wanted another daughter. If I could have chosen one, it would have been you."

Honor could no longer restrain her tears; they flowed down her cheeks in shiny silver trails. She reached up to wipe them away. "I—I...ever since my mother got sick, I've looked to you as a mother. I love you very much."

Ida Edwards closed her eyes. Honor gazed at her. Her clothing was bloody, but there was no way to stanch the blood's flow. It came from too many places at once, finding passages through the rents in the dress that Mrs. Edwards wore. Whatever had struck her had done so with a great force.

All around Honor, people were moaning or crying out. She didn't know what had happened, but it must have been horrible. There were bodies strewn as far as she could see. People's clothing and skin were burned, with tattered, blackened edges framing exposed muscle tissue. Some bodies were still burning; whoever could was hastening to smother the flames.

Tears welled in her eyes and spilled over her eyelids as she watched Mrs. Edwards draw her last breath. "Oh, please, don't die," she murmured over and over. She slid the woman's head into her lap and smoothed her blond hair. Like Miriam, Mrs. Edwards had pretty gray eyes, but they were now closed forever in death.

How could she tell Miriam that her mother was dead? Miriam had no one except her mother. Where would she live? What would she do? She couldn't remain in her own home; there were several British officers billeted there. It wasn't proper. It was dangerous.

Honor and Miriam had always been like sisters. "Now we will be sisters," Honor vowed through the blur of her tears. She rocked back and forth, praying that Miriam would never see her mother in death. The blow would be too cruel. "Mrs. Edwards, now Miriam and I will truly be sisters. I'll take care of her, I promise."

* * *

Dylan ran as fast as his bad leg would allow him. He'd heard the explosion; it had shaken his warehouse, broken some windows. He could see and smell the smoke. But worse, he could hear the cries of the injured and smell the stench of burned flesh.

"Dylan!" shouted a voice he recognized as Paddy's. "Stop!"

Without stopping, he scanned the people around him for Paddy and spotted him in a live oak. Worming his way through the now-surging mass of people, Dylan got to the tree. "What happened, Paddy?"

"Explosion. Don't know." Paddy climbed down out of the tree and grabbed Dylan's hand. "Honor... come with me."

A fear that he had never suspected could live within his body tore through Dylan like a bolt of lightning, shattering every pretense of composure. "Lead on."

As they ran through the crowd, Dylan even faster than before, now ignoring his injury completely, he called, "Is she hurt badly? Is... Paddy, what's wrong with her?"

Before the boy could answer, they found Honor. Her apron and bodice were covered with blood, as were her face and hands. Dylan closed his eyes for the briefest of moments and prayed that her injuries weren't severe. One glance at the woman in Honor's arms told of a different fate. The woman was dead.

Dylan fell to the ground beside Honor and enfolded her in his arms. "Oh, Honor, my darling, what happened to you?"

Her wet gaze, a blank stare that showed no comprehension, met his. "Mrs. Edwards... Miriam's mother... she's dead."

He nodded, wondering if Honor had been stunned and was unable to understand what he was asking her. "Yes, she's dead, but what of you?"

"I'm... Oh, Dylan, what can I tell Miriam? Poor, sweet Miriam. What will she do? I must go to her. Yes, I'll go right now, as soon as I've taken care of Mrs. Edwards."

Dylan realized that Honor wasn't thinking clearly at all. Distraught, she was more concerned about Mrs. Edwards and Miriam than herself. He wiped her tears and was glad to see that the blood on her face came away and wasn't replenished by fresh blood from a wound. That left the injury to her chest and stomach and legs. "Honor!" he exclaimed, as if to startle her into hearing him. "Listen to what I'm saying. Does your body hurt, Honor? Talk to me. Tell me where you're injured."

"Me? No, I'm not hurt. Mrs. Edwards . . . she's dead. Oh, God, she's dead." Honor glanced around at the writhing bodies. People were burned beyond recognition, crying out in agony. Each cry brought a shudder to her own form. "Oh, Dylan. So many people dead. The burning! Dear God, the burning. Can you smell it? People burning all around me. I couldn't do anything to help them. Oh, dear God, let this be a dream."

Soldiers began to file in, helping those who were injured. Army surgeons and Charleston's doctors went from body to body, person to person, checking to see who had survived and who hadn't, giving aid to those who still needed it.

Dr. Peterson, the doctor who had treated Dylan when he fell, stopped by Honor. "Let me see, child."

He knelt beside Honor and began to examine her for injuries. Honor brushed away his hand and pointed to Mrs. Edwards. "She's dead, Dr. Peterson."

"My Lord, it's Ida Edwards." He glanced at Dylan and several other men who were trying to help the victims. He motioned for them to lift her.

"We'll take care of her from here, Honor." Dr. Peterson turned to Dylan. "Young man, will you see that Honor gets home safely? I'd do it myself, but there's too much to do here. I'll send her something to help her sleep."

Dylan nodded, gently but firmly disengaged her from Mrs. Edwards and helped her to her feet. He and Paddy walked along with her, leaving the carnage behind. Honor could hardly walk. She stumbled along, barely noticing where she was going until they walked into the yard at the inn.

Della was standing at the fence, looking in the direction of the explosion. When she saw who was walking with Dylan, she screamed, "Lord, have mercy, my girl's been hurt!"

"No, Della, no, she's just stunned." Dylan didn't want a hysterical woman on his hands when Honor needed him so badly. "Help me get her to her room." Dylan noticed the anguished look on the boy's face and knew he had to get him away from Honor. "Paddy, go to the kitchen."

Della led Dylan up the stairs to Honor's room. "Set her down on the bed, Mr. Alden. I'll bathe her and put her to bed."

"No!" Honor protested, trying to rise. "I've got to go to Miriam."

Shaking her head, Della said, "You aren't about to go anywhere. You just sit right there and let me—"

Honor struggled to her feet. "You don't understand. Miriam's... Mrs. Edwards is dead. I've got to go and help Miriam."

Della squinted as if she was deep in thought. "Mr. Alden, you sit with her a minute."

Dylan pulled Honor's head against his chest and held her closely. After a few seconds, he realized that he was rocking back and forth with her almost as if she were a sick child. He was whispering soft words into her hair and dropping gentle kisses onto her forehead when Della returned.

She'd noticed this man's interest in Honor before, though she doubted if either of them was aware of his or her feelings yet. Shaking herself out of her romantic thoughts, Della said, "Here. Let me give her a dose of this."

Honor glanced up as the spoon plunged into her mouth. She grimaced and glared at Della. "What was that?"

"Protection." She turned to Dylan. "Now, Mr. Alden, leave us alone. I'll take care of her like I always have."

Dylan had no choice. He could leave peacefully, or the Irish woman would throw him out bodily, and he instinctively knew that she would if she felt that he was threatening Honor in any way. "I know you will, Della. Thank you."

Relinquishing his hold on Honor wasn't easy. She clung to him for a long moment, seemingly reluctant to let him go, but gradually the laudanum—and the shock of her experiences—took effect and her head lolled to one side. Her grip lost its strength.

Dylan left the room. He never would have imagined that it would take all his strength to do so, but it did. He hovered there in the hallway, like a hummingbird over a flower, for a long time, but finally gave up. Della wasn't about to leave Honor alone while she was in this condition.

After a while, Dylan went downstairs. There was nothing he could do for Honor right now, or for anyone else, for that matter. He sat down at a corner table and stared into a tankard of ale.

"Dylan," Jeffrey called from across the room. He walked over and stood by the table where Dylan sat.

"Hello, Jeffrey. Please sit with me for a while." Dylan didn't really want the company. He would rather have sat alone, but Jeffrey represented an opportunity for Dylan to build a friendship that might ultimately be of value.

"I saw Paddy." Jeffrey pulled out a chair and sat down. "He told me about Honor. Is she really all right?"

"I guess so." Dylan tilted his tankard, but didn't drink. He just allowed the lukewarm beverage to moisten his lips. "When I got to her, she was bloodied, but the blood came from Mrs. Edwards, according to Honor."

"That's about what Paddy said." Jeffrey waved to the serving girl and she brought him an ale. "What a tragedy!"

Dylan looked at Jeffrey closely. "Do you know what happened?"

Jeffrey shrugged and nodded. "I think so, though I'm not sure we'll ever be certain. The story I got was that one of the British soldiers accidentally discharged a musket down where they were storing all the confiscated arms and ammunition. It caused all the powder to explode."

"As if this city wasn't already in enough pain," Dylan said, gulping down nearly half his ale. "Carelessness, Jeffrey. God's blood, how many people are dead and how many others injured badly?"

"The early estimate is about two hundred dead." Jeffrey drained his mug and motioned for another. "Where will it end?"

"That, my friend, is a question that thousands upon thousands of people would love to have the answer to." Dylan smiled a wry smile. "Just one more thing for the Americans to hold against the British when this is all over."

Jeffrey nodded. "Not that we need anything else. God knows we have more than enough already."

Dylan didn't respond to that. This discussion could lead down paths he didn't want to follow this night. "Did you know the Edwards woman?"

"Yes, I did. Second-best seamstress in all of Charleston."

"Second best? Seems to me that Miss Miriam said something about the Edwards' shop being the finest."

"It is. Only Miriam is a better seamstress than her mother ever was." Jeffrey grinned. "Mrs. Edwards started to take in sewing when Miriam's father died. The business grew quickly, especially after Miriam began to help her mother."

"What of Honor?" Dylan asked. "How did she and Miriam get to be such good friends?"

"Who knows? They've always lived close to each other, were the same age. Naturally gravitated to each other, I guess." Jeffrey considered the question for the first time in his life.

"And you?" Dylan watched Jeffrey more carefully with this question.

"Oh, I lived about halfway between the two. We played together as children." Jeffrey leaned back in his chair and thought of his childhood years, the freedom of youth and no responsibility. "I've always been in love with Honor, but she never cared for me in the same way."

"What makes you so sure?" Dylan asked, edging forward on his seat.

"She's told me more than once." Jeffrey laughed wryly. "I've come to accept it. I always thought she'd change her mind, but now I can see that she's found other interests."

"Oh?" Dylan was stunned that Jeffrey would say such a thing. "I don't know what you mean."

"I think you do, Dylan Alden." Jeffrey looked down at his drink for a long time. "And I'll kill you if you ever hurt her."

Dylan lay on his bed and stared at the ceiling. Everything seemed to be going awry. Honor was lying in a near-catatonic state from a disastrous accident that had stunned her so badly she'd had to be sedated. A man he hardly knew was threatening his life because of her. Dylan had never been in such a position.

He cared for Honor, of course he did. Anyone would. She was an intense, intelligent young woman with a good sense of humor. She worked hard. But Dylan acknowledged that there was more. His feelings went beyond the simple friendship that he knew Honor felt for Jeffrey.

Dylan knew that her feelings were deeper for him, too. This relationship shouldn't . . . couldn't be allowed to develop any further. He and Honor were on opposite sides in this war. She might even forgive him for that, but she could never forgive him for using her, and that was exactly what he was doing.

He had become friends with her simply because she was a woman who knew many people. That was it—he had grown close to her because she was an important link in his espionage system. He had to keep staying at the White Point because it was the most popular inn in town. Dylan had a job to do and he was doing it to the best of his ability. Honor was nothing more to him than a contact. That was all. Just a contact. Nothing really personal.

Even as he told himself that she meant nothing to him, he knew he was lying to himself. Dylan would continue to lie to himself. It was the only way he could continue to do his job effectively.

Honor lay in her bed, her pillow bunched beneath her head. Outside her window, a mockingbird was singing. How her head ached. How her eyes burned. How the vision of the carnage was emblazoned on her eyelids. She'd cried and cried, but now the tears refused to come.

When her mother had become ill, Mrs. Edwards had become a second mother of sorts. She'd helped Honor choose her clothing, had advised her about relationships and had comforted her when times demanded it. Now Mrs. Edwards was gone.

Rising from her bed, she swayed back and forth from the effects of the medicine Della had forced down her. Honor stood at the window and looked over the city. From her vantage point, she could see none of the damage done by the explosion. What had happened to cause the explosion? Would she ever find out?

And poor Miriam must be distraught, her only living relative gone in a moment's time. When the sun rose, Honor would go to Miriam's and comfort her. After Mrs. Edwards's funeral, Honor would bring Miriam back to the inn to live. *We will be like sisters,* she had promised Mrs. Edwards. Honor's tears streamed anew. Over the past few years, she'd forced herself to think that her own mother would die first because her health was so poor. Now the woman who'd been the substitute mother, a vital woman brimming with good health, was dead, while Honor's mother still lay in her stupor, her mind vacant most of the time.

Honor couldn't bear to think of Mrs. Edwards and Miriam any longer. She needed to think about something good, something positive, or she would go mad. Her thoughts turned to Dylan. Wiping her wet cheeks on the sleeves of her nightgown, Honor wondered how he felt about her.

Dylan must think you a fool, she chided herself. Honor didn't remember all that had happened, but she did recall bits and pieces of the walk back home and of him helping her upstairs. There, her mind got fuzzy. Had she heard him call her "darling"?

When he had held her in his arms, rocking back and forth, had he kissed her again and again, whispering sweet words of love to her? How could she ever find out?

What else could happen? Her city was occupied. Her best friend's mother, along with countless others, had been killed. Her own mother didn't even know she was alive. Surely the end of misfortunes had come.

"What?" she shrieked, glowering at Jeffrey. "You're mad!"

"Honor, you must. You have no choice." Jeffrey pulled her into the deep shadows beneath the live oak and clamped his hand over her mouth. "Many lives depend on you."

"Jeffrey, you know I can't tell such a lie. Not even to Clinton's men." Honor's lungs burned from lack of oxygen and she inhaled deeply when she realized she was holding her breath.

"Honor, every person who works must sign."

"You're saying I have to sign an oath of loyalty to the king in order to work in my own father's inn?" she asked incredulously. In the darkness, she could barely see his face, but she knew that his forehead would be wrinkled with consternation.

"Exactly. Everyone must sign or they can't get a work permit." Jeffrey placed his hand on Honor's arm and squeezed slightly. He knew how she felt about the British, especially since Mrs. Edwards's death. "Everyone, Honor. No exceptions. Those who don't sign will be treated as hostile and subject to a variety of punishments, not excluding imprisonment.''

Honor leaned against the tree trunk, her head bowed with indecision. She'd agreed to be nice to the soldiers, even to flirt with them, but to sign an oath of loyalty to a king she had sworn to help defeat? The implications were far-reaching. She didn't know if she could actually force her hand to sign the paper.

Her world seemed to be collapsing around her, and there was nothing she could do to prevent it.

Chapter Nine

Honor smiled at the soldiers. They teased her and flirted, and she returned their banter. Miriam remained silent, still stunned over her mother's death. Honor gazed up at them, fluttering her dark lashes. "Tell me all about London. Is it the most wonderful place in the world?"

One of the men began to regale her with tales of London's glory. "It's the most fascinating, cosmopolitan city in the world, miss."

"Oh, I do wish I could see it for myself." Honor pointed to the line where Miriam should sign. "There, Miriam, write your name." She looked up at the two soldiers and whispered, "Poor thing. Her mother was killed in the explosion down at the magazine."

The two men nodded. The other soldier handed Honor a paper. She read the oath, blanched as she scrawled her name on the line. "Well, please stop by the White Point to see us sometime. That's my papa's place."

"Oh, we will," they assured her in unison.

Honor ushered Miriam out of Clinton's headquarters, formerly Miles Brewton's home, and forced herself to be calm until she reached the inn. Miriam followed along without saying a single word. When they reached the inn, Honor sat Miriam at a table and brought her a glass of milk. "Here, drink this."

The funeral was long past, but her friend didn't seem to be recovering from her shock as quickly as Honor thought she should be. While Miriam drank the milk, Honor straightened the changing room in preparation for supper. There would be a houseful tonight, she thought.

"Was she in pain, Honor?" Miriam finally asked, staring directly at Honor, her eyes filled with pain.

Honor gave up her chores and sat down. She took Miriam's hands in her own and held them for a few seconds. "I don't think so, Miriam. She—she wasn't burned like so many of the others. I think she was struck by flying debris that sort of knocked the wind out of her when it did whatever... She said—she said to tell you how much she loved you."

The two women sat there for a long time, not talking. For a while, tears flowed, but they gradually subsided. Their grief was undisturbed as they reached out for each other, the only people who truly grieved Ida Edwards's passing. She hadn't been a leading citizen of the town, a planter's wife or the daughter of a wartime general. She was simply a kind woman who did what was necessary to rear her daughter as a lady. Ida Edwards had loved Miriam with all her heart, had loved Honor as well. And they loved her.

Honor enjoyed having Miriam live with her. Even though the room was small, the bed was large enough for the two of them. As the days progressed, they became more like sisters and better friends. They shared everything.

One evening when Jeffrey stopped by and sat with Miriam and Honor, the three of them talked about the war. Miriam, having gotten over the initial shock of her mother's death, said, "I hate them. This is all Clinton's fault."

In spite of the fact that Honor felt almost the same way, she touched Miriam gently and shook her head. "Miriam, it was an accident. Clinton didn't do this."

"Oh, I know that," Miriam agreed, sliding into a slouch in her chair. She fidgeted with her scarf for a moment. "But I can't help believing that if Clinton hadn't taken Charleston, we'd still...Mother and I would still be sewing side by side in our little shop." She hesitated for a long moment. "It's so lonely now."

"I know," Honor murmured, looking at Jeffrey, her eyes imploring him to find a way to help Miriam through this difficult time in her life.

He shrugged and finally said, "I'm sorry, Miriam. There was nothing any of us could do to prevent what happened."

"Thank you, Jeffrey. I know all the soldiers did their best." She rose and started to walk away from the table. "It just seems like there must be some way to—to get rid of him—Clinton. All of them." She turned to Honor. "I think I'll go up to bed now."

Honor saw that she was going to get no further help from Jeffrey. "I'll—"

"No!" Miriam pressed her hand to Honor's shoulder, to keep her from rising. "You go on and talk. I know how busy you've been lately."

Watching Miriam leave, Honor felt her mind spinning. She waited until her friend was out of hearing and then turned to Jeffrey. "We can use her, Jeffrey. Lots of soldiers come into the sewing shop."

Jeffrey shook his head. "She can't do it, Honor. She's too emotional. You can see everything she's thinking on her face."

With a sigh, Honor realized that Jeffrey was right. It wouldn't be fair to expose her to the dangers of spying, because she'd be too easily caught. "Well, there must be something she can do."

Dylan joined them. "How is Miriam? I met her on the stairs and she didn't even acknowledge that I was there."

"Oh, she's better, but a little distracted this evening." Honor's thoughts shifted back to the day of Mrs. Edwards's death. Honor could almost feel Dylan's arms around her again. She remembered that night on the roof, when he'd kissed her. There had been many nights since then that she'd lain awake thinking about his kisses.

"Sorry to hear it."

Dylan and Jeffrey started talking, but Honor had to leave. Across the room, a soldier was beginning to look fidgety. She understood that to mean his mug was nearly empty. Her work never seemed to end since the soldiers had moved in.

When she could stop again, she took her seat. "What's going on with you two?"

Jeffrey and Dylan looked at each other and then at Honor. Jeffrey spoke. "Dylan tells me that Clinton's revoked the paroles, Honor."

Honor's eyes grew wide and her mouth flew open. For a few seconds, she couldn't speak. "He couldn't. I mean, that's dishonest."

"Dishonest, but true, Honor." Dylan's mouth was set in a grimace. He didn't like what he'd learned any more than the American soldiers did. Unfortunately, he liked many of them. Well, it wasn't his job to inform on them. He was trying to obtain information on the continued resistance.

"You said Clinton was an honorable man." She stared straight ahead, seeing nothing, her mind a whirl of angry activity. Then she faced Dylan. "Is this what they call 'honorable' in England?"

"That's not fair, Honor." Jeffrey came to Dylan's defense. "It's not Dylan's fault he was born in London."

"No, you're right." Honor's anger cooled somewhat. "I'm sorry, Dylan. You don't deserve my wrath. You've been here every time I needed you for something. You're a true friend."

Soon, Jeffrey left. He didn't like staying around with Clinton's soldiers all about, especially in light of what he'd just heard. When Jeffrey was gone, Honor sighed and looked at Dylan. "Doesn't Clinton know that this sort of thing is likely to have the exact opposite effect from what he wants?"

"I don't know, Honor," Dylan said dryly. "Who knows what he's thinking?"

"Does this mean that everyone who—who signed the paroles now has to give himself up?" Honor thought of the men who hadn't lifted a hand against the British, but who'd been forced to sign the paroles anyway. Her father, Paddy, Dylan. "They may have to fight against... Oh, Lord, this is awful. Dylan, those men might have to fight against their own brothers or their friends if Clinton forces them into service."

"Hard to believe, I know." Dylan pushed back from the table and rose. "I wish my leg would get better so I could fight. Sometimes I feel so tired of sitting back and watching from afar."

Honor watched him limp across the common room and up the stairs. Right now, Dylan was the only steadfast person in her life. She instinctively felt that she could trust him with anything.

Honor needed to get away. She wanted a chance to think, without having to run for more ale or rum. When the common room was nearly empty during the late afternoon, she sneaked out the back door. Not caring where she walked, she followed one street until it intersected with another, and then changed direction.

She found herself near a house that had been demolished by the cannonading. The house had been a splendid specimen of architecture, with stately white columns rising from the first floor to the third. The curved brick staircase that led to the piazza still stood, with beautiful marble lions sleeping on the curves. Located near the water, this lovely home had taken several direct hits. What wasn't damaged by cannonballs had been burned and charred by fireballs. The wrought-iron gate was open, so Honor walked in.

There was a pretty garden, left now for the weeds to take over. Since the owners weren't around, and weren't likely to be, Honor skirted the ruins of the house and took the little brick path that led into the garden.

The gardens were beautiful, fragrant and bursting with blossoms that would soon fall prey to the weeds that were already as high as Honor's knees. The path wound around, past several clusters of shrubs and flower beds once as pampered as the lady of the household, past marble statues of Greek gods and benches with ornate wrought-iron designs. When she discovered a bench set in a small glade that was closed from view of the street by high boxwoods, she sat down to think.

The fragrance of jasmine wafted to her, mixed with the delicate scent of roses. Honor looked around, feeling a sweet sense of peace steal over her. How could anyone sit in this garden for long and walk away still carrying fear and hatred in her heart? A little arbor supported the Carolina jasmine and the fragrant climbing roses. Someone had planned this place to be one of solitude and serenity, exactly what Honor needed right now.

She'd felt restless and useless. So far, she'd discovered little that would help restore Charleston to its former glory as the cultural center of the south. Clinton's grasp on the city was too tight . . . for now, at least. Honor leaned back and closed her eyes, letting the peace of the quiet garden settle over her like a comforting blanket.

Then she heard someone coming down the walkway. At first, she glanced about for somewhere to hide, but there was only one exit. If it were night, she could hide behind the arbor, but not during daylight. She could only hope that who-ever was in the garden meant no harm.

The footsteps were light, almost like a woman's soft kid boots on the brick walkway. What woman besides herself would be out at this hour, walking in a stranger's garden? Maybe someone who wanted to escape the sight of Clinton's men as much as she did, she told herself.

She hoped that whoever it was would bypass this small, shaded glade for a more ornate area, but it was not to be. When a figure appeared in the narrow opening in the box-woods, Honor gasped out loud.

The woman appeared to be just as surprised to find Honor there. "Hello, honey," she said, and took another step for-ward. She glanced around, as if expecting to find someone else. "Mind if I join you?"

It was the prostitute who had spoken to Honor and Miriam one afternoon in town. "Uh, no, not at all." Honor scooted over on the bench, wondering what she should do. "I'm . . . how nice to see you again, Miss Echo."

Echo sat beside her and laughed. "Honey, just call me Echo. Everybody does."

Honor, still uncertain as to what she should do, simply nodded. "I'm Honor Richmond."

"Honor. Now that's a right pretty name." Echo studied Honor for a few seconds. "What are you doing out here all alone?"

"Oh, just getting away from everything, I suppose." Honor didn't really know how to explain her feelings. Even if she could put them into words, she wasn't sure whether or not she should tell Echo. "Clinton's revoked the paroles. One awful thing after another keeps happening. I just wanted to get away from it for a while, I guess."

"That sounds good to me." Echo settled her skirts grace-fully about her, though a good amount of her ankles showed beneath the hem. "I hate what's happened here. Friends dy-ing. Cannonballs blasting through our houses. Explosions killing innocent people. It ain't right."

"I agree, but there's not much we can do about it."

"Oh, there's ways and then there's ways of getting things done." Echo leaned closer to Honor, as if to whisper a se-cret. "Especially with men."

Honor didn't understand exactly what Echo meant, but she ╵iled anyway. She felt that since the conversation wasn't ╵aking sense to her, she should change the subject. "Why did ╵ur mother name you Echo? That's rather an unusual ╵me."

Echo nodded and her blond hair bobbed up and down. ╵ure is. I guess my mother was a lover of fine literature. I ╵lieve Echo was a character in some of the Greek myths."

A prostitute's mother educated enough to know names ╵om mythology? Honor's mouth dropped open in surprise. ╵Who was your mother?"

"Oh, I don't guess you'd know her. She was a beautiful ╵oman who... Well, none of that makes much difference, ╵arie." Echo smoothed the satin of her dark red dress. "She ╵as a lover to one of the planters. Never loved nobody else, ╵e didn't. Taught me to read, too." Echo chuckled and raised ╵r eyebrows. "But I don't get much of a call for reading to ╵y clients."

Honor laughed with her. "Well, I'm impressed, nonethe-╵ss."

"Lots of girls take on fancy names when they enter the ╵ade, but I figured my name was perfect."

"How's that?"

"Well, echo...I echo everything the men want to hear." She ╵ughed and arched her eyebrows suggestively.

"I see. I think you're right." Honor thought the name was ╵actly right for her. It seemed to fit her somehow, and fit her ╵ob even better. "What are *you* doing out here alone?"

"Honey, I'm just getting away, the same as you."

"Don't you... If I'm being too personal, just tell me to stop ╵king questions. You see, I never—"

"There's not much about my life that's too personal." Echo ╵ughed again and took Honor's hand. "Pretty hands, but ╵ey show signs of hard work." She held up her own hand for ╵onor to see. "Not a sign of redness or irritation here. Your ╵ade is reputable, but you work hard, ruin your skin. I have ╵othing to do but pamper mine."

"Doesn't seem fair, does it?" Honor found that she liked ╵e prostitute. Of all the people she'd talked to in Charles-╵n, this woman was the most forthright. "Does it bother you ╵hen... well, I mean, when ladies turn away from you?"

"I admit it used to." Echo's smile faded for a moment, but returned even brighter. "But I think I have the upper hand Most of their husbands have visited my bed more than once What do you think?"

"I think you're right. But don't you want children or husband?" Honor asked.

"Heavens, no. What would I do with a passel of brats t tend to?" Echo gazed at Honor for a long moment. "I'n going to tell you the truth, dearie. I like what I do. I enjoy m work. What do I care if a bunch of stuffy old matrons skitte off like crabs when I walk on their sidewalks?"

Honor nodded. She'd seen the women Echo spoke of, do ing exactly that. "But, Echo, what about...I mean, m' mother speaks of her 'wifely duty' as being a burden. Not tha my father ever exercises his 'husbandly prerogative' any more, I don't believe. My mother's been ill for a long time.'

"Do you believe everything your mother told you?"

"Yes, don't you?"

Echo thought about the question for a minute, ther laughed out loud. She laughed so hard, she nearly fell off th bench. Finally, when she had composed herself, she nodde vigorously. "I certainly do. A girl *should* believe her mother But they don't exactly speak the truth on this one, dearie. I'l tell you this, if I didn't enjoy it, I wouldn't do it."

"You know, Echo, I like you."

"I like you, too."

"But that's another thing my mother told me." Hono shook her head. "She said never to associate with women lik you."

"I reckon she did. Every mother worth her weight in sal tells her daughters—and sons—that." Echo grinned again "You know, even my mother said it."

The two women laughed. Finally, Honor said she had to b going. "I look forward to seeing you again some time." Sh stood and started to move away. "I live at the White Poir Inn. My father owns it. Where do you live?"

"Here," Echo whispered, with a catch in her voice. "Ur til Clinton came along."

Honor sank back to the bench and put her arm around he "I'm so sorry. This was a lovely home."

Echo dabbed at the corners of her eyes with the ruching on
er sleeves. Honor took her handkerchief out of her pocket
nd gave it to the woman.

"Thanks, dearie." Echo sniffed into the white cotton
quare.

Honor looked back in the direction of the ruined home.
"You...this is where you..." Her voice trailed off. She didn't
ven know how to ask the question.

"Oh, no. This is where I lived, where I always went to get
way." Echo dabbed at her eyes again and stared at the
andkerchief. "I'll get another one to you. Anyway, don't you
emember? I showed you the pink house on East Bay the first
me we met. There's a small sign that says Night's Pleasure
nn just above the door."

"Oh, yes," Honor said, vaguely remembering something
bout a pink house. "Where are you staying now?"

"Oh, I guess I'll live there until I can rebuild here." The
oman looked around. "This garden was well kept. Not a
eed to be seen. Now look at it."

"It's lovely, Echo. That's what drew me inside your gate."

"Thanks, Honor. You're a nice girl." She stood and pulled
Honor up with her. "Now, it's time for you to be going. I'm
re your parents—your father, anyway—will be looking for
ou."

"Goodbye," Honor said, once again starting to walk away.
I enjoyed talking with you."

"If you ever need me, you know where to find me," Echo
alled after her. "I promise I'll help any way I can."

All the way back home in the dim summer's light, Honor
ought about the things Echo had said. Even though she was
...a woman of soiled reputation, she was intelligent. Honor
new instinctively that not much got past her. She was some-
ne who would know how to deal with almost any situation.

During the next few days, Honor had an opportunity to
verhear a few conversations that might influence the Pa-
iot movement. Unfortunately, Jeffrey had gone into hid-
g. He was nowhere to be found. She'd looked, and so had
addy.

As she and Paddy sat in the barn one afternoon discussing the problem, she picked at a piece of straw, bending it and folding it. "I wish he'd told us where to look."

"Yeah, me, too. How we gonna find him?"

"I don't know, Paddy." Honor flicked the bent straw away and leaned back. "He did it to protect us. If someone thought we knew where he was, they'd...well, with Clinton doing the things he's done, there's no telling what they'd do. Cornwallis is no better."

She remembered hearing about the massacre at the Wax haws and shuddered. Tarleton had slaughtered Buford's men who'd been surrendering with white flags raised. Was that the fate Cornwallis held in store for the men he caught? Since the day in June that Clinton had returned to New York, Cornwallis had been searching frantically for Francis Marion.

"Honor," Paddy said, frowning in thought. "What *about* us? Everybody knows we're good friends of Jeffrey's."

Honor wrapped her arms around him and pressed her head against his. "I don't know, Paddy. We'll just have to be careful, that's all I can say right now."

Long after Paddy had gone, Honor pondered the queries he'd raised. The boy was intelligent, no doubt. His very questions had been the same as hers, though she hadn't voiced them for fear of frightening him.

She was still restless and had been ever since the British marched into town. She tried to sleep, but often failed. Trying desperately not to awaken Miriam, she'd creep from her bed and wait to see if her friend moved.

That night was especially hot. Sure now that Miriam hadn't awakened, Honor couldn't stand the confines of her room any longer. She tiptoed to the door, peeked out, and upon seeing no one about, slipped to the room from which she'd first seen the British. For another long moment she listened to see if she'd awakened anyone, but she finally crawled through the window to the roof.

From there she commanded a view of the city. The steeple of St. Michael's still rose like a dark obelisk above the trees, but had been further marred by the glancing blow of a cannonball. She could pick out the demolished houses, great yawning vacancies among the groves of live oaks and pa

ettos. Here and there, a soldier rushed on his way to some
ask, no doubt another tactic to harass or frighten the
Charlestonians.

A carriage rolled by, lurching when it found the deep crev-
es made by the cannonballs. Honor watched it until it dis-
ppeared from view. Somewhere behind her, the Ashley and
Cooper rivers merged to form Charleston Harbor, a normally secure place that had protected the city until a few
months ago.

So much had happened. So much was yet to come. Where
did she fit into the plans for the future of Charleston?

A sound distracted her, and she turned slightly to see a head
merge from the window. "Honor," came Dylan's whisper.
"Are you . . . there you are."

His eyes had adjusted to the darkness as he'd made his way
stealthily up the stairs and down the hallway. He now slipped
silently through the window and scooted over to where she
sat. "I heard your footsteps and thought you might be com-
ng out here. Hot tonight, isn't it?"

She picked up a twig with dried leaves still on it and fanned
herself. "Sultry."

Dylan stole a glance at her. Honor's hair hung in a neat
braid that reached midway down her back. He longed to run
his fingers through it, to see it wild and free about her face.
Now that he was here with her, he didn't know why he'd
come. He'd vowed time and again to avoid her, except in the
company of others. Once again he'd violated his own rules
where she was concerned.

"What are you doing out here?" he asked, stretching his
bad leg out before him and flexing his foot. "There's not
much going on now."

"No, there's not. I just couldn't sleep." Honor was beginning to wonder herself. Somehow, she felt better when the
fresh sea air swirled around her, chasing off the stench of liv-
ng in an occupied city. "What about you?"

Dylan shrugged. "Couldn't sleep," he lied. He had been
nearly asleep when the floor above him creaked. He'd lis-
ened to the soft footsteps until he determined that she was
headed for the window, and then he'd followed. "Nice view."

"Yes, now that we've no cannonballs to dodge." Honor
ooked around, falling in love once again with Charleston in

the moonlight. "Come here," she whispered, motioning for him to follow.

Very carefully, she edged her way to the other side of the gable and peered out over the harbor. The moon floated directly above the water, sending its image shimmering like pearls across the dark surface. Diaphanous clouds, like a bride's gauze nightgown, trailed across the moon, enfolding it in a cocoon of silver so fragile that she thought the clouds would tear in the force of the breeze that fluttered the live oak leaves.

"That feels good," Dylan murmured, studying her profile. He never tired of looking at her. Honor's expressive face was everchanging, though he could rarely tell what she was thinking.

"Yes. I hope it keeps up." She felt his gaze upon her and turned to face him.

For a moment, time hung between them, as if suspended from a delicate thread that would unravel if either of them moved or spoke. Neither did for a long time. Then Dylan advanced ever so slightly toward her. She tilted her head the tiniest bit, to accommodate the kiss she knew was coming.

The night was magical. The gentle breeze off the harbor wafted something like fairy dust all around them, cloaking them in an opaque gossamer mist. Their lips touched, tentatively, wondrously, softly, and then their bodies seemed to meld together, like two figures of soft wax pressed into the same mold.

Honor wasn't breathing. Her lungs burned in protest, but she dared not pull away and spoil the precious moment. Dylan's fingers found her back, massaging it, kneading it, and then slowly moved to unbraid her hair. Finally, binding her ebony hair around his fists, he drew her even closer, until she could no longer tell where he ended and she began. Her entire body cried out, wanting more, wanting that something that eluded her still.

Dylan fought the impulse to ravish her right there on the roof. She was an innocent, yet so apt a pupil. He felt his body respond to her as his need arose, demanding and urgent, but he steeled himself against giving in to his passionate nature. One day, perhaps, the time would come, but not now. Not here on the roof in view of anyone who might pass by and glance up.

What was he doing? He was actually thinking of reasons not to make love to her on the roof, as if it mattered where the deed was done. His body belied his doubts, moving slightly closer to maintain contact. Then he drew away from her, feeling the breeze suddenly turn chill against the moistness where her lips had been. How could he even consider such a thing?

"The hour grows late, love," he whispered, burying his face in her hair and stroking her tresses as if to memorize their texture and fragrance. He couldn't remember ever being stirred by a woman as he was by Honor. "I fear if we remain here any longer, I will be unable to maintain control."

Honor didn't trust herself to speak, so merely nodded. She didn't want him to maintain control. Glancing once again toward the harbor, she noticed that the iridescent pathway painted by the moon rolled and churned in the wake of one of the Royal Navy's ships, dispelling the beauty of the moment for her.

The beauty of the moment, but not of the memory. Dylan's kisses, his passionate embrace, his use of the word *love* were emblazoned in her mind as if branded there by scorching metal. When he edged back toward the window, she shivered from the chill of the sea breeze ruffling the hem of her nightgown.

Color flooded into her cheeks, and she was thankful for the darkness that hid her embarrassment. She was hardly clothed to be entertaining company. When she climbed back through the window, she found Dylan waiting for her.

"I couldn't leave without . . ."

His words were muffled by the kiss he placed ever so gently on her lips. Honor felt like a mass of warm jelly, lacking the substance to remain on her feet. She felt almost as if she were fuzzy around the edges, her eyes and emotions not quite focused as she wavered there in the darkness.

And then he was gone.

Honor hugged herself and recalled the words Echo had spoken, "I enjoy my work."

If this prelude to the passion Echo referred to was a sample of what was to come between a man and woman, Honor might just change her mind about marrying. The trouble was, Dylan was the first man who'd ever made her feel this way.

When she was in his arms, she was as light as the sea foam that floated on the waves and sometimes caught the breeze.

She stared into the darkness where he'd been and smiled broadly. Her conviction that everything had taken a turn for the worse in her life had been wrong. Dylan Alden was proof of that. Her life was changing, there was no denying it. With Dylan at her side, she could stand anything.

Anything. Even Clinton and Cornwallis.

What a kiss!

Chapter Ten

Recalling her exciting night, Honor hummed as she served the men meeting in the private room upstairs in the tavern, even though she'd had a long, hard day. The sun had risen, sending the temperature above a hundred degrees, and the moisture in the air was palpable. She brushed a few stray curls off her face with the back of her hand, and they stuck against her scalp as if they'd been plastered there.

In the heat, the odor of the stew was nearly revolting to her, but she trudged up the stairs bearing several more plates of it and rice. The heat was taking its toll on the food stores of Charleston once again, spoiling hundreds of pounds of beef.

Honor tried not to smile as the men discussed the problems of food shortages. Colonel Nisbet Balfour, now commandant of the board of police set up by Clinton, sent soldiers into the countryside foraging for food. In addition to his soldiers, he had the citizens of Charleston to feed, as well as the Continental soldiers imprisoned on ships in the harbor. General Leslie and his staff, at first imprisoned on Haddrell's Point, had been sent to Philadelphia.

Balfour's men were a surly bunch this evening as Honor placed their plates of stew before them. She hummed and smiled, flirting with them as she was accustomed to doing. They were used to her and most ignored her, except when she brushed against them as she placed their plates on the table.

Honor enjoyed her work. These men, many dressed in their red woolen uniforms, were being roasted alive. Though she considered it almost indecent, she'd adopted sleeveless attire for these particularly hot days. Whatever breeze flowed through the wide-open windows of the inn cooled her bare arms, but did little for the soldiers except to bring in swarms of mosquitoes and flies to pester them even more.

She hadn't seen Jeffrey in almost a month. She feared that he'd been captured and sent to Philadelphia. Though he wasn't a uniformed soldier, he'd nonetheless been deeply involved with the Patriot effort to maintain Charleston's freedom.

Late that night, Honor saw someone go into the barn. She believed the man to be Jeffrey. Knowing that Dylan heard every sound she made, she slid out of bed and over the windowsill, without touching the floor. Somehow, she had to find a way to climb down off the roof.

Her answer was the live oak that had broken Dylan's fall. Carefully maneuvering herself down the steep slope of the roof, she edged out onto the largest limb she could reach. The venerable tree, whose branches extended higher than the chimney, provided a safe exit, though climbing down took her a long time.

When Honor's feet touched the ground, she crouched there, eyes searching the darkness around her. Once she was sure that nobody was following her, she crept stealthily toward the barn. The thirty or so feet between the umbrella of the live oak and the barn door posed her greatest threat, as the moon was bright. If she could cross it undetected, she would be safely inside.

Praying that nobody would see her and that the man in the barn was indeed Jeffrey, she took a deep breath and scampered across the exposed area. Once inside the barn, she waited until her eyes adjusted. She didn't really know what to do. She couldn't see anyone nor hear anything.

She hesitated. Had she really seen someone slip into the barn? Maybe he'd left while she was climbing down the tree. Honor took a step forward, and someone grabbed her, clapping a hand over her mouth to keep her from screaming.

She couldn't scream, but she could kick and bite. And she did. With all her might, she lashed out at her captor, biting his hand at the same time.

"Damn it, Honor, this is Jeffrey," he whispered fiercely. "Have you turned cannibal since I saw you last?"

"Jeffrey, thank the Lord, it is you." Honor reached up and hugged him impulsively. She clung to him for a moment. "We thought Balfour had shipped you off to Philadelphia with

General Leslie. There are soldiers billeted here. You must be more careful.''

He drew Honor further into the shadows. "No sense giving ourselves away, then."

"Where have you been?" she asked, peering at his face in the semidarkness.

"You said *we*. Whom were you referring to?" Jeffrey asked, pulling her down into the hay. He'd wanted to do that a thousand times, but tonight it was simply a way of resting. He'd been out of Charleston for several weeks and had just returned, having to outrun several soldiers in the process.

"All of us, but most particularly, Paddy and me."

"I've been in hiding, mostly." He inhaled the clean fragrance of her hair and wished that she would smile at him in the same way he'd seen her smile at Dylan.

Jeffrey mistrusted Dylan, though the man had been around for quite some time. There were others in Jeffrey's organization who wished to bring the man into the group, give him a job to do. Honor liked and trusted Dylan, though Jeffrey was certain she hadn't given him any sensitive information.

"Honor," he said finally, "what have you for me? Have you heard anything that will help us?"

She shrugged. She'd heard many things during his absence, some of which it was too late to act upon. "I heard this evening that Balfour is sending out foraging parties about every two days. They go north one day, west two days later and then south. They're having to go farther and farther to find food."

Jeffrey nodded. "From what I can gather, the British have been a bit close with their information. Hardly anyone knows anything."

"I also heard that several wagons of supplies were suppose to be sent out to Cornwallis in about a week. Shoes, lighterweight clothing—that sort of thing."

"That's good. Keep that kind of information coming."

"There's one other thing, though I don't know whether you can use this or not," Honor said, wondering if she was being foolish in reporting it.

"Let me judge. When you hear something, pass it on regardless."

Honor smiled. He hadn't heard what she had to say. "Well, there was a soldier in here the other day bragging about how he was being sent to train some raw Tories. He didn't say exactly where he was going, or maybe he was too drunk for me to understand him. Maybe he was just exaggerating. I thought I heard him say 'Anderson' several times.''

"Fort Anderson, maybe?" Jeffrey asked, wondering about the significance of the name. "Could be another soldier. Did you get the name of the man he was talking to?"

"No," Honor said, feeling a little deflated. "He kept saying something about 'up to Anderson.'"

"Has to be Fort Anderson, then." Jeffrey considered the information. "Being held by raw Tory recruits, eh?"

"I can't answer that for sure. He was awfully intoxicated."

"Honor, this may be a breakthrough for us, if it's true." Jeffrey kissed her on the cheek and grinned. "Keep your fingers crossed."

"When will I see you again?"

He thought about it for a long moment. "I don't know. We need to devise a method of letting me know you need to see me."

"I could leave you a note here," Honor offered, her thoughts racing for ideas. "No, I believe that would be too dangerous for both of us."

"Exactly. Nothing can be written down. Maybe later, but for now, you must pass the word orally."

"What about Paddy?" Honor remembered that the boy was helping Jeffrey. "What can I tell him?"

"Nothing. He and I will work out our own signals." Jeffrey bowed his head wearily. His entire body ached from sleeping on the ground under bushes. The mosquitoes had nearly drained his body of blood, and he was exhausted from all the travel, from staying up all night. "For now, you can set a candle in your window. Don't light it, just put it there. I'll find a way to talk to you."

"Jeffrey, what about Miriam? She's still grieving so deeply. Please, can't we give her something to do?"

"Honor, I told you. She can't keep a secret. Her face is too readable."

Honor crossed her arms over her chest and sighed. "I'll find something for her to do that will break her out of these doldrums."

"Go now, Honor. When you reach the house, go straight to your room and don't look back here." Jeffrey held her close for a few moments. "If someone notices you, I don't want them to see you looking back at me."

Inhaling deeply, Honor stood at the barn door, just within the depth of shadows that would keep her hidden from view. When she had watched long enough to assure herself that nobody was about, she ran across the yard and into the changing room.

There was a faint glow from the banked fire, but no sounds to indicate that anyone was awake. To be sure, she sat down in a chair near the fire for about thirty minutes. If someone spotted Jeffrey and came down to investigate, maybe they wouldn't associate her with him. That way, both of them might be safe.

As she sat there rocking, she nearly fell asleep. Now that she knew Jeffrey was safe, she was more relaxed than she had been in weeks. After the half-hour interval had passed, she rose and walked quietly to her room. She decided that she didn't want to try to sneak back upstairs for fear someone would think she was doing something wrong. Nice, normal tiptoe, she chanted to herself as she walked barefoot up the stairs.

Miriam was wide awake when Honor reached her room.

"Where have you been?" she whispered urgently. "I was afraid something had happened to you."

Honor considered her situation. Miriam would probably know if she lied, so she decided to tell the truth, or at least a part of the truth. "Miriam, I've been talking to Jeffrey."

"In the middle of the night?" Her friend's eyes narrowed, and she stared at Honor in disbelief. "What's going on here, Honor? I can tell when you're hiding something from me."

"Miriam, how serious are you about...revenge against the British?" She held her breath as she awaited Miriam's response.

"What do I have to do? Kill one of your 'house guests' to make you understand how serious I am?" Miriam pulled her down onto the bed. "Now, you're not moving until you tell me what this is all about."

Honor began to explain, leaving out several pertinent points—especially Jeffrey's connection with Paddy. "I think

I know a way you can help without really endangering yourself."

"Anything. Tell me what you want me to do."

"I want you to make me some clothes."

"What!" Miriam gasped, scowling at Honor for her foolish suggestion. "What can we possibly gain by my making clothes for you?"

"Miriam, I've told you that I'm... trying to obtain information about the British troop movements." Honor tried to explain without giving any more details than were absolutely necessary. Jeffrey was correct in his assessment of their mutual friend. "Certain women in this town can be in certain places, and the soldiers and men never really take notice of them. In other words, they don't guard their words as carefully as they do among other men."

"Costumes?" Miriam's mouth tilted into a smile. "I see. You want to look like these women who... like who, for instance? What sort of costumes are we talking about?"

Honor braced herself for Miriam's reaction. "I want you to make me look like—like Echo."

"Honor!" Miriam clapped her hands over her mouth. "You want me to—to make you a dress that shows your... Lordy, that dress was indecent."

"Well, at least it won't take as much material." Honor knew her argument was useless, but she made it anyway. It would probably take two or three days for Miriam to see that she had struck upon an excellent idea.

Her friend giggled. "Well, you did say that those women were the only ones with money to spend. I'll do it if you promise to tell all your lady-of-the-evening friends who made your dress."

With that, Honor fell into a fit of giggles, too. She and Miriam buried their faces in pillows until their giggles turned to snickers and then to smiles. "I'd better get some sleep. I've been awake almost all night."

"Honor, how will you... I mean, you don't really intend to let the men..."

Honor's face flamed. "Of course not, you goose. I've got a bottle of laudanum. I'm going to put them to sleep." Honor thought for a moment. "And if you don't turn over and go to sleep yourself, I'm going to use it on you."

"Honor," Miriam whispered, leaning close so she wouldn't have to speak very loud. "Was Jeffrey all right."

Honor sat bolt upright in the bed and spun around to stare at Miriam. "You're in love with him, aren't you? You promised never to fall in love, and you've done it."

"Hush, Honor. Someone will hear you."

"I never would have believed it." Honor lay back on the pillows and crossed her ankles comfortably. "Does he know? Maybe it was you he came to see and not me."

"He doesn't know, and if you tell him, I'll sew your chemises together at both ends with stitches so tiny, you'll never be able to get them out."

"All right." Honor smiled. She really liked Jeffrey and knew that he'd loved her for years. Maybe with a few hints here and there, she could redirect his feelings toward Miriam. It was certainly worth a try.

With Clinton gone back to New York, her life was looking better all the time. Now, she had a real opportunity to discover some helpful information for the Patriots. Her friends, Miriam and Jeffrey, were going to get married, though neither of them knew it yet. And most of all—best of all—she, Honor Carlotta Richmond, might be falling in love with Dylan Alden.

Dylan listened to the giggles that filtered down from Honor's room and wondered what in the world could be happening. He knew that the two women were having to sleep together, but he thought they would have outgrown their girlish giggles by now.

Honor's laugh was lovely. Its musical quality rang like the purest chime, sending its enchanting melody through the air for all to hear.

He should rightfully be upset that the women exhibited no care for the other people in the inn, but he wasn't. He was merely curious.

The memory of Honor's kisses slipped silently into his mind, filling him with a warmth that tingled through him like liquid lightning. His response tonight was equal to the evening when they'd sat on the roof, staring across the harbor, and had suddenly found themselves in a passionate embrace.

"Damn!" He cursed and sat up. Why was that woman always on his mind?

If he wasn't sure that this inn was the best place to obtain information, he'd leave immediately. If he didn't feel so strongly about the colonies belonging to England, having been nurtured and protected until they'd become prosperous, he'd leave Charleston. Look how Britain had been paid back. The colonies, in his opinion, were as much a part of England as . . . well, as London. He owed his king his best effort.

That effort demanded that Dylan remain at the White Point Inn and Tavern. Seeing Honor every day was a pleasure he wanted to avoid if possible, but he knew he couldn't. She was every bit as important to him as the men who frequented the place. She was the invisible master spy, so to speak. Men seldom noticed a serving girl unless they were looking for a tumble in the hay. Honor had made herself invisible. Her quiet service had gained her entry into the most private of conversations, he was certain.

Dylan simply had to find a way to tap that information without her realizing that he was using her. Damn, but he hated the idea. He genuinely liked her. Using her was something he had no choice about. Maybe one of these days he'd be able to make her understand, though he doubted it. Nonetheless, she was important to him. Her friendship, if properly focused, could provide him with the tools necessary to defeat the remaining militia in South Carolina and the Continental Army. He was sure of it.

He'd just have to make sure that he didn't kiss her again. He'd have to make sure that he could ignore that glorious fragrance of hers. Friendship, not lovers. Professional interest, he kept telling himself; though as his eyes closed in sleep once again, he wasn't sure he was convinced.

Honor and Miriam rose early the next morning. Miriam hustled off to her shop, while Honor completed her morning chores. The hours seemed interminable to Honor. She changed beds, swept floors, served meals and gave instructions to the other help.

When the tavern was nearly empty, she hurried out the door and almost ran the several blocks to Miriam's shop on Tradd

Street. She burst through the door, frightening several ladies who were examining a length of satin.

Miriam motioned for Honor to go into the small room at the back of the shop where patrons weren't allowed. The room had been Miriam's and her mother's special place, where they'd gone to chat or to plan their days or to sketch a new gown for one of their clients. Honor had always enjoyed visiting them there. The room had many happy memories for her, and she suspected that it had for Miriam as well.

When Miriam had bid her customers goodbye, she locked the door and hurried to join Honor. "Look! I've sketched a dress there. What do you think?"

Honor took the papers from Miriam's hand and examined them carefully. "Miriam, you're a genius. This will be perfect. How will we get the material?"

"I've just received a shipment of lovely fabric. Mrs. Wentworth, the old Tory cow, wants a dress and cape." Miriam showed Honor the sketches. "If I cut her dress and cape the way I've shown here, I can fit your dress into the same length of fabric. The problem will be talking her into using that exquisite shade of purple satin."

"Purple?" Honor asked, wondering what in the world Miriam could be talking about. "Why purple? Can't we just use any color she chooses?"

"No. She'll select some conservative color—a brown stripe or dark green taffeta." Miriam shook her head confidently. "It's got to be purple. What else would Charleston's newest prostitute wear?"

Honor stared at her blankly. The plan was an excellent one, but what if the laudanum didn't work? What if she couldn't get away without...without losing her virginity? When she'd devised this ingenious ploy, she hadn't stopped to consider the cost to her.

Now she did. Honor thought about the ramifications of misjudging the amount of laudanum necessary to put someone to sleep. Maybe she should discuss this with Dr. Peterson before she made a mistake.

But even if the unthinkable happened, she wouldn't shirk what she considered her duty. Too much damage had been done, too many people had suffered, too many lies had been told for her to back away now, not when she'd discovered a second perfect way to obtain information.

Could she actually go through with it if she had to? Honor remembered Dylan's embrace, the passion and response each of his kisses had evoked. Would it be so with another man? Echo had said she enjoyed her work. Honor was torn inside, frightened of what might happen, yet determined to eradicate the British threat at all cost, no matter how degrading or how personal.

Another thought occurred to her. Maybe she should find a way to make love to Dylan first. Deliberately lose her virginity... The idea shocked her. Could she do such a thing? She'd have to ponder about the situation more.

"Honor! Wake up!" Miriam reached over and shook her arm. "Where are you? You know, you're so distracted these days, I think you're in love yourself. Don't come teasing me about my feelings for Jeffrey. You're worse. At least I can keep my mind on what I'm—"

"All right, I hear you." Honor tried to be interested in all the details about the dress, but she didn't understand half of what Miriam said.

"I think this is going to be the most exciting thing I ever made. Image it, me making a dress for a spy."

Honor took her arm, her gaze level and serious. "Miriam, you can't tell anyone of this. Maybe after the war is completely over, we can talk about it, but not now."

"I won't tell anyone, honest. I don't know why you're so worried." Miriam smiled cheerfully. "Thank you for letting me do this, Honor. It's given me something to take my mind off... well, myself."

"I know. I appreciate your help." Honor smiled and hugged her friend. "We'll make a great team, you and I. The sensational spy and her dressmaker extraordinaire."

"Oh, I have another dress for you." Miriam led Honor to the small room where completed dresses were waiting to be picked up by their owners. She pulled a gown of rose-colored silk from the peg where it was hanging. "This is perfect for you. Exactly to fit and everything."

"You made this for me?" Honor played with the fine fabric, letting it slide through her fingers like liquid rose petals.

"No, silly. I couldn't afford anything like that. But someone paid for it and never picked it up." Miriam held up the dress for Honor to see.

"It's stunning." Honor eyed Miriam thoughtfully. "Why didn't the buyer pick it up?"

Miriam turned away and pretended to brush a speck of dust off the gown. "She died. It was for Sally Caterman. Her house...everything was leveled by the cannonballs. You know they lived nearer the hornworks than almost anyone."

Honor sank back into the chair. "Oh, Miriam, I hadn't heard. I'm so sorry. I can't take the dress."

"Sure you can. Who else could wear it?"

"Where would I wear such a fine gown? I'd look rather foolish serving drinks at the tavern while wearing this dress, wouldn't I." Honor looked longingly at the dress. All her life she'd dreamed of owning such a lovely gown, but even after being given one, she couldn't accept it. "Miriam, you can sell it to someone else."

Miriam crossed her arms over her chest and shook her head resolutely. "Honor, that dress is made for you. It's perfect for your coloring."

"Miriam, listen to me. It's lovely, and you're sweet for offering it. But I don't have any place to wear it."

"Listen to yourself." Miriam hung the dress back on the peg and sat down again. "You're going to pretend to be a prostitute. Why on earth can't you pretend to be a planter's daughter or somebody's cousin?"

"Everybody would know. The first time I tried to act like a lady, I'd be found out and ridiculed." Honor leaned back and stared at the dress longingly. She could almost imagine herself at a ball, wearing that gown, Dylan asking her to dance... Someone asking her to dance, she corrected mentally. "Even if I tried, someone would—might—ask me to dance, and then what? I would trip over my big feet."

"Your feet are small and you're graceful." Miriam refused to give up on this. She'd made her decision after Honor had fallen asleep last night.

"But, you sweet girl, I don't know *how* to dance." Honor turned around. She couldn't look at the dress or her resolve would melt away.

"Well," Miriam said with a glint in her eye, "you're not so simple-minded. Maybe you could learn."

"Simple-minded? Miriam, I—"

"Calm down, I was teasing."

"All right, if we work on the assumption that I'm graceful and not *too* inept, who would teach me?" Honor was sure that with this question the discussion would come to an end. She could feel herself beginning to succumb to her friend's persuasive abilities.

Miriam scowled and toyed with her shears. "There must be someone. Don't we know someone who—who maybe is fallen from the favor of the planters?"

"There are thousands of us who don't find favor with the planters. In fact, Charleston is teeming with—" Honor stopped speaking. She turned to gaze at the dress. "There might be someone. What about Echo?"

"Honor, be realistic. She's even farther from being the darling of society than we are. No," she said firmly, "it's got to be someone else."

"She might be farther from society than we are, but her mother was the mistress of a planter." Honor saw her plan coming clear. She could be many people. All she needed was the proper disguise, and Miriam could help her with that. "I need to talk to her."

After the busiest part of the evening passed, Honor stepped to the backyard for a breath of air. Not a breeze stirred to refresh her after a long, hot spell in the changing room. The sun rode low on the horizon, its last slivers of light filtering through the live oaks.

Honor needed to walk. Her muscles were bunched up, complaining of the strain of bending over tables, squatting to pick up dropped cutlery, charging up and down stairs. She headed out of the yard, not stopping to tell anyone where she was going.

As she walked toward Bay Street, she thought of the Night's Pleasure Inn and considered stopping by to talk with Echo. Deciding that now would be the busiest hour of the woman's evening, she walked on. Down by the wharf, she met a drunken man who staggered into her, knocking her off her feet and falling with her to the hard-packed dirt walkway.

Honor scrambled up, glaring at the man, who still lay sprawled on the ground. He attempted to rise, but fell back again and scowled at her as if it were her fault.

"Eh, miss, you be lookin' fer a gent sich as meself? We could find us a bit of a spot and 'ave a good time, we could." He got slowly to his feet, swaying unsteadily. "Well, I'm available, I am."

"Sir, you are contemptible, to say the least. Your presence is reprehensible to me and I wouldn't go anywhere with you even if you had the money to pay me." Honor turned to walk away, but he caught her arm.

"I gots a few coin, I 'ave," he said in a heavy accent. "You've no call to act like you's better'n me, neither."

Honor wheeled around to face him once again. He was several inches taller than she and much stronger. Fear welled up in her. How could she get away from him? Her only hope of escape, if he chose to grab hold of her, would be due to his drunken state. She might have an advantage because of that. "Sir, if you truly have money enough to buy a lady's presence for the evening, perhaps it would be wiser to spend your coins on a bath. You smell worse than a goat yard."

When she turned to leave, he reached out and caught her arm. "Now, that ain't a nice way to treat a visitor 'ere. Come with the soldiers, I did. You should be a little friendlier to—"

Honor waited no longer. The situation might soon pass the point at which she could escape. She smiled and swung her fist as hard as she could, catching him under the chin. The astonished man's teeth crashed together and he fell straight backward, unconscious.

"Sweet dreams," she whispered as she turned and walked away as quickly as she could.

"Honor, wait for me," Dylan called, rushing along after her. He caught her arm and swung her around. "What are you doing out here all alone? Don't you know how dangerous it is to walk unescorted?"

Wondering if he'd seen her strike the man, she nodded her head in agreement. "It certainly is dangerous. Look at that man lying there. He was walking all alone, and a demure young miss, who shall remain nameless, struck him a solid blow, rendering him unconscious."

His eyes growing wide in disbelief, Dylan turned to look at the man Honor was pointing to. "You did that?"

"I'm sorry, but I'm not able to give any more specific details on the matter." Honor laughed, her fear evaporating now that Dylan was with her. "I'm afraid the man's jaw will ache for a few days. Perhaps he will be missing a few teeth as well."

Dylan chuckled and took her arm. "I believe, Miss Richmond, that we should be moving along before the drunken gentleman wakes up and realizes what you've done."

As they strolled along Bay Street together, Dylan kept glancing over his shoulder. He was clearly concerned about something. "Is someone following us, Dylan?"

"No, what makes you ask that?"

"You keep looking over your shoulder, as if you expected someone to creep up behind us or something." Honor turned and gazed at the darkened street they'd just walked. "What is it?"

"Nothing, I assure you." Dylan didn't want her to know how worried he was about the man she'd struck. The swaggering drunk was well-known on the wharf for his temper. "I was simply making sure your friend wasn't following us."

"I see. But I don't believe you should be concerned. We'll be nearly home before he is well enough to come looking for us." Honor wasn't worried. She'd handled drunks before. This one was nothing new to her.

"I hope so." Dylan didn't slow his pace. The man had a nasty temperament and wasn't above gathering a group of men to come searching for Honor. Sure enough, it wasn't long before he heard the sound of an angry mob behind them. "I think our respite is about over."

Honor, too, heard the unmistakable sound of a rowdy group of men heading their way. "What shall we do?"

"Look for somewhere to hide until they pass." Dylan hurried along, glancing left and right for an adequate spot.

"I know just the place." Honor took his hand and began to run. When she reached Echo's demolished house, she pulled Dylan through the wrought-iron gate and then along the brick walkway. "Even if they come in here to search the grounds, I know a private glade where we can hide."

In the darkness, Honor almost passed the narrow entrance to the little garden she had found a few days earlier. "See, here it is."

The silvery crescent moon slumbered peacefully in the sky and, about the time Honor and Dylan reached the bench, drew a cover of wispy clouds over herself. The gnarled branches of a live oak hung low over them, providing a tent of darkness in the little garden.

Dylan could hardly see Honor. "How did you find this place?"

"I was walking, spotted the abandoned garden and came in to look around. I was feeling pretty angry then—just after Mrs. Edwards died." Honor sat on the cool bench and watched the narrow entrance to make sure they hadn't been followed. "Even if they came into the yard, I don't think anyone could find this place in the dark."

"Just the same, I'd prefer having some cover or something to hide behind." Dylan glanced around, his eyes adjusting to the darkness. "That thing should do nicely."

He pointed to the arbor, overgrown with roses and Carolina jasmine. Honor nodded and stood up.

"Here," Dylan whispered, placing his coat on the ground. "Sit on this."

Without speaking, she settled herself on his coat. The grass beneath had grown tall and cushioned her as she sat there waiting. The fragrance of the flowers was enchanting, almost magical, drawing her into some private world of the senses, where, after a moment's hesitation, Dylan joined her.

Sitting there, their legs touching, Honor could smell his clean, masculine scent. Combined with the fragrance of the garden, it was intoxicating, but not nearly so much as Dylan's presence.

His arms went around her, of their own volition, he thought, knowing he should move away. He wouldn't kiss her. He hadn't lost control of himself to the point that he couldn't make up his mind to do something and not follow through. He wouldn't kiss her, no matter what. Filled with resolve, he sat there, holding her protectively against whoever had gathered against them.

Tenderness, friendship, affection. Those were the words that expressed his feelings for Honor. Love and passion were not applicable. Love he had forsworn completely. Passion he could find with any prostitute.

With his arms around her, he could feel the swell of her breasts. He felt a tightening in his groin and tried to think of something else while he casually adjusted his position. When he moved, she did, almost making matters worse.

Dylan cursed himself for being a lascivious man, bordering on taking advantage of a defenseless young woman. What was wrong with him? Had they not been followed, he would have torn himself away from her and left, never to see her again. But he couldn't leave her. She might believe otherwise, but she was as defenseless as a newborn kitten against the likes of those men. She'd merely been lucky when she'd hit the drunk earlier.

He heard the sound of men tramping through the weeds and shrubs, and pulled her closer into his embrace. No matter what happened, he couldn't risk letting her be seen. Since he could see the entrance to their little glade, he knew he could be seen as well.

He lay back on his coat, pulling her down with him, with a cautioning finger across her warm, soft lips. Stifling a groan, he gave in to his desire and kissed her. This time, his need surged forth, and he kissed her long and hard, filling her sweet mouth with his tongue, caressing her tiny body until he felt her response equal his.

His hunger demanded fulfillment. Dylan wanted nothing more at the moment than to rend her clothes asunder and fill her with his passion, until she cried out for relief. Somehow, they were lying face-to-face, heart-to-heart now, her arms encircling his neck. His hand slid inside her bodice, cupping her breast and catching her taut nipple between his thumb and forefinger. Nothing could prevent him from making love to her; he was past the point of return.

Honor's gasp of surprise was muffled by Dylan's lingering kiss. In the privacy of the little garden, she was about to give to Dylan that which she'd thought to maintain until her death. Reality had long since escaped her mind, its place assumed by soft, fuzzy images of his face, his scent, his hands, his body, hot and writhing next to hers.

To her astonishment, she wasn't afraid. This moment was one that would undoubtedly change her life, but she moved forward, embracing that tantalizing secret held only by married couples and a few women like Echo. Her breath came in ragged gasps between kisses, and her fingers threaded through his hair as control of her body passed from her consciousness to his.

In that moment, she realized that she loved him. She knew little about him, but could no longer deny her feelings for him. She had loved him for some time. That discovery fueled her desire for him. *Dear God, let this be wonderful,* she prayed silently, and then wondered how she could have such nerve. What she was about to do was a sin, as surely as murder and theft were sins. But maybe God would forgive her this once.

Dylan became absolutely still, his body rigid. Someone was inside the little glade with them. He felt Honor tense and knew that she, too, realized they were not alone.

The crescent moon provided little light and that was almost obscured by the canopy of live oak that protected most of this garden. Dylan willed the moon to remain hidden while the intruder searched the tiny area. The flowers and vines were so thick that, unless the man had been there before, he wouldn't recognize that the small space behind the arbor was large enough to accommodate two bodies.

Whatever the outcome of the search, Dylan knew one thing for certain. No matter the strength of his passion, he and Honor had to leave the moment the men departed from the garden.

Relief flooded over him. His normal senses returned, but he was wary of each movement she made, steeling himself against her seductive body.

This night is another that will find me staring at the ceiling with an itch in my groin.

With that thought, Dylan listened to the sounds of the search party moving away from them. He held Honor down, refusing to allow her to rise until the men had been gone for more than thirty minutes. He wasn't willing to risk her life because of a moment's haste, but those thirty minutes were the longest and most tormenting he had ever lived through.

Chapter Eleven

Honor stood at her window, peering across the yard as she recalled the exquisite moments with Dylan the previous night. She had thought to lose her virginity, but circumstances had prevented it. Now, looking back, she was glad.

She, like many before her, had been caught up in a moment's passion, one that would fade for Dylan as quickly as a cube of indigo dropped in the harbor. But what of her? She had acknowledged that she loved him, if only to herself. Did she?

So sure of her feelings last night in the intoxication of the moment, she quailed before her quick conclusion. What had brought her to that point? What rational thinking had dispelled her resolve never to fall in love?

Was there anything at all rational about her emotions? And what of Dylan? How did he feel?

She turned and stalked out of her room. Honor knew she needed someone to talk to, someone who knew of these things. She instinctively went to her mother's room, but found her parent staring out the window with tears rolling down her cheeks. Fighting tears of her own frustration, Honor ran down the stairs.

Life wasn't fair. First, her own mother had been taken from her by some mysterious disease, and then Clinton had attacked, terrifying her so badly that it seemed to have robbed her mind of its powers. Then her substitute mother had been killed in an explosion caused by some careless British soldier. Where was the justice in life?

Honor strode forward, though she didn't know where she was going. The morning sun glittered on the water as she walked along the fortifications and up East Bay Street until she found herself standing in front of an ornate pink house. A small, neatly lettered sign proclaiming Night's Pleasure Inn swung from a wrought-iron post.

After looking up and down the street to see who might be out this early, Honor screwed up her courage and opened the gate. Once inside, she hurried along the brick walkway and up the steps. A moment of indecision overtook her, and she almost turned away, but Honor wasn't a coward. She paused a few seconds as she tried to decide whether to knock or to go on inside. Though she had a good education for a working-class woman, she felt remarkably ignorant concerning the etiquette that pertained to such a situation.

"When in doubt, knock," she told herself, and rapped smartly on the door.

A young black woman opened the door and peered through the narrow opening. "Yes'm?"

Honor knew her voice would abandon her, but she managed to utter, "Miss Richmond to see Miss Echo."

"Miss Echo don't see nobody this time of day. Come back . . . this afternoon."

The young woman started to close the door, but Honor jammed her foot inside. "Look, young woman, this isn't an easy thing for me to do. Will you please do as I say? I realize this is an inconvenience for Miss Echo, but . . . this is rather an emergency."

"Let her in, Wilma," came a voice from within.

Wilma stood aside and let Honor pass. When she reached the parlor, Honor tried to keep from gawking, but she couldn't. The room was opulent beyond anything she'd ever seen.

An intricate cut-glass chandelier hung in the center of the room and caught her eye immediately. From there, her gaze took in several bright red-and-gold-brocade sofas that looked to be as soft as a feather mattress.

Sprawled across one sofa like a woman from an old Greek drawing, Echo smiled at Honor and beckoned her to come in and sit. "Well, dearie, what can I do for you?"

"Miss Echo—"

"Echo," the woman corrected.

"Echo, I've—I need help and I don't know who I can turn to, except you." She seated herself and bowed her head. "I don't even know where to begin."

But begin she did. The words spilled out of Honor like a kettle of oyster stew boiling over. At times they were accompanied by tears, at others by anger and at still others by frustration.

Something about Echo instilled trust in Honor. She couldn't determine the reason, but she knew that of everyone she knew, Echo could be trusted with all the secrets that now welled up within her.

Sometime during the expurgation of Honor's hidden thoughts, Echo moved over to sit with her. Wrapping her arms around her guest, she listened quietly, never commenting, never judging, never questioning, until the words finally stopped coming.

"I'd say you've got quite a plateful for a woman your age." She signaled for Wilma to bring some refreshments and sat quietly for a moment. "Fortunately, these are things I might be able to help you with."

Honor raised her chin and smiled timorously. "Do you really think so?"

"Some things I know about and will help you with right away. Others might not be so easy." Echo watched Wilma come in with a silver tray laden with sweets and coffee. "We'll talk about it after breakfast."

During their meal, she refused to allow Honor to discuss her troubling questions and problems. As she ate, Honor began to feel a little better. They laughed and talked like old friends, just as Honor had suspected they would. The more they talked, the more convinced she became that she'd done the right thing.

"All right. Now, let's take this one step at a time." Echo considered the problems. "Let's deal with the easiest ones first."

Honor smiled and shook her head. "None of them sound easy to me."

"Don't you worry about anything. We'll work this out." Echo leaned back into the plush depths of the sofa and thought for a few minutes. "Now, you're just about the smartest girl I've ever met. You're exactly right, how these men brag about what they do for the British army. I haven't been paying much attention to them, but I will from now on, and I'll pass the word on to you. I'd do anything to get even with them for them ruining my beautiful house."

"That's wonderful. That'll save me from having to explain being out of the house a lot." Honor breathed a sigh of relief. Ever since that afternoon in the glade, Honor had known that Echo would be willing to help the Patriot cause. She had, in fact, wondered if Echo was already involved in some way. "My father depends on me to run the inn most of the time."

"Well, he shouldn't. You should be out having a good time while you're young." Echo grimaced and laid her arms casually across the back of the sofa.

Honor watched the prostitute, unable to tear her gaze away from the woman's graceful demeanor. It didn't matter to her that Echo was considered less than a dog by most of Charleston society. Now they were friends. Even without the thick makeup, Echo was a beautiful woman.

"Well, back to the issues at hand." She sipped her coffee thoughtfully. "If something comes up—say, someone I think you should hear personally—I'll send for you. You know Wilma now. I'll entice the gentleman back for a second evening, gratis, and you can listen to him. How's that?"

"That sounds wonderful." Honor liked Echo more and more. Her intelligence was quite remarkable, and once again, Honor wondered why the woman had chosen prostitution as her career.

"Right. Now, about the dancing." Echo rose and whirled about the room, humming a jaunty tune all the while. "You'll do fine under my tutelage. I'm an excellent dancer. Stand up."

Honor obeyed and was soon dancing nearly as gracefully as Echo. "You're wonderful," she said at last, breathlessly.

"And you're a good student," Echo said, collapsing on the sofa. "Now, about the last matter. The one that's troubling you the most."

"Yes. You're right," Honor admitted. She'd come under the guise of enlisting Echo's help in obtaining information from the British, but Dylan was foremost in her mind. "Can you help me to understand my feelings?"

"I hope so, baby." Echo pulled Honor down into her arms, cuddling her like a little girl, and began to talk in sweet, soft tones. "Honor, every woman feels these things eventually. No matter how we harden our hearts against it, some wonderful young man comes along and with one glance shatters those walls we've spent so long erecting.''

"But how do you know if he's—''

"Shh! Just listen. You can ask questions afterwhile." Echo stroked Honor's hair and continued to talk in quiet tones that seemed to soothe Honor's fears away. "Once we meet that young man, our entire outlook changes. We see things we never saw, birds never sang so sweetly, jasmine never smelled so fragrant. It's as if the whole world is fresh and new just for the two of you.''

Honor let the words flow over her like the warm summer tides in the harbor. Silken and comforting, Echo's voice went on, and Honor let her eyes close.

"And then that special feeling arises. That quickening of the blood that makes us feel like a million butterflies are caught inside our skin every time he comes around." Echo paused for a moment, remembering her first time. She'd fallen in love, desperately wanting him to love her in return, but he'd used her. She'd gotten over the bitterness. Now, she used men for her own purposes. She allowed them to use her body, but in turn, she used them for other things. She was a wealthy woman, a woman who had many favors to be called in one of these days.

"There's nothing in the world like that feeling," she continued. "Ah, love is a wondrous thing, Honor. Tread carefully, baby. Make sure this is the right man.''

"How will I know?" Honor's voice was barely above a whisper.

"You'll know. Nobody else can make you feel the same way he does. You can't stand to be without him even for a few minutes. You live in constant frustration—first you're committed to him, then you're not sure. When you're with him, you love him. When he's away, you can't quite recapture that feeling.''

"That's the way I feel. I was so sure..." Honor's voice trailed away. Then she told Echo about hiding in the garden, about the surge of passion that had threatened to send her past the point of reason.

"Honor, I'm not a mother. I'm not even the motherly type. Never will be.''

Privately, Honor disagreed with Echo's assessment, but said nothing.

"But listen to this well and heed my words. Men are less in control of their bodies than women. Don't allow yourself to be placed in such a situation again, unless you're ready to give something most precious away." Echo hesitated, wondering where all this sage advice was coming from and wishing that she'd been privy to it when she'd lost her own virginity. "Once your innocence is gone, you can't get it back. Don't make the conquest too easy for him. Make sure your man is worth the cost to you before you give yourself to him."

Dylan hurried home. All day long, the need to talk with Honor had been strong within him. He felt the urgency to discuss their situation so that they wouldn't lose control again. Last night had been a dangerous evening, in more than one way.

He wanted to pack his clothing and leave the inn, but knew he couldn't, no matter how hard he tried. His towering strength of purpose, his unbreachable willpower turned to a quivering quagmire in her presence, one that seemed intent on pulling him down more deeply.

All night he'd lain in bed, tossing and turning as he tried to make some sense of his feelings for her. Even if there was some remote chance of—of his being in love, he had nothing to offer her. By now, the family estate had probably been sold, his brother basking in the wealth it had brought. Dylan had a meager income, but hadn't withdrawn any money from the account since he'd left England. Now, even if he wanted to, he couldn't.

Maybe later, after he'd earned enough money to buy a plantation, he could consider marriage, but he doubted it would ever happen. He had seen firsthand what a woman could do to a man when she got angry. Physical punishment had nothing to do with the agony his mother had inflicted on his father and him.

Dylan clutched the little package in his hand. He realized that giving her the trinket it held was no way to apologize for how he'd treated her last night, but he wanted her to have it anyway. Maybe she could sell it when the war was over and have some extra money to help support herself.

As he approached the inn, he spotted Honor walking slowly toward home. "Honor," he called, feeling his heart quicken as he neared her.

She turned around and looked at him as if he'd just materialized before her out of thin air. His thickly corded muscle rippled elegantly as he hurried to join her. He was quite a masculine specimen to behold as he strode closer.

Dylan hastened his footsteps and caught up with her, his heart beating faster at the sight of her softly curved figure. Steeling himself against her magnetism, he smiled as if nothing untoward had happened between them.

"Hello," she said as he approached. "I didn't realize you were so close behind me."

"I wasn't until just now." Immediately upon reaching her, Dylan caught a whiff of her lovely scent and backed away again slightly.

Honor gazed at him, at his broad chest, rising and falling quickly as if he'd run a great distance. From somewhere nearby, she heard the screech of gulls as they fished for their dinner, and she thought of Echo's words.

Dylan noticed her smile. It was as if she were remembering something amusing. "Is anything wrong?"

"What? Oh, no." Honor looked into his blue eyes, the same color as the sky over the harbor. The wind ruffled his hair, flicking a curl here and there across his forehead. "I was just remembering something a friend told me earlier today."

"Oh? Something I'd be interested in?" Dylan became alert at the possibility of information that could help him. After all, that was his job. That was why he was living in the same house with Honor.

"I doubt you'd find it very amusing. Women's talk, that's all." She turned and walked through the gate, with Dylan trailing after her. *Don't make the conquest too easy,* Echo had said. Instead of throwing herself into Dylan's arms as she really wanted to do, she was walking away from him, and he was following. It gave her a nice feeling. Maybe he did care, after all.

They went into the common room and Dylan took a chair. There were few patrons this early in the afternoon, so Honor poured them each a cup of milk and sat down to talk. "Did you find out who was chasing us last night?"

"No, haven't heard a thing." Dylan watched her as she scanned the room to make sure she wasn't neglecting any of the customers who might need a refill. "Probably won't. They're undoubtedly not the sort of men who would talk about it. After all, their intentions weren't exactly honorable."

"I suppose not." Honor considered the problem. She'd almost decided that she needed to stay away from the wharf area for a few days, just in case the man remembered what she looked like. "Maybe I should avoid the area. What do you think?"

"I think that's a sound idea." Dylan covered her hands with his. "Honor, that sort of man is dangerous, day or night. I shudder to think what might have happened had they caught you alone."

"I don't exactly like to think about it either, but I can't lock myself away forever. Sooner or later I'm going to run into him." Honor tried to smile reassuringly, but failed. "Maybe he'll forget me."

"With enough bad rum in him, he will," Dylan agreed. Then he chuckled. "He's probably interested in someone else by now. Be alert, but don't dwell on it."

"I won't." Honor knew he thought he'd saved her from a terrible fate. "Thank you, Dylan. I don't know what I would have done without you."

Dylan's smile brightened his entire face. A dimple appeared in his chin and his eyes shimmered like a sunny afternoon. Honor decided she'd done the right thing, even though she knew she could have escaped just as easily alone as with him, maybe even more easily.

"I'm glad I could be there when you needed me." Dylan reached into his pocket and brought out the little package he was carrying. "I brought this for you."

Honor took the package and removed the paper. She opened the little box inside and gazed steadily at the contents. A garnet necklace. "Oh, Dylan, this is lovely, but I can't accept it."

He knew her reasons were rooted in custom, but he didn't give a sand flea for custom. "Sure you can. Why would you think otherwise?"

"It's too expensive," she explained, lifting the necklace from it's velvety bed and holding it up. The light streaming

through the window caught the facets, and the deep red stone
glittered brightly. "It's stunning."

"Honor," Dylan said, realizing he'd have to find a way t
convince her to accept the gift, "this is made for you. And i
you—if you won't wear it, keep it. After the war is over, yo
may need some money. You can always sell it."

"Sell it?" Her gaze rose to meet his. "Dylan, if I keep thi
lovely necklace, you can depend on my having it forever. It'
far too precious to sell."

"I just want you to—to be happy." He felt as though h
was buying her off. The necklace wasn't of really great valu
and he'd taken it in trade, so it meant little to him. But Hono
could use it to help make her future more secure. He didn'
like the idea of her waiting on tables in a tavern for the rest o
her life. She deserved better.

"Look, Honor, keep it." His hands closed around hers a
they held the necklace. "I might not always be here, and
want you to have some security for later. Maybe you won't sel
it. Maybe you'll never have to, but at least I'll know you hav
that option."

Honor realized then what he was saying. He was giving he
the necklace because he was leaving. But why? She had n
claim on him. He'd made no promises, offered no future fo
her. A chill danced down her spine and she slowly disen
gaged her hands from his and put the necklace back in th
box. She started to hand it back to him, but hesitated. Th
necklace would lend authenticity to the gown that Miriam ha
provided as a costume for Lynx. This would be the finishin
touch the outfit needed. With a chill in her voice that matche
the one darting up and down her backbone, she smiled pret
tily. "Thank you, Dylan. I have just the perfect use for this."

Dylan watched as she rose, slid the box into her pocket an
walked away. Something had just happened that he didn'
understand, and he wasn't sure that he ever would. Wome
were too complicated for men to fathom, he decided, an
finished his milk.

Honor now knew that her feelings for Dylan were muc
deeper than his for her. Lying across her bed and staring int
the largest garnet of the necklace he'd given her, she decide
that maybe this was true with almost all relationships.

man's feelings simply weren't as complex and focused as a woman's.

Focus was a word that brought Honor back to the present. Her attention must be focused on obtaining information to stop the British. For now, she would have to put aside her own feelings and concentrate on her job. But with Dylan constantly around, it would be difficult.

She knew, with as much confidence as she could muster, that she loved him. Marriage was another matter entirely; she still wasn't sure about whether or not she wanted to enter into that union.

In some ways, Echo's life was much more interesting. True, there were times when the prostitute might not enjoy a particular affair, but she could choose to make love or not. A wife, Honor suspected, didn't have that choice.

Honor knew she could never enjoy the sort of lifestyle Echo seemed to like. There were too many reasons that held her back, even if she'd been so inclined. Echo's life was dangerous and, in reality, immoral. Long ago, Honor had decided to live up to her own name, though it wasn't always easy. She might enjoy impersonating a prostitute, as long as she didn't actually have to submit to the intimacy that the job entailed. And she was determined that she'd never have to face that problem.

With Echo's help, along with Ruth Richmond's seemingly endless supply of laudanum, she would get along nicely. Echo had promised that after Honor pretended to take a gentleman to bed, liberally dosed with laudanum in his rum, one of Echo's girls would take her place. Simple and well planned—she hoped.

She hid the necklace and returned to the common room to do her job. By now, the tavern should be filling up with hungry people. Her father would be angry if he had to come looking for her and remind her of her duties.

When she reached the common room, Paddy was there, shining Dylan's boots. The boy did a good job, she noticed as she walked by. During the span of the evening, Paddy went from table to table, shining boots of anyone with a coin for him. Smiling and winking at him, Honor realized he could make a lot of money if he kept up his pace.

The crowd this night was loud and boisterous. Several men took the small, private dining room upstairs to avoid the

overly noisy common room. Dylan accompanied them at thei
invitation. Honor went along to serve them all. While she wa
taking their orders, she overheard one of them say that Gen
eral Horatio Gates had assumed command of the Southern
army.

She perked up a little, even though she knew these men t
be Patriots. She probably wouldn't hear anything to pass on
but she liked to keep up with everything concerning the war.

"Why the bloody hell didn't they send Greene?" One man
asked, scowling at the rest.

Another shrugged and said, "Why didn't they listen t
Washington? He's the commander of all the Continenta
forces. Seems to me he'd have convinced them."

"Gates did a fine job at—"

"Luck, I tell you. Gates is an oaf."

"Right. Not to be depended upon."

"And what about that little party our officers had over t
Haddrell's Point? Did you hear about it? On July fourth, ou
men, being prisoners and all, took to celebrating our free
dom from British oppression. Our independence. Some o
'em still had pistols. Shot 'em off."

"I'll bet that made them British guards happy."

Honor listened as she placed food on the table. The six men
bantered General Gates's reputation back and forth across the
table like a child's ball. She didn't know much about the gen
eral, but thought that Congress must have known what the
were doing. They probably had information about Gates tha
the common people didn't have.

Before long, Honor had to leave to bring more rum to th
men. Knowing that she might miss something, she hurrie
down the stairs, filled several pitchers with rum and returned
as quickly as possible. When she returned, the men were dis
cussing a Patriot victory and laughing about it.

"Said they took the fort without firing a shot."

"I been to Thicketty Fort. The lot of us could have de
fended it."

Dylan shifted uneasily in his chair. He, too, had heard o
the siege of Fort Anderson, which these rebels were callin
Thicketty Fort. He understood that Captain Patrick Moore
a Tory from North Carolina, had surrendered against a fa
superior force of militia. Dylan kept silent. Anything he sai
to defend the soldier would bring suspicion upon him.

One man swilled down the last of his ale and said, "Just goes to show them fancy Englanders is yeller unless Clinton's got his sword pointed at their backsides."

"Yeah," another man agreed, "too bad he didn't go back to New York before they attacked Charleston."

Honor's gaze went to Dylan. She noticed the color rising in great splotches on his neck and cheeks. He was undoubtedly angry about the man's reference to the British being cowards. But, Dylan was now a Carolinian . . . an American by choice. Maybe it was due to the room being so hot. August was a nearly intolerable month with its intense heat and high moisture content in the air.

"Fort Anderson up at Thicketty took without a shot being fired. Who would have thought it?" one man finally said, slamming his empty tankard on the table.

Honor rushed over to refill it, wondering if she'd heard the man correctly. Could Fort Anderson and Thicketty Fort be the same place? How could she find out without making herself obvious? She hurried around the table, filling each cup as she came to it until she reached Dylan.

"Dylan," she said as she reached for his cup, "I don't understand. I thought they were talking about a place called Thicketty Fort. Now that man said Fort Anderson." She shrugged and knitted her brows together. "I'm confused. Which is correct?"

"Both are correct, Honor," Dylan explained. He was weary of the bragging and angry about the remarks about the British soldiers. "Fort Anderson," he whispered, so as not to call attention to Honor and himself, "is located at a place called Thicketty Creek."

"Oh, I see. This war stuff is so confusing." Honor could hardly contain her glee as she continued around the table, filling glasses.

Her information had done some good. At least she thought it had been her information. If Jeffrey had passed it on in time, then Honor had truly helped the Patriot cause. She prayed that it was so.

She stood in the shadows at the corner of the room, thinking ahead to the conclusion of the war. No matter who won, the people who lived in America would have to find a way to get along. With tempers running so high, and resentments so rampant, how could they ever manage to live together amicably? She was happy the government didn't depend on her to find the answer to that problem.

Honor lost count of how many times she trudged up and down the stairs carrying trays of food and drink. She learned nothing of value that night, but she couldn't have refused to serve them. Someone who was paying attention to her habits, and Jeffrey had told her that the British had spies everywhere, might have figured out her pattern if she served only the British. She couldn't afford to have her duties come under that scrutiny, so she continued to serve all small parties that took private rooms.

At last the men began to leave. They'd consumed a great deal of rum and ale, so the evening had been profitable for the tavern at least. When she finally returned to the common room, most of the customers were gone.

She regretted that she'd had nothing to pass on to Jeffrey these past few days, but she couldn't manufacture information. Honor hoped he would understand.

One afternoon, Wilma stopped by and asked to see Honor. The young black woman smiled shyly as Honor came to the door and handed her a small bouquet of roses. "My mistress sent them to you. She knew you'd enjoy looking at them and *smelling* them," was all the girl would say.

Honor thought the bouquet a very touching gift from Echo and thanked the girl. She found an empty pitcher, filled it with water and placed the roses in it. "I'm going to take these to our room," she said to Miriam, who'd just come in for supper.

When she got to her bedroom, Honor placed the roses on the table by the window. With the heat the way it was, they wouldn't last very long. She leaned over to smell them and noticed something white inside one of the buds.

Curious, Honor picked the object out and saw that it was a piece of paper. She tiptoed back to the door and locked it before unrolling the tiny scroll.

Client needs special attention tomorrow night.

                                                            Echo

Honor felt a rush of blood to her temples and sat down on the edge of her bed. This was to be her first attempt to seduce information from a man. Her fingers shaking, she took the note downstairs and tossed it into the small fire in the changing room.

She then turned to Miriam. "We need to talk."

Miriam looked up from her biscuit with a puzzled expression on her face. "What about?"

"Before it gets dark, we need to deliver a certain dress you just finished." Honor didn't want to be more specific. She didn't know who was in the common room or outside the door. Anyone could easily hear them talking.

Nodding, Miriam popped the last of her biscuit in her mouth and licked the strawberry jam from her fingers. "I'm ready."

Miriam explained to Della that she had to deliver a dress and needed Honor to go along for the sake of propriety. Della glanced from one of the women to the other, but didn't say anything.

As they hurried along the street, Honor told Miriam about Echo's note. "Isn't that clever?"

"I suppose," Miriam said, feeling suddenly sorry that she'd agreed to help her friend. "Look, Honor, I really don't think this is such a good idea. What if something goes wrong? And it could, you know."

"Don't worry, Miriam. Everything will go as planned. Echo is very adept at this sort of thing. You'll see." Still, Honor felt apprehensive about the whole venture. Not that she distrusted Echo, but Miriam was right. Anything could happen.

They retrieved the dress from the shop on Tradd Street and hurried on toward East Bay. Honor suddenly wished Dylan had made love to her. If she had to sacrifice her virginity for the cause, then she wanted her first time to be with someone she cared a great deal about. Since she couldn't very well come right out and ask him, she'd have to find another way. Somehow, she knew that everything would be all right. Brimming with confidence, she led Miriam directly to Echo's place of business, Night's Pleasure Inn.

"Do people really stay here overnight?" Miriam asked as they walked up the steps.

Honor shook her head. "I don't think so. Most people would get one look at the interior and know what sort of place it is."

"What's it like? When did you see it? Have you actually been inside? Honor, have you?" Miriam was full of questions, which tumbled out of her mouth like a startled covey of doves.

"Shh. See for yourself." Honor knocked on the door and Wilma opened it. "Miss Edwards is here to deliver a dress for one of Echo's... I mean, for Miss Echo."

"Come in. I'll go get Miss Echo." Wilma showed them into the parlor and hurried away.

Miriam turned slowly around, her eyes wide with curiosity and astonishment. Her gaze fixed on a portrait of a beautiful naked woman.

Honor glanced at the portrait and then stared at it. The woman was Echo. Nobody could dispute the likeness. Her lush body was draped only slightly by a transparent gauze shawl, but her breasts were clearly visible, as was the curly thatch of blond hair at the apex of her legs.

The reality of what she was about to do came down on Honor full force. She sank into a chair, her mind spinning with possibilities and horrors. Sure now that she'd made the wrong decision, she rose and started to grab Miriam's arm to leave, but Echo came into the room.

"Honor, dear child, how good to see you." Echo hugged Honor and kissed her cheek. "And you've brought your sweet friend, Miss..."

"Edwards," Honor supplied, hardly able to speak.

Echo spoke with Miriam for a few moments about the dress. "Miss Edwards, this is absolutely lovely. Such fine workmanship, too."

"Thank you, Miss..."

"Call me Echo. Everyone does." The woman continued to examine the dress and then held it up to Honor. "Dearie, this is perfect. Wherever did you get the pattern?"

Miriam beamed with pride. "Well, if you recall the day Honor and I spoke with you, you were wearing a similar gown. I added a few touches that made this one unique, and here we are with this creation."

Echo studied Miriam for a moment. "Would you make dresses for me? If you think it will be a problem, I won't do it, but maybe we could arrange for private fittings, that sort of thing. My seamstress isn't very creative or talented."

Nodding, Miriam agreed. "We can work something out, I'm sure."

"I can be quite discreet, Miriam," Echo assured her. She led the two women to the door. "It wouldn't be appropriate for you to be here when our clients start to arrive, so be on your way. See you tomorrow, Honor. Come early in the afternoon and we'll finalize our plans. Oh, don't worry about the laudanum. I have some sleeping powders."

Honor walked home in silence. The full weight of her plans was now upon her. When first conceived, the strategy seemed to be fun and exciting, but now she was wary of many things. There was the possibility of being discovered. There was a possibility of being injured.

There was the probability of losing her virginity to a man she didn't even know.

Honor shrank from such an eventuality, no matter how remote. Though she'd never really considered her virginity as the most sacred part of her, she hadn't intended to give it to a stranger. Once again she thought of Dylan. His kisses filled her with an intense longing unlike anything she'd ever known.

What would making love with him be like?

She weighed the choices before her. She could either abandon her plan completely, or she could risk having her virginity taken by some drunken patron at the Night's Pleasure Inn. The third possibility intrigued her.

She could seduce Dylan Alden.

Chapter Twelve

Honor was puzzled by her feelings for Dylan. The relationship between her parents had never caused her to believe that marriages could be happy. Yet here she was, contemplating that very thing. Marriage.

The chaste existence between her parents seemed cold and uninviting, a far cry from the heated passion that blossomed uninhibitedly for her when she was with Dylan. His kisses, the memory of those luscious moments with him, stirred something within her even as she stood there staring out her window.

With Dylan in her heart, everything seemed possible. Loving Dylan, as she was now convinced she did, gave her sworn duty new meaning. Whatever oppression Dylan had left to come to America, she wanted to insure that he never had to endure it again. She would do whatever was necessary.

Loving Dylan gave her courage.

The more she considered the evening planned for the Night's Pleasure Inn, the more she realized she would have to make love to Dylan first. What would he think of her, she wondered, if he knew of her plan? The mission to Echo's might end in Honor's being raped, but she was now convinced that she had to go through with it.

The success of her tip to Jeffrey about Fort Anderson reinforced her feeling of importance. She was as integral a part of this war now as any man who hefted a musket. And she was proud of herself for having the courage to do a job that needed to be done, a job that only she could do.

* * *

Tonight she would make love to Dylan. She would wait for him to come to supper, to sit in the common room and talk with the other men. Then she would flirt with him and later follow him to his room.

About midway through the evening, he stuck his head in as if to see who was there, but he didn't remain. Honor watched, puzzled, as he retreated up the stairs, and decided that he would return later.

She served table after table of hungry and thirsty men, but still Dylan did not come to supper. Honor's temper was growing shorter as the evening progressed, and she saw her plans evaporate like water from a puddle beneath a grueling summer sun.

Honor had been so busy, she hadn't had time to eat her own supper, though she was beginning to feel hungry. Dylan had appeared on the staircase several times, but had always returned to his room. She decided that he must be looking for someone.

Finally, people began to leave in groups of twos and threes, until the tavern was nearly empty. She cleaned off tables and began to sweep, angrily swishing the broom to and fro. She wanted to complete her chores before sitting down to her own supper.

"Excuse me, Miss Richmond," Dylan said from the staircase. "I require supper for two in my room. Stew and milk will be fine."

He turned and left without saying anything else.

Though Honor was puzzled by his strange request, she nonetheless went into the changing room and filled two bowls with rice and a spicy vegetable stew cooked with a ham hock. She headed up the stairs with the meal, wondering all the time who he was having in for supper.

As she walked down the hallway, she decided with a sigh that she would have to postpone her plans for seducing him. She could hardly do so if he had company. She stopped short, so abruptly that she nearly tipped over the cups of milk. Maybe Dylan's guest was a woman!

If that was the case, then everything changed. All her well-laid plans dissolved in her mind and simply drained away before they could be implemented. Why hadn't she thought of that before? Though she'd known Dylan for some months now, she'd never asked him if he had a lady friend—or even a wife. Honor had never seen him with a woman, but that meant nothing. He was sometimes gone from the inn for long stretches of time.

Lifting her chin as if she hadn't a care in the world, she took the few steps that brought her to his door and, balancing the tray on one hand, knocked gently. *When he opens the door, hand him the tray and leave. Just leave. You don't really want to know who's in there,* she told herself.

He swung the door wide and smiled broadly. "Come in."

Honor glanced past him, but saw nobody else. Still, she wasn't taking any chances. For all she knew the woman could be Miriam. "Here's your supper. I hope you and your—your friend enjoy it."

"Oh, I'm sure we shall. The food here, as you told me yourself when I first came, is excellent." Dylan gestured for her to enter. "Come in, please."

Praying that the woman would be someone she didn't know, Honor stepped inside the small room. She glanced around and saw nobody besides Dylan. "Aren't you...having company for supper?"

"I am, indeed." Dylan took the tray out of her hands and placed it on the small table near the curtained window. "Please sit, Miss Richmond."

"Me?" Honor exclaimed, a question in her voice.

"Yes, you. Whom did you think I would invite to supper?" Dylan still wasn't sure about what he was doing. He had paced back and forth all day, trying to put all this . . . this business with Honor in some sort of perspective, and had failed. "I've been waiting all evening for you to finish your work."

"Oh," she said limply, and sank into one of the chairs. "Why?"

"It occurred to me that we've never really shared a meal together." Dylan sat across from her and smiled cheerfully. He wanted to put her at her ease. Under no circumstances did he want her to be afraid of him. Somehow he had to put their relationship back on the right track. He didn't know exactly how it had come about, but in the past few weeks, something had changed their friendship into more than he'd ever thought possible.

"We have. We've eaten together many times." Honor was puzzled by the way he was acting. This turn of events would make her task easier tonight, but she was uncertain of what he had in mind. Had he lured her here to seduce *her?* She chuckled, thinking how odd it would be if both of them had the same thing in mind.

"Yes, technically speaking, we have. But not exactly as I have envisioned it." Dylan was having trouble explaining his reasoning to her, primarily because he didn't understand himself. "There have always been other people around."

"I see." That explained exactly nothing to her. They'd been alone together several times. What had eating to do with the matter?

"Here, eat before the stew gets cold." Dylan tucked his napkin in his shirt and began to eat. "Be sure to tell Della what a wonderful stew she makes."

"I will, though you should do it yourself." Honor sipped the broth of her stew and watched him pensively. "I think she likes you."

"I'm glad to hear that. Someone who cooks as well as she does is a good friend to have."

They ate almost in silence after that. Dylan kept thinking of questions to ask her, but many were too personal, while others were too impersonal. For some strange reason, there seemed to be no common ground that evening.

She was beautiful. The fresh, creamy color of her skin shone in the light of the candle he'd placed on the table. Her eyes glittered like black diamonds set in iridescent pearls. Though she might be a serving girl, she ate with all the grace and refinement of a lady. Her delicate hands fascinated him at every turn. He'd held them and knew them to have slight calluses from hard work, and yet they were elegant as they lifted the spoon, as they touched the napkin to her mouth.

Her mouth. Lips the color of summer roses in the twilight, deep-colored and lush, soft and kissable. Damn it, he cursed himself, stop thinking of kissing her.

But he could not. His gaze was drawn magnetically to her lips, parted slightly as she watched him, her eyebrows knitting together as if she thought something was wrong. He smiled to reassure her, but felt as if he were being dishonest. In his attempt to inspire her confidence, he wanted to take her in his arms and assure her that nothing was wrong, that he'd care for her forever. But that was untrue.

Everything about him was false. He hated himself for lying to her, for misleading her about his loyalties. He hated himself for taking advantage of her.

He pushed back from the table and threw down his napkin. Nothing seemed to work right. He had invited her here to talk seriously, and now all he was doing was thinking of making love to her.

Knowing that he could establish nothing permanent, he had meant to tell her that their relationship could not be. But he hadn't the heart.

What should I do? she wondered. For a time, they sat in silence, neither apparently willing to break the tenuous thread of tranquility that seemed to be embedded in separate thought channels. Her palms grew damp and clammy. Her mouth was as dry as if she'd eaten cotton for supper. Her heart pounded like the surf against the shore.

Honor watched him, puzzled by the quickly changing expressions on his face. It seemed as though his mind were a butterfly, flitting from flower to flower and still not finding what it sought.

Well, this is one butterfly that will find what she wants and take it. Honor put down her spoon and wiped her lips before placing her napkin beside her plate.

Very calmly, she rose, walked over to him and leaned down to kiss him. As she came closer to him, his expression changed once again. He looked thoroughly bewildered as her lips touched his.

"Honor, please, you don't know—"

Her lips smothered his protest. For a few seconds, she thought he would push her away, but he didn't. And then his arms were around her, pulling her down into his lap. All the plans she'd made for seducing him were unnecessary. Dylan was as willing as she.

The moments lengthened as her kiss lingered. Curled in his lap, she felt her heart begin to pound even harder and louder. Its rhythmic tattoo filled her blood, her ears, her mind with a desire to touch, to embrace, to—to do more than she'd ever done before.

Honor felt his thumb come to rest against the swell of her breast. For a few seconds, it didn't move, but remained still, as if he was content merely to touch her. But the desire that beat so steadily in her own blood seemed to rage in his as well, for his hand soon cupped the breast and then was inside her bodice.

Dylan was astonished by her behavior and would have stopped her, but his body denied him the right to interfere. Pleasure, passion, desire flooded through him, and all the stolen kisses, compounded by the evening in the little garden, were as nothing compared to the way he now felt and crowded out all rational behavior.

He couldn't have stopped her if he'd wanted to.

And he didn't want to. Lust, he reassured himself. Pure, unbridled lust drove him as he slid his hand inside her bodice and then began to remove her clothing. She couldn't be a virgin. Not with such passion spent so freely. He hesitated for a few seconds, feeling a sense of jealousy of whoever had been with her before, but decided he didn't care. She belonged to him now.

He'd never found petticoats and chemises and bodices so infuriating, nor so uncooperative, until that moment. In his haste to rid her of the offensive garments that kept him from attaining his goal, he tore her dress.

Honor smiled and rose. If she allowed him to continue, her dress would be in shreds. With a confidence born of need and trust, she removed her clothing and dropped it to the floor. Praying that she wouldn't appear foolish to him, she stood there naked for a moment and then blew out the candle.

Her brazen behavior stunned even Honor. Where she got the courage to do such a thing, she would never know. After she extinguished the candle, she took his hand and led him to the bed. By now she was shaking, not out of fear, but out of anticipation. The moment of truth had come.

Dylan threw off his clothes more quickly than he could ever remember doing. For all he knew, or cared, he might have tossed them out the window. By that time, she lay in the bed waiting. What nerve! he thought, realizing he liked a woman who went after what she wanted.

Honor continually surprised him at every turn. Moonlight from the winds pierced the darkness, playing across her body as the breeze moved the curtains. Dylan lay with her, kissing her deeply, plunging his tongue inside as he plundered and played in his newfound excitement.

He couldn't remember ever being so zealous in his haste to make love to a woman. Even so, he forced himself to go slow. She might not be the virgin he'd thought her to be, but she wasn't nearly as experienced as some of the women he'd courted in the past.

Honor shuddered as Dylan stroked her body and delicious waves of excitement shimmered through her like tiny rivulets of quicksilver. He kissed her lips, her cheeks, her eyelids and then her neck and her ears. Each touch of his mouth on her left a trail of liquid fire as he continued down her neck and caught one nipple between his lips.

With a moan, Honor clasped his head in her hands and began to run her fingers through his hair. More insistent now, his mouth tugged on first one nipple and then the other until she could no longer tell the difference. Her entire body was his to use as he would.

She writhed beneath his touch, each caress sending her into a more primitive world of sensation, each moment an exploration of her own passion.

Dylan looked down at her. "Honor, my darling, do you understand...?" His gaze met hers, full of determination and brimming with unspoken passions.

And then he slid over her, all hesitancy and protest dissolving in the heat of their desires. Her warm moisture welcomed his throbbing manhood and she seemed to be urging him on. Dylan lost all sense of reason and plunged inside her. To his astonishment, he met with a resistance that told him he'd been wrong about her experience.

"Honor, why?"

"I wanted you to be first." She pulled his head down and kissed him. "Don't ... stop."

"I—I'm honored," was all he could manage to say.

Other conversation was lost in their lovemaking. After the initial shock of losing her virginity, Honor discovered the true enchantment of loving and being loved.

He guided her carefully through that wonderful maze of sensations, building and then slowing their pace until both of them were nearly frenzied with want of each other. Waiting until he was sure she was ready, he kissed her long and hard, caressed the rest of her body, and then allowed their lust to blossom into a miraculous flower of passion.

For a long time afterwards, Honor lay there in his embrace, a place where she was as sheltered as if she were in a cocoon of silk, as she basked in the sweet aftermath of their lovemaking. She knew she couldn't remain in his room all night, but she was reluctant to go, reluctant to break the spell that seemed to bind them together.

They'd shared few words this night, letting their love speak for them, she thought. And it had spoken loudly and eloquently, never to be quieted again, she hoped.

She rose, pulled on her dress, tucked her underclothes under her arm and kissed him goodbye. "Until tomorrow, Dylan," she whispered and disappeared through the door.

After she left, Dylan cursed himself for being such a weakling. He should have realized she didn't know what she was doing. A virgin. He'd seduced a virgin. Damn, he exclaimed to himself, rising to stare out the window. He hadn't been so foolish since he was a boy.

No matter what transpired here tonight, he vowed, we cannot... I cannot allow it to happen again.

Honor fairly danced down the hall, hugging herself. When she reached her room, she hesitated. Would Miriam sense what had happened? Could she tell?

Suddenly, Honor wondered if everyone would look at her and know what she'd done. Telling herself to remain calm, she slipped into the bedroom and dropped her clothes. She pulled on her nightgown and slid into bed, hoping her friend was asleep.

"And where have you been all evening?" Miriam asked, yawning, vestiges of sleep still evident in her soft voice.

Honor didn't know how to answer, but realized that if she didn't do so, Miriam would come fully awake. She didn't want that to happen. "I was serving a large party."

Miriam yawned again. "That's nice." Then she sat up. "Honor, there was no party. I looked for you."

"Hush, Miriam, before you wake up everyone in the house. As I was saying, I served a large party and then went for a walk."

"Oh." Miriam lay down again.

Honor was thankful for the darkness. At least Miriam couldn't see her face and know she was lying. Miriam would know. They had been friends too long. Either one of them could tell when the other was lying. Too many secrets and dreams had passed between them for it to be otherwise.

"Miriam," Honor said, knowing that she had to tell someone or burst, "the truth is I made love to Dylan tonight."

"You what?" Miriam exploded from the bed and stared at Honor in the moonlight filtering through the curtains.

"Keep your voice down," she whispered fiercely. "I'm going to tell you everything."

In a quavery voice, she did just that. She kept nothing back, telling Miriam of the fears that had led her to do such a thing. Honor told of her feelings for Dylan and of her fears that he didn't return her love.

"He's the most foolish man alive if he doesn't." Miriam drew her knees up and wrapped her arms around them. "Tell me something, Honor, and be truthful."

"What?"

"Was it wonderful or awful?"

Honor had feared that Miriam would ask for details and was happy to answer this simple question. "It was the most wonderful experience of my life."

Paddy met Honor early the next morning. "Jeffrey wants to see you."

"Where is he? In the barn?" Honor asked, putting down the tray she was holding.

"No. I'm to take you to him."

Though Honor had hoped to see Dylan this morning, she followed Paddy out of the house and the yard. They walked along, laughing and talking as if they had nothing more on their minds than having a good time. Honor flirted with soldiers they met, some of whom came into the tavern, and nodded or spoke to nearly everyone else. She felt glad to be alive.

After a few minutes, she began to wonder where they were going. They'd just been down this same street before, heading the other direction. She looked skeptically at Paddy, but he smiled and teased her about some nonsense, and she realized that he was checking to see if they were being followed.

Finally they walked down a narrow alley that paralleled the river, and from there took a path that was overgrown with sea oats and rushes. Honor spotted a shack that looked as if it would fall apart if the wind blew hard. Paddy told her go to inside, while he remained outside to keep watch.

Jeffrey was waiting for her. "Honor, I'm glad you could come."

"What is it, Jeffrey? Are you all right?" Honor looked him over to ascertain for herself his physical condition. "What's wrong?"

"We have a problem." He brushed off a rickety old chair and tested its strength. "Here, sit down."

When she complied, he sat facing her. "We have a spy in our group."

Her eyes widened in fear. "What happened?"

"Every time we get a good report, the British are there at the same time or even ahead of us." Jeffrey leaned back, staring at the door for a moment.

Honor's thoughts raced. Could Echo be the one? No, she didn't really know enough to tell anyone anything. Besides, she had a great deal to be angry with the British about. What about Miriam? She knew much more than Echo, but had an even better reason to hate the British. Besides the two other women and Paddy, Honor didn't know any of Jeffrey's spies. "What should I do?"

"Don't do anything." Jeffrey chewed his bottom lip for a moment. "Someone has infiltrated our organization and is passing information to the British. We've got to find out who he is before we go any further."

"But, Jeffrey, how can we find out who it is?" Honor thought of all the men who came to the tavern. There were men of both sides, but they never mixed. Someone who came there might be the spy.

"I don't know yet. The problem is that if the spy passes on false information to one of our people, and we act on that tip, then the identity of that person will be known to the British."

"Oh, I see." Honor thought of her coming assignation at Echo's house. "But, Jeffrey, I've got a contact that I can't miss. I mean, this is important. This man is highly placed."

"No, Honor. We can't take a chance." He sighed. All the work he'd done to organize the network would have to be done again. He didn't mind the work, but he did mind the risk to his people, particularly Honor. "It's just too risky. It won't take me long to figure out who this man is, and then we'll be free to go back to work. Until then, you must not pursue this contact, nor should you try to make others."

"But, Jeffrey, this is already set up and it's important. Otherwise—"

"No, Honor. It's too dangerous for you and everyone else. I'm stopping all operations until further notice, do you understand me?" His voice was stern, edged with fear.

"Yes, Jeffrey, I do."

"Good." He hugged her briefly. "Now go. Don't go back the way you came. Walk down the river a ways and then cut through. Paddy can lead you."

"Goodbye, Jeffrey. Take care of yourself." She rose and started to leave.

Jeffrey stared at her. She'd heard him, had agreed with him, but he doubted if she intended to heed his words. "Honor, I'm serious about this. I realize how committed you are to our cause, but I will not risk your life. Do I make myself clear on this matter?"

"Of course you do. You've spoken very eloquently and clearly, as usual." Honor kissed his cheek and walked out the door. "Oh, Miriam and I are moving into her shop. There are two spare rooms in the upper story. There are so many people coming in and out of there that you could probably stop in without anyone noticing you. Miriam would be pleased to see you, too." This was the first chance for Honor to plant the seeds of her idea. Jeffrey and Miriam would be perfect together. He just had to think of it as his idea.

As she and Paddy walked back to the inn, she decided that no matter what Jeffrey said, this meeting tonight at Echo's had to take place. She couldn't afford to back out at this late hour. Knowing the risks Jeffrey had mentioned, she would take extra precautions to maintain her anonymity. She would be as safe as a babe in its mother's arms.

Dylan paced about his office and cursed himself. How had he let such a thing happen? Clearly, it was all his fault. If he hadn't forced himself upon Honor that night while they were hiding, she wouldn't have initiated their lovemaking last night.

"Damn, but you're a fool," he exclaimed, slamming his fist down on his desk. "Any idiot could have found a way to stop the progress of this situation before it was too late."

"Sir? Were you talking to me?" Dylan's clerk, Otis Renfrew, opened the door between their offices and stared at him.

"Er, no, just arguing with myself about something—something personal. Nothing to do with you or business, Mr. Renfrew." Dylan felt doubly foolish. He'd failed to maintain a proper distance between himself and the subject of his scrutiny and now he'd embarrassed himself before his clerk. "Go on about your duties. I'm fine."

"Yes, sir." The clerk started to close the door, but changed his mind. "Oh, sir? The salt is ready to be shipped tomorrow night."

"Fine," Dylan said, waving his hand in dismissal.

There was another irritant. Now that he owned this warehouse, he was obligated to smuggle merchandise to the Patriots. Otherwise, he'd have no way of maintaining his position as a Patriot supporter. He had no hatred for the rebels at all, but he knew that the more supplies they received, the longer the war could go on.

The British army, on the other hand, was dependent on planters who shipped their goods to Charleston, or to be more specific, had their goods confiscated and sent to Charleston. The planters were paid in vouchers that could be exchanged in town, but many of them were living on revoked paroles and couldn't come to Charleston for fear of being captured and imprisoned.

To Dylan, the system was a parasitic one, but he'd yet to determine who was the host and who was the parasite in this system.

His clerk was another sore spot. Through his contacts with the British authorities, Dylan knew Otis Renfrew considered himself to be a British spy. The man was intelligent enough, but he was also a drunken braggart, which was why he could not be relied upon for more sensitive espionage. Sometimes the information about Dylan's smuggling reached the British authorities, sometimes it did not.

Dylan was forced to give the man some help, so to speak. On the pretense of sending salt to the rebels, Dylan was actually smuggling it to Cornwallis. Somewhere above Georgetown, a British contingent would overtake the wagons and reroute the merchandise.

He considered his plan an excellent one. Mr. Renfrew thought he was spying for the British, but in truth the man was merely an excuse for all Dylan's shipments that got way-laid by the Tories. During some of the suppers at the inn, Dylan would curse the fact that he must have unknowingly employed a spy. He couldn't, of course, discover the man's identity and relieve him of his duties outright, for that would give him away. Dylan argued that he had to find a way around the man, whoever he was.

Honor was another story. He was nearly overcome by her admission that she'd selected him to be her first lover. What could she possibly mean? He knew her well enough to believe that she wouldn't sell herself as a common prostitute, but if not that, what was she about? The rationale behind her actions eluded him.

He tried to imagine her in one of the bawdy houses near the wharf, but couldn't. Every time he thought of her in another man's arms, he got furious. "You haven't the right to tell her what to do with her life. Nor with whom she can make love."

Dylan began pacing again. He needed to talk with Honor, to make sure he understood her purpose. Perhaps, since her mother was ill, she didn't know of the relationship between a man and woman. "That's it!" he exclaimed, dropping into his chair. "She doesn't know about intimate relationships. I'll talk with her tonight."

Honor and Miriam moved into the house where the sewing shop was located. She explained to her father that he could rent her room to another soldier. He didn't like the idea, but she didn't give him much of a choice.

She and Miriam spent much of the day carrying their belongings from the inn to the shop and arranging their new rooms. Then Honor had to leave for Echo's. She pulled on a large bonnet that covered her head well, its protruding brim shadowing her face. Maybe she wouldn't be recognized if she encountered someone she knew.

As she walked along the brick sidewalks, she kept remembering what Jeffrey had said. Her own intuition told her that this wasn't one of the situations that he'd spoken of, that she'd be all right.

Honor slowed a little as she walked down East Bay Street. At this time of day, in the strong heat of an August afternoon, there were few people out walking. Most Charlestonians did their outside chores early in the day to avoid the sultry summer weather. For that, she was glad. When she noticed that she was practically alone on the street, she charged through the gate and up the steps. This time she didn't knock. Echo had told her to enter straightaway, so as to avoid being seen and recognized from the street.

As she walked through the doorway, Wilma came down the stairs and smiled. "Miss Echo is in her room. She says for you to come on up."

Honor nodded and started up the stairs. "Excuse me, Wilma, but which is her room?"

"Top of the stairs, at the front of the house. It's the room on the right."

Honor moved quickly up the stairs and down the hallway. The house was tremendous, with five rooms opening off this corridor and a staircase leading to another floor. The closed draperies were plush velvet, even though it was summertime and most Charlestonians had brought out their lighter, cooler curtains. Candles in the chandeliers and sconces burned against the darkness of the hallway, casting great long shadows that danced on the walls as she walked. The thick carpet muffled her footsteps.

When Honor reached Echo's room, she knocked lightly. "Come in," came a call from inside.

Honor opened the door and went inside. This room, freshly decorated, from the appearance and smell, was completely different from the rest of the house that she'd seen. There were no dark, plush velvets here, no gaudy reds and golds, but a rich mauve and hunter green decor dominating the room. The wallpaper was hand painted, a delicate floral that caught the muted colors of the breathtaking Aubusson carpet.

"Hello, Honor. Come in, my dear," Echo said, sitting at a dressing table that had three large mirrors. "Please, make yourself comfortable."

Honor saw the sofa and seated herself. She was still a little afraid of her coming assignation, not for physical reasons, but for mental ones. "Thank you, Echo. I . . . you've been very kind to me. I hope that one day I can repay your kindness."

Echo turned around and faced her. "The job you've undertaken is payment enough for me. You're a courageous girl, Honor. There aren't many like you."

"I'm just doing whatever I can . . . for the cause." Honor didn't know exactly where the women who worked for Echo stood in this war. She didn't want to endanger anyone by mentioning the words *Patriot* or *partisan* or *rebels*.

Smiling, Echo nodded. "You're a wise woman. Now, let me see what we need to talk about." She rose and walked to the corner, where she tugged on a long tapestry bellpull. "We'll talk over cakes and coffee."

After Wilma brought up the tray, Echo explained about how her house was run. She mentioned the qualifications she looked for in her girls, the things that made them stand out above other prostitutes. "You see, Honor, a fallen woman isn't necessarily a bad person. Frequently, my girls come from fine families. I require excellent manners and cleanliness, and comely appearance, of course."

"How . . . what happens to make a girl come to you?" Honor asked the question that had been burning within her ever since she first met Echo.

"Money. Loneliness." Echo shrugged and took a bite of strawberry jam on a little cake. "I don't ask. If they tell me, then I listen. That's another thing. We must be good listeners."

"Me, especially," Honor said and laughed, but it came out as a shrill, stilted sound, unlike her usual musical quality. "It's the rest that I'm a bit leery of."

"Honor, child, with your intelligence, you could be the most profitable of my girls if you came to work here." Echo sipped her coffee and looked at her over the cup. When she put it down, she shook her head. "There aren't many who're smart and beautiful."

"You're very kind." Honor felt awkward talking about herself. She steered the conversation back to the things that would help her.

Echo told Honor more about how the girls were expected to behave when the clients started coming in. "Oh, yes, don't act surprised when you see someone you know. We'll make sure you aren't recognizable."

"How will you do that?" Honor asked, suddenly wondering what she *would* do if someone she knew came in. What if someone did recognize her? She would be ruined forever.

"Don't worry. We'll style your hair, put on makeup and dress you like a pretty doll." Echo grinned and rose. "Let's start with your hair."

She rang for Wilma and asked for the curling tongs to be heated. Honor, Echo and Wilma spent the rest of the afternoon perfecting the appearance of Lynx, Echo's newest girl.

Honor stood still while the two women pulled the new, deep-purple satin dress over her head. The satin gown was trimmed with black lace flounces and had sleeves, though the bodice plunged nearly to her waist, exposing the pearly swell of Honor's breasts. A single ribbon of black lace was tied around her throat, with a tiny bouquet of artificial flowers for decoration. Her hair was piled high in a mass of curls, interwoven with purple-satin ribbon, paste gems and more flowers.

When they were done, Echo allowed Honor to look at herself in the mirror. "Why, Echo, I'm beautiful," she exclaimed. "A bit gaudy, but beautiful."

Chapter Thirteen

Dylan waited all day for Honor, but she didn't come back to the inn. When he went to question Della, she only shrugged.

"She took herself off to live with Miriam. Just the two of them by theyselves. It ain't right, I'm thinkin', it just ain't right." Della pounded the dough she was rolling for biscuits. "I don't know what that girl's problem is, but something sure is bothering her."

Dylan knew, or thought he knew. After last night, she couldn't face him. What a fool he was for allowing that to happen. He set out to find her.

"I don't know exactly where she went." Miriam smiled sweetly and glanced around. She didn't like having Dylan question her about Honor's whereabouts. She didn't like to lie and she didn't do it very well. "But I'm sure she'll be back . . . sooner or later."

Darkness had settled on the city, and Honor was out wandering the streets of Charleston. And it was his fault.

The man's eyes were large, gray orbs that widened when Echo introduced him to Honor. "Sorry to keep you waiting, Otis. I hope one of the girls gave you the drinks I sent down." She turned to Honor and gestured. "This is one of our finest girls, a real lady, saved especially for you. Lynx, this is Mr. Renfrew. I want you to be *very* nice to him this evening."

"Good evening, Mr. Renfrew," Honor said, with a quaver in her voice. She handed him another drink, as Echo had instructed earlier. The man wasn't bad looking, but the idea of walking up those stairs to the bedroom beside Echo's was frightening. Honor almost wished she could gulp down a cup of rum herself. Instead, she held out her hand to him, and he lifted it to his lips.

"My, what a lovely girl you are."

"Yes, and such a shame," Echo said, shaking her head sadly. "She's the daughter of a planter. Her parents were killed by that awful Swamp Fox and his band of renegades. Her house was plundered and then burned. Poor dear had nowhere else to turn." Echo leaned over to Otis Renfrew and whispered, "She's a virgin, so please be careful."

When the man looked back at Honor, he licked his lips as if in anticipation of a great feast. He wavered slightly, as if he were having difficulty standing. "Sh-shild, I'll take extra shpecial care of you tonight."

Honor bit her lower lip. She could hardly keep from laughing, because she knew what Echo had told him. Honor also knew that the two drinks Otis Renfrew had consumed were laced with a seemingly magical powder Echo had obtained.

Otis Renfrew drew Honor away from Echo. "Come, my dear, 'llow me introdush you to the enchanting world of intimashy."

His slurred speech was comical to Honor. She'd heard many men speak so after they'd consumed several cups of rum or ale, but Otis Renfrew hadn't had enough to make him drunk. The powder must be working.

Honor led him to the stairs, walking with him as well as was possible with his lurching and staggering. She hoped he wasn't already too sleepy to talk. "Here is . . . my room, Mr. Renfrew. Won't you come in?"

He stumbled over the threshold and followed her into the room. It was, in truth, Echo's private parlor, partially converted for Honor's use. Most of Echo's furniture remained, but a bed with posts carved into rice stalks had been brought in for Honor. She seated him on the bed and proceeded to blow out most of the candles.

She turned her back to him and stared out toward the harbor. "Please, Mr. Renfrew, make—make yourself comfortable."

From where she stood, she could hear him tearing off his clothes. Taking a deep breath, she moved closer to the windows, her short skirts swishing and whispering with each step and allowing cool air to seep inside the bell shape. She glanced down at the part of her legs that showed below the hemline and wondered why women didn't adopt this attire all the time. It made walking much easier, and was certainly cooler.

Now was the time for her to try her hand at espionage. She turned slightly and saw that he was in bed already, covered to his chin. "Excuse me if I seem a little nervous, Mr. Renfrew. You're such an important man—Echo told me how important you are—working at one of the large warehouses and all."

"Well, yesh, my dear. I sh'ppose you could describe me as an important man."

Honor knew from the sound of his voice he'd be asleep in moments. She needed to act quickly. "What—what exactly do you do? I suppose you keep the British authorities posted on the supplies that you export and important things like that."

"Sh-shure, I do." Otis sagged back against the pillow and patted the bed. "C'mere, girl. What wash your name? Don't matter."

Steeling her nerves against what might happen, Honor walked to the bed and got in on the other side from Mr. Renfrew. "I'm still a little nervous. It's this war. Why don't the British do something about that awful man?"

"Damn shlippery fool. Can't catsh him." Otis tried to lean up on one elbow, but couldn't remain there for long. "Coursh, I'm helping all I can. Boss don't think I know he's shending stuff to damn rebels. Fooled him. British army cuts him off above Georgetown. Gotsh shtuff...shalt and clothes going out tomorrow night. Thinksh I'm a fool."

Otis closed his eyes briefly. " 'nuff talk, girl."

He caught her arm and pulled her down with him on the bed. For a moment, Honor thought she would scream, but she managed to avoid his lips by cuddling up next to him and sniffling. "I'm so afraid."

"Don't be 'fraid. Otish good...good. Take care his girl...good..."

Honor opened her eyes wide and watched him for a few minutes, until he started to snore.

Gently, she disengaged herself from his arms and went over to the door that connected with Echo's chambers. She tapped lightly. The door swung open, and Echo pulled her into the dressing room.

"What happened? What took so long?" Echo nearly dragged Honor into the adjoining bedroom and looked her up and down, as if she expected to see tears in the dress. "Are you all right?"

Honor smiled brightly. "I'm fine." She fairly danced around the room. "It worked, Echo. He talked, and then he went to sleep as if by magic."

"Did you hear something helpful?"

"Yes." She dropped onto the sofa. "Now all I have to do is figure out a way to get the information to my contact person."

"Well, a clever girl like you should be able to do that." Echo sat beside Honor and hugged her. "I'm real proud of you, Honor. If you ever need a job, you've got one with me."

Echo sent for a girl who looked a lot like Honor. "Alice, you go in there and take a nap. When Mr. Renfrew wakes you up, start to cry as if he'd hurt you real bad. I'll come right in."

Echo helped Honor to undress. She and Wilma combed her hair, leaving it hanging loose down her back. Honor scrubbed her face clean and then looked into the mirror. "It's me again."

Before she left, she told Echo about the change in her address so that if another important man came along, Wilma could find her. She started out the back door, then turned around and smiled. "Thank you, Echo. You're a good friend. And a lady."

As she rushed down the street toward Miriam's shop, Honor hoped the man she'd encountered that night with Dylan wasn't lurking about. She was no more than a block away from her destination, when she saw a man coming toward her.

"Oh, Lord, don't let it be..." Honor eyed him carefully, ready to duck into someone's yard if necessary, but then she noticed the man was limping. It was Dylan.

She didn't know which was worse, meeting the drunk man that she'd struck or Dylan. Tense and tired, she wanted nothing more than to go home and fall into her bed. As Dylan approached, her mind raced, trying to think of a plausible excuse. She could find none that were really believable, but one might be acceptable.

"Hello, Dylan," she said, trying to gauge his eyes in the semidarkness.

"Honor!" he exclaimed, taking her in his arms and holding her tightly against his chest. "What are you doing out here alone at this hour? Don't you realize ... that man could ... Have you gone daft?"

"Nice to see you, too," she teased, hoping he wouldn't stay angry with her for very long.

Dylan didn't answer. He crushed her mouth with his kiss, a kiss born from fear and anger. When he finally drew back, he was ashamed of himself. "I—Honor, I apologize for my behavior. I was so damned—excuse me—worried about you. I've been combing the streets for hours looking for you."

Honor circled her arms around his neck and smiled up at him. "Then I'm amazed we didn't run into each other sooner."

"What do you mean?" he asked, peering down into her luminous dark eyes.

"I've been looking for Paddy. Have you seen him this evening?" she asked anxiously in turn. Behind Dylan's head, her fingers were crossed.

"Paddy? You were out looking for Paddy?" Dylan was incredulous. "Miriam said she didn't know where you were."

Honor shook her head. "No, she probably didn't. After my last trip to the inn, I went to the little market to order some supplies. Then I started to wonder about Paddy, so I decided to look for him."

"That was a foolish thing to do." Dylan was so delighted that she was safe that he couldn't stay angry with her for very long. "Next time, find me and I'll go looking for him."

"All right," she said contritely. "Let's go home. To Miriam's."

Dylan tucked her arm under his and they walked the block down Tradd to Miriam's shop. "Why did you move over here?"

Honor didn't really want to talk about this. She knew she was on dangerous ground. Dylan was much more alert than her father and might pick up on some nuance of her story that Henry Richmond had missed. "Miriam and I were having to sleep in one small bed. Since her mother isn't...I mean, since she passed away, well, Miriam didn't need these extra rooms for her business. So we decided to move in here. And Papa can rent that extra room to someone else, now that I'm out."

"I see." Dylan didn't know exactly why, but he felt disappointed, when he should be happy. He'd liked knowing where Honor was, that she was safe. Now, with her living alone with another young woman, he couldn't be assured of that. "I think you should reconsider. At this time particularly, your move could prove dangerous. I mean, two young women living alone. What if that drunk finds out where you live? How will you defend yourself?"

"With a darning needle?"

"Honor, this isn't a laughing matter. The man is a potential threat to you." Dylan didn't really want to frighten her, but he wanted her to understand the situation she was in. Moreover, he wanted her to stay at home in the evenings instead of prancing around the streets alone.

"Dylan, come in. I'll fix you something . . . milk or coffee." She opened the door and stepped inside. "Come on. We don't need to argue about this. It's not a problem."

Eyebrows knit together in doubt, Dylan followed her into the little parlor, past a little swinging gate and through a doorway into a tiny room that served as a kitchen. Miriam was sitting there in her dressing gown, apparently waiting for Honor to return.

"This wasn't . . . Oh, hello, Miriam. I didn't expect you to still be up." Honor glared at her friend with what she hoped was a significant expression. "I didn't find Paddy."

"No? Too bad." Miriam rose and started to walk out of the room. "I'm sure you'll excuse me, Mr. Alden, but I'm hardly dressed to receive visitors."

"Of course, Miss Edwards." Dylan tactfully looked away as Miriam hurried from the room. When he heard the tread of her footsteps on the staircase, he smiled at Honor. "She said she didn't know where you were."

"She didn't. I already told you." Honor hoped he wouldn't continue to question her. She was becoming uncomfortable. She studied him for a moment. "There's something else bothering you. You can tell me. What is it?"

Dylan waited until she finished her preparations for making coffee. "Why don't you sit down?"

"Oh, this doesn't sound too good." Honor seated herself near the small fireplace. "Good thing there's a fire going or we couldn't have coffee."

"Honor, forget about the coffee for a moment. Forget Paddy. Forget Miriam." He began to pace again. He felt sure that he was wearing out his boots from all the walking he'd done lately. "We need to talk about what happened between us last night."

Honor felt warm all over, as mention of their lovemaking brought back memories of that wonderful event. She tried to smile. He was concerned that he'd done something wrong. There were two reasons Honor had allowed him to make love to her. First, she wanted her first time to be with someone she cared about instead of an accident at Echo's place. The second reason was that she loved him. She stood and caught his hand as he walked near her. "Dylan, it was glorious. I'm sure I left before I thanked you properly."

Before he could say anything, she stood on her tiptoes and kissed him, a long and leisurely kiss that sent the wonderful memories of their intimacy flooding over her again, with almost the same potency as the actual event.

Dylan let himself drift farther into that secret place of passion where he'd locked his feelings for Honor neatly away. For a moment, he allowed her kiss to deepen, sending wave after wave of sensations through him. But he'd vowed never to make love to her again. He couldn't succumb. He simply couldn't. He drew away from her, hating the sudden rush of emptiness that flooded over him like a tide before a storm.

"Honor, we can't continue to…this must stop." He walked around the table until it was squarely between them. Maybe that would help. He held himself erect and steeled himself against her charms. It wouldn't happen again. No discussion was needed.

Honor fluttered her eyelashes at him and tilted her head to one side, a pout on her mouth—exactly the way Echo had showed her. His mouth softened slightly. "Dylan," she said, her voice a throaty whisper that only he could hear, "why are you being so mean to me?"

"Mean?" Dylan nearly choked on the word. "For the love of all that's holy, Honor, I'm protecting you."

Her smile was tantalizing, her lips slightly parted. She was playing with him, flirting as he'd never seen her do before.

Where had she learned such tricks? Or had she been hiding them? No, he was sure she'd been a virgin. There could be no doubt about that.

"From what?" she drawled, leaning forward so that her breasts jutted against her bodice. She would love to see the expression on his face if he ever got to see her in her lady-of-the-evening attire.

"Honor, I demand that you stop this—this ridiculous posturing immediately." Dylan regained control of himself, not trusting himself to look at the curve of her breasts. She began to move toward him, slowly and seductively. "Honor, damn it, stay where you are. We have to—"

But she reached him before he finished his speech and he lost his willpower. Such a potent force from such a tiny person, he thought as he carried her up the stairs to her bedroom.

When they were lying in her bed together, Honor whispered, "Now I can thank you properly."

As Dylan walked toward the inn much later, darkness cradling him in anonymity, he mulled over the problem of Honor. She was lovely, an innocent, and he'd corrupted her—there could be no doubt about that issue. What he could do about it was another. "I swear that I will avoid that house, and its inhabitants, as if my life depended on it."

Honor rose early the next morning to search for Jeffrey. Even though she'd put a candle in her window, he hadn't stopped. Honor had known he wouldn't. With the threat of a spy within their network, Jeffrey had steadfastly refused to implicate her. But this was important, too important to miss.

She took a circuitous route to the ramshackle house where she had met with him last, but he wasn't there and there was no trace of him. At a loss about what she should do next, she began a search for Paddy.

She found him at the White Point Inn, sweeping the floor of the kitchen. Honor suffered a hug from Della and teased the older woman. "I've been gone but one day, and you treat me as if I've gone off to England to become the consort of the king."

"Hush your mouth, speaking of sinful business like that. The Lord'll be reluctant to forgive such talk." Della glowered at Honor, but hugged her tightly again before releasing her. "I'm going to send one of the girls over to help you out. Tisn't right you living over there by yourselves without chaperons, and you both spinsters. Begorrah, but everybody in town'll be talkin' about ye."

"Della, we don't need—"

"Don't need, maybe, but I reckon you're going to have anyhow." She crossed her arms, and her expression fairly dared Honor to challenge the edict.

"All right. Send her over. Now, I need to see you, young man. Della, he'll be gone with me for a while." Honor caught Paddy by the arm and led him outside. She walked away from the kitchen and other buildings, down to the kitchen garden. "Paddy, I need to talk to Jeffrey immediately."

"Can't do it, Honor. He said not to come to him until he gives a sign." Paddy's brows wrinkled in thought. "What's wrong?"

"I have something to report to him. And—and I need to talk to him about something else." Honor gazed at Paddy, willing him to understand the urgency of her message.

"He said—"

"Yes, I'm sure he did," she interrupted, placing her hands on her hips. "*I'm* telling you that if you don't take me to him—"

"All right, don't holler at me."

Honor walked slowly along with the boy. At times, she wanted to reach out and shake him, to somehow let him know how urgent her messages were. He picked up a stick and dragged it across an expanse of wrought-iron fence. He walked down to the river and tossed oyster shells into the water. He found stones and threw them, clacking, down the brick sidewalk.

Her patience nearly at an end, Honor realized they'd come down this same street three times. Paddy seemed to be a child at play, with nothing on his mind other than his boyish pursuits. "Paddy, now this is really too much. I—"

"Can't catch me, big sister," he called, and ran as fast as he could down a narrow alley.

Honor hurried after him, knowing she shouldn't call his name. He wasn't really playing—at least, she hoped he wasn't

"When I catch you, I'm going to whale the daylights out of you. I'm stopping to break a hickory stick now."

She broke a flexible branch from a shrub and ran along after him. "Did you hear me?"

"Can't catch me. Ha, ha, ha, can't catch me."

Honor ran faster, wondering if he wasn't using this ploy to tire her out enough to lose her completely. "Stop right now. I mean it, you spoiled little . . . monster."

Then she saw the shack sitting in a deep grove of live oaks. Part of it was tumbled down, scarred from a fire that had probably begun as a result of the fireballs. Honor hurried along, wondering if this was where Jeffrey was hiding.

She glanced behind her to see if they were being followed, but saw no sign of it. Still, it wouldn't hurt for anyone who might have seen them go down the path to think that she was still scolding the boy. "Don't you go near that house. It's falling down and dangerous. Do you hear me?"

Honor herself went past it and entered from a jagged, gaping hole on one side that looked as if a giant had eaten the corner of the building. The place smelled of fire, acrid smoke clinging to everything. "Paddy? Jeffrey?" she whispered, wondering if she wouldn't be better off to leave.

She turned around, glancing at the burned furniture and scarred walls. A staircase behind her looked stable enough, but she didn't know whether or not to risk climbing it. Though light filtered through gaping cracks in the wood, the room was still fairly dark. As she made her decision, Jeffrey stepped out of the darkness.

"Honor, why have you come?" he asked, his face a tapestry of anger and concern.

"I—I . . . where is Paddy?"

"He's never allowed in here. He led you here and then ran on past." Jeffrey motioned with his hand. "He's probably hiding out there in the undergrowth somewhere. Why are you here?"

"Jeffrey, something happened that I had to tell you about." She didn't like being treated like a naughty child, but she *had* gone against his orders.

"I know what happened, or most of it, anyway." Jeffrey took her hand and led her to a mattress he'd dragged into a closet that opened beneath the staircase. He motioned for her to sit. "What I want to know is *why* it happened."

Honor was stunned. How could he know what had happened? "How do you . . . maybe we're talking about two different things."

"We're both talking about your visit to Echo's place." Jeffrey sat cross-legged beside her. "How could you be so foolish?"

"You know about Echo?" she asked simply, her excitement draining from her body. "But how?"

"Echo and I have been friends for a long time." Jeffrey stared at Honor, as if daring her to ask the obvious question. "She, too, is working for the cause."

Honor smiled brightly. "I knew there was a reason I liked and trusted her."

"Therein lies the problem, Honor." Jeffrey took her hands. "You *didn't* know if you could trust her. She could have easily been working for the other side."

But Honor shook her head. "No, Jeffrey. I knew she was one of us. She said things I understood, things that touched my heart and my soul. I saw her pain. There was never any danger with Echo."

Jeffrey shrugged. "I don't deny that you have good instincts, Honor. Neither do I know what she told you, but I do know her to be an honest woman, so I can't scold you too badly for befriending her."

"Nor should you. Jeffrey, I've done something wonderful." Honor wriggled with excitement.

"No, you've done something foolish." Jeffrey fairly growled the words. "I can't imagine how you could do such a thing. To—to prostitute yourself—"

"But I didn't!" she exclaimed. "I did nothing wrong."

"What are you talking about? Echo told me very specifically that she set you up with a man and that you took him upstairs." Jeffrey's brow furrowed with doubt. "She doesn't lie, Honor. You've gone too far."

"Certainly not in that regard, anyway," Honor teased, chuckling at his discomfort. Maybe Jeffrey wasn't as aware of a prostitute's ability to bend the truth as she was. "But we gave him sleeping powders. I talked to him a little and then he fell asleep. He likes me a lot, Jeffrey."

"I don't give a damn if he likes you!" Jeffrey exploded. "You will not, under any circumstances, go back to that place."

"You may not tell me what to do, Jeffrey. I can obtain valuable information there, possibly information that we can't do without." Honor lifted her chin and stared directly into his eyes. "I am not a dog to obey your every command."

"Honor, you don't…there are dangers of which you can't possibly be aware." Jeffrey's voice became pleading, and he took her hands in his own and held them tightly.

"I am well aware of those dangers, Jeffrey, and I accept the risk." She never took her eyes off him. "I've…lost my mother to this war, thanks to Clinton's first attack." She squeezed her eyes shut to stop the tears that threatened. When she had regained control of her emotions, she gazed at him steadily. "I've lost a woman who was like a mother to me. I've lost good friends, either killed, wounded or in prison ships. I've lost the city I love to a bunch of scavengers who're raping Charleston as if she were no more than a common wharf woman. I've lost my personal liberty. *I shall not be denied my part in ridding this city of its vermin.*"

Jeffrey opened his mouth to speak and then closed it. There was nothing he could say to rebut her speech. "I'll do whatever I can to make your quest more safe."

"Now," she said more cheerfully, "let me tell you what I heard."

For the next few minutes, she related the details of the wagon train and what lay in wait for it, along with other details of troop movements or shipments that she'd found out about. When she finished, there was a look of dismay on Jeffrey's face, one that silenced her completely.

"We can't act on any of this information, Honor," he said flatly, and then hung his head. "None of it."

For a moment, Honor couldn't speak. When she finally found her voice again, she touched his chin. "Why not, Jeffrey? Why not?"

"Because of what I told you. We've an infiltrator. We don't know who yet." He stretched his legs out before him, groaned and rubbed them briskly. "If this information is a part of his trap, then we're doomed and Charleston is doomed."

"But, Jeffrey, all that salt!" Honor's face blanched, all the color draining away. She felt cold inside. "Think of what our people could do with it. Think of the meat that will spoil without it."

"Honor, this is difficult for me, too." He closed his eyes briefly, resting them against the pain that showed in her eyes. "But we cannot act. We can't risk losing everything for one shipment of salt."

For the next few weeks, Honor continued to work at the White Point Inn and Tavern, helping her father and the women he'd hired to serve the customers. She heard interesting remarks, obtained information that might be useful to the rebels and passed it on. She occasionally spent an evening "entertaining" at Echo's and always discovered details that were bound to be helpful.

Jeffrey thought he had found his infiltrator and reorganized the network. Once again, he had an efficiently operating group. Though he was still careful to avoid the British at all costs, he didn't hide in shacks, nor did he move as often. He even stopped by Miriam's shop occasionally to talk with them.

Dylan, though he tried desperately to stay away from Honor, frequently stopped by to see her, but never at night. He tried to be content with the times he talked with her at the inn, but there were other moments when he needed to be alone with her, not for intimacy, but for her sweet friendship.

One evening when Honor was serving a large group of British officers, Dylan waited for her. He could hear the raucous laughter, the lewd remarks, and see the pinches and touches the drunken men attempted. He marveled at how well she managed to evade their grasp, and half wished that she'd evaded his own touch as well.

As he watched her thread her way among the tables, her hips swinging gracefully, he felt a tightening in his loins. Dylan had never suffered for female companionship until recently. He simply couldn't find anyone he was interested in— except Honor. He'd even gone down to the Night's Pleasure Inn, but hadn't gone inside.

When he could bear no more of the soldiers, he decided to go upstairs for a spell. There he could wait until it was almost time for her to go home and then he'd accompany her, for her safety, of course.

Honor noticed Dylan slowly mount the stairs and decided that it was just as well. She hadn't had any time to talk to him that evening at all. The rowdy group of soldiers were content to swill down more ale than anyone would have ever thought possible, and it was a full-time job for her to serve them and avoid their grasping hands.

Knowing she'd have black-and-blue places on her bottom, she continued to hover as close to the table as she could, hoping to hear something useful. Then one man mentioned King's Mountain.

"'Eard we was took by surprise."

"Not so. Ferguson knew the rebels were about. He could have summoned aid from Tarleton, who was no more than thirty or forty miles away."

Another man shook his head. "Tarleton's got the fever. Came down with yellow fever. Was in bed about to die for better than two weeks, as I hear it."

"So what happened at King's Mountain?" a man asked, throwing up his hands in disgust. "Let's don't get mired in them details. Tell us what happened."

"Well," the first man said, bowing his head sadly, "Ferguson and 'is men were atop the mountain. Good solid view of the 'ole area. Best fighting position around."

"So how come 'e lost?" another man asked.

"I'm getting to that. Anyway, I 'eard that Ferguson said nobody could get 'im off that mountain, not even God. Well, I guess God showed 'im. The rebels buried Ferguson right there."

"Why didn't he get help? We've got men all over the place."

"Lord Cornwallis was in Charlotte. Tarleton, too—not far away. Ferguson should have sent for help."

"He did. Sent for the Highlanders at Arness Ford. Sent the letter on the sixth of October. Battle started on the seventh."

"'Ow many men did we lose?"

"Around 150 killed. Total more than a thousand wounded, killed and captured."

Though Honor couldn't be sad for the Tory loss—some of those men were probably acquaintances of hers—she *was* sorry for the men who'd been killed or injured, and their families. Those captured, like the Patriot men located at

Haddrell's Point or in the prison ships, would be released at the end of the war.

She continued to serve drinks to the crowd, but her thoughts were on the victory. Even though these men weren't too concerned with the impact of the Patriot victory, she was. Honor believed that the war was turning in their favor.

"There's more bad news, maybe worse," the knowledgeable officer said. "The American Congress has appointed Greene to command the Southern Continentals. He'll turn and run, same as Gates did after Camden."

"I doubt it. Nathaniel Greene is a fine soldier. We shall have trouble with him."

"I 'eard we lost a boatload of provisions and another of injured men to a band of rebels who had nothing but a few muskets and a cannon they carved out of a tree trunk."

"A Quaker cannon? That's what they call them things."

"Yeah, I 'eard 'bout that."

The men finally began to leave. Dylan had been sitting at his window watching, and when he saw the tavern begin to clear out, he went back downstairs. Honor was preparing to leave.

"May I walk you to your quarters, Miss Richmond?" Dylan sounded as serious as he possibly could. "I fear it's dangerous for a lady to be on the streets alone at this late hour."

"How very kind of you, Mr. Alden, but I'm perfectly fine alone." Honor didn't want to impose, even though she wanted his company. She'd seen him leave earlier and thought he might be tired.

Dylan glanced about to see who might be listening. "I have another errand, Miss Richmond, so walking with you would be my pleasure."

"I'll get my cloak." Honor found her cloak and pulled it closely about her shoulders. The October nights were chilly, and she didn't relish the idea of going out into the cold wind. For the first time since she'd moved to her own house with Miriam, she regretted her decision.

Dylan and Honor strolled along as if they were walking down a country lane, admiring the spring flowers, instead of fighting a brisk, chill wind that made the moist air seem doubly cold.

"Did you hear about King's Mountain?" she asked him as she pulled her cloak tighter about her neck.

Nodding, Dylan said, "I heard. Quite a Patriot victory."

"Does it seem to you like the tide of this war is turning a little toward the Patriots?" Honor asked. She still tried not to commit herself to strangers, but there was no real doubt whose side she was on to those who knew her.

"I can't tell, Honor. We hear reports, but they're weeks after the event occurred. How can we know what's going on?" Dylan privately agreed with Honor, but he didn't like it at all. His security was being threatened by the Patriot victories. "I only know one thing—that I miss you when you're not around."

Honor looked up at him and smiled. "I miss you, too, Dylan. Terribly."

Honor's life was a series of exciting moments. Her friendship with Dylan had deepened into something much more serious, though she wouldn't label his feelings for her as love, not yet. She continued to work with Jeffrey, enjoying the experience of relaying information that was helping to win the war.

And Christmas was coming.

The months of November and December had been filled with fighting throughout the war zone, but the best news was that General Nathaniel Greene had finally marched into South Carolina. Honor couldn't remember being so excited about an event in the war.

She set about making presents for everyone. She and Miriam combined their efforts and made kerchiefs for the ladies and handkerchiefs for the men. Honor embroidered Dylan's herself.

Henry Richmond invited his guests to have Christmas supper with the family. At a big table in the common room, Henry, Jeffrey, Della, Paddy, Miriam, Dylan and Honor celebrated the season with a ham, fresh roasted oysters, sweet potatoes and a flummery. The serving women and Joseph ate at a nearby table, enjoying the same good food.

When they were done eating, Honor and Miriam rose and handed out their presents. Everyone liked his or her gift.

"We made them ourselves," Honor and Miriam said simultaneously.

Honor realized, as they were opening their own gifts, that neither of their mothers was present, and she felt sad. She shook off her dark mood, however, and tried to make the best of what she had. After all, here she was with good friends, celebrating the birth of Christ.

With the season being one of joy and news from the war good, it was easier for Honor to be happy. After the tables were cleared, she went upstairs to her mother's room. She sat down in the dimly lit room and gently placed a new kerchief around her mother's shoulders. "Mama, I don't know if you can hear me, but I love you. So much has happened since— since you went away from us. I've fallen in love with a nice man, Mama. I wish you were here to talk to me about him. I need to talk to you, Mama. I wish just for once you'd come back...just for a minute or two."

Honor looked down at her mother's glazed eyes and sighed. She fought back tears as she bent down and kissed her mother's cheek. "Merry Christmas, Mama. I miss you."

Later that evening, Dylan walked Honor and Miriam back to their house. "It was a lovely supper, wasn't it?"

"Sure was," Miriam agreed. "I don't think I'll ever be able to eat again."

Honor nodded her agreement. "Della is the best cook in all of the Carolinas."

"Who could doubt that?" Dylan asked, smiling down at her. "Perhaps in all the world. I must admit to feeling very full after one of her finest meals."

When they reached the shop, Dylan hesitated. He looked at Miriam and then at Honor. "Maybe I should return to my lodgings."

"Nonsense. Come on in for a while." Miriam smiled at him and winked at Honor. "I'm very tired. The two of you can stay up and talk."

After Miriam went up to her room, Honor smiled shyly at Dylan. "I'm glad you like your handkerchief. I embroidered it myself."

"It's wonderful." Dylan reached into his pocket and pulled out a little box for Honor. "I brought something for you."

"What is it?" she asked breathlessly.

"Open it and see." Dylan smiled in anticipation. He'd looked hard for just the perfect gift for her. He wanted something special.

She opened the box and found a little ivory-and-lace fan with a small scene painted on the handle. "Oh, Dylan, it's lovely. I . . . it's too lovely for words."

"Not nearly as lovely as you." He was pleased that she liked his gift so much. It made him feel much better about their relationship. "Not nearly."

Dylan reached over and tilted her chin up so he could look into her eyes. He immersed himself for a moment in their warm, whiskey color, memorizing every plane of her face as if he'd never see her again. He slowly lowered his head until his lips touched hers.

The contact sent shivers of excitement down Honor's spine. She always felt a thrill when Dylan kissed her, though he seldom did. It seemed that he was wrestling with himself over his feelings for her, but she could wait. Honor was confident that he would make the right decision eventually. When the kiss was over, she smiled at him and then looked at his gift.

She sat there for a long moment, staring at the fan. "We've known each other a long time, it seems."

"Yes," Dylan agreed and took her hands in his. "We've been through a great deal together."

"Dylan, when will it end? The war, I mean." Honor sat on the sofa and stared at the sputtering fire. "It's gone on so long now."

When he settled himself beside her, Dylan wrapped his arms around her and rested his chin on her head. He loved the sweet fresh scent of her. "I can't say, Honor. One day the Patriots seem to have the upper hand, but on other days, the British do. We just have to hope that the war ends while there is still enough of America to fight over."

"So many have died. At King's Mountain, at the Waxhaws, at Camden, here in Charleston. Even innocent people like Mrs. Edwards." Honor felt tears wet her cheeks once more. She looked up at Dylan through glistening eyes. "I'm glad we're on the same side, Dylan. I don't think I could bear it if we were not."

Chapter Fourteen

Christmas supper at the inn had been difficult for Dylan. Seated between Honor and Miriam, he'd felt like a traitor, though he was the only one among the group who wasn't. Everyone there, with the exception of himself, was a staunch Patriot supporter. He didn't belong with them.

And then, after he'd walked Honor and Miriam back to the shop, Honor had said the one thing that could make him feel even worse. There were many times when he'd cursed himself for being on the opposite side of this war, even though everyone thought otherwise, but her words had ripped through his heart with the swift strike of a double-edged knife.

He hadn't remained long after that. He couldn't.

Assuming his identity as London the spy, Dylan slid into the shadows beside the old wharf. From there, he commanded a view of the entire area. Cedric was due to arrive any time.

He heard someone coming, a slight scraping of boots on the rocks, and drew further back into the darkness. He didn't like meeting Cedric in town. This must be important.

When the man came into view, Dylan recognized his contact. He reached out and jerked Cedric by the cloak, pulling him into the shadows as well. "What do you want?"

Cedric straightened and glared at him. "Well, old boy, I'd just like to find out if you've heard anything more about what Greene's doing."

"Do you mean to tell me that you jeopardized our entire operation just to ask that question?" Dylan felt his anger rise as it seldom did. "If I knew anything, I'd pass it on to you as quickly as possible."

"Well, as you don't, I'll just take meself on down the street a ways. Got a notion to drop in at the Night's Pleasure. Been a while, if you know what I mean."

Dylan watched him go. When he got about fifty feet down the street, Cedric began to whistle. Dylan had known all along that his contact was different from the other men in the British espionage system, but now he knew he was positively dangerous. Something strange was going on with Cedric; the man would bear watching.

Honor smiled at Dylan. Ever since Christmas, he'd been much more...approachable. Nearly every evening he walked her back to the shop after the tavern closed. Nearly every evening, he came inside for a few minutes. He hadn't made love to her again—something was holding him back—but Honor knew he would if given the opportunity.

As they walked home, he slid his arm around her to ward off the cold, biting January wind. "I heard something today. Do you know who General Daniel Morgan is?"

"Yes, why?" Honor asked. Dylan didn't usually discuss the events or participants of the war with her, and she wondered why he was bringing it up now.

"Morgan and his men, including Andrew Pickens and William Washington, defeated Tarleton at a place called the Cowpens." Dylan opened the door of the shop and followed her inside. He removed her cloak and then his. "It was a major defeat."

"Oh, Dylan, how wonderful!" Honor threw herself into his arms. "Was Tarleton killed?" she asked finally.

"No, he got away, but a great many of his men were captured. This is . . . really bad news for the British, Honor."

"Does this mean the war is over?"

"No, not even close, I'd say. Tarleton's saying he's going to get Morgan if it's the last thing he does." Dylan remembered the red-haired officer with distaste. A cold-hearted man, Tarleton was rumored to have captured several women and beaten them, accusing them of spying. The idea was preposterous to Dylan.

"He's more than earned his nicknames," Honor said. "I hope this was his last battle."

For a short time, neither of them spoke. Dylan longed to tell her of his allegiance, but knew that such a thing was impossible. He could only hope that after the fighting had ended, the two of them would be able to talk out their differences. Dylan's feelings for her were growing stronger, in spite of his promises to himself. So far he'd managed to stay away from her bed, but it took a force of willpower he wouldn't have thought he possessed. He didn't know how much longer he could maintain his distance.

The touch of her lips on his, her fragrance, the soft press of her breasts on his chest all were saboteurs to his vows to remain apart.

Dylan began to talk about England, about his family's estate. "Honor, it's the most beautiful place I've ever been. Verdant fields, trees, a home that rivals some of the most opulent in Charleston. It should have been mine."

"It sounds wonderful, Dylan." Honor recognized the signs of homesickness. She realized that encouraging him to talk about it might help lessen the pangs. "Tell me more about it, about your family."

"We had horses and cows, coppices and fields. Several tenant farmers worked the land. My brother left before I did. He went to London to live. He didn't like the country." Dylan smiled ironically. "But my father left everything to my brother."

Honor knew little of the ways of wealthy people, but she couldn't understand why a man would do such a thing. "Why, Dylan? Why would he give the estate to a son who clearly didn't want it, instead of to a son who did?"

"Tradition. The eldest son inherits." Dylan practically spat the words, like epithets. "I receive a small monthly allowance, which will rot before I take any of it."

"I never thought that wealthy people had problems." Honor chuckled and shook her head. "Tell me about the—the rest of your family. What happened to your mother? What did she say about all this?"

"There's another sad tale. My mother left us when I was very young." Dylan shook his head sadly. "I suppose my brother takes after her. She went to London to stay, too.

Hated the country. Finally, she—she killed herself, because my father wouldn't give her a divorce.''

"Oh, Dylan, how tragic." Honor began to understand why Dylan was so skittish about permanent relationships. "My parents haven't exactly had a blissful marriage, either."

"What of them? I thought your mother had been ill for some time."

"Oh, she has," Honor admitted, looking up into Dylan's eyes. "But they never got on well. My father had . . . other alliances. My mother didn't want him in her bed, but she didn't want him in anyone else's, either." Honor considered the implications of what they'd both revealed about their mothers. "Makes women sound a little self-centered."

"Whether you are aware of it or not, Miss Richmond, most women are quite selfish." Dylan kissed her forehead and cuddled her against his shoulder. "Don't pout. I know you're not."

He kissed her mouth, to stop her retort. He was so hungry for her. He needed her so badly that there was no stopping him this time. No amount of willpower could have prevented him from taking her up to her room.

Honor knew that his reaction was probably due to his homesickness, but she didn't care. Once in her room, she removed her clothes quickly, lest he change his mind. Snuggled with him beneath the covers of her bed, Honor turned into his arms and kissed him, first on his mouth, then his face, then his neck and broad chest.

Honor took the tiny pebble of a nipple into her mouth and sucked gently, teasing it with her tongue and teeth as he had done with hers. When he groaned, she nearly cried out with happiness. Honor knew nothing about pleasing a man, but with Dylan's patience, she was determined to learn.

He drew her on top of him, her slight weight hardly noticeable as he wrapped his arms around her, relishing the silken feel of her skin against his body. He slid his hands down her back, cupped her buttocks and then rolled her onto her back. Desire surged in him as never before as he plunged his tongue into her mouth.

Honor could hardly breathe. Dylan's kisses were powerful, taking her breath away. His fingers played down her body, teasing and toying with her until she thought she would

scream out with passion. Throbbing between them, his manhood hardened, and she shyly reached down and touched it.

Dylan gasped, but continued to kiss her, finally pushing her
hand away and plunging into her moist sexuality. "Oh, God,
Honor, I love you, my darling."

"And I love you, Dylan. I have for a very long time."

Their pace quickened. Honor moved with him, her body
not her own to command. She felt much like a rhapsody, his
to direct and give meaning to. Her self-expression became his
to govern as she smothered him with her kisses.

Dylan suddenly felt free. He had said the words, words that
had hovered on his tongue like moths seeking the brightest
flame. All the months of pent-up passion flamed through him
like volcanic eruptions, until he could contain himself no
more and spilled his seed into her.

He realized that she hadn't experienced the same level of
gratification, so he continued to move within her until her
own explosion came seconds later, wracking her body with
wave after wave of pleasure. When she finally began to
breathe normally again, he slid to one side and kissed her.

Dylan knew he'd told her that he loved her. With those
words came a kind of release he never expected to find. The
entire act of making love had been lifted above, far above, the
ordinary. He couldn't brush off what he'd said as simply
words uttered in the throes of passion, for even though he'd
never acknowledged his feelings to himself, they'd been there.
Nothing, he realized, would ever be ordinary with Honor.

A woman as independent as she certainly was might be
difficult to live with, but Dylan felt he was up to the task. And
for once, he truly looked forward to something. "Honor, I
meant what I said."

"I know, Dylan," she said quietly. "I've known it for some
time. I was waiting for you to discover it for yourself."

"I love you. And you love me, too?" Dylan let the words
roll off his tongue. Once said, they came more easily, as rep-
etition makes a task effortless. "Remarkable."

"Yes, I do." Honor snuggled against his chest, reveling in
the feeling of loving and being loved by a man like Dylan Alden.

"Honor, no matter what happens—no matter what occurs
in the future—we won't allow it to come between us." Dyl-

an's thoughts shifted to his occupation, to his loyalties. "Swear to me that you won't turn your back on me."

"What could possibly happen that would—"

"Promise me, Honor." Dylan held her close, as if when he let go she'd disappear. "I need to hear your promise."

"I promise, Dylan. I won't ever turn my back on you."

"And I make you the same vow. Whatever happens in the next few months, nothing will come between us." Dylan kissed her to seal their pact. He could only pray that when she discovered the truth about him, she would remember their promise.

Honor had never considered marriage until recently. And she wouldn't now, except for the fact that the two of them were very much alike. They could get married and work for the Patriot cause together.

She wondered if she should tell him what she was doing, her contribution to the cause. She didn't want to spoil the precious moments of soft edges and gentle touches and buoyant feelings that followed their lovemaking, however. She smiled as if she had achieved something wonderful. She was learning to please the man she loved in a way she'd never expected. Honor slid her fingers across his chest, playing with the thatch of light-colored hair.

Once again his kisses became urgent, demanding. Honor felt the passion rise in her, bidden by his touch and filling her with a scintillating charge that sped through her like fire through dry grass. His fingers, his kisses were magical, elemental, able to kindle her most energetic and sensual responses.

The scent of their lovemaking mingled with her flowery fragrance, and Dylan gazed down into her eyes, a shaft of moonlight filtering through the window to highlight her face. Perfection. That was Honor, in so many ways.

He guided her to a second, more exhilarating level of satisfaction, blending his fluids with hers in a sweet mixture of love. Her body glistened with pearlized droplets of perspiration, salty to his taste when he kissed her breasts. He felt her shiver beneath him as she floated down in the sweet cocoon of the aftermath of their lovemaking.

Suddenly, Dylan felt humbled that this woman should love him, that she could be wise enough to allow him to come to his own decision, without pressing him to make up his mind. An extraordinary woman, no doubt.

For the first time in his life, Dylan looked forward with pleasure to the future, one that seemed much less bleak than what he'd always envisioned. The prospect of beginning a new dynasty, breaking ground for his own crops and living in the warm glow of love with Honor shattered his feelings of distrust for women. His heart basked in the new freedom of love that welled within him, unbidden, but welcomed by this enigmatic woman who'd taught him that experiencing his emotions wasn't necessarily a painful venture.

With her cuddled in the crook of his arm, Dylan felt his body relax. All the tensions melted away as if her touch was somehow a purgative, ridding him of all that would hold him captive. Smiling, he inclined his head toward her and inhaled deeply. He would never again smell flowers without thinking of her.

At dawn, Dylan slipped down the stairs and left through the back door. He didn't want anyone to see him leave. Honor's reputation was something that he would guard as viciously and rigorously as he knew how. Though she'd given him the precious gift of her love, he didn't want it to taint their relationship in the years to come.

The thought of marriage went with him as he strode silently through the swirling mist toward his lodgings. They would have to talk about the details later. Dylan realized that he had nothing to offer her, nothing but his love. He understood that, for Honor, that would be enough, but it wasn't for him. Within the next few weeks, he would find out where the most fertile lands were around Charleston and begin his quest to purchase a place for them to begin their life together.

For now, he must be content to see her when he could. Marriage, until the end of the war, was out of the question. His job was too dangerous. Dylan refused to expose her to the possibility of becoming a widow within days after they married. She probably wouldn't expect to be married right away, but she would believe that the event would take place in the near future.

Even with Honor, he couldn't relate the details of his part in the war, not until all was decided. His work was too critical, especially now that the tide seemed to be turning in favor of the Patriots. For the next few months, he would be busy in his dangerous task of obtaining and passing on information. He would have to wait to tell her.

Honor awoke and Dylan was gone. For a long time she lay there, hugging the pillow where he'd laid his head. A warm and lovely feeling of contentment filled her as she snuggled against the pillow and breathed in the scent of him. Closing her eyes, she could almost feel his touch again. What a wonderful night she'd spent.

Then she jumped out of bed and peered out the window.

Outside, the mist swirled, hiding anything or anyone who might be standing down there on the street. Like a tangible cloud of mystery, the moisture enveloped Charleston in its silver-gray depths, daring her to venture into its heart to see what awaited her.

She thought that the mist was a little like her relationship with Dylan. As the sun rose, the mist would lift a bit here and there, exposing new insights into the complexity that she had discovered between them. Unfolding as the relationship warmed, the sweet mysteries beckoned her to press on, to discover more and more.

That unveiling, she decided, would have to be up to Dylan. He'd said he loved her. Honor hugged herself and somehow knew that everything would be all right. She recalled his promise to her, and hers to him. Having made those vows made her feel like she already belonged to him, and he to her. It was a wonderful feeling, one she wanted to revel in for the rest of her life.

During the next few days, scattered reports of skirmishes filtered through the tavern. Honor listened to them and to the men who told the stories, but found nothing that would help her cause.

Jeffrey stopped by the shop early one morning, and she poured him some coffee. He sat there, staring into the steaming liquid as if he didn't intend to say anything at all, but merely wanted her company. Honor knew that when he was in such a mood, her best option was to wait for him to say something. Chattering would only distract him.

After a few minutes, he looked up at her, as if he'd just realized she was there. "Oh, Honor. I'm sorry. Forgive me for . . . being so doltish."

"There's nothing to forgive, Jeffrey. We're friends." Honor smiled. "Have you noticed how nice Miriam looks these days? I'm sure she's about the prettiest girl in Charleston."

"What?" he asked, as if her comment was the last thing he would have expected her to say.

"Miriam. Don't you think she's pretty?" Somehow, Honor had to get Jeffrey interested in their friend, who was as in love with Jeffrey as Honor was with Dylan. "I think she likes you a lot."

"Me?" Jeffrey stared at her for a few seconds. "Honor, what are you talking about?"

She leaned forward slightly. "Jeffrey, I think she loves you."

"You're teasing me, of course." He smiled and rocked back in his chair. "Are you sure?"

"No, I'm serious." Honor sighed. Why were men so thick skulled? "Jeffrey, I think you should be nicer to her."

"Miriam?" Jeffrey repeated, as if the idea of becoming closer to her was suddenly appealing.

"Well, anyway, why are you here?"

"Oh, yes. Something's wrong, Honor." Jeffrey stood and began pacing. "The information we're getting is wrong about a third of the time."

"You mean the things I tell you—"

"No, not so much the information I get from you. But someone is passing us wrong details intentionally, I believe."

Honor considered the implications. "Gracious! I never expected anything like that. What can we do?"

Jeffrey sighed and shrugged. "Nothing, really. The problem is that if we start to pick and choose the items we believe are real, then we run the risk of eliminating the effectiveness of the organization."

"We do have a problem." Honor thought about it for a little while, resting her chin in her hands. "Maybe we should act only on information we obtain from more than one source. Didn't you say you often get the same tips from several people?"

"Yes, but the trouble is, some of the best information we've gotten has been from a single source...like your report on the salt and supply wagons."

Honor's head jerked up, and she stared at Jeffrey for a few seconds. "You sent someone! Even though you told me you couldn't."

He grinned sheepishly. "I couldn't pass it up. We need salt too badly, along with the other things we got."

Honor jumped up, hugged him, and began to dance around the room. "And I thought my first foray into the field of prostitution had been worthless."

"Nothing is really worthless. Even the erroneous information. Eventually, it will help us to track down the man who's been supplying it. I'm just afraid we don't have enough time."

"What do you mean?"

"I now keep a record of where I obtain each piece of information. If it turns out to be erroneous, I can go back to that person to ask a few questions."

"What a wonderful idea." Honor settled back into her chair. "We should know very quickly then."

"Maybe." Jeffrey studied her for a long time, sipping his coffee wordlessly. After he'd emptied his cup and accepted another, he grimaced. "Honor, there's something else."

"What?"

"I'm changing your position—promoting you, so to speak. I want you to concentrate on what I'm telling you. From now on, forget merely listening for tidbits of information."

Honor was intrigued by his words. He was promoting her. "And? Tell me what you'd like instead. I'll do whatever you say—as long as it's not quit, or something like that."

"I think there's a British spy who's as good as you are, maybe the man I'm searching for." Jeffrey gazed at her, never breaking eye contact. "We've got to find out who he is and eliminate him."

The breath flew out of Honor with a whoosh. "Eliminate?"

Jeffrey stood up abruptly, overturning his chair. He righted it and started to pace again. "This isn't my idea. Do you remember the day you came to Lincoln's office looking for me?"

Honor smiled faintly, recalling the event well. "I must say I did a fine job of acting."

"Too fine, it seems." He came to stand beside her, peering down into her eyes. "One of my superiors happened to witness your little . . . entertainment. He thinks you're the only person we have who can get close enough to this man without him realizing we're looking for him."

Her eyes closed briefly. This was really the first time that an accolade had come her way. To her, it was a compliment of the highest degree. "I'll do it. What do we know about him?"

"Nothing," Jeffrey admitted, sagging back into his chair. "Nothing at all. The only thing we know for sure is that he knows whatever *we* know, most of the time. And he's got to be stopped."

"But, this could take months. Where do you suggest I start?" Honor asked, recognizing the monumental task she'd been handed.

"I believe you need to use all the sources you currently have. You can't ask questions—that would immediately draw suspicions. You need to listen more critically, especially for names—possibly ones that sound like code names."

"Like Lynx?" she asked, smiling again.

"Exactly. Except I doubt that the British have a woman as lovely as you, one who could be called a 'lynx-eyed spy.' "

After Jeffrey left, Honor began to devise her plan to trap whoever this man was who was sabotaging the Patriot efforts. She would have to divide her time between the White Point Inn and the Night's Pleasure Inn, she decided. She hoped that the patrons from one place wouldn't recognize her if they frequented the other.

Honor needed to think. She wanted to go somewhere to be alone, to feel the cool air swirling around her. Her Charleston lay out there, and she succumbed to the urge to go out and enjoy the cool winter's day.

The city was waking up, its silence giving way to workers traveling to their businesses, to soldiers marching to their posts. Honor pulled her cloak about her, drawing the hood over her head.

The overcast, pearlescent sky was vigorous with misty movement, as if the winds were conducting a ballet. Toward the west, the clouds were darker, billowing and swelling as they gained strength. The weather was changing. Soon there would be rain.

Honor hurried her footsteps, breathing deeply of the cool, fresh air that smelled of the coming rain. The palmetto trees rattled their swordlike fronds in eager anticipation of an early-morning drink.

For a time, Honor didn't pay attention to where she was going. Her feet were merely following the most convenient way—straight ahead—until she reached the Ashley River. The Ashley's usually gentle movement was more frenzied today, almost a match for Honor's mood as she skirted a grove of palms and edged along the high-water mark to avoid getting her skirts wet.

She loved the river. As a child, she'd often played there with Miriam and Jeffrey, while Della and Joseph dug for clams and oysters or fished. As she walked along, the wind picked up, throwing sand in her face, and the palmettos thrashed back and forth, their fronds shrieking and rattling. Rain began to fall in tiny droplets, tossed about by the mounting air currents.

It soon began to fall in earnest, pelting her face, and the wind threw her hood back, allowing the downpour to drench her hair. Behind her, the surging tide raked across the beach, obliterating all trace of her footsteps. If something happened to her, nobody would ever know where she'd gone.

Honor smiled at her gloomy fantasy, but glanced toward the churning water nonetheless. She realized, too late, that she shouldn't have walked so far from home. A quick stroll around the area near the shop would have sufficed. Hurrying along, she spotted the shack where Jeffrey had met her several months before, when he was hiding out from the British. Though its condition was decrepit, she would, at least, have some protection from the wind and rain.

Praying that the building wasn't inhabited, she yanked the door open and stumbled inside. "Not fit out for anyone. The average fool would have known better than to venture out into the hostile elements," she scolded herself.

She looked around. The room had been a fisherman's shack at one time. There was little in the way of furniture, except for a table in one corner and the rickety chair she'd sat in when she'd talked with Jeffrey. Rain poured through the roof in so many places that she might just as well have tried to make it home.

Wondering if she should even bother to stay, she glanced again at the darkened corner where the table sat. It was too dark for her to tell, but she thought the earth under the table might be dry. She walked over, bent down and tested it with her hand. "Dusty," she muttered, weighing her options. She could either make a dash for home, stand there beneath the sieve that served as a roof or crawl under the table and sit in the dust.

After glancing out through the crack in a broken board, Honor opted for the dust. Her cloak would be damaged beyond repair when its wet fabric combined with the dust and sand on the floor, but she had no real choice: outside, the wind howled like a predator, closing in on its prey. Huddled beneath the table, she waited for the storm to let up.

Dylan cursed himself for not waiting to meet with Cedric. Anyone with common sense would have postponed the meeting, but his news was too important. Battles did not wait upon good weather.

Cedric was late. Dylan hid in the brush as he usually did, peering up and down the riverbank to make sure he hadn't been followed and that Cedric wasn't, either. Accused by many of being too cautious now that the British controlled Charleston, Dylan nonetheless continued his meticulous ritual regarding these meetings. Just when he was about to decide that Cedric wasn't coming, the man appeared, struggling along the bank against the wind.

Dylan waited until he was close enough to be recognized with certainty, then strode forward to meet him. "Let's go inside," he called, his voice captured by the wind and sucked up into the swirling rain.

Honor's eyes grew large with fear. Who was outside? The muffled sounds of voices teased her, but she couldn't recognize either. Then the door flew open. Two men surged into the room, stamping their feet and shaking their clothes, and then apparently, examining the room, to see if they were alone.

Holding her breath, Honor saw them both slowly turn their heads, practiced in their search. Both of them saw the table, gazed at it for a few seconds and then completed their inspection.

When they were satisfied that all was well, they began to talk—and Honor began to breathe again, inhaling in tiny breaths that sounded to her like they vied with the wind for its raucous quality.

"Better," the first man said, banging the door shut.

"I say, chum, you'd better 'ave a good story for your old pal, Cedric, to git me out in this blaster," the second man fairly shouted. He was nearer to Honor, standing between her and the other man.

Trying desperately to see and hear everything, Honor sat motionless in the deep shadows under the table. She would have given anything to see the two men's faces. The first man sounded like a British gentleman, though she couldn't hear him well enough to recognize his voice. He sounded slightly familiar, but with the howling of the wind and pounding of the rain, she could hardly even hear herself thinking.

The second man shouted, "Can't 'ear a bloody thing."

Again, Honor couldn't hear much of what the first man was saying. Something about a British supply post. Then she heard him mention supplies. Was he with the British government, perhaps in charge of sending supplies to their outposts? She would have given her left leg to hear everything, but couldn't, no matter how hard she strained.

She thought of Dylan and wondered if his bad leg troubled him more in this kind of weather. Della claimed that weather affected wounds. The man's voice sounded a little like Dylan's, but she'd seen this fellow rush through the door, stamping his feet. And Dylan never wore a hat.

She heard the man say something about getting ready to ship the supplies to Wadboo Bridge when the rain let up. Honor perked up a little more. The man was in charge of supplying the British outposts. He was sending something up to Wadboo Bridge, one of the supply posts.

So excited now that she could hardly keep still, she held her knees tightly to her chest. She wanted the men to leave so she could report to Jeffrey. He'd told her to forget this sort of thing, but supplies were important to the Continental army right now. What with Morgan racing through North Carolina with his men to meet Greene, more supplies than ever would be needed. The Continental army was growing larger and hungrier every day. Her report might help to alleviate part of that problem.

As Honor thought of her new mission, she wished again that she could see these two men's faces. One looked to be nearly six feet tall and the other just above. The shorter man's hair was brown; the taller man's head was obscured by a hat that covered most of his hair and shadowed his face. Even if the lighting in the shack had been better, she could not have seen his face very well.

The wailing of the wind, combined with the dangerous situation, made her feel like shrieking loud enough to be heard in heaven. Her fingers shook, which she told herself was due to the cold, though she knew herself to be lying. Honor refused to give in to fear. She'd been through too much, had lost too much, had come too far, to do so. She was a true Patriot, she told herself inwardly, a soldier worthy of the trust of her superiors and of her countrymen.

Thinking such thoughts made her feel better. She strained once again to hear, though the two men weren't talking much now. Honor wished they would leave. Her legs ached and her head was becoming stopped up. She was afraid she might sneeze at any moment.

The taller man finally strode across the room and peered out a crack in the wall. Then he hurried back to join the other. They stood there for a moment and then opened the door. Rain dashed into their faces, but the taller man left.

Through a loose board beside her, Honor watched the man run up a slight incline and disappear over the hill. The second man waited a few minutes, an eternity to Honor, and then slipped out into the elements in turn. Honor, through her loose board, watched him leave the way he had come, from somewhere toward the harbor.

How long should she remain? Was it safe for her to leave her hiding place? Suppose they'd spotted her, and the first man was circling back to catch her? Indecision beat upon her as steadily as the rain beat upon the shack.

Honor stayed hidden for about thirty or forty minutes. When she could crouch under the table no longer, no matter what happened, she crawled out and gratefully stretched her numb legs. Rubbing them vigorously, she began to feel the pins and needles that brought the feeling back.

* * *

Dylan squatted in the reeds and sea oats, watching for Cedric to leave the shack. The eerie feeling that had haunted him while he was there remained with him, but he hadn't seen anyone enter the building, nor had there been anyone inside. When Cedric had gone, Dylan waited still longer, just to be sure about his feelings. He wasn't often wrong.

After thirty minutes of pounding rain and vicious wind, he rose and walked away. As he neared the edge of town, his limp became more pronounced. Soaked to the skin, he hurried to his lodgings to change clothes and have a nice bowl of Della's hot stew.

Chapter Fifteen

Honor put a candle in her window the moment she arrived home. In fact, she put candles in every window, and prayed that Jeffrey would remember their signal. If he came by.

The dreary day continued as it had begun, alternating between deluges of rain and then periods of misty fog. Honor paced back and forth, peering out first one window and then another. Jeffrey, and in all likelihood, Paddy, like other normal beings in the city, was closeted away, toasty and warm by some fire as they waited for the storm to pass.

Miriam sat by the fire in the kitchen, sewing happily, humming as she did so. "Honor, you're worrying me to death. Why don't you sit and get warm."

"You don't seem to understand, Miriam," Honor said, pausing to stare at her friend. "I've got to find Jeffrey now."

"As much as I'd like to see him, I don't envision him traipsing out through the rain to drop in unexpectedly." Miriam put down her sewing and looked at the serving girl. "I can't do anything with this wild-eyed woman. Can you?"

The girl put down the onion she was dicing. "Ever since I knowed you two, you's been as different as the sun and the moon. I can always count on Miss Miriam to sit and sew, quiet like the moon. Then there's Miss Honor. She be just like the sun, pacing there, ready to explode."

"What would *you* do, Miriam?" Honor asked, dropping into a chair to prove that she didn't have to pace back and forth to think.

"Well, I can tell you for sure I wouldn't go out in a rainstorm like this—"

"Achoo!" Honor snatched her handkerchief and dabbed at her nose.

"—and catch my death of cold." Miriam rose and went to the shelves. She fetched a jar of honey and a bottle of rum. Mixing the two in a cup, she glared at Honor. "Now, I want you to drink this and go to bed. I'll get the warming pan right now."

"Miriam, I can't—"

"Drink it, or I'll send for Della." Miriam crossed to the door and took her shawl off the hook. "She'll see to it that you take your medicine. I don't believe you want the kind she'd bring."

Honor wrinkled her nose, remembering the awful potions Della had dosed her with when she was a little girl. "No, you're right. I'll have some of this, after all. Thank you very much. Please sit back down."

Miriam chuckled and resumed her needlework. "Have you seen Jeffrey lately, Honor? Has he said anything about me?"

"Yes and yes." Honor sipped the honey and rum, wondering if Jeffrey had ever kissed Miriam. "I think he likes you, Miriam. He just doesn't know how much yet."

"Well, that Mr. Alden sure likes you." Miriam eyed her friend closely over the shirt she was working on. "Has he...mentioned marriage?"

"Miriam!" Honor exclaimed, jumping up and toppling the cup of honey and rum. "How can you suggest such a thing? I—we...Mr. Alden is a nice man, a gentleman. What would he want with the likes of me?"

The serving girl looked from one woman to the other. "I b'lieve you two're gonna be arguing when you gits to heaven...if you gits there." She stared significantly at Honor. "If you don't do more going to church and praying, and less giggling and flirting with them men, you ain't neither one gonna ever see them pearly gates."

Honor opened her mouth to speak, but thought better of it. She leaned down and picked up the cup. "I'll mop this up. Don't worry about it."

Glad she'd consumed most of the potion, she grabbed a rag and wiped the floor. "There. That should be fine."

A little later, the sky lightened a bit and the rain stopped. From the banks of clouds over the Neck, Honor realized it would begin to rain again soon. She could wait no longer.

"I'm going to find Jeffrey," she announced, grabbing Miriam's cloak.

"Honor, don't you get my cloak wet!" Miriam called as she slammed the door.

Jeffrey was living in the cellar of a house out near the edge of town. The old widow who lived there had been a friend of Jeffrey's parents and was happy to let him stay. The building was in poor condition, so the British hadn't found any use for it.

Honor went down one street and up another, backtracking and checking to see if she was being followed. There were few people on the streets and none of them was interested in her. She hurried along, reaching her destination before the rain started again.

Knowing that he was in the cellar, Honor went to the cellar door and banged on it. After a long hesitation, she called softly, "Jeffrey, are you in there?"

The door opened and Jeffrey jerked her inside. "What in bloody hell are you doing out on a day like this?"

"Looking for you." She wrenched free of him and turned to glare. "You don't think—*achoo! achoo!*—I'm out for a stroll—*achoo!*—for nothing, do you?"

"Sounds to me like you're taking a cold." Jeffrey looked more closely at her and placed his hand on her forehead. "You've got a fever."

She brushed his hand away. "It's nothing."

"Don't say that. You could have some—"

"Jeffrey!" she exclaimed, sneezing three more times. "Listen to me. I've some news for you."

"About the spy?" Jeffrey led her across the tiny room and they sat down. "What?"

"No, it's not . . . well, it might be." Honor couldn't say for sure if one of those two men was her spy or not. "I can't be certain. I just can't. But listen to this."

"I'm listening."

"I went walking this morning and wound up down at that old shack on the Ashley River about the time the deluge started."

"Speaking of deluges, let's start back toward your house. I think the wind is picking up again, and I want to make sure to get you home before the rain begins."

Honor rose and they walked toward the door. "Jeffrey, they were talking about sending supplies up to the Wadboo Bridge supply post."

Jeffrey stopped and stared at her for a long moment. "You're sure?"

"As sure as I could be. I was crouched under that table in the corner while they were talking. The wind was shrieking and howling and the rain was pounding, but I tried to hear as much as I could." Honor felt another sneeze coming on and lifted her handkerchief to her nose.

Opening the door, Jeffrey peered out into the yard. "Maybe if we hurry we can make it."

As they rushed along, Honor told him about the name she'd overheard. "'Cedric,' I'm sure. He sounded very British. Like he'd just arrived recently."

"What did he look like?"

"I don't know. It was too dark in the cabin. The other man had on a hat that shadowed most of his face." Honor hurried along, Jeffrey's long legs taking such great strides that she had a hard time keeping up with. "Slow down, I can't walk that fast."

He slowed his pace and took her arm. "It's starting to sprinkle a little. We need to go as fast as we can."

By the time they reached the house, the rain was coming down steadily. Honor hurried inside and removed the damp cloak. "Not too wet, Miriam," she said, hanging up the woolen garment by the fireplace.

Miriam smiled brightly. "Well, hello, Jeffrey. How good to see you."

Honor watched the two of them for a minute and decided that the time had come for them to be alone. "Miriam, I feel simply awful. I think I have a fever."

Miriam crossed the room to her and placed a cool hand on her forehead. "My goodness' sakes alive! You're burning up. Get upstairs right now and put yourself in bed."

Honor hadn't intended for Miriam's reaction to be quite that strong, but she obeyed anyway. She did feel bad. Her head was stuffed up and her body was wracked with shivers.

After stripping Honor's clothes off and tucking her firmly in bed, Miriam went back downstairs. She stopped by the kitchen to talk briefly with Jeffrey, and then went to find the servant Della had sent over. She sent the girl straight to the White Point Inn.

Della was in the common room, making sure the women who worked there were doing their jobs. "Honor done took sick. She's coughing and sneezing and her forehead is hot as can be. Miss Miriam say come quick."

"I knew I shouldn't have let that child leave this house. Her pappy ought to be whipped for letting her go." Della told the serving girls where she was going, went back to the kitchen and found her heavy cloak, one that had once been Honor's. She picked up several jars and tied them in a kerchief and handed it to the girl. "Let's go."

When they reached the sewing shop, Della marched straight in the door and back to the kitchen. She saw Miriam and Jeffrey sitting there talking quietly. "Mr. Jeffrey, what are you doing here when there ain't no chaperon for my babies? You know better than that."

"Uh, sorry, Della. I—I was just going to leave. I was—was keeping Miriam . . . Miss Edwards company until the girl returned," Jeffrey stammered, hating himself for doing so. But ever since his childhood, she'd treated him like he was her child, too. Nobody else in the world had the power to make him feel like Della did. "I'll go, now that you're here."

Della chuckled and shook her head. "Harrumph. Up to no good, I'll warrant." She glanced at Miriam and saw the blush that warmed the girl's pale cheeks. "I reckon you can stay, since we're back. If you behave."

"Yes, ma'am."

With a grin, Della hurried up the stairs, following the serving girl. "That boy ain't never gonna grow up."

"You scared him to death," the girl said. "You scares us all, sometimes."

Della stared at her for a second. "It's a good thing, too. That boy always was a handful of trouble." Della stopped outside Honor's door. "Honor and Miriam is gonna be like my own babies till they die."

Without knocking, Della burst through Honor's door and crossed her arms over her chest. She glanced around the neat room, and a hint of a smile touched her lips. She quickly repressed it. "Honor, what have you been doing to get yourself sick?"

Honor opened her watery eyes and peered at Della, feeling better just hearing the woman's voice. "I got caught out in the cold rain this morning."

"That ain't gonna make you this sick. Takes a mite longer and a lot more than that." Della studied Honor for a minute. "Must be some of them folks come in the inn gave this to you. Everybody is sneezing and coughing these days."

"It's just a cold, Della. I don't know why you're so worried." Honor didn't feel like answering a lot of questions or doing a lot of talking. Her throat felt dry and scratchy. "But thank you for coming."

"Harrumph! You've got no more sense than a bantam hen. Hopping off in the rain like some toady frog." Della began to open jars, continuing her diatribe about Honor's ways.

Dylan peered out the window. The weather had changed little since he returned from his visit to the warehouse. Even though the afternoon skies had lightened, as dusk drew on the rains reappeared, and the winds continued, with no signs of letting up. There seemed little respite from the cold deluge, even in the common room.

He wanted to see Honor. The day had gone badly, since his shipment was late being sent out. The British desperately needed the supplies that had been scheduled to go out this afternoon, but hadn't because of the weather.

Tomorrow would be better. He'd make sure the shipments left and then he'd stop in to see Honor. That should improve his mood.

Dylan's foul mood was due to several things. First was the impossibility of getting the shipment out as planned. The second was his meeting with Cedric, who had seemed distracted. Dylan was certain something was wrong, that Cedric might have been holding something back. And last was the continuing momentum favoring the rebels.

That hurt most of all and put Dylan into a dark frame of mind that pervaded everything he did. He'd worked so hard for his cause, spending nearly every minute possible to assure a British victory in the war. Even the defeat of Charleston had been tainted somewhat. Dylan didn't approve of Clinton's dishonest tactics, nor of Tarleton's savagery. Cornwallis wasn't much better.

Dylan felt that the momentum gained by the Patriot forces was directly due to the mismanagement of the Southern campaign. It was one thing to defeat an enemy, but another to flout the victory in the faces of the losing soldiers. That, along with Tarleton's outright butchery of surrendering soldiers, had given the Patriots new rallying points.

Unable to stay cooped up in the inn any longer, Dylan pulled on his cloak and darted out into the damp night. A visit with Honor would cheer him when nothing else would.

"But, Della, I'm perfectly able to come down to supper." Honor blew her nose and glared at the woman who was more like a mother to her. "Go home. I'm sure Papa needs you. Don't worry about me."

"Well, if you didn't think you were a duck, I wouldn't have to be here. Now I am. I sent a girl to help your pa. You just keep under those covers and drink this hot broth." Della crossed her arms over her chest and sat there staring at Honor. "Do you want me to spoon it into you?"

"No, thank you, I'll manage." Honor realized that her attempts to make the woman leave were wasted. Della intended to stay until she was better.

Miriam poked her head into the room. "Honor, Dylan is here to see you. What shall I tell him?"

Della came to her feet and squared herself in front of the bed. "You tell that man that Honor won't be seeing him anytime soon. Then you tell him it isn't proper for him to call when . . . I'll tell him meself."

Honor watched with horror as Della hurried down the stairs. "Stop her, Miriam. Don't let her be mean to Dylan."

Miriam giggled as she turned to leave. "You should have seen Jeffrey when Della came in. He was six years old again."

Alone, Honor struggled into her skirt and bodice, pulling a heavy shawl about her shoulders. Della could do a lot of things, but keep her from seeing Dylan wasn't one of them. Her head swimming from her sudden movements, she rushed down the stairs. As she neared the kitchen, she heard the Irishwoman scolding Dylan.

"And another thing. No real gentleman calls on a lady who doesn't have a proper chaperon." She leaned forward slightly, her finger near Dylan's nose. "My girl isn't no wharf woman you can come in and see any time you please. I'm not gonna have you ruining her reputation."

"The furthest thing from my mind," Dylan said, trying to reassure the woman. He didn't understand what had gotten into the her, unless it had something to do with Honor and Miriam living alone. Until now, she'd been all friendly and sweet, but apparently something had happened to change her opinion of him.

"It had better be." Della opened her mouth to continue, but Honor touched her arm.

"I'd like to speak to Dylan, if you don't mind, Della." Honor felt a little unsteady and sagged down into a chair. "Please sit and have some hot soup and coffee."

Dylan glanced at Della, as if he expected her to charge at him and throw him out. "Well, if you're sure it's all right."

Honor glowered at the woman, hoping to quell any further outbursts. There was precious little chance of that, Honor knew, if Della had anything left to say. "Of course, it's all right."

The older woman said nothing, but poured a cup of coffee and brought him a steaming bowl of soup. "Mr. Alden, I have one thing left to say to you. If you ever did anything to hurt my girl, I'd hunt you down and—"

"Della!" Honor exclaimed, jumping up and immediately losing her balance. She fell toward Dylan, and he caught her as she launched into a fit of coughing.

"Honor, by all that's good and decent, why didn't you stay in bed?" Dylan asked, helping her back to her chair. "I'm perfectly capable of taking care of myself." He looked at Della and raised his eyebrows. "I believe this young lady should be in bed. Would you mind if I escort her upstairs? I promise I'll return immediately."

"I'm not even worried." Della almost smiled, but she caught herself in time. "I know I can trust you, Mr. Alden."

He lifted Honor and carried her, protesting, up the flight of stairs. "Honor, you should be more careful. This cold could easily turn into something worse."

"I'm fine. I simply have a winter cold." She smiled brightly, but her nose was red and her cheeks were flushed with fever. "Don't worry."

Leaning over to put her in bed, he kissed her forehead and then covered her up. "I suppose someone *else* will help you change clothes."

Honor nodded. "I believe that would be best, particularly since Della is likely to come storming up the stairs at any moment to see what's keeping you."

"Well, I'll stop by tomorrow to check on you." He kissed her on the forehead once again. "We'll talk when you're better."

When Dylan returned to the kitchen, he found Della waiting. She eyed him speculatively, but said nothing. He ate his soup and talked with Miriam for a few minutes, but without Honor's cheerful presence, there was no reason for him to linger.

He slipped out into the damp, chilly night, feeling very alone. At least the rain had almost stopped.

Walking slowly down the street toward the White Point Inn, he realized he was being followed. Taking deliberate care not to frighten away whoever had decided to make him his target Dylan moved into a narrow street that had several houses set behind tall brick fences. As soon as he turned the corner, he darted into the first recess and waited.

The sound of muffled footsteps continued, and Dylan huddled in his hiding place, waiting to see who might have followed him. The moments stretched into minutes as his pursuer rounded the corner and then stopped, apparently wondering what had happened to his prey. Dylan held his breath. Then the footsteps began again, hesitant at first and then with more confidence.

Dylan wished there was a moon to cast shadows. Had there been, he might have determined how much farther the man had to come before reaching him. Finally, he reached the wall where Dylan was hidden. Dylan took a deep breath and jumped out in front of him, grabbing his coat. "Why are you following . . . Cedric! Why are you following me?"

"Take it easy, mate," Cedric said, trying to free himself from Dylan's grasp.

For a second, Dylan didn't release him. When he finally did, Cedric looked annoyed, but Dylan didn't care. "Why are you following me?" he repeated.

"Got a bit of a problem to discuss." Cedric straightened his coat and waited.

"Well, get on with it." Dylan glanced up and down the street. He didn't like the idea of Cedric coming specifically to look for him. "I don't like this above half."

"Seems that some of our superiors believe there's a spy for the Patriots what's finding out too many of our secrets."

"My opinion is if they learn *any* of our secrets, it's too many." Dylan knew that trying to hurry Cedric was as useless as trying to get past Della would have been a short time ago at Honor's house.

"Got to git 'im." Cedric stared at Dylan, as if to gauge his response.

"What do you mean?"

"You. You got to git 'im." Cedric grinned maliciously, obviously enjoying putting Dylan in the position of being recognized with him. "Got to be stopped, and you're the man to do it. 'E's too good."

Dylan considered the situation. The Patriots, apparently, had a spy who was stealing British secrets, one man who was better than all the others. "What do you mean by 'stopped?'"

Cedric drew his finger across his throat. "Give 'im a proper smile, that's what."

Suddenly, Dylan's blood ran cold. He'd never killed a man, except in self-defense. Now he was supposed to discover this man's identity and kill him...no, murder him. "Who sent this order?"

"'Fraid I ain't at liberty to say, chum." Cedric drew back slightly, as if he suspected that Dylan might strike him. "You know that."

Dylan knew well the orders concerning the passage of names from one level to the next, but he felt that this was one command that deserved special treatment. "I won't do it, unless I know who gave the order."

Without waiting for a reply, he turned and walked away. He knew that Cedric would either follow after him or return and report Dylan's refusal to obey a direct order.

Cedric caught up with Dylan and turned him around with a jerk. "I didn't say it was a request, *London*. You've been given an order. You know the penalties for refusing to obey. Sounds like treason to me."

"Not you nor anyone else can expect me to kill a man on suspicion. Nor will I do so without knowing who gave the order." Dylan poked a finger into Cedric's ribs. "Now, you just go back and get permission to tell me."

"I'd say yer makin' a huge mistake, chum." Cedric brushed away his hand. "You might say that we 'ave a l'il insurance that you'll do what we say."

For the second time, Dylan felt the cold pounding of his blood through his veins. "And what do you mean by that?"

"Oh, just the matter of the tarts what lives in the shop you just left. Might git to like spendin' a l'il time in prison. I bet their 'ealth would suffer a bit, 'specially that wisp of a dark-haired wench."

Fury flew through Dylan like wildfire and he threw Cedric against the brick wall. As he drew back to hit him, reason took over. Without a doubt, if he hit Cedric, then Honor, and maybe Miriam, would suffer. Gripping the man's coat with the steely grasp of rage, Dylan glared into his eyes. "If you ever harm either of those women, I will hunt you over the Earth and kill you with a great deal of pleasure."

Fear palpable in his countenance, Cedric slid away from Dylan and shook himself slightly. "Well, chum, I'd git to lookin' fer the man you was told to find, if I was you."

He slipped away in the darkness, apparently hurrying to escape Dylan's wrath. For a long time, Dylan stood there, his forehead touching the bricks Cedric had recently been pressed against. Long ago, he had recognized the possibility of this event, but he hadn't foreseen what had finally caused it.

He had vowed early on that when his spying became a danger to his friends, he would stop. Now it wasn't quite that simple. Dylan considered his role in the war to be noble. He understood that because of the task that had been assigned to him, he would make lifetime enemies of the "friends" he made in Charleston. But he'd hoped for understanding on the part of the people of Charleston. None of that had come to pass—yet. The enemy he'd made was on his own side.

He never doubted for one second that Cedric would follow through with his threat. For now, Dylan's only choice seemed to be the path that Cedric and his faceless, nameless superior demanded of him. Could Dylan comply?

For several days, Honor felt miserable, but the cold gradually relinquished its hold on her and she felt better. Her father had been furious with her for two reasons. First, she wasn't working. Second, Della refused to leave Honor while she was sick. None of her father's blustering could convince the Irishwoman to budge one iota.

When Honor finally returned to work, several of her regular customers voiced their approval. The new serving girls weren't nearly as efficient and good-hearted as Honor. She went about her regular tasks, serving food and drinks, charming everyone as she went.

Every day, Honor found time to spend with her mother, who seemed increasingly weaker. There were days when she'd smile, but most times she simply stared. No matter what her mother's condition, Honor talked to her as she always had, as if she understood every word. She frequently talked about Dylan, hoping that somehow her words would break through that barrier and reach her.

She enjoyed her work. Though she was always tired at the end of the day, Honor went happily about her tasks, teasing and flirting, once again listening for information that might lead her to the man for whom she was searching.

Most nights, Dylan watched her, happy again to have her nearby. He continued to walk her home every night—for fear of Cedric's trying to fulfill his promise, he told himself. But deep down inside, he knew it was because he loved her.

On March 1, 1781, ratification of the Articles of Confederation occurred, though Honor didn't hear about it until more than a week later. Privately, she celebrated, for this was one more sign that the war was being won by the Patriots.

She went about her task of discovering the identity of the British spy. Her inquiries met with little in the way of results that pleased her.

One afternoon she decided to visit with Echo. She hurried down to the large pink house and knocked at the door. Wilma opened it and smiled happily. "Good to see you again, Miss Honor."

"I'm happy to see you again, too. Is Echo here?"

"She's in her room. I'll tell her you're here."

Honor waited in the foyer. The house seemed still and quiet compared to the last time she'd been there, when the parlor had been bustling with activity. The place had a certain charm in spite of its riot of vibrant color, so unseemly compared to the pale pink exterior walls.

"Miss Honor, she says come up."

Honor knew her way and went straight to Echo's room. With a quick glance toward the room she'd used when she'd entertained Otis Renfrew, she tapped on Echo's door.

"Come on in," Echo called from inside.

She was seated at her dressing table once again, and Honor realized that even though she might be a genuinely nice person, she was a bit vain. Since women in her position relied on their appearances for their income, Honor smiled and overlooked that particular shortcoming, which in Echo somehow seemed endearing.

"Hello, Echo," she said, crossing the room to hug her friend. "I've missed you."

"I heard you were ill." Echo stuck a ten-inch hairpin into her coiffeur and then turned to look at her. "You seem a little pale to me."

"I'm feeling much better. It was just a cold." She sat down on the sofa and waited for Echo to finish with her hair. "Though Della treated it like a serious illness."

"You can never be too careful."

"I think she takes things to the extremes, though." Honor felt a bit uncomfortable talking about her own health.

"Well, so be it," Echo said, patting the last curl into place. "Let's talk. What have you been doing?"

"I've been working hard." Honor explained about having to work doubly hard for her father after her illness. Echo nodded with understanding. "But I have something else to talk with you about."

"What is it?" Echo looked at Honor for a moment. "This is business?"

"Yes." She considered several ways of approaching the matter and decided that the simplest way was always best. "Echo, I've been given the job of finding a British spy. He's probably the one who has caused us the most trouble, infiltrating our system, discovering our secrets. I've got to find this man quickly, before the British find a way to regain their lost momentum."

Echo nodded slowly, as if she were considering the implications of Honor's assignment. "I agree with that, but it's a little like checking every dog in Charleston for fleas. Where do we start?''

Honor looked at her friend, dressed now in gold satin and black feathers, and smiled. ''This is a job for a woman. A devious woman. And I happen to know two of them.''

Chapter Sixteen

"I'm so tired I could fall down on the walk and fall asleep right here," Honor said, wondering if her feet would ever stop aching.

"You shouldn't work so hard," Dylan said, wishing he could do something to make her life easier.

Honor nodded in agreement. "You're right, but I don't have much of a choice."

Dylan cursed himself inwardly. If he weren't so involved in espionage for the British, he could do something about the situation. He could marry her, if she'd have him. In the past few days Honor had been a little distant and he wasn't sure why. When they reached the house, she hesitated. He slid his arms around her and held her close, saying nothing for a long time.

"My darling," he whispered against her hair as he inhaled deeply of her enticing fragrance, "if I could, I'd marry you today and end your slavery to your father."

His words echoed through Honor's mind, touching every part of her with sadness. She didn't know why Dylan couldn't marry her, but she knew why *she* couldn't marry *him*. She had a difficult and dangerous job to do, one that she couldn't shirk, even for her own gratification. "Don't worry, Dylan. We'll work this out . . . later."

He'd expected her to be upset with him. After all, she was his wife in every way except for carrying his name. They'd made love; they'd acknowledged that love. Only the formality of sealing their vows before God was left to be done. *Maybe she's so shocked over hearing that I can't marry her that she doesn't know what to say.* "Honor, soon, I promise.

When all this...all these battles are over—when there is peace once again—we can begin to make plans.''

She smiled at him. He obviously thought she'd rant and rave about his taking advantage of her or some such nonsense. She stood on her tiptoes and kissed him lightly. "Don't worry, Dylan. I truly understand. I know we can't make any foolish commitments now. Our time will come."

After kissing her good-night, Dylan walked away. He stopped on the corner to evaluate his thoughts. He was happy that she understood that he couldn't marry her, but disturbed that she'd taken the news so calmly. Somehow, it hurt his feelings, and he didn't know why.

Honor put her discussion with Dylan out of her mind. She didn't know his reasons for wanting to wait for marriage, but she was glad he didn't press the issue.

Discovering the identity of the British spy turned out to be much more difficult than she had ever imagined it would be. For days, seemingly without end, she had listened to every conversation at the inn, until she felt that if she heard one more word of boasting she'd start laughing hysterically. One evening she returned to her room, sat down and removed her shoes. Her feet ached and she rubbed them vigorously as she talked to Miriam.

"I simply don't understand how this man works. It's almost as though nobody in the entire city of Charleston knows who he is—on either side." Honor wriggled her toes and leaned back, allowing herself to relax for the first time all day.

Miriam stopped sewing and watched Honor thoughtfully. "It seems to me that you're working at this too hard. One of these days, someone will say something that will set in motion your—your whatever it is inside you that makes sense of all you hear. Don't be so impatient."

Honor gazed at her friend. Never in all the years that they'd known each other had Miriam sounded so calm and logical. In the past few days, she had changed considerably. "What's going on, Miriam?"

Picking up her needlework, the seamstress shrugged. "I don't know what you mean."

"Yes, you do. You know exactly what I mean." Honor leaned forward and eyed her friend suspiciously. "Is something... Are you and Jeffrey... that's it!'' she leapt to her aching feet, hardly noticing them. "Tell me everything. Every detail.''

The servant winked at Honor. "That boy's been underfoot so bad I can't get my work done. I done tol' Miss Miriam that she gonna have to git shed of him so we can work. Else we ain't gonna have nothing to eat.''

"Now, he hasn't been here that much, and you know it. Why, he's hardly—"

Honor laughed and held up her hands in protest. "She's just teasing you, Miriam.''

"Oh." Miriam smiled meekly and returned once again to her sewing. When she looked up, her face was red. "The two of you are being mean to me, and I don't know why. Jeffrey is just being nice.''

"Of course. I'm sure that's all it is." Honor winked at Tilda. "We understand.''

Feeling happy that she'd done something good for two dear friends, Honor went upstairs to bed. She lay there for a long time, thinking that maybe the world was changing for the better. She was glad to be a part of it.

Dylan stood in the shadows, thinking about Honor. When he'd walked her home, she'd seemed distracted. That she was tired, he had no doubt. The tavern had been even more crowded than usual, and one of the serving girls hadn't come to work in several days, forcing Honor to work doubly hard for longer hours.

These days, he spent a great deal of time wondering how he was going to tell her about his part in the war, though he couldn't be assured that he'd ever have to. With Cedric's increased peculiarity, Dylan wasn't sure what would happen.

Being discovered by the opposite side would probably prove fatal. Cedric had lost all sense of security. He seemed to care little if their association were made known but Dylan still cared. Without anonymity, his usefulness would come to an end, not to mention his life. Even in a city occupied by the government he worked for, there were too many rebels for him to escape unscathed.

His thoughts kept returning to Honor, and her response to his statement that he couldn't think of marriage. Why had she been so calm about it? Why hadn't she shown more emotion? It almost seemed to him that she was relieved, but that was impossible.

The sound of footsteps brought him back to the present. Leaning forward slightly, he looked down the street. A man was sauntering toward him, as if there were no cares in the world, not to mention a war going on. The man was Cedric.

Dylan waited until Cedric was close enough to touch and then pulled him into the shadows. "God's blood, man, what are you about?" He peered up and down the street to see if anyone had noticed them, while Cedric disengaged himself.

"I say, mate, yer a bit touchy this evenin', ain't you?" He straightened himself and stared angrily at Dylan. "You'd think you was in a den of thieves."

"Cedric, *my friend,*" Dylan began, placing a strong emphasis on the word friend, "we're in an occupied city—a place that may be the biggest stronghold of the Patriot cause. Whether you choose to believe it or not, these people merely tolerate us while they wait to be freed by the rebels. I suggest you understand that and act accordingly."

"I've never run across anyone as scared of shadows as you."

Dylan bristled at the slur, but decided against making an issue of it. "Listen, Cedric, we're here for a purpose. What have you to tell me?"

"I was just coming to that." Cedric lit a cigar and puffed a couple of times before speaking again. "As I mentioned before, we thinks there's a rebel spy what is as good as me boss thinks you are. I thinks 'e's better."

With a quick glance around, Dylan nodded, ignoring Cedric's insult. "You told me before, or have you forgotten? Are there further instructions or more information?"

"You've been picked to find 'im."

"What are you up to, Cedric? We talked about this before. I know my assignment." Dylan was still surprised that he'd been given a task that might ultimately reveal his identity as a spy to the Patriots.

"As I said, if you'd been listening, me boss thinks yer the best we got." Cedric watched the glow of his cigar die in the misty air. "I 'ave me own opinion, but I guess it don't count."

Once again, Dylan ignored Cedric's barb. "Are there other orders? Any clues or suggestions? Why are we meeting again about this?"

"I told you all we know. Somebody for the damned rebs has been pilfering our information. Yer job is to find out who and eliminate 'im.''

Eliminate. The word resounded once again through Dylan's mind like thunder. "Cedric, you've told me nothing new. What is going on?"

"Nothing, mate. Just want to make sure you understand the orders.'' Cedric shifted his weight from one foot to the other, as if he were uncomfortable with the subject. "Just want to make sure you ain't got soft.''

Dylan straightened and glared at the man standing nervously before him. "I understand my orders. What I want to know is why you've chanced exposing us for nothing."

Cedric grinned a bit lopsidedly. "You just worry 'bout doing yer job. I don't never do nothing for nothing, chum.''

For a long time after Cedric drifted into the mist, Dylan stood there staring after him. All his instincts told him that the man had acted suspiciously. Suddenly, he wondered if Cedric might have gone over to the other side. If so, had he attempted to expose Dylan by signaling for this senseless meeting?

His last words resounded through Dylan's mind like thunder: *I don't never do nothing for nothing, chum.* What could he possibly mean by that? Were the Patriots paying Cedric now to act on their behalf? Would Cedric actually change sides? To the last two questions, Dylan had no answers, but his suspicions pointed in that direction. From now on, he'd have to be extremely careful.

Honor placed steaming bowls of oyster stew on the tables. She'd worked so hard to determine the identity of the British spy, but still had nothing to show for her efforts except for sore feet and aching muscles. She was beginning to believe that the man was a myth, but the evidence proved otherwise. Many of the same secrets that she passed on to Jeffrey miraculously got passed on to the British.

The same news about shipments of goods often resulted in the British and American forces meeting and battling to control the supplies. Honor had poured over every scrap of information, every informant in an attempt to discover the name of the spy. Once she had a name, even a code name, she could close in.

This night, the small dining room was full of bawdy talk and boastful tales. She hated serving these particular men, even though she'd gleaned good information from them in the past. One man, a surly looking man with scraggly brown hair and hazel eyes, swilled down measure after measure of rum, hardly paying attention to the men around her.

He kept eyeing Honor, studying her as if to memorize everything about her. She'd handled drunks before; she'd handled forward men on the street; she'd handled potentially dangerous men, such as the one on the wharf. But she felt instinctively that this man was one she should be wary of.

And then he spoke. She'd heard the voice before. Where?

"And I says to 'im, 'Chum, it's yer job. Do it.'" The man rocked back in his chair and allowed his gaze to follow her around the room.

Honor went downstairs and filled her tray with more cups of rum, more stew and more bread. Her mind was busy, darting about like a firefly on a warm summer's night. Who was he? Where had she heard that voice?

As she neared the room again, she could hear the man talking. Just as she was about to open the door, she froze. He was one of the men on the riverbank, that morning when it had rained so hard! He was one of the men in the shack where she sought shelter from the storm!

"Don't know where the bitch has got to. Be hell to pay if she don't come back soon with our food."

Honor held her breath for a second. He sounded mean. She consciously calmed herself as much as possible, put on the carefree smile she always wore when serving her customers and opened the door. No matter what happened, the man must never find out that she'd been hiding that day in the shack. He would kill her without hesitation.

"Here we are, gentlemen." She placed the food on the table and began exchanging empty glasses for full ones. She noticed a spill and wiped it up, all the while listening to the continuing conversation.

"Name's London, you say?" one man asked, plunging his spoon into the stew.

Honor perked up a little, but didn't divert her attention from the spill. She carefully wiped one way and then the other, folded her cloth and repeated her motions. The silence that followed seemed protracted, and Honor could no longer make a pretense of wiping the table. She threw her cloth onto her tray and surveyed the room.

Most of the men were paying no attention to her. The man with the dark hair and surly expression was watching every move, however, almost as if he knew what she would do next. The other twenty or so men, packed into a room designed to accommodate no more than twelve, were looking at him.

Without appearing to hurry or to dawdle, Honor forced herself to walk from the room at her normal pace. *London.* She knew the name was significant or the men wouldn't have watched the surly fellow so expectantly. She knew, deep inside, that London was no ordinary man. The speaker had been too secretive, too precise in his gestures and movements, too alert to her every move to be a normal, everyday customer.

With conviction arising from her instincts, Honor realized that London must be the man for whom she was searching. She fought hard to keep the excitement from her eyes as she continued about her duties, so as not to raise anyone's suspicions. Her heart fluttered in her chest like dragonflies hovering over a pond, and she was sure that someone would notice.

When she went into the common room, Dylan was there. He smiled at her, but she hardly had time to speak to him. Finally, she became free for a few minutes and went over to apologize. "I'm so sorry. We have a private group in one of the rooms and I've been so busy running in and out that I've hardly had time to think."

"I'm here to walk you home, not intrude on your duties." Dylan looked around the still-crowded room. "Looks like you won't be ready to leave soon."

Honor's gaze followed his. "No, I doubt it. Maybe you shouldn't...you don't have to walk me home, you know. I'll understand."

"Not walk you home? Nonsense." Dylan looked at the men still drinking and talking. "I have a brief appointment near the wharf. I had thought to walk you home and then take care of my rather unpleasant business. If you think you'll be here for another thirty minutes, I'll rid myself of this task and come back."

"Judging from the rate they're drinking, I'll be another hour." Honor smiled at him. She really didn't want to impose. He always seemed to be so busy. "No. I insist. I can walk home alone."

"I'll be back. You wait for me." Dylan rose, tossed a few coins on the table and walked out.

Honor didn't have much time to think about him. Her customers kept her so busy that she forgot everything except the task at hand and the name London. If she finished work before Dylan returned, she would go to find Jeffrey. He needed to know of her discovery at once.

She was saved the effort. Jeffrey came in a few minutes after Dylan left. Honor collected payment from her customers and then hurried over to sit with Jeffrey as they left. "Jeffrey, I've discovered something."

"What?" He edged forward on his seat, leaning closer to hear what she had to say.

Honor waved at several men who were leaving, including the man with the familiar voice. She waited until the door closed after them. "I know the name of the British spy you asked me to find."

"You do? How did you find out?" Jeffrey clasped her hands in excitement.

Honor let him wait a moment in anticipation. "His name is London. I heard some men talking earlier."

"London," Jeffrey repeated, his brow wrinkling in thought. "I don't know a man by that name."

Sinking back in her chair, Honor shook her head sadly. "Neither do I, but it's a start."

"You know, Honor, maybe that's a nickname or—or alias...or a code name. Something like that. Maybe we're approaching this wrong."

Honor's eyes widened with excitement. "You're right. I'm sure you are."

"Don't be so quick to agree." Jeffrey leaned back slowly and considered the situation. "We can't afford to overlook anything, so we must consider the possibility that the man's name actually is London."

"I understand, but the way the word was said led me to believe...wait, Jeffrey!" Honor sat up straight, her hands clasped before her excitedly. "The man said, 'Name's London, you say?' I really think we are talking about an assumed name."

"Still, I don't want you to miss the truth because you've excluded a possibility."

With a smile of accomplishment, Honor nodded. "I won't. This is exciting."

Jeffrey sighed. "Honor, please take care. This isn't a game, as I've said so many times. These men are serious."

"I know that, Jeffrey." She could hardly wait to begin her search, now that she had her first real clue. She'd spend the next few evenings at Echo's place, and talk her father into hiring someone new to replace her.

When Dylan returned, he was disheveled, having slid down an embankment while looking for his contact. The man had never turned up, and all Dylan had to show for his effort was a mud-stained cloak and trousers.

Honor stared at him as he came in the door. "Gracious, what happened to you?"

He muttered something and walked over to where she sat talking with Jeffrey. "Hello, Jeffrey. Good to see you again." Dylan looked at Honor and grimaced. "Fell. On my way to meeting my friend. Can you wait a moment for me to change clothes?"

"Yes, I'll talk with Jeffrey for a few minutes longer."

Nodding, Dylan left the common room. When he was gone, Honor gazed after him for a moment. "Jeffrey, why not ask him to help us? He's clearly on our side and—"

"Honor, don't go telling me how to recruit men for our network." Jeffrey waited a few seconds for the words to take effect. "I've told you we can't hazard bringing in someone new right now. This is too critical a point to risk our entire operation. Nobody new—do you understand?"

"But, Jeffrey, we've known him—"

"Honor, promise me." Jeffrey gripped her hands and held tightly. "Promise me that you won't bring in anyone else, no matter how loyal they seem."

"I promise, Jeffrey, but I think we're making a mistake." Honor watched the doorway for a minute. "He would be an excellent spy."

"Who can say?" Something about Dylan still rankled Jeffrey, and though he attributed it to jealousy, he refused to give in to Honor. "Think of everyone else. Supposing he's a spy. Are you willing to risk the lives of all the people along the network?"

With a sigh of resignation, Honor turned back to him. "All right. Maybe we'll have this conversation again after the war is over and you can tell me how wrong you were."

"Or maybe, when we have this same conversation, you can tell me how right I was."

Dylan took Honor's arm as they walked along the darkened street. "What were you and Jeffrey talking about when I arrived?"

Honor felt color come to her cheeks. She'd promised Jeffrey she wouldn't reveal anything to Dylan, but she didn't like lying. "Nothing much. Just how many people had been in, the weather, Miriam—that sort of thing."

"Oh," Dylan said and wished he could see her face more clearly. She didn't sound very convincing. "It seemed to me you were having a rather serious conversation."

"Hmm," Honor said, as if trying to remember what they could have been talking about that was serious. "We must have been talking about Miriam, then. It seems Jeffrey likes her more than he ever imagined he could."

"So he's decided if he can't have you, he'll take Miriam."

"How did you know about that?" Honor asked, wondering if her personal life was as open as it appeared to be.

"I knew it the first time I saw him. The way he was looking at you was unmistakable." Dylan chuckled. "He even told me he'd do me physical harm if I ever hurt you."

"Dylan!" she exclaimed. "You've been talking about me to someone . . . to Jeffrey?" Her statement came out as a question.

"Not really." Dylan didn't want to tell her the extent of the conversation, nor mention the severity of Jeffrey's threat. "Just men talking. He loves you."

"Loved. Past tense." Honor wondered if Dylan might be a little jealous. The thought pleased her. "You're not jealous, are you?"

Dylan swallowed hard and tried to smile, though he wasn't certain she could see his face very well. "Of course not. Why would you ask a thing like that?"

Honor's smile widened. He *was* jealous, no matter how vehemently he might deny it. "Oh, I don't know. Curious, maybe."

They walked on a little farther and Dylan slid his arm around her. "I admit it. I am jealous. I can't stand the way some of those men look at you."

Feeling like leaping up to the roof of the nearest house and crowing, Honor tried to maintain her dignity. "And I'm jealous, too, so be careful."

They stopped simulteneously beneath the deeply bowed limbs of a live oak that grew near her house. Dylan leaned down and kissed her, holding her as close as possible. When he finally drew away, he looked at her in the near darkness. "Honor," he whispered, wishing that times were different. "Don't give up on us. We'll . . . our time will come."

"I've never doubted it. Besides, I'm going to make sure that—" Honor stopped midsentence. Someone was lurching drunkenly down the street toward them. The person, small in stature, stopped near her front door and fell. "I wonder who that is?"

Dylan, too, had seen the figure. "Too small to be a man. Must be a woman or a—"

"Boy!" Honor exclaimed, breaking free of Dylan's embrace and rushing toward him. "It's Paddy."

Dylan reached Paddy before Honor did. Even in the pale moonlight, he could see that the boy was badly injured and unconscious. Dylan lifted him carefully. "Honor, open the door, quickly."

Tears streaming down her cheeks, Honor obeyed, snatching the candle that lit the reception room of the shop. "Come with me." She fairly ran up the stairs, calling to Miriam as she went. "Here, put him in my bed." She tore back the bed covers.

Placing the boy on the bed, Dylan noticed that he was bleeding in several places and had bruises on his face. "Send for the doctor."

Honor rushed into the hallway, where she met Miriam coming out of her room. Tilda, the serving girl, was coming downstairs from her little loft bedroom. "Go get the doctor. Paddy is injured badly."

While they waited for the doctor, Honor bathed Paddy's face. Dylan removed most of the boy's clothes, and she grimaced at the knife wound in his abdomen. "My God, Dylan, can he live with an injury like that?"

"I don't know, Honor. Only the doctor can judge."

Honor went into the hallway and looked down the stairs. "What's keeping them?"

Dylan pulled her back into the room and pushed her into a chair. He thought for a moment that she might faint or grow hysterical. "Now, Honor, don't be ridiculous. Tilda hasn't had time to even get to the doctor's house yet."

"But he's just a boy. Who would do such a thing to a child?" Honor looked past Dylan. Paddy looked so young and fragile lying there. She gazed up at Dylan. "I'm all right. Let's try to stop that bleeding."

They worked side-by-side, one pressing clean cotton squares over the wound and the other wiping away the blood, which seemed to gush no matter what they did. After a few minutes, it slowed to a steady seep.

Honor watched the circle on the cloth turn red. She kept thinking of Mrs. Edwards and all the blood that had flowed out of her. "Do you think it's slowing down because we've succeeded in stanching the flow, or because he's got so little blood left?"

"I don't know, Honor, I—"

The door slammed downstairs and was followed by the sound of heavy footsteps on the staircase. Dr. Peterson burst into the room. "What happened? Your girl told me that this child had been injured."

"It's Paddy, Dr. Peterson." Honor stood protectively by the boy, unwilling to relinquish her position. "Is he...do you think it's bad?"

Dr. Peterson firmly moved Honor out of the way and lifted the pad. Blood continued to seep from the wound. "Knife wound, looks like. Clean entrance and exit. The bleeding is slowing down, but he's lost a lot of blood."

For a few minutes, Dr. Peterson examined the boy, making sure they'd missed nothing in their earlier search for injuries. "Looks like this is the worst of it," he said, returning to the knife wound.

"Is he going to be all right?" Honor asked, praying that the answer would be affirmative.

He applied a coating of salve and then a thick dressing. "You'll have to change this bandage frequently." He turned to face Honor. "Who is going to nurse him?"

"I will . . . *we* will," she amended, knowing that Miriam would want to help. "Della will probably help us, too."

"Good. She's an excellent nurse." the doctor stepped back and examined his handiwork. "Make many clean bandages. He'll need plenty of beef broth, spooned into him a little at a time. Beef makes blood."

After Dr. Peterson had left, and the other two women had gone to their rooms, Dylan stood there for a few minutes. "Honor, would you like for me to stay with him?"

Honor smiled wanly. "No, thank you. I'll do this. You need your rest."

"If you need me for anything at all, send someone." Dylan kissed Honor good-night and left.

Long after she was alone with Paddy, Honor stood over him, gazing down at the boy. Someone had meant to kill this child. Honor realized that this wasn't an accident or a case of mistaken identity. He was too small to be taken for another man.

"Whoever did this knew what he was doing," she said, drawing the covers closer around Paddy's shoulders. "Some vicious animal, not a man, chose to kill this boy. Who would do such a thing?"

Honor watched her patient awhile longer, noting his ragged breathing. After a while, she changed the dirtied pad. He looked so young and innocent, with his brown hair tousled about his face.

Who would intentionally harm a child? she asked herself again. *Someone who knew this child was a spy.* The answer came full blown into her mind.

Paddy had nearly been killed for being a spy. But who would do a revolting thing like that?

London.

Chapter Seventeen

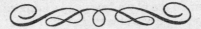

Honor nursed Paddy with all the dedication of a mother, though she'd never considered herself to be much of a candidate for that position. The rare smiles that filtered through the pained expressions rewarded her in a way she never expected possible.

Over the next few days, his condition began to improve. Dr. Peterson seemed pleased. "Honor, I attribute his recovery to you."

"I did nothing that anyone else wouldn't do," she protested, still happy that he felt that way. "Paddy's a fighter, Doctor."

"I can see that." Dr. Peterson closed his little leather bag. "Keep him still as much as possible. He needs his rest."

Honor found that task more difficult than she at first anticipated. Paddy was used to wandering as he chose and resented being cooped up against his will. "But, Paddy," she explained for the fifth time in two days, "you must remain still or that wound will break open."

"Honor, how come somebody did this to me?" the boy finally asked.

"I don't know, Paddy. I wish I could answer that question." Honor not only wished she could answer the question, but wanted to know with surety who had done it. She still suspected the man London, but had no proof.

"Do you think it's because I help Mr. Jeffrey?" Paddy's lustrous brown eyes were weak and watery, hardly the bright and alert pair that she remembered.

"I'm almost sure of it, Paddy." She breathed deeply and tried to smile. "I won't let anything else happen to you."

"I'll be looking out next time," he promised, wriggling in the bed. "Can't I get up for a while?"

"Not today." Honor watched him sigh and glance out the window at the signs of spring. "Soon, though. Paddy, do you have any idea who might have done this to you?"

He squirmed and shook his head. "No, but if I did, I would go and beat him up."

"No, Paddy, you mustn't." Honor was afraid from the grim expression on the boy's face that he intended to look for the man as soon as he was able to get out of bed. "Don't even consider the idea. It's too dangerous."

"But, Honor, he may try to hurt me again." the lad crossed his arms stubbornly. "I'm going to get him first."

"No, Jeffrey won't like it if you try to do that. You're . . ." Honor tried to think of something to convince Paddy of his value to the organization. "You're too important. You're the best ears Jeffrey has."

Paddy grinned and then gripped his side in pain. He slid back down on the pillows. "Maybe you're right. I'll have to think about it, though."

"You can't remember *anything* about the man?" Honor asked, hoping the boy could think of some detail, no matter how small, that would lead her to his attacker.

"No, he jumped on me down by the wharf in the dark." Paddy wrinkled his brow. "There was two of them, actually. One said something about 'London' just before they started hitting me. I wish they'd go back there."

Honor felt an icy realization descend on her with all the weight of a battleship. She was right; London was the nasty culprit. She'd get him if she never did anything else. Paddy was too small to seek vengeance, so Honor would do it for him.

Dylan entered the room. "How's Paddy today?" he asked with a smile.

"I'm fine. Getting strong." Paddy always brightened when Dylan was around.

"He's really doing much better," Honor confirmed, vainly attempting to forget what Paddy had said about London. She motioned for Dylan to sit down for a visit. "Talk to Paddy. I'm afraid he's tired of my prattle."

Eyeing her for a moment, Dylan chuckled. "I doubt that. You've never appeared to be the sort of woman who would bore a man. What do you think, Paddy?"

"Naw. She's fun, except she won't let me get up."

Dylan glanced at Honor, who was about to speak. "Now, Paddy, I'm sure she's doing exactly what Dr. Peterson said to do."

"That's right, Paddy. Remember what he said when he was here yesterday? Maybe you can come down to the parlor tomorrow."

"But I feel better today."

"Don't be giving Honor a difficult time, Paddy. She's stayed here with you ever since your attack." Dylan watched the boy's expression change to one of reluctant acceptance. "Do you know who did this?"

Honor listened to Paddy answer the same questions for Dylan in the same way he'd answered them for her. She had no reason to doubt that he was telling the truth, but she wanted to know if he'd remembered some detail he'd forgotten to tell her. Anything would help. But his story remained consistent. She was glad that he didn't mention the name of his assailant. If Dylan discovered who had committed this crime, he might go after the man himself.

Honor wanted to take care of the villain.

Accepting that he knew no more than he was telling, Honor began to think of other ways to discover what had happened. As soon as Paddy was well enough to be left alone, she planned to go and visit Echo. The two of them could come up with something if they tried.

Honor learned from Jeffrey that the Americans had launched a siege to retake Augusta. "But, Jeffrey, why won't you tell me the outcome?"

Jeffrey gazed at her. "The battle is still going on, Honor. We may not know for a long time. Remember how long it took the British to take Charleston?"

"Yes, but Charleston is larger than Augusta." Honor was impatient, but she couldn't help it. She knew that if the Americans were successful in taking Augusta from British control, then Charleston must surely follow. She could hardly disguise her excitement. "We've ratified the Articles of Confederation already. How much longer must Charleston wait to be freed?"

"Well, we're doing all we can do." Jeffrey hated these conversations with Honor. She was bright, too bright for him to gloss over the details. She wanted to know everything. He considered Dylan for a moment and almost chuckled. The man loved Honor, Jeffrey was sure of it. He wondered if Dylan knew what he would be getting if he married Honor.

"Well, I'm working on my task. I think I've got a plan for discovering the identity of our mystery man." Honor told Jeffrey about her decision to alternate between the tavern and Echo's, hoping to find someone who knew the code name. "I think Echo will agree to let me sit in the parlor."

"Honor, that's too dangerous. What if someone you know comes in? What if someone recognizes you?" Jeffrey groaned. "You take too many chances. Look what happened to Paddy."

"No, I don't. I'm just doing my job the best way I know how." She studied him for a moment. "What *about* Paddy? You're not planning to let him continue as a spy, are you?"

Jeffrey looked down at his hands. He felt some considerable guilt over Paddy's attack. "I don't honestly know, Honor. Paddy isn't the sort of boy who is likely to allow me to make demands. If he thinks he's still useful, he'll continue to spy."

"I thought you'd say that." Honor thought of the small boy, still unable to go out and play like normal children. "He's never had much of a childhood. I . . . we can't let him get hurt again, Jeffrey."

"I'll do all I can, Honor, but somebody knows who he is."

"London," she said flatly. "It has to be him."

"We don't know that. It could have been anyone. Even someone trying to rob him."

Honor's gaze was piercing. "Do you honestly believe that drivel? Who would rob a poor boy? Anyone who looked at him would know he had nothing of value."

"You're right, of course. I just hate to think that there's a man out there with no scruples about murdering a child."

Honor couldn't think about it anymore. She'd agonized over the same thought for days without arriving at any logical conclusion. She decided to change the subject.

"So what's going on with you and Miriam?" For a few seconds, she thought she caught the signs of a blush. "Come on, tell me."

"What makes you think that anything at all is going on?" Jeffrey finally asked, hoping she would drop the subject, though he realized that was almost as impossible as asking the waves to stay up on the beach.

"I recognize the signs. You have them and so does Miriam." Honor leaned forward to whisper, "Tell me, or I'll drop her a little hint that I saw you with someone else."

Jeffrey blanched. "You wouldn't."

"I think you know—"

"All right. You're a hard woman to deal with, Honor." Jeffrey grinned. He knew that she was only asking because she cared about both of them. "I'm falling in love with her. Do you think she likes me very much?"

"Jeffrey, you're as slow as a sea turtle crossing the sand." Honor placed her hands on her hips. "I mean, how long does it take to realize you love someone?"

"I confess. I do love her, but I can't marry her now."

"And why not?" Honor asked, wondering if she should admonish him to conduct himself as a gentleman. Miriam had nobody to make that speech for her. "Jeffrey, be careful with her feelings. Miriam does care a great deal for you. Don't . . . why can't you marry her now?"

"I'm a spy. If I married her, I might endanger her life. I wouldn't want to make her a widow the first year of our marriage."

"That's a ridiculous—" Honor stopped short. Wasn't that the exact same excuse she'd used with herself to justify her own reluctance to marry Dylan? And what about *him?* What was keeping Dylan from marrying her? Did he think that his warehouse position was so dangerous that he might be killed? She looked back at Jeffrey with understanding. "All right. I know you're right. Just don't do anything to hurt her."

Honor sat in Echo's parlor, more anxious than she'd been in some time. Jeffrey had been correct in his assessment of the danger to her. Though she and Echo took all sorts of precautions to prevent her from being recognized, there was still a chance she would be.

She glanced around the room. It was too early yet for many guests to be there, but she hadn't wanted to miss anything. Echo had decided that if someone approached Honor, she would simply say that her services had already been reserved for the evening and she was merely waiting for her "friend" to arrive. In the case that Honor took someone upstairs, the same arrangement as before was planned.

The time passed slowly, creeping by with the speed of honey dripping off a cold biscuit. Honor smiled a great deal and declined several offers. She wanted to remain in the parlor where she could hear the conversation. Dressed in her purple satin and black lace dress, she sat on the sofa and listened.

Several lively conversations were going on around her while men waited for girls to become free, but she didn't join in. She sat as quietly as possible, hoping to fade into the background enough to encourage unrestrained speech.

Suddenly, she heard her name—her code name—being called. "Lynx!" Otis Renfrew rushed across the room to her. "I've been looking for you for several weeks."

"My, whatever for?" she asked, fluttering her eyelashes at him. She hadn't anticipated Otis coming in. This could either be a complication or a godsend, she decided, and she didn't know which.

Then she saw the man from the tavern—the one with the scraggly hair. Honor turned her head slightly, so that he couldn't get a good look at her. If anyone recognized her, it would be he. She smiled at Otis. "Dear Otis, would you like to...spend the evening with me?"

"Why, yes, my dear. How kind of you to offer." Otis glanced past her and nodded slightly. "I was hoping you'd be free this evening."

Wondering if Otis had been signaling to the man who'd just come in, Honor rose with her back to the latter. She couldn't afford to take a chance on him coming over to talk to Otis. "I'll just ask one of the girls to bring you a drink." She leaned down so that he got a full view of her cleavage. "I had a prior engagement, but I'll see if Echo will cancel for me."

Otis gazed at her full bosom and licked his lips hungrily. "Yes, please hurry."

Honor signaled to Wilma, who brought Otis a drink. Honor hurried up the stairs to prepare for him and to escape recognition. She still couldn't be sure whether the man from the tavern had seen her or not, but she didn't want to take any chances.

She flew up the back stairs and crept along the corridor to her room. Once inside, she went straight to the door that adjoined Echo's room and tapped lightly. "Echo, it's me."

The woman opened the door. "What's wrong?"

"Two things." Honor glanced behind to make sure she hadn't been followed. "Otis Renfrew is here."

"That's no problem. He'll understand that you're—"

"That's not really a problem, Echo." Honor felt her mind rushing, touching on details and establishing plans more quickly than she ever thought possible. "I saw someone from the tavern, a man who would most assuredly recognize me, so I invited Otis upstairs. Wilma is fixing him a few drinks."

"I see. Then, you'll have to stay the night with Otis." Echo grimaced and looked at her. "I don't know how else to get out of this, since he recognized you from before."

Honor considered her options. She could abandon the search for London—at least the part of it that she executed from the Night's Pleasure Inn—or she could spend the night with the repulsive Otis. She smiled. "How long do you think the sleeping potion will last?"

"Until morning," Echo answered with a frown. "You're not seriously considering this, are you?"

"I am. I got information from him before. Who knows, I might discover something interesting. He may even know who London is." Honor smiled bravely at the thought. "If you can arrange to come in very early and demand that Otis leave, this might work."

"I can do that without any problem. I'll think of some plausible excuse." Echo began to reconsider. "This *might* work, Honor. I'll invent something. You cry or—or something like that. I'll come in and throw him out. By the time he realizes what's happened, it will be too late. He won't remember whether he hurt you or not." Echo hesitated. "Honor, don't do this. It's too risky."

Honor smiled and hugged her. "You're a good friend, Echo, but little Paddy was almost killed by the man I'm looking for."

"You don't know that for sure."

"I know deep down in my heart that he's cold-blooded enough to do it. I can't imagine anyone else who is." Honor paused a moment, allowing her anger to subside. "Besides, Paddy said one of the men mentioned London."

"He could have been talking about the city of London."

Honor shook her head vehemently. "You know he wasn't, Echo. You know that he was calling the other man London. It's too much of a coincidence."

"Well, right or wrong, you have Otis Renfrew to deal with this night. I wish you luck, Honor." She started to close the door between the two rooms. "You're a brave woman."

"No more than you," Honor replied, thinking about all the things that had happened during the past year. "I think, Echo, that some of us never realize what we can really do in life unless there's some catastrophic event. Given the chance, our heroic sides rise to the surface."

"Very philosophical for a young woman dressed as a prostitute," Echo said flatly and grinned. "But I expect you're right. Maybe we're the lucky ones."

Honor stood calmly by the window, looking out over the Cooper River. In the moonlight she could see the masts of several ships, reaching for the sky like dark fingers as they bobbed up and down on changing tide. Leaning against the windowsill, she remained there thinking about her earlier statement to Echo. She must be a horrible person to be thinking of war as something of a benefactor, but somehow she did. Because of the war she was learning more about herself. Because of the war she had met Dylan.

"Life is so...complex," she whispered to the moon. "We're in an intense love-and-hate, play-and-fight kind of life. How do we really know who we are unless we're tested?"

Before she could pursue her thoughts further, a tap on the door distracted her. She walked to the door, filled with a sense of dread for what she knew she must do. She'd already poured another drink for Otis, mixing in the substance Echo had given her. Had enough time elapsed for Wilma's drinks to take effect?

Summoning all her courage, she opened the door and let him in. Honor smiled her brightest smile, took his hand and led him into the room. "How very good to see you again, Otis."

He swaggered slightly and bent to kiss her. Honor turned slightly and he placed a wet kiss on her cheek. Before he could rectify the matter, she backed away and motioned to the turned-down bed. "Make yourself comfortable. I'll fix us a drink."

With her back to him, she could hear the sounds of his getting undressed. She went through the motions of pouring a drink while she listened for the cessation of noise that would indicate he was finished. She smiled as she turned around. "My, you must have been busy. I haven't seen you in ages."

"Been busy. Lots going on."

Dismayed that his speech wasn't slurred, she noticed that her hands trembled as she handed him the drink. "You're a very important man. I just know you are. All this war business is so exciting." She paused a few seconds and fluttered her eyelashes at him, then walked around to the other side of the bed and sat down on the edge. "Can't you help me understand? Most of the men who come in here aren't smart enough to explain things, but I know you are."

Otis beamed with pleasure. "Of course, my dear. Let'sh shee."

Closing her eyes briefly, Honor said a silent prayer of thanks that his speech was beginning to slur. He was beginning to feel the effects of the drink. She tried to look extremely interested in what he was saying. He droned on and on, primarily talking about how important he was to the war effort and how his information was so vital to the British, though his employer didn't know.

Honor had heard all that before. She continued to encourage him to talk, nodding and smiling as if his words were the most fascinating she'd ever heard.

"And I've found thish man, Cedric, who ish deeply embedded in the shpy organization. He pash-passes my news on to the proper pershon, who then acts on it." Otis sat there, his bare chest puffed out with pride.

Instead of choking him like she wanted to do, Honor said, "Oh, Otis, isn't that dangerous? I mean, what if someone found out what you were doing?"

He brushed aside her concerns with a wave of his hand. "I can handle anything that—comesh my way."

For better than an hour he boasted about his importance. Honor thought he would never fall asleep. When he finally did, she rose and went to Echo's room.

"He's a simpleton, Echo. How can the British use such a man? He was telling me things that he should never talk about, even before the drinks started to take effect on him." Honor paced back and forth as she spoke. She was angry that she'd wasted so much time on so little information.

"Honor, calm down."

She sat on the sofa and tucked her feet beneath her. "I'm sorry. I know I should be thankful that I got one little tidbit. A name is better than nothing."

"What's the name?"

"Cedric," Honor answered, leaning back and staring at the ceiling. "Otis apparently doesn't know Cedric's last name, if indeed Cedric is his name and not an assumed one."

"Sounds frustrating. You don't even know whether the man you're looking for is the very one you've been talking to. He could be, you know."

"You're right. I have to be careful." Honor considered the possibilities. "This Cedric could be the same person as London. He could be someone completely different. These could be assumed names or they could be correct names. Grr!" She groaned, jumping to her feet and starting to pace again. "Sometimes I think this situation will drive me mad."

"It is a puzzle, I admit." Echo stood and caught Honor's arm as she started past her. "Stop pacing and think rationally. You're not doing anyone any good like this, least of all yourself."

"I know, Echo, but it seems as if I'm getting closer and closer, but just can't reach out and grasp that last bit of vital information. This man has got to be stopped." Honor sagged down into a chair and propped her chin in her hands. "All right. We now have a new lead. I need to discover the identity of this Cedric. I'll take this step by step and solve this problem once and for all."

Honor slept most of the day. Her experience at Echo's had left her drained, too exhausted to even get up for meals. The fatigue came from the tension generated by seeing the man from the tavern, a man who would surely have recognized her. The closer she came to identifying London, the more dangerous her job would become.

She realized now, as she lay there, that she would have to be more cautious. If she went to the Night's Pleasure Inn again, she'd have to take extra steps to disguise herself. The excitement thrilled her, but frightened her, too. This job was more serious than she'd ever thought her part in the war would be.

At suppertime she dragged herself from her bed and went downstairs. Miriam and Tilda were talking in the kitchen. Miriam was sewing, as usual. This time she was attaching buttons to a man's shirt.

Honor glanced at it and asked, "Whose shirt is that?"

"Dylan Alden's," Miriam answered, never looking up. "He was by to see you last night."

Stunned, Honor whirled around and stared openmouthed at her friend. "What did you tell him?"

Miriam put her sewing down and looked at her. "I told him where you were, of course."

"You didn't!" Honor exclaimed, sinking into a chair. She was too astonished to be angry. "What did he say?"

"Oh, he said he'd stop by to see you when you felt better."

"What?"

Miriam chuckled and gazed at Honor. "I told him you weren't feeling well and had gone to bed early."

Honor clasped her chest, hoping to slow the pounding that threatened to break through her ribs. "Oh, Miriam, don't scare me like that."

"I'm sorry. I couldn't resist." She picked up her sewing again. "He's a nice man. Handsome, too."

Tilda looked up from her cooking. "Did I hear somebody knock on the front door?"

Honor glanced down at her nightgown. "Maybe you'd better go to the door."

Nodding, the girl hurried off.

Within seconds, Honor heard Dylan's voice. "Is she feeling better?"

"Yes, sir, Mr. Dylan, she's much better," Tilda said, speaking loudly enough for Honor to hear. "But she ain't dressed for company. She's been in bed all day. Just got up."

"Oh, well, I suppose I'll come back . . . tomorrow." Dylan glanced through the doorway and saw Honor sitting in a long white gown with tiny blue bows. The idea of her in a near state

of undress excited him. "Please tell her that—that I'll visi
with her then."

As he walked away, Dylan felt nonplussed. Just the sight o
Honor in her nightgown had excited him much more than h
ever thought possible. The gown covered more of her bod
than the dresses she wore when she worked in the tavern
Damn, but he wanted her.

Early the next morning, Dylan sat at his office table peer
ing across the river. He had another shipment scheduled t
leave for the Ninety-Six District, where Greene's men wer
amassing supplies to be sent to the fighting Continentals nea
Augusta. It grated on him to ship goods to the Americans, bu
he had little choice. If he suddenly changed sides, then hi
disguise as a Patriot sympathizer would be gone and he woul
be forced to give up his spying.

His leg was all but healed, and he had difficulty remem
bering to limp. Dylan didn't mind the limp. It separated hi
from his persona of London, who didn't favor his leg.

There came a light tapping at his door. He glanced up
wondering where his clerk had gone. "Come in," he called
wondering who would come calling at this time of day.

Honor opened the door and stuck her head in. "Are yo
too busy to see me?"

"Honor!" Dylan rose quickly. "Please, come in and sit fo
a while."

She walked to the chair he indicated and sat on the edge. A
the way there she'd argued with herself about whether or no
she should come. "I'm so sorry I wasn't dressed for receiv
ing callers last night."

"I hope you're feeling much better."

They talked about her illness, the one she didn't have
Honor felt guilty for lying to him and was tempted to tell hi
the truth, but she couldn't. She'd promised Jeffrey. Dyla
brushed back a lock of sandy blond hair and smiled. Hon
felt as if she could tell him anything. Jeffrey was being to
suspicious.

After a few minutes of trivial conversation, Dylan walke
over to Honor and drew her to her feet. He wrapped his arm
around her and kissed her soundly. "I've wanted to do th
for days. I've missed you."

"And I've missed you," she confessed breathlessly, clinging to him as if she never wanted to be away from him again. How she longed for all this to be over, for the strife and conflict to be past, so that she and Dylan could marry and settle down.

She loved him with all her heart. He loved her; he'd said as much on several occasions. They belonged together—she'd known it from the first day she'd met him. She'd always known he was different from other men.

The tenderness she sensed in him almost overwelmed her. Honor had never felt so safe, so secure in all her life. Looking back, she realized it had been that way for some time. Maybe that was a part of love—trust and security.

Nothing could come between them now. As soon as the war was over, their lives would be merged into one beautiful existence, and their happiness would last a lifetime. Nothing could prevent that. Nothing.

After a few moments, she extricated herself, smoothing her hair and clothing with nervous hands. "I—I really have to go. Will I see you tonight?"

His kiss was her answer. "Yes, I'll stop by. Let me walk you to the door."

"Don't worry. I'll find my way." She stepped through the door into the foyer. "Goodbye."

Dylan smiled and returned to his work as Honor walked through the small reception area and out the little gate. Then her heart stopped. Otis Renfrew was coming out of another door, and there was no way she could escape being seen by him.

"Lynx!" he exclaimed, rushing over to her. "What are you doing here?"

"Otis . . . I—I came looking for you." Color sprang to her cheeks, and she wondered how she would ever get out of this situation. "I—I wanted to apologize. For the other night. You see, I fell ill and—"

"Oh, you have nothing to apologize for." Otis glanced over his shoulder at Dylan's door. "I need to return to work. I'm afraid my employer will call me and—"

"Oh, I'm sorry. I shouldn't have come." Honor started toward the door. "I'll . . . shall I see you again soon?"

"Yes, you certainly will." Otis smiled broadly. "Maybe sooner than you think."

Honor hurried away, praying that Dylan wouldn't open his door. If he saw her talking to Otis, he might become suspicious and start asking questions. That would be a disaster.

Dylan heard voices. He listened carefully. Otis was a spy, or presumed himself to be one. Maybe he knew the man Dylan was searching for. "Otis!" Dylan called. "Come in for a moment, won't you?"

Otis glanced over his shoulder and rushed into Dylan's office. "Yes, sir?"

"Were you talking to someone?" Dylan watched the man's face, searching for a hint that the man might be lying.

"Er, yes, sir. I was." Otis swallowed hard and glanced around. "Is something wrong?"

"No. Who were you talking to?" Dylan didn't want to sound too interested, but he would like to know who Otis associated with.

A blush brightened Otis's cheeks. "A lady, sir."

"A lady?" Dylan asked, now more curious than ever. Could Honor still be out there? "What lady?"

"She's a . . . just a lady friend."

Dylan glanced past Otis, but saw no one in the outer office. "Would that be Miss Richmond?"

"Miss Richmond? Oh, no." Otis shook his head vigorously as he shifted his weight from one foot to the other. "Her name is . . . she's a . . . she works at the Night's Pleasure."

"There was a prostitute in the outer office?" Dylan gaped at Otis. Had Honor encountered the woman? Was she embarrassed or angry? Would Honor think that the prostitute was there to see Dylan?

"Only for a moment, sir." Otis sensed that his employer was in a mental turmoil. "Are you ill, Mr. Alden?"

"What?" Dylan asked, suddenly seeing Otis again. "Oh, no. I'm fine. Tell me something, did you see another lady in the office?"

"No, sir, should I have?"

"Not necessarily. It's just that I had a visitor, and she left only moments before you returned." Dylan let out a sigh of relief. Of all things that could happen, he wouldn't want Honor to be embarrassed. Dylan looked at Otis. "Mr. Renfrew, in the future, please see that your lady friends visit you at your lodgings instead of here."

* * *

Honor almost ran home. How could she have been so blind? Otis had told her a great deal about her employer, the Patriot sympathizer who shipped goods to the American troops. Why hadn't she realized that he must mean Dylan?

She shivered when she realized how close she'd come to getting caught in the web she'd woven for Lynx. From now on, she'd be even more careful.

What she'd thought could never happen almost had.

Honor had almost lost Dylan because of her foolishness.

Chapter Eighteen

Never had kisses thrilled Honor so. Dylan's fingers traced wispy trails along her breasts and stomach. All the anguish she'd suffered throughout the day because of her encounter with Otis was almost gone, save for the memory of her discomfort, which was fading quickly.

When Dylan made love to her, nothing else mattered. The war, the strife, her problems—everything seemed to be pushed into the background while she enjoyed Dylan's exquisite ministrations. Her body burned for him, yearned for him in ways she never would have thought possible.

Love, trust, friendship—all those emotions were a part of her feelings for Dylan and made their physical relationship all the more powerful. She wondered how she could have been so lucky to find a man so compatible with her, one who cared so ardently about the same things, one who loved her both physically and emotionally.

And what love. Dylan brought her to the edge of the precipice, letting her taste the sweetness that lingered just over the rim, but brought her back down again. Teasing her, taunting her with his expertise, he plied her body and mind with love.

Soaring like the fluffy clouds that dotted the springtime sky at sunset, pink and warm and wonderful, Honor clung to him, moving with him as one. Her fingers caught his hair, played with and caressed his cheeks, drew lines and circles on his chest and back. Honor opened her eyes. In the shaft of moonlight that filtered through her window, she could see him, one side lighted, one side shadowed.

When she felt as if she could stand no more, Honor pulled him close. "Now, Dylan, love me now."

"I do, Honor. I do love you." Dylan slowly increased their pace as an orchestra leader increases the tempo of a rhapsody. Their music became faster and faster until their rhythm burst forth in an exquisite climax, filling them both with unbounded passion.

Honor lay there, eyes closed as she reveled in the feeling of being well loved, cosseted now in the soft music of a lullaby. She lay nestled in the crook of his arm, dreaming of the day when they could be together forever. The word *forever* brought her back to reality. Their forever couldn't begin until her job was done.

Honor moved quickly among the tables, thinking about how often she'd done this very thing. She'd been serving here all her life, or so it seemed. These men, some of them, had been coming into the tavern for many years.

"Aye, Miss Honor, you're lookin' verra handsome this evenin' and I'll be wonderin' why." One of her customers, a Scot, winked at her and studied her.

Honor hugged him impulsively and teased him: "Because I'll be servin' a verra handsome Scotsman."

"Tease me if you will, miss, but I been noticin' yer quick smile. Somethin's made you a happy lass."

Without saying something that would give her away, Honor could do nothing but smile. She hurried on her way, talking and teasing as she always did. The banter was familiar and friendly.

Dylan came in. Within a few moments, several other men entered and went to his table. When it became apparent that they needed more space, Honor took them to a small dining room off the common area. "You'll have more room here, gentlemen."

For some reason Dylan seemed to be displeased with the presence of the men, or some of them. He went silent, and his face hardened into a blank glare.

Moving efficiently among them, she took the orders of the men she didn't know. She knew several of them and knew what they wanted to drink. When she returned with their beverages, she placed them on the table and took their orders for supper.

One of the men was the one who'd been watching her so closely for the past few days, the one she'd seen in the parlor at Echo's. Honor tried very hard to pretend that she didn't notice his scrutiny, but it was difficult because he made her feel so exposed, almost naked.

She threaded her way among the tables in the common room, having to serve in both dining rooms. She was puzzled by the presence of the man who kept watching her. Without doubt, he was on the side of the British, but here he was, sitting with Dylan, a known Patriot. If she ever could have doubted it, she'd seen the truth when she went to his office, and Otis had confirmed that the man he worked for was a Patriot sympathizer.

She felt as if she should warn Dylan to say nothing that he wanted to keep a secret, but remembered that he had never let slip anything of his plans. His rum didn't affect him as it did others. No matter how much he drank, he remained close with his secrets. Still, a word of warning might be in order.

Dylan was furious. Cedric should never have come here. To be seen in public together was unforgivable. Still, if Cedric had something to tell him, something urgent, maybe he had no choice.

During supper, Cedric kept watching Honor. Dylan bristled visibly. He realized that Cedric was threatening him by being there and ogling her. It was the man's way of telling him that his own progress on finding the Patriot spy wasn't developing quickly enough.

As the evening passed, Cedric eyed her carefully. When she was out of sight, he whispered, "Now there's a sweet one. I'll wager that she would give a man a romp worth fighting for."

Dylan choked back his anger. "Cedric, you've made your point. Why don't you leave?"

"I've got a bit of news. Does the name Lynx mean anything to you?"

"No, I don't recall ever hearing of anyone with that name."

"We've a bit of information that says the name of the spy is Lynx, but we don't know anything else. It may be a false lead."

Dylan watched Honor return with a tray laden with drinks. He looked at Cedric, who was again eyeing her with interest. "I'll begin immediately to verify this." He caught the man's arm to get his full attention. "Don't touch her, Cedric. Our relationship has always been tentative. I don't like your methods and you don't like mine. I'd hate for you to do something foolish that would destroy our 'friendship' beyond repair."

Cedric chuckled and tried to remove Dylan's hand. "Just do yer job and leave the skirts to me."

His grip tightening, Dylan glared at the man. "Harm her in any way and I'll hunt you down like the mad dog you are. Leave her alone. Do I make myself clear?"

Honor lounged seductively in the chair, one leg slung casually over the arm. The evening had been dull thus far. There were too few patrons at Echo's to liven up the evening, but she still had hope. For more than a week she'd been here as frequently as possible, watching and listening.

For the past few nights, she'd forsaken the wearing of her purple-and-black dress. Miriam had remade the rose silk into one a bit more seductive, and Honor, along with a blond wig and plenty of Echo's pasty makeup, had been sitting in the parlor listening. Occasionally she served drinks, but Echo felt that it would make it easier for someone to recognize Honor if she were doing something she did at the tavern.

Then the man came in. Something about him made her leery of him. His countenance spoke of anger, of violence. She'd seen it every time he'd been in the tavern lately. He held himself aloof most of the time. In fact, the evening he'd joined Dylan and his friends was the only time she'd ever seen the man with anyone else. Most of the time he simply stared at her.

Honor knew that this man held important secrets; her instincts told her he did, and she trusted them. Why was he here? Did he recognize her? Was he following her? If so, what did he want?

Then Otis came in. Honor froze, not knowing exactly what she should do. From her past experiences with him, she realized that he had some contacts within the British spy network, but she didn't know how deep they went. She couldn't afford to have him recognize her in her new disguise. Indecision confounded her for a few moments.

Then she decided that she'd have to at least talk to Otis. Maybe he would even know who the other man was. She smiled at him, and he came over.

"Have you seen Lynx?" he asked, looking around.

Honor could have crowed. He didn't recognize her. "No, sir, I don't believe she's here this evening. I'm waiting for someone, but if you'd like, you may sit with me until you . . . find someone else who strikes your fancy."

Otis looked uncertain, as if he might leave, then he changed his mind. He sat down and smiled. Wilma brought him a drink before Honor could signal that she wasn't going upstairs with him. She supposed it didn't make much difference. After a few minutes of pleasant conversation about the springlike weather, she asked the question she'd intended all along to pose to him. "Who is that man over there?"

Otis glanced across the room. "Him? His first name is Cedric—that's all I know." He looked at Honor as if he wanted to impress her. "And—" he leaned closer, dropping a kiss on her cheek "—I believe he's a spy."

"Spy?" Honor repeated, as if shocked by the revelation. Her hand went to her breast and she looked at Otis with such sweet innocence that she almost laughed. "You mean he's passing information on to those—those rebels?"

"Oh, no, miss." Otis leaned back smugly. "He's with us. He's managing our network. Very important man. Cold-blooded, though." He studied Honor for a moment and then whispered, "Don't ever go upstairs with him. I understand he's a bit brutal."

Honor felt like kissing Otis. He might be a talkative drunk, but he apparently did care for the safety of the girls at Echo's. "Thank you, sir. I won't."

"Is that you, Lynx?" he asked, gazing at her more closely. "It sounds like you."

"Oh, Otis, how did you guess?" She smiled sweetly, leaned closer and whispered confidentially. "The gentleman Echo has arranged for me to . . . meet prefers blond girls."

"Oh, I see." He stared at her critically. "I think you're much prettier natural."

Otis drifted away with a pretty black-haired girl, and Honor continued to study Cedric surreptitiously. When he rose from his chair and walked toward her, her heart thundered in her chest like a wild bird seeking to escape its cage. She forced herself to smile as he sat beside her.

Honor didn't know what to say, but she didn't have to. He spoke first. "'Aven't I seen you somewheres before?"

"I'm sure I would have remembered you, sir," she said honestly. "Perhaps someone else looks like me."

"Name's Cedric."

"How nice to meet you." Honor felt as if she were sitting in a kettle over a roaring fire. "Do you come here often?"

"Often enough." He continued to study her.

Honor stared at Wilma, hoping she'd understand what was happening. Wilma mixed a drink and brought it over. "Compliments of Miss Echo, sir."

"What did you say your name is?"

"I didn't." Honor knew that she shouldn't tell him her name, but every second she hesitated made matters worse.

Otis stepped back over to her. "Excuse me, Miss Lynx, but remember what I said."

"Thank you, sir," she said limply. She had the feeling that despite all her hard work, her carefully constructed disguise was crumbling like the houses that had been struck by the cannonading.

"Lynx, is it?" Cedric leaned back and slid his arm around her. "I know a man what wants to meet you."

Of all the things he might have said, that was the last thing Honor expected. "Oh? Who?"

"Man name of London," Cedric answered, studying her face for any change of expression. "Ever 'eard of 'im?"

Honor knew that he was testing her. "London? What is his first name?"

Cedric chuckled. "I think you know. Maybe I should just set up a little rendezvous for the two of you. Might prove to be an interesting evening."

Dylan saw Otis coming out of the Night's Pleasure Inn and smiled. The man was certainly loyal to whatever woman he'd found there. "Evening, Otis."

"Hello, sir." Otis looked around. "What are you doing down here?"

"Oh, just walking." Dylan gestured toward the ornate pink building. "Come to . . . see your friend?"

"Lynx?" Otis asked, looking a little let down. "Yes, but—but she was busy tonight."

Lynx? The name echoed through Dylan like a clap of thunder. Was the most effective Patriot spy working out of the Night's Pleasure Inn? It made good sense. There, and at similar places, men were known to drink heavily, loosening their tongues. They also tended to boast a lot to impress the women. Suddenly the reason he'd been unable to discover her identity came clear: he had been searching for a man.

"A woman!" Dylan exclaimed to himself when Otis had walked on. "She's a woman. Imagine that. The Patriot's most effective spy, a woman. I never would have thought it." He jumped when he heard a sudden footstep behind him.

"Women're always devious." Cedric, who'd come up to him out of the shadows, grinned maliciously. "Might be fun, eliminating a tart like that."

Dylan stared straight ahead. He'd been wary of Cedric's tactics for a long time, but the idea of killing a woman was impossible for him to believe. "Surely you don't mean to kill her?"

"Look, chum, we've wasted two months looking for this wench. She's trouble, I tell you. We could both give 'er a tumble and then slide the shiv between her lovely breasts."

After Cedric left, Dylan sat there in the shadows, wondering what he could do. There was no doubt in his mind that he couldn't kill a defenseless woman, though this one might not be quite as defenseless as most.

He considered trial and imprisonment, but that option was almost worse than killing her outright. If she were put in one of the prisons, she'd be used worse than... But she *was* a prostitute; maybe it wouldn't make any difference. Dylan stopped. What was he thinking? Just because she was a prostitute didn't mean she should be thrown into a prison where she would likely be used by guards and prisoners alike until she died of exhaustion or worse.

He couldn't do that. Dylan would simply have to find a place to hold her prisoner. He'd find someone who would keep watch over her until the war was over. Maybe he could use his warehouse. There were several small rooms that would do. He could move out there himself, to watch her more closely, though he hated to isolate himself from Honor, as he knew this move would be likely to do.

Satisfied that he had solved his dilemma, he moved furtively out of the shadows. It was too bad that Cedric had discovered her identity as well. Of all the people involved in this scheme, Cedric would prove the hardest to deal with. Dylan had to find some way to circumvent his contact's plans. He was definitely up to something devious.

Honor found Jeffrey still in bed. She burst into the room, ignoring his state of embarrassment as he raced to find something to put on. "We've got a problem!" She excaimed.

"What, Honor?" He pulled on some trousers and a shirt. "What could be so—so damned urgent that you have to awaken me at this ungodly hour?"

She sagged into a chair and tucked her left foot beneath her. "Jeffrey, I have a contact who is setting me up with London."

"What?" Jeffrey almost tripped as he rounded the bed, straightening his clothes as he went. "Who? When?"

"The man's name is Cedric. I've seen him around several times. He looks..." She tried to think of a way to describe him succinctly. "He looks vicious."

"Vicious?" Jeffrey settled into a chair. "Honor, maybe we should proceed slowly on this. I don't like it."

"So you think it may be a trap, too?" Honor leapt to her feet and began to pace. "What should we do? We can't risk missing an opportunity to catch London. He's done far too much damage already." She stopped and stared for a moment. "I can't forgive what he did to Paddy."

"I agree, but I think we should examine the possibilities closely."

"We haven't much time." She inhaled deeply and looked at her friend. "I'm meeting him tonight."

"Tonight? Honor, we'll have to postpone this meeting. It's too dangerous." Jeffrey crossed his legs, tapping his fingers on the arm of the chair. "I won't let you do it."

"Look, Jeffrey, we don't have much of a choice." She sat down in the chair beside him. "We can make this work. I have a plan."

"I'm not giving in, you understand, but tell me your plan."

Honor began slowly. "You and a few other men can be waiting in a room nearby. When London comes in, I'll bash him over the head with something. Wilma will already have him drugged. Then we'll take him someplace safe."

"What then?"

Thinking about Jeffrey's question, Honor sat back and stared at him. "I'll have to go, too, Jeffrey. I think the time has come for Lynx to retire. This man Cedric knows who I am, or at least suspects, I'm sure. My usefulness is over."

"I agree on that point."

"I don't think I can stay on in Charleston."

Jeffrey considered the situation for a long time. "You can go up to my plantation," he said finally. "There are still a few servants there. You'll be safe. I'll leave a few men to guard London."

Honor nodded. "That sounds like an excellent plan. I want Paddy to go as well."

"That's not a good idea. Remember what the British did to him? I'll arrange for him to stay with someone else and then devise a way for us to get out of town." Jeffrey rose and started to pace. "Honor, if we're careful, we can reverse their trap. It's a risk, though."

"I know, Jeffrey, but it's a risk we must take."

Honor's mind was a flurry of activity. Should she leave? Was this a trap? She instinctively didn't trust this fellow Cedric, but her plans were in place. Right now, a man wearing his hair tied back with a light blue ribbon should be entering the parlor downstairs. A man with blue eyes and sandy hair.

He would go to Wilma.

Dylan spotted the black woman serving drinks immediately. He felt a little foolish wearing the light blue tie in his hair, but it was the signal that Cedric had agreed upon. He walked over to her and smiled. "I'm here to see Lynx."

Wilma smiled back and handed him a drink laced with some of Echo's sleeping potion. "She'll be ready in a few minutes. Help yourself until she sends for you."

Before she sent word to Honor that London had arrived, Wilma stirred three other drinks and set them aside for him. Echo had decreed that the man should get no farther than three steps into Honor's bedroom before he lapsed into unconsciousness.

Wilma left the room quickly after that. She hurried up the stairs and slipped into Honor's room. "He's here."

Honor's heart fluttered and her blood pounded through her veins like the hoofbeats of a runaway horse. The urge to flee splashed her neck and cheeks with color, but she quelled her fears. "Wilma, go ahead as planned. I'll alert the others."

Jeffrey and his men had sneaked into the Night's Pleasure Inn early in the afternoon through the back entrance. They now sat in Echo's bedroom, waiting for the signal. Honor stepped inside and found Jeffrey pacing back and forth like a caged wildcat. "Go easy, Jeffrey. Everything has been planned to the last detail. Nothing can go wrong."

Honor stood at the window as she had several times before, but this time was different. This would be her last evening as one of Echo's girls.

Dylan knew that the Patriots were aware of his identity. There was no other answer to this peculiar invitation. Cedric had somehow managed to give him away, perhaps intentionally. Dylan was useless to the British as a spy any longer, but he could make one last effort toward the cause, one that would save considerable time, effort, supplies and casualties. He would rid them of the woman who had been his arch rival, though he'd never realized her gender until yesterday.

At first, he'd decided to keep the Lynx at his warehouse, but after considerable thought, he realized that to do so would endanger both of them. He had to take her to a safer place. The land that he'd bought, hoping to build a home for his family in future years, had but one small cabin. He and the Lynx would live there until the war ended.

The black woman, Wilma, handed him another drink. "She'll be ready for you in a minute."

Had Lynx discovered that he knew who she was? Would she expect to surprise him by rendering him unconscious? Dylan looked at his drink, wondering if it could contain some sleeping powder. If so, it was too late. This was his third cup of rum.

He needed to act while he was still in control of his facilities, if, indeed, his drink had been tampered with. When Wilma signaled that she would take him up, he followed quickly, feeling the effects of the drink begin to take hold.

Honor gazed out the window. By now, Wilma was on her way up the stairs with London. The window where she stood was but three feet from Echo's door. Honor would lure London there, and Jeffrey would take care of him. It seemed so simple.

She heard a tap on the door. Without turning, she called, "Come in."

"A gentleman to see you, miss."

Honor nodded, catching a slight glimpse of a man out of the corner of her eye. She still hadn't turned to see him fully. She was savoring the moment of her victory.

The door closed and heavy footsteps brought the man closer, almost to her side and within reach of Jeffrey. London's wary, she thought, and turned to see him fully. "Dylan!" she exclaimed, her eyes widening in horror.

"Honor?" came Dylan's astonished reply.

"No!" she shrieked, but it was too late. The butt of Jeffrey's gun crashed down on Dylan's head and he crumpled to the floor.

And with him, Honor's entire future crumpled into the murky depths of despair.

Chapter Nineteen

Echo and Wilma examined Dylan's head. "Hit him hard, but he'll be all right. The drinks and powders will keep him asleep until you get out of the city."

"Goodbye, Wilma," Honor said, hugging the black woman impulsively. "I'll miss you."

Wilma sniffed and whispered, "Bye, Miss Honor."

Honor turned to Echo. She had but a few seconds to offer a lifetime of gratitude for what the woman had done. "I couldn't have done this without you, Echo. If I live through this and you ever need anything, come to see me at the White Point Inn and Tavern."

Echo wiped a tear from her eye. "I wish you the best of luck, Honor." She laughed and swiped at the stream of tears again. "And if you ever decide to take up the trade, I'll be happy to take you in. You'd be a helluva prostitute."

Blinking back her own tears, Honor kissed Echo's cheek and left quickly. Jeffrey and his men had already reached the back of the house and were placing Dylan in the bottom of a boat. "Careful," she admonished them.

Jeffrey grimaced and climbed in after he'd helped her board. "I don't like this, Honor. This isn't exactly what we expected."

"That's the truth if I ever heard it." She moved over and slid down near Dylan, so that she could rest his head in her lap. She felt like a traitor. Guilt plagued her, and the tears began to flow. She was glad of the darkness, which hid her crying, but it didn't make her feel any less awful.

They reached a low dock and glided to a stop. Some of Jeffrey's men secured the little boat and helped Honor out, then lifted the still-unconscious Dylan. They carried him to a wagon nearby. Jeffrey took Honor into a small shack where she changed into black clothes of mourning.

When she returned to the wagon, Dylan was nowhere to be seen. A man hammering a nail into the large box on the back looked up. "Coffin's sealed."

The words numbed Honor, for they held more than one meaning for her. The coffin was sealed for her on several parts of her life. She could no longer go home, for fear of endangering her family. She couldn't return to Miriam's or Echo's for the same reason. Her life as a spy for the Patriots had come to an abrupt end tonight. But one of the most important parts of her life was physically nailed in that coffin, and now that relationship was dead as well.

"Honor, we must hurry before Dylan awakens." Jeffrey helped her into the wagon.

Tears were streaming down her face already, tears meant to be forced as they reached the troops guarding the road. In accomplishing her goal to stop the spy London, she had destroyed the one thing that had more meaning to her than anything else: her love for Dylan.

The wagon lurched to a stop at the British outpost, and Honor glanced around, oblivious to her surroundings. Jeffrey was there, holding the reins. A black man sat in back with the coffin.

A soldier approached them. "Papers, sir?"

Honor's voice cracked as she tried to speak. "I—I have none, Soldier." She threw back her veil. In the lamplight, she knew the tears would be visible on her face, silvery streaks in the flickering light. She noted the reaction of the soldier. "Kind sir, my husband..." She choked on her words, fresh tears gushed forth and she buried her face in her hands. "The Patriot spy... Lynx, a woman of low character—" Honor steeled herself, lifting her chin and straightening her back with righteous indignation. "That—that loose woman murdered my husband."

"A woman? Who would have guessed. Reckon that's why they had so much trouble finding her." The soldier obviously had heard of the Patriot spy. "You say she killed your husband?" He looked at Jeffrey and then at the black man.

"A friend and a loyal servant of the crown, sir. My husband is... he's in—"

The soldier walked back to the coffin. "I'm sorry, ma'am, but I have orders to search every shipment coming through here."

Honor waved her hand slightly and the servant pried open the coffin lid. Animal blood of some sort had been splashed liberally over Dylan's shirt. The bright red blood had been dulled by time, and the shirt looked brown and stiff. As stunned as she was, drained of all feeling, Honor thought that they might well have used her blood instead of an animal's. She could hurt no worse than she did now.

Praying that the soldier wouldn't look at Dylan too closely, Honor let out a wail. "Oh, God, take me, too! I don't want to live without him!"

She rose up in the wagon and would have pitched forward in a contrived faint had Jeffrey not caught her. He turned to the officer. "Can't you see you're killing this woman by letting her see the man's body?"

"You mean she never—"

"No," Jeffrey snapped. "Why should we make matters worse by showing her this gruesome sight?"

"Oh, you're quite right." The soldier looked uncertain. "Where are you taking . . . the deceased?"

"To the family burial ground on her plantation. That is if that devil, Francis Marion, hasn't destroyed it." Jeffrey hoped that their remarks, designed to make the soldier believe they were Loyalists, would work.

"Well, sir, without papers, I—"

Honor leapt to her feet again and nearly vaulted down onto the road beside the soldier before Jeffrey could catch her. "Shoot me then, right now. I demand it. Or I'll throw my body upon your bayonet. I have nothing left to live for. Nothing. The babe that dwells within my belly will be better off never gasping for his first breath. Oh, the horrors of it! That awful woman."

Her last effort spent, Honor crumpled in a heap at the soldier's feet. Jeffrey leapt from the wagon and gathered her into his arms. "Do you see what you've done? Not only is her own life in danger, but her child's as well. I swore to this man as he lay dying that I would care for his child. I'll not let you—"

"Sir, if you'll place the lady in the wagon and leave before my captain hears the commotion, I'd appreciate it."

The soldier turned and went back to his duty station. Jeffrey wasted no more time. He laid Honor on the wagon seat and climbed up beside her. Within seconds, they were pulling away from the outpost.

Honor lay as still as possible. She didn't want to think. She didn't want to sit up, because Jeffrey would want to talk. She just wanted to awaken from her sleep and let this horrible nightmare be over.

She recalled the last time she'd made love to Dylan. How sweet and wonderful it had been. Their love had been a fragrant blossom, opening slowly as the sunlight of their newborn feelings warmed it, coaxing it to life. Now, in the flash of a second—the moment of their recognition of each other at Echo's—that blossom had withered and died.

Dylan would hate her. And she'd only begun to wrestle with her feelings for him.

Even if she could get past his treachery, his deceit, she couldn't forget the way he'd treated Paddy. She would never forget the child's bruised and battered body. Even if she could overlook everything else, she couldn't convince herself that a man who could inflict so much mindless pain on one child wouldn't do it to another—perhaps even his own.

Tears streamed down her face anew. In accomplishing the goal she'd set out to reach, she'd destroyed her own life.

After they'd ridden a short distance, Jeffrey pulled off the road and the other man opened the coffin. While Honor watched dazedly, they bound Dylan's ankles and wrists with leather thongs, carefully concealed beneath his clothes in case someone else got curious.

Precautions, Honor thought. Precautions to prevent the man I love from escaping. How ironic. Had their relationship progressed, he might never have considered escape. They might have spent the remainder of their lives living in ignorant bliss, neither knowing of the other's treachery. At that moment, she would have accepted blissful ignorance—almost.

Dylan's head ached with the force of thunder, and his mouth was as parched as a dusty summer road. He struggled to awaken, still confused by the darkness surrounding him.

He seemed to be drifting—no, lurching was a better word—
along in the darkness. He moved restlessly.

Suddenly, he came alert. His hands were bound, as were his
feet. He raised his head and it met with a low wooden object.
Where was he?

The memory of that excruciatingly painful moment as-
saulted him almost physically. Honor. She was the Lynx. She
had done this to him. He was her prisoner.

The motion finally stopped. He closed his eyes at the sudden thwack of wood splitting as the lid was pried off his
prison.

"Yes, suh, he's awake," a deep voice announced from
above him.

Dylan knew it was useless to pretend to be still unconscious. He opened his eyes to the white-hot glare of the
morning sun beating down on him. He could see two figures
standing over him, but because of the light behind them, he
couldn't see who they were.

One man was black—he could tell from the voice. But the
other had yet to speak. The black man helped him to his feet,
and Dylan found himself face-to-face with Jeffrey Sheridan.

"Jeffrey, how nice to see you again," Dylan proclaimed
facetiously, staring directly into his eyes. After a moment, he
glanced around, but Honor was nowhere to be seen. Too bad.
He wanted to confront her directly about her part in this.

"Dylan, I'm sorry about hitting you so hard," Jeffrey said
uncomfortably. Over the past year, they'd almost become
friends.

"Really?" Dylan moved his head slightly, but the pain
caused him to wince. "I'm not sure I believe you."

"Come on." Jeffrey opened his coat to let him see that he
carried a pistol. "Don't be troublesome, Dylan. If not for
Honor, we'd probably have finished the job."

"Ah, yes, Honor." Dylan felt a pang in his heart that had
nothing to do with his injuries. "And where might the little
tart be now?"

Jeffrey turned abruptly and punched Dylan in the stomach. "Don't ever call her that again! She's a lady and you
know it."

Dylan glared at Jeffrey, not willing to let the man know how
badly he was hurt. "Oh, yes. I, of all people, know what a
lady she is."

Jeffrey led them up the stairs and into the house they'd stopped in front of. He took Dylan to each downstairs room and showed him the locked shutters on all the windows. "We made the place secure enough to keep intruders out, but it works just as well to keep prisoners in."

With failing hopes, Dylan eyed the shutters. The wood seemed to be strong and nailed firmly in place. It would take a huge man, perhaps the black man trailing after them, to break through the thick shutters.

"My grandfather, who built this house, barely escaped during the Yemassee Indian wars, so he made sure it was impregnable." Jeffrey led Dylan up the stairs. "Don't get any ideas. Dr. Deek, here—" he indicated the servant "—is the only man other than me who knows the way in and out after I seal this place. Don't give him any problems."

Dylan glanced at the huge black man. "Why do they call you *Dr.* Deek?"

The black man grinned, showing several gaps where teeth had once been. "When I was a young'un, I took care of the little animals with broke bones and stuff. Got to be purty good."

Jeffrey grimaced. "He was usually the one who broke the bones first. Fortunately, he got over that mean streak—well, pretty much. I still wouldn't want to make him angry."

Neither would Dylan. He hurried on after Jeffrey. The black man posed a menacing threat that he didn't want to test, not until he got to know him better.

As he had downstairs, Jeffrey took him to every room upstairs except one, showing him the futility of attempting to escape. Dylan stopped before the last door, a little puzzled. "Why didn't you take me in here? Is this the room that contains the elusive escape route?"

Jeffrey strode back to where he stood and glowered at him. "That room, sir, is off-limits to you. It has nothing to do with escape. Feel free to make yourself comfortable in the rest of the house."

Dylan walked slowly away from the door, wondering why that one room was so special. Suddenly, he knew. Honor was there. She had to be. Her effectiveness in this war had come to an end, as had his own. In effect, they were both prisoners. With a derisive smirk, he mused that justice had somehow prevailed. He'd done what he'd set out to do, though he'd backed into his success rather than meeting it head-on.

"Now, to continue. There are no weapons in this house, except, of course, Dr. Deek. No knives, even at table. You may attack Dr. Deek at any time you choose. He probably won't kill you, but he'll make you wish you were dead, in all likelihood."

"What do you mean, attack?" Dylan asked.

"He likes to fight," Jeffrey said simply, and then smiled. "He'll be happy to take you on whenever you want."

"That right, Doctor?" Dylan asked, smiling at the black man. Of all the things he might do while he was here, Dylan realized that challenging the black man would be the most foolhardy.

"I sho' does. I'se whupped three or four at the time, I has. I reckon I'd whup the devil hisself, if I got the chance."

Dylan chuckled nervously. "You might, at that."

Jeffrey opened the door of the last room in back. It had no windows and the door was of heavy hardwood. There was a narrow mattress on the floor and no other furniture. "Here is your home for most of the time, especially during those short periods when Dr. Deek has to sleep. He will be your constant companion."

Honor, still wearing her mourning attire, went down to supper. This would be her first opportunity to see Dylan since they'd arrived. She was visibly nervous.

When she reached the dining room, Jeffrey, the black man and Dylan were already there. She lifted her chin and strode into the room as if there was nothing at all unusual about the situation.

Dylan stared at her. In black, she was more beautiful than he'd ever seen her. Her face hinted at a sadness he didn't quite understand. She should be gloating at her recent victory over him and the British.

"Good evening, gentlemen," she said, walking to her chair. She clamped her mouth shut to keep her teeth from chattering with her nervousness.

Dylan leapt to his feet and pulled out the chair. "Allow me, *Miss Lynx.*"

She fought to keep control of herself and sank into the chair as gracefully as she could. Her words were hardly more than a whisper. "Thank you, sir."

Supper was a chore. The conversation was stilted; the food edible and little more. When it was over, Honor excused herself and went to the parlor. It was a pretty room, a room that might have been sunny had the shutters not been nailed shut. The draperies were of wine-colored velvet that matched a tone in the thick carpet. The furniture was comfortable. She sat on the sofa, staring at the cold fireplace.

Dylan entered and sat across from her. She knew that they needed to talk about their situation, but she didn't know how to begin to explain her feelings. They were simply too complex for her to understand.

"Honor," Dylan said finally, "it seems that we're to be living here for some time. We need to establish some sort of arrangement between us to make it tolerable."

She met his gaze, wallowed briefly in the icy cold of his blue eyes and then glanced away. "What do you suggest, Dylan?"

Jeffrey walked into the room and looked at the two of them. "What's going on?"

Honor glanced at Dylan and noticed the pulsing of the muscles in his jaw. She turned to Jeffrey. "We're—we're discussing our arrangements for living here, Jeffrey. I think this would be better done in private. We have a great deal to talk about."

Jeffrey nodded. He truly felt sorry for them. Both of them were nice people, firmly believing in their chosen sides in the war. They were in love. He'd resented that fact once, but now he had Miriam. They'd be married soon, if all went as he planned. "I have some advice for you." Jeffrey walked a little closer so he could watch both of them as he spoke. "Forget the past and start over. Neither of you is right and neither is wrong. We've all made choices according to what we believe in. You can't fault each other—or me—for that."

After he left, Honor and Dylan talked at length about their differing loyalties. "Dylan, can't you see that you're wrong?" she demanded.

He leapt to his feet and glowered at her. "Honor, you are a subject of King George. You were born a subject of England's rulers. What you're doing is treason."

"You told me you loved America and her people. Why would you subvert her attempt at freedom?" She sprang to her feet in turn and stared up into his face.

"Because it is illegal. America is as much a part of England as London is." Dylan winced as he used his code name. "We're citizens of the same government, Honor. Can't you see that?"

"A government that allows us no representation? Why should I remain bound to that sort of government? Do they treat us as equals? No, we're somehow beneath them, much like the people who work for your family—the people who bring the land to life so that your father can squander his wealth on your brother."

Dylan bit his tongue to keep from yelling that she knew nothing of that problem, but calmed himself a little before speaking. "Honor, I admit that there are problems, but insurrection isn't an answer. Think of the deaths that have resulted. Is killing even one person worth it? The better answer is in dialogue with the government, in open communication. This can be resolved without war."

It wasn't until just before sunrise that Honor went up to bed, their problems unresolved. They'd both defended their actions, both decried the other as being a traitor. Now the pain bit even more deeply into her soul. Dylan was an honorable man. He'd fought for his side—fought to win—fully believing he was fighting for the right side, just as she had. The gulf between them seemed to have widened.

And there was Paddy. As she'd looked at Dylan and listened to him, she'd been unable to broach the subject. It was too painful. She couldn't bear to hear him confirm what she already suspected.

They would be cooped up here together for some time, so she decided to avoid speaking of their duplicity in the future. If they could find some common ground upon which to resume their friendship, if not their relationship, then she would be happy. The discussion of Paddy's beating would have to come later. She simply couldn't stand any more painful revelations.

Several days passed with an uneasy truce existing between them. Honor took her meals with Dylan, even after Jeffrey went back to Charleston. Dr. Deek was always around, lurking there as if he expected Dylan to bolt. Jeffrey had assured her that the man was as gentle as a lamb, but she wasn't sure. He looked awfully vicious.

Finally, she could stand the silence no longer. The truth had to be told. She confronted Dylan in the parlor. "You beat Paddy. How could you do such a thing?"

Dylan spun around to stare at her in disbelief. "What did you say?"

She crossed to stand behind a wingback chair, suddenly feeling the need to have something solid between them. "How could you purposely injure a child? One who adored you?"

"You think that I..." Dylan flew across the room and jerked her to him, his hand drawn back to strike her.

"Go ahead. Hit me. Are your targets always women and children? Is that why you slither about like a snake instead of fighting like a man?" As soon as she'd spat out the words, Honor wished they could be retracted, but they could not. They hung there like a double-edged accusation, one that would destroy them both.

For a moment, his anger was almost uncontrollable. He finally forced his fist to open, however, and pressed his hand on her shoulder. Her words had raced through him like wildfire, blistering and burning everything with devastating heat. Pain ripped through him like a million shards of glass, biting into him. No matter what he'd done, how could she possibly think such a dastardly thing?

When Dylan finally spoke, his voice was low and threatening. "I never lifted a hand against an unarmed person, much less a child. Until this moment." His gaze held hers, willing her to listen to him, to hear what he said. "Whatever you think of me, know this, I never struck Paddy. I never ordered such a thing."

Tears stung her eyes, but she refused to allow them to fall. Lord, how she wanted to believe him. How she wanted this chasm between them to heal. She needed him worse than she'd ever needed anyone or anything. When the misty haze dissipated from her eyes, she stared directly into his clear blue ones. No matter what had happened between them, she knew he was telling her the truth. The impact of that knowledge burst through her like a falling star, blazing in glory but for a few seconds. "If you didn't—and I must believe you...I do believe you—who did? Who is vile enough to do such a thing to an innocent child?"

Dylan's hands dropped to his sides as he finally realized the truth. "Cedric."

Honor remembered Otis's words about the rumors of Cedric's brutality. "You're right. What shall we do about it?"

"We'll get word to Jeffrey." Dylan returned to the fireplace, knowing that what he was about to say and do was treasonous. "I'll tell him—"

"No, Dylan." Honor understood what he was about to say. All his arguments for the British side flooded through her mind. "Don't say anything more. That way, if you're ever questioned about this, you won't know anything."

"Honor, you don't know him. He's a ruthless killer."

"I'll get word to Jeffrey. He'll find Cedric and take care of him for us."

Honor went to find Deek. She told him that she needed to get word to Jeffrey immediately. After writing a cryptic note that couldn't fail to be understood by Jeffrey, she sent Deek on his way, though the black man insisted upon locking Dylan in his room before he left.

Several days passed before she got a note in reply that read, "Well done, Lynx. Problem solved with aid of Echo. Paddy coming to visit you."

Her heart soaring, she went to show Dylan the note. His smile convinced her that she'd been right about doing this her own way.

He grinned. "I'll be happy to see Paddy."

"Me, too." Honor slipped into a chair. "I think the country air will do him good."

One evening they were sitting in the parlor after supper, and Honor sighed softly, wishing that just once more she could feel Dylan's arms around her, loving her as he'd claimed. How could he hate her after what they'd done? It didn't seem possible. Her initial shock had worn off, and she now viewed him as a friend, or tried to. What could she do to repair the damage to their relationship? Could they ever forgive each other and be happy again? Honor realized that she no longer cared about the war. She loved him and that was that. She'd have to find a way to overcome both their doubts.

Dylan, too, agonized over the same questions. He adored Honor, no matter if she was the spy Lynx. Was he willing to throw the love of a woman like Honor away because of political differences? He felt his resolve to remain aloof evaporat-

ing as he watched her sit there night after night and stare at
that cold fireplace.

"You know, Honor," he said suddenly with a wry smile, "I
have to admit that you were good at your job."

"What?" she asked, drawn from her silent ruminations by
his voice. She couldn't have heard him correctly.

"You were good at your job."

"My... as Lynx? Is that what you mean?" She was surprised by his admission.

"Yes, that's precisely what I mean." He moved over to the
couch to sit with her. "I can't concede that you were right in
what you did, but you did it with skill and courage."

For the first time in days, Honor smiled, really smiled.
"Why, thank you, Dylan. That's very kind of you to say." She
looked up at him and saw crinkles around the corners of his
eyes. "You were good, too. I searched high and low for you
for several months before I got my first clues."

"How did you get involved with that woman at the Night's
Pleasure?" he asked, edging closer to the real question he
wanted to ask, the question that burned within him.

Honor giggled nervously. "I met her one night as Miriam
and I were walking. She warned us to be careful of your soldiers. Later, I talked with her again. I liked her."

"I never met the woman, I don't believe." Dylan wasn't
sure whether he wanted to meet her or not. "How—how did
you... work?"

The smile faded briefly from Honor's face. "Do you mean
to ask if I ever..." She jumped up and spun around to face
him. "How can you ask such a thing?"

He stood and placed his hands on her arms. "I didn't mean
to imply—"

"Yes, you did." Honor's face blazed with color and her
eyes flashed fire. "What a—a bastard you are."

She turned to run from the room, but he caught her and
pulled her into his embrace. "Honor, I—"

He kissed her. Their hunger for each other transcended all
the ramifications of their past disagreements, of their oppos-
ing loyalties. Dylan gathered her into his arms, still kissing
her, nearly overcome with need of her, with the need to confirm that she still loved him as he loved her.

He pushed open the parlor door and found his jailer
standing there with his arms crossed and his eyes glaring. "Dr.

Deek, if you know what's good for you, you won't bother us this night."

Honor felt as light as lacy foam riding on the crest of a wave. Her dark hair hung around her shoulders as Dylan carefully removed each of her garments. She stood there, taking her turn and disposing of his. The hunger grew to unmanageable proportions and they nearly tore each other's clothes off in their rush to rid themselves of everything that stood between them.

When he laid her on the bed, Dylan allowed himself a moment to memorize every facet of her lovely body. "Honor, in spite of everything, I love you."

"And I you, Dylan." She felt warm inside, so warm, and then sensed a tiny quickening in her stomach. She'd ignored it for as long as she could, and now she had to face another problem, possibly alone.

Their lovemaking was frantic and frenzied and glorious. Neither wanted it ever to end, but gradually, Dylan let her come back to the world around them. He continued to ply her body with kisses, reawakening that hunger that hovered so very near the surface of her emotions. She was a passionate woman, more passionate than any he'd ever known.

He finally chuckled and drew her into the curve of his arm. "You know, you might have made a good prostitute."

Honor punched him. "That's not a nice thing to say. But what are we going to do, Dylan?"

Their experience had surprised her. For the span of one exquisite hour, they had put aside their political views and reveled in the passions that had been pent up for so long. For more than a year they'd known each other, enjoyed each other. The other times they'd made love had been hasty, with the exception of one unforgettable evening, and she'd always felt her inexperience shadowed their joining. Not so this time. Now all she had to worry about was keeping her hostage from escaping and explaining about the child that grew within her. Her performance for the sentry when she'd smuggled Dylan out of Charleston had not been totally an act.

"Honor, we must put all this behind us." Dylan propped himself on one elbow and stared down at her. "Lynx and London are officially retired from this war. Neither of us could be effective any longer, even if we tried. But that's too dangerous. We'd both be killed before a week was out."

"Jeffrey told me that one of the keys to winning the war was to eliminate the spy London." She snuggled in his arms. "I've done my job."

"That's interesting. Cedric told me the same thing, about you, of course." He smiled. "So it seems that we have each reached our highest calling for the war effort."

"Dylan, we've managed to put our differences aside, but what of others?" Honor felt the pressure of the future intrude on their happiness. "How will we cope with other people?"

"I don't know, Honor, but we'll manage. We'll have to. I want to get married as soon as possible." He kissed her again, relishing the sweet taste of her lips, the soft touch of her fingers on his chest. "We'll surely fight, but we'll enjoy making up."

"We can't return to Charleston—not now, anyway. Where will we go?" She felt the sensation once again in her belly and smiled. What would he say when she told him he was to be a father?

Dylan thought for a moment. "I've got some land with a tiny cabin, big enough for just the two of us."

"We'll need a bit more room than that," she said, kissing him lightly. "Dylan . . . don't forget about Paddy."

He gazed at her, knowing that she'd been about to say something else. What could possibly stand between them now? Hell, as if the war weren't enough, now there was something more—judging from her expression, something far more serious. "What, Honor? What are you keeping from me?"

Her eyes closed briefly as she considered how to tell him. The words stuck in her throat. Finally, she opened her eyes and stared levelly at him. "I'm carrying your child."

Dylan's own eyes widened in surprise and he inched back to look at her stomach. If he looked carefully, he could see that it wasn't quite as flat as it had been when he'd first made love to her. With a mist of tears in his eyes, he gazed at her with sweet longing.

"The child of compromise, Honor. Our child will help heal the division, the pain. Our child will be born of peace."

"Do you really think so?"

"I know so. We are his parents, though we're from opposite sides. Others like us will come together to forge a new generation. There's hope, Honor. There's always hope."

Epilogue

April, 1784

Honor shifted slightly to hide her nursing daughter from Charleston's curious eyes. The tiny baby, nearly two months old now had captured her mother's heart, as well as her father's. Their older child, a son named for his father, slept against Dylan's chest, comfortable in the safe haven of his arms. Paddy, feeling that he was grown now, stared eagerly at the city they were entering.

Since the end of the war, Honor and Dylan had resisted coming back to town, content to remain at their little cabin, which had grown rapidly from its first single room to a respectable four rooms. Soon, the larger house would be completed, a plantation to equal any in the area. Honor had never known such contentment, such happiness.

Humming a soft lullaby, she gazed out the window. "My, but everything has changed so much. I hardly recognize . . . Oh! There's Miriam's. Do stop, Dylan." She covered her breast as the baby fell asleep.

Smiling indulgently, Dylan called to the driver and the carriage rolled to a halt. He opened the door, shifted little Dylan to Paddy's lap and got out. After helping Honor and baby Carolina from the carriage, he reached back in and took his son. Paddy jumped to the brick walkway and followed them to the door.

"Do you think she's changed? I wonder if she and Jeffrey got married and had children." Anticipation sparkled in her eyes.

"Do calm down, Honor." Ever the doting father, Dylan smiled, glancing proudly at each member of his little family. "I'm sure that we'll find out soon enough."

The door swung open, and Jeffrey bustled onto the piazza. "By the Gods, it is you! I told Miriam that—"

"Jeffrey, who is... Honor!" Miriam shrieked, shoving Jeffrey aside and throwing her arms around Honor and the baby. "Dylan! And Paddy! Well, do come in."

A chorus of happy greetings echoed all around as they entered the neat shop and filed back to the little parlor. Honor glanced at the familiar surroundings. "I see everything's the same."

"Almost," Miriam said, blushing effusively. "We're expecting our first child." She smiled at Honor and gestured. "Come in and sit down for a while. I see you're ahead of me again. Let me hold the baby."

"This is wonderful, Miriam." Honor handed her daughter to Miriam and took a seat. "This is Carolina and this is Little Dylan. We keep saying we won't call him 'Little Dylan,' but we do."

The men were talking animatedly as they sat down nearby. For a moment, Dylan had wondered how Jeffrey would react to his onetime enemy, but there seemed to be no residual animosity. "How are things in Charleston?" he asked curiously.

"Well, everything is going well. Business is good. We're gradually rebuilding." Jeffrey ruffled Little Dylan's hair. "How about with you?"

"We're just about finished building our new house. Our cabin is a bit cramped with all of us." Dylan looked at Paddy, who seemed to be uncomfortable. "What's wrong, Paddy?"

"Nothing. I just sort of wanted to look around. On my own." Paddy's dark eyes gleamed with anticipation. "Do you mind?"

"No, go ahead. Meet us at the White Point Inn in a little while." Dylan watched as the boy darted out the back door. "Don't slam the—" the door banged shut "—door," he finished lamely.

Jeffrey laughed. "That's a good boy. I'm happy that you and Honor are keeping him with you."

Dylan chuckled and nodded. "He's a good boy, all right. A big help, too." He sobered a bit and studied Jeffrey. "I owe you a debt of thanks, Jeffrey."

Jeffrey tilted his head to one side in surprise. "For what?"

"For taking care of some very unpleasant business for me."

"I don't understand."

Dylan hesitated. If he brought the subject up, he would be opening the door to questions and recriminations, but he had to express his gratitude. "You took care of Cedric for me. As I recall, I was rather tied up at the time and unable to handle the matter myself."

Jeffrey laughed out loud, clapping his knees with his hands. "I wondered if you knew about that. Honor's note didn't give any details."

Dylan glanced at Honor. "I owe her a debt of gratitude as well. She prevented me from doing something that for me would have been an act of treason. I was fully prepared to contact you myself, but she wouldn't allow me to even voice my feelings. I guess she understood me even better than I understood myself."

"An extraordinary woman." Jeffrey thought wistfully of the time when he'd been in love with Honor. Even though he was happily married to Miriam, there were moments when he thought of Honor and knew he'd never forget the love he still held for her. He stood, walked over to the fireplace and stared into the ashes. "I'm delighted that we all came out of this alive." He turned to face Dylan again. "And still friends."

Honor looked at the two men. She'd wondered how they would manage to get past their individual loyalties, but now realized that both of them were intelligent enough to forgive and forget. "We're all still friends."

Jeffrey glanced from Honor to Dylan. "Did she ever tell you about the time we talked about bringing you into the Patriot spy network?"

Dylan stared at him. "You're joking, of course."

"No, not in the least. We discussed it several times." Jeffrey grinned at Dylan. "Honor felt that we should bring you in, but I guess . . . well, I think I didn't for my own reasons."

Dylan remembered the day he'd realized that Jeffrey loved Honor. That had been the main reason Jeffrey refused to talk to him about spying for the Patriots, he was sure. "I suppose it's a good thing."

"I guess. Everything has a way of working out."

Honor rose. "As much as I'd like to stay and talk, I'm afraid we need to hurry on. We haven't been to see my parents yet."

Amidst kisses and promises to visit, Honor, Dylan and the children finally were on their way. As they neared the White Point Inn, Honor grew more excited. She hadn't been home in nearly two years. She leaned back. Home. No, Charleston wasn't home anymore. Her little cabin in the peaceful countryside was home.

The carriage stopped in front of the inn. For a few seconds, Honor couldn't force herself to move. Questions flooded over her. Would her father welcome her with open arms? She hadn't been home since her mother died. Would things be different? Would Della be here? Was—

"Honor? Aren't you going to get out?" Dylan was already standing beside the carriage with his arms outstretched to help her down.

"Oh, yes. I was thinking of so many things. Dylan," she whispered as he lifted her and the baby from the carriage, "I'm afraid."

Though he knew her fears were real to her, he sensed that the moment she entered the inn, everything would be all right again. He chuckled and hugged her. "Honor Carlotta Richmond Alden afraid? I doubt it. She tackled the famous British spy London and captured him single-handedly. Why would she be afraid of anything?"

Honor lifted her chin and smiled at him. "You know what I mean."

"Yes, my darling." He reached into the carriage and picked up Little Dylan. "I must admit that greeting my in-laws for the first time as your husband has caused a few, shall we say, second thoughts on my part?"

With a glint in her eyes, she tucked her arm in his. "Are you saying that the British master spy, the infamous London, is afraid to walk into a tavern?"

Dylan studied her for a long moment. "Hmm, I seem to have lost control of my wife. The little spitfire Lynx has taken her place." He leaned down and kissed her. "I love you, my darling. Everything will be fine."

The door of the tavern opened and one of the serving girls ran down the walk. "Miss Honor! You and the babies is come home."

Dylan smarted that he wasn't included in the warm greeting. "Hello to you, too."

"Hush yore mouth and hand me that child. He's the spittin' image of his daddy." The girl took Dylan from his father's arms. "I cain't wait for—"

Della appeared in the doorway and hurried toward them. "My darlin' girl has come home."

She hugged Honor, clinging for a long while, and then Dylan. She scowled at him through her tears. "You should be ashamed of yourself, keeping them away all this time."

"Well, Della, in my own defense, I did have Honor's condition to consider." Dylan laughed at the Irishwoman. "You'd have killed me if something happened to her. I remember distinctly that you told me—"

"Sure you're not holding that against me, after all this time?" Della grinned. "Give me that baby. Looks like she's starvin' to death." Della took Carolina from Honor's arms and cradled her against her ample bosom.

Before Honor and Dylan could reach the door, Henry Richmond was standing on the steps. "For the love of a bottle of rum, Della, you're acting like a mother hen."

The woman looked up at him and scowled. "Henry Richmond, if you think you're going to keep me from playing with these babies, you can go soak your head in a rum keg or I'll do it for you. Now get out of my way."

Henry stepped aside and shook his head. He chuckled and shook Dylan's hand. "Son, don't ever let a woman learn that she's important to you. See what happens?"

Honor stared at them in amazement. The relationship between her father and Della had certainly changed. She remembered back to the day when she'd realized—that Della and her father were in love. The interplay between the two of them now confirmed her beliefs.

Henry turned to Honor. "Daughter," he whispered, his voice catching in his throat. "I'm glad you've come home."

Honor allowed him to hug her, relishing the comfort she found there. She knew in that moment that a great deal had happened, and that she would never hear all of it from him.

She didn't care, either. He seemed to be happier than she could ever remember him being. "I'm glad to be here."

He stepped back and surreptitiously wiped a tear from his cheek. "Women. I'll never understand them." He peered into the tavern after Della. "I'd better get in there and meet my grandchildren."

Dylan and Honor stood for a long while watching Henry and Della as they played with the two small children.

After a while, Paddy came in. Della nearly crushed him in her embrace. "Faith and begorra, where have you been? You're skinny as a well rope."

"Della," Paddy finally said, struggling free of her grip, "I'm a man now. You don't hug a man."

"You just as well get used to huggin', because I'm always going to do it." Della looked at the little group, together for the first time in two years. "Who's hungry for some stew?" She scowled at Honor. "Well, miss, are you plannin' to starve? Can't you see I'm busy with this baby?"

Honor grinned and looked up at Dylan. She laughed, picked up a tray and headed toward the kitchen. "Some things never change."

* * * * *

Harlequin® Historical

FIRST IMPRESSIONS THAT ARE SURE TO ENDURE!

It's March Madness time again! Each year, Harlequin Historicals picks the best and brightest new stars in historical romance and brings them to you in one exciting month!

The Heart's Desire by Gayle Wilson—When the hunt for a spy pairs a cynical duke with a determined young woman, caution is thrown to the wind in one night of passion.

Rain Shadow by Cheryl St.John—A widower in need of a wife falls in love with the wrong woman, an Indian-raised sharpshooter more suited to a Wild West show than to a farm.

My Lord Beaumont by Madris Dupree—Adventure abounds in this tale about a rakish nobleman who learns a lesson in love when he rescues a young stowaway.

Capture by Emily French—The story of a courageous woman who is captured by Algonquin Indians, and the warrior whose dreams foretell her part in an ancient prophecy.

Four exciting historicals by four promising new authors who are certain to become your favorites. Look for them wherever Harlequin Historicals are sold. Don't be left behind!

This March,
Harlequin is proud to bring you

~~by~~ *Request*™

Three complete novels by
your favorite authors!

Temperature
Rising

What every doctor needs—a great bedside manner!
What every doctor *doesn't* need...
The quintessential male chauvinist as a patient
A handsome malpractice lawyer with a personal grudge
A sexy male housekeeper with a private agenda

The *doctors'* Temperatures are Rising!

Relive the romance....

Three complete novels in one special collection:
LOVE THY NEIGHBOR by JoAnn Ross
UNDER THE KNIFE by Tess Gerritsen
AN UNEXPECTED MAN by Jacqueline Diamond

Available wherever
Harlequin and Silhouette books are sold.

HREQ4

Harlequin® Historical

**A SON OF BRITAIN, A DAUGHTER OF ROME.
ENEMIES BY BIRTH, LOVERS BY DESTINY.**

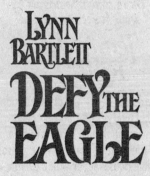

LYNN BARTLETT

DEFY THE EAGLE

From bestselling author Lynn Bartlett comes this tale of epic passion and ancient rebellion. Jilana, the daughter of a Roman merchant, and Caddaric, rebel warrior of Britain, are caught in the clash of two cultures amid one of the greatest eras in history.

Coming in February 1994
from Harlequin Historicals

Don't miss it! Available wherever Harlequin Books are sold.

Harlequin proudly presents four stories about
convenient but not *conventional* reasons for marriage:

- ◆ To save your godchildren from a
  "wicked stepmother"

- ◆ To help out your eccentric aunt — and her sexy
  business partner

- ◆ To bring an old man happiness by making him
  a grandfather

- ◆ To escape from a ghostly existence and become a
  real woman

Marriage By Design — four brand-new stories by four
of Harlequin's most popular authors:

CATHY GILLEN THACKER
JASMINE CRESSWELL
GLENDA SANDERS
MARGARET CHITTENDEN

Don't miss this exciting collection of stories about
marriages of convenience. Available in April, wherever
Harlequin books are sold.

MBD94

HARLEQUIN®

Don't miss these Harlequin favorites by some of our most distinguished authors!
And now, you can receive a discount by ordering two or more titles!

HT#25409	THE NIGHT IN SHINING ARMOR by JoAnn Ross	$2.99	☐
HT#25471	LOVESTORM by JoAnn Ross	$2.99	☐
HP#11463	THE WEDDING by Emma Darcy	$2.89	☐
HP#11592	THE LAST GRAND PASSION by Emma Darcy	$2.99	☐
HR#03188	DOUBLY DELICIOUS by Emma Goldrick	$2.89	☐
HR#03248	SAFE IN MY HEART by Leigh Michaels	$2.89	☐
HS#70464	CHILDREN OF THE HEART by Sally Garrett	$3.25	☐
HS#70524	STRING OF MIRACLES by Sally Garrett	$3.39	☐
HS#70500	THE SILENCE OF MIDNIGHT by Karen Young	$3.39	☐
HI#22178	SCHOOL FOR SPIES by Vickie York	$2.79	☐
HI#22212	DANGEROUS VINTAGE by Laura Pender	$2.89	☐
HI#22219	TORCH JOB by Patricia Rosemoor	$2.89	☐
HAR#16459	MACKENZIE'S BABY by Anne McAllister	$3.39	☐
HAR#16466	A COWBOY FOR CHRISTMAS by Anne McAllister	$3.39	☐
HAR#16462	THE PIRATE AND HIS LADY by Margaret St. George	$3.39	☐
HAR#16477	THE LAST REAL MAN by Rebecca Flanders	$3.39	☐
HH#28704	A CORNER OF HEAVEN by Theresa Michaels	$3.99	☐
HH#28707	LIGHT ON THE MOUNTAIN by Maura Seger	$3.99	☐

Harlequin Promotional Titles

#83247	YESTERDAY COMES TOMORROW by Rebecca Flanders	$4.99	☐
#83257	MY VALENTINE 1993	$4.99	☐
	(short-story collection featuring Anne Stuart, Judith Arnold, Anne McAllister, Linda Randall Wisdom)		

(limited quantities available on certain titles)

	AMOUNT	$
DEDUCT:	10% DISCOUNT FOR 2+ BOOKS	$
ADD:	POSTAGE & HANDLING	$
	($1.00 for one book, 50¢ for each additional)	
	APPLICABLE TAXES*	$ _____
	TOTAL PAYABLE	$ _____
	(check or money order—please do not send cash)	

To order, complete this form and send it, along with a check or money order for the total above, payable to Harlequin Books, to: **In the U.S.:** 3010 Walden Avenue, P.O. Box 9047, Buffalo, NY 14269-9047; **In Canada:** P.O. Box 613, Fort Erie, Ontario, L2A 5X3.

Name: _____

Address: _____ City: _____

State/Prov.: _____ Zip/Postal Code: _____

*New York residents remit applicable sales taxes.
 Canadian residents remit applicable GST and provincial taxes.

HBACK-JM